Requiem: A mass for the repose of the souls of the dead.

A musical composition setting parts of a requiem Mass.

An act or token of remembrance.

PROLOGUE

"AGAIN. HARDER. FUCKING *MEAN* IT."

I strike the boxing pad with everything I've got, pouring all of the hatred and pain synched tight around my heart into the blow. As always, my aim is true; the impact of the hit rattles up my arm and through my shoulder, so hard that it makes my teeth crack together, but from the look on Ruth's face, my efforts this morning aren't even close to meeting her standards.

"This is the problem, Sorrell." She grabs hold of my braid—my hair is so thick and long that I *have* to tie it back to work out—and gives it a vicious tug. "If you'd spent more time training instead of sneaking out to parties, Rachel wouldn't be dead right now. She'd be here, where she belonged. You both would have been safe. Focused. Dedicated." The look in Ruth's distant blue eyes is even colder than usual. It isn't every day that the head of Falcon House deigns to come and train her wards. Usually, we train as a group, led by Sarai or even Gaynor, but ever since my best friend's death, ageless Ruth, with her dark brown hair tied back into a severe bun, and her calloused hands, ramrod-straight posture and her ever-present air of disapproval, has been working with me personally, one-on-one. That is to say, she's been making my life a living hell. As if it hasn't been hell enough.

Rachel was more than my best friend; she was everything. I wouldn't have survived the past four years without her. Now that she's gone, I'm honestly not sure I'll make it through the rest of this week. Not with Ruth so intent on breaking me.

I bite the tip of my tongue, knowing that my mentor is right. On paper, Falcon House is a foster home—a very *large* foster home. In reality, it's so much more than that. This place is a sanctuary. We train our asses off here. Learn to fight. Learn to protect ourselves. Plenty of resources were available to Rachel and I. We should have spent more time running drills and practicing the floorwork, but Rachel was never one to conform to Ruth's rules. And then she'd left to study at that fancy private school on a scholarship, anyway, and that had been that. No more training sessions together. I'd barely seen her at all. Months had slipped by with only text messages to keep our friendship alive. When she'd returned to Los Angeles last month, all keyed up and ready to party, I hadn't had the heart to deny her.

"What's one night?" she'd said. Six hours away from the house, without our fellow sisters watching our every move? It hadn't seemed like such a big deal at the time. Ruth makes it sound like we were tiptoeing out of the house every weekend to get fucked up, but that couldn't be further from the truth. The house party Rachel insisted we go to was literally the *first* party we'd ever been to.

I should have known better, though. It was my duty to tell my friend no, err on the side of caution, and insist that we stay on House grounds. It had never been easy to say no to Rachel. I'd relented to her ceaseless badgering in the end. We'd drunk too much. Gotten high. Gotten into a car with a group of guys we hadn't known. And now Rachel is dead.

It's that simple.

I hit the pad again, a right jab, left hook, uppercut combination, trying to throw Ruth off with a set we haven't practiced today, but the woman who picked me up off the streets and saved my life is no fool. She sees my maneuvers coming a mile off and positions the pads strapped to her hands accordingly, once again disappointed. She shakes her head, and the weight of her disapproval is an unbearable yoke around my neck.

"You can forget about going to the funeral," she says.

I drop my fighter's stance, straightening. "Ruth! You're not serious. I *have* to go to the funeral!"

"You're too distracted. There are only four days left until you leave, and I will not send you out into the world unprepared. It's already reckless to send you to that school in this state. I still think it would be better to send Margo—"

I set my jaw, hands clenched into even tighter fists, my body locking up. "I'm going to Toussaint. *I'm* going to be the one. You're not sending Margo."

Rachel hated Margo. Everyone hates Margo. The girl's a grade A bitch with a chip on her shoulder the size of Mount Rushmore. I won't have her or anyone else leaving Falcon House to avenge *my* best friend. I'll slip away in the night if I have to. Ruth's right; I should have protected Rachel, and I didn't. She's dead because I didn't stop her from getting into that car. I'll be damned all the way to hell and back if I fail her in this now, too.

Ruth flares her nostrils, eyes roving over the determined features of my face. "You can stay here and train until your hands bleed, so that you're ready for what comes next, or you can go to the funeral. No, wait. Let me phrase it another way. You can make things right for Rachel, or you can go and stand by a grave site, and sulk and cry like it'll change anything. Your call. But I know what *my* decision would be."

Rachel's already been dead a month. The coroner refused to release her body for weeks; the squat old man in charge of determining Rachel's cause of death dragged his feet and then some. I'm not the only one who's been waiting to attend Rach's funeral in order to bid her a proper goodbye, but I am the only girl at Falcon House who loved her the way I did. Most sisters aren't as close as I was with Rachel. It feels like a betrayal not to attend the service now, to see her pale face at peace, witness her lying there in her open casket, to watch them close the lid and seal it shut. To see her safely lowered into the ground, where she'll decay and rot and never grow old, while I am left behind to navigate this waking nightmare of a life without her.

But avenging her is more important.

I adopt the fighting stance that's been hammered into me since the first day I arrived at Falcon House and launch myself at Ruth and her pads. She staggers back a step with my first strike. The second unbalances her less, but she still needs to right her own stance to compensate for my fury. I rain down blow after blow, throwing all of my hurt, and guilt, and pain behind my fists until I finally do something I've never done before: I catch her off guard.

My left fist connects with Ruth's jaw—a sweeping backhand that takes her by surprise. Her eyes widen, her head whipping to one side, and a small spark of satisfaction blooms to life inside me, when a pearl of bright red blood swells from my mentor's bottom lip and trickles down her chin.

I've split my knuckles open with the hit, but the bright flash of pain I feel is nothing compared to the roaring chasm of hurt within me that tears open a little further every time I remember that my friend is gone.

I will gladly shed my own blood if it enables me to avenge Rachel.

I'll shed Ruth's.

I'll shed Gaynor's blood, and Sarai's, and the blood of anyone else who stands in my way.

I make this promise to the universe as I charge again at Ruth.

Even if it means that I can't go and be with Rachel when she's interred into the ground. Even if I have to stay on my feet, locked in this training room for four solid days, until Ruth is satisfied with my progress and I put her on her ass. I'll do whatever it takes…

Because the guy who killed Rachel is still out there, walking around, free as a goddamn bird, and I will not tolerate that injustice. Theo Merchant is going to bleed, too, and I won't stop bleeding him until there isn't a drop of blood left in his body.

Ruth smiles, sharper than the edge of a blade. "Good. Now we're getting somewhere."

SORRELL

ALLEGEDLY, Toussaint Academy is one of the best private schools in the country. Eighty percent of its graduating students go on to attend Ivy League institutions, who then go on to become astrophysicists, and politicians, and doctors, and bankers. Rachel applied to the school as a joke, never thinking she'd be awarded a scholarship, but I wasn't surprised when she'd come racing down the hallway one morning, screaming at the top of her lungs, brandishing an acceptance letter in her hand. She was smart. Like, *genius* smart, with a photographic memory. She volunteered at soup kitchens. She was in the Big Sister program. Of course stuck-up, pretentious, ridiculous Toussaint Academy wanted her. She was the perfect candidate on paper—underprivileged enough to make them look good, like they're giving back to the community, but smart enough to keep their numbers up and ensure their stats remain stellar.

Lord knows how Ruth swung me a spot. I am *not* smart. Not like Rach. I can hold my own and take care of my assignments, but I'm not special like she was. I'm of average intelligence. I do not volunteer in any soup kitchens. You will never find my ass signing up for a Big Sister program—I'd be a horrible influence on impressionable young minds. Ruth must have done some digging and straight-up *blackmailed* someone in order to pave the way for me to complete my senior year at a place this prestigious.

Five hours outside of Seattle, nestled away in the topmost eastern corner of Washington State, Toussaint Academy is the last bastion of civilization nestled at the center of one point five million acres of the Colville National Forest. One point five *million* acres.

There's one road in. One road out. No townships to speak of. No stores. No malls. No Starbucks. No cell phone reception. I'm going to have to connect to the school's shitty satellite internet to be able to message and call Ruth for our daily check-ins, for fuck's sake.

The drive is interminable and boring as fuck. Two hours out from the Academy, Gaynor, who drew the short straw and is accompanying me across state lines, turns the radio off and yawns, shaking her head.

"If you turn the music off—" I begin.

She holds up a hand. "I can't hear myself think, Sorrell. If I have to listen to one more Rage Against the Machine song, I swear to God I'm going to cry."

"Put something else on then."

"Let's just have some quiet for a second. Why…why don't you hum something peaceful? My nerves are shot from all that shouting."

Jesus, she is so *old*. I zone out after a while, watching the tiny towns flash by the passenger window in a blur. After a while, I'm so damned bored that I *do* start humming, just to try and piss her off.

"That's pretty. What is that?"

"Hmm?"

"That melody. It sounded like…'*Brahms*?'"

"I dunno. It was just in my head. It's not *Brahms*, though. I swear I've never listened to *Brahms* in my life."

"So uncultured. Oh! Look. Over there. That's the last café before we enter the National Forest. We should get you a coffee. I doubt they're gonna have any at the school."

I swivel in my chair, gunning her down with an incredulous look. "I beg your pardon? What do you mean, you doubt they'll have any?"

"It's a boarding school, Sorrell. I doubt they're going to give a bunch of teenagers access to stimulants that will keep them up all night and make them loopy."

"I can't survive without coffee."

"You're gonna have to."

Fear grips me by the throat. "Pull in. Pull in right now. Maybe they sell the ground stuff."

Gaynor chuckles remorselessly as she swings the car into the parking lot at the last minute, slamming me up against my door. "Stay here," she tells me, when she parks. "Watch the car."

"No one's going to steal the car. We're in the middle of freaking no—"

She slams the door closed, mouthing at me through the window to stay put. I get out anyway. "Good lord, child, can you never do as you're told?"

"I'm staying with the car! I'm just stretching my legs!"

She pulls a face at me as she disappears inside.

It's fucking cold. I sit on the hood of the Subaru Outback, hands stuffed into the pockets of my leather jacket, waiting for Gaynor to emerge from the run-down café, and it hits me again—the almost out-of-body weirdness of this situation. A month ago, Rachel and I were singing along to trashy pop songs on Spotify, dancing around the bathroom, getting ready to go out and have some fun. She'd been so excited. Told me there was someone she wanted me to meet. A boy, of course. We'd snuck mouthfuls of Sarai's corked Chardonnay straight from the bottle, wincing at the sour taste of it, giggling like idiots as we'd fled the kitchen. We'd talked about 'The Plan' for after graduation. We were going to get summer jobs and save up as much as we could, then take a year off and go backpacking through Europe. I wanted to spend the first month in Paris. Rachel had wanted to hit London and work under the table some more before we headed to France. 'The Plan' was a work in progress, but we were figuring everything out. We basked in the sunshine and spent every moment we could at the beach, ogling shirtless dudes playing volleyball…

I blink, and my memories of the week proceeding Rachel's death fracture and dissipate, leaving me behind, planted back on top of Gaynor's Subaru, stunned by how quickly life can flip upside on a dime if you're not careful.

No more beach.

No more summer jobs.

No more Paris or London.

No more *Rachel.*

Fuck.

I clench my jaw, swallowing hard, refusing to give in to the stinging in my eyes. If I start crying now, I'll likely cry forever. I won't be able to stop. I'll drown in my sorrow, and my friend won't be here to drag me out of my depression.

Staring down at my worn leather ankle boots, I try not to think about Rachel. I try not to think about anything at all.

"Jesus, Sorrell. I can't tell if the black cloud hanging over your head is just normal Washington weather or if you manifested it with your crappy mood." Gaynor thrusts a to-go cup at me, steam rising out of the little hole in the plastic lid; the coffee she's procured for me is piping hot but I don't give a fuck. I take a giant swig and embrace the pain of the searing hot liquid, scalding my tongue and throat. It hurts like a bitch, but this is a quantifiable sort of pain. My mouth is burned because I gulped down extremely hot coffee. Great. Makes total sense. I've experienced this kind of pain before. I know approximately how long it will last for. I know that I shouldn't suffer any serious lasting damage, and by tomorrow I'll probably have forgotten all about it.

This other pain I'm experiencing—the pain of losing my friend—is new. I can't quantify it. It doesn't make sense. I don't know when or *if* it will go away, or if it will leave me unscathed. I feel like I'm being crushed to death by it. That any second I won't be able to stand the awful pressure and I'll succumb to it, and that will be the end of Sorrell Voss.

Frowning, Gaynor *tsks* at me, slapping a hand at my boots, wordlessly requesting that I remove my shitkickers from her fender. She rolls her eyes, giving up, when I blatantly ignore her, though. Sighing, she hops up beside me onto the hood of the car, positioning herself next to me, then takes a sip of her own coffee. She's a tiny woman. The top of her sandy blonde head barely grazes the top of my shoulder. She looks like she's being slowly eaten by the puffy, two-sizes-too-big blue coat that she's wearing. The woman's mascara is always a little smudged, always a little clumped together. In her late forties, she normally looks good for her age, but the grim, overcast day today makes her look washed out, her skin pallid.

"You look like shit," I tell her pleasantly.

Her response is immediate. "Cheeky mare! You're one to talk. You look like Casper the not-so-friendly ghost. Your face is the color of curdled milk. Your hair's too black. You should get some highlights or something. Soften it up a bit. You look like you've gone full dark side. What color would your light saber be if you were a Jedi?"

"What do you think?" I ask, laughing.

"Red!" she replies. "It'd be *red!* Sith Lord in the making. Where the hell's your tan, huh? You spent enough time at the beach this summer."

My smile fades at the mention of the beach.

Life is an obstacle course these days. One minute I'm doing really well, navigating the challenges I'm presented with. I've jumped the gap. Grabbed the rope. Swung across the water. Scrambled up the vertical wall. And then someone says something small and inane that shouldn't matter, and I'm falling flat on my face. The rope is ripping through my bare hands. I'm falling into deep and treacherous water.

I spent the summer at the beach with Rachel.

I will never spend a summer at the beach with her again.

Gaynor notices me deflate and shrinks in on herself a little with me. "You've seen him, then, I take it," she says.

I know which *him* she's referring to, naturally. I clear my throat. "Yeah." My voice cracks. I clear my throat again. "*Yes.*" I say it more firmly this time. "I studied the file Ruth put together before we left. He looks like a real piece of shit."

Gaynor chuckles, hiding her face in her own coffee cup. She stops laughing pretty quickly, covering her mouth with her hand. "Ohhh. Ahh! Ow! Hot, hot, hot!"

She'll live. I squint at her a little. "What? What's funny?"

She grimaces, eyes watering. "Well, he's not too bad to look at, is he? Very handsome. Rich. Plays the violin—"

"*Cello,*" I say, correcting her.

She rolls her eyes again. "He's on the lacrosse team. He was voted most popular kid in the school or something—"

"No, he wasn't," I scoff.

Gaynor shoots me an annoyed sidelong look. "Whatever. He's one of the popular ones. Privileged. People like Theo Merchant don't take too kindly to strangers fucking with them and causing trouble—"

I sip my coffee, not tasting it, my tongue far too scorched. "I'm not gonna cause trouble. I'm gonna be very, very nice—"

"Yeah, yeah, yeah. And then you're going to poison him in his sleep or something?"

I shrug noncommittally. "Haven't decided yet."

"Well, don't expect me to come visit you in prison, sweetheart. Not up here anyway. Too cold," she grumbles, hiding her chin inside the collar of her jacket. "If you do plan on murdering him, at least do it back in California. San Quentin's no fun but at least it'll be warmer—"

"San Quentin's a men's prison," I tell her. "And you're forgetting something."

"Oh? What's that?"

I poke myself in the chest with my thumb. "*Minor.*"

Gaynor laughs, shaking her head. She stares off into the trees that crowd the horizon, her gaze distant. "Know what I think? This is all some bad business. No amount of revenge is going to make you feel better. I think you know that already, don't you? And…if you hurt this boy and get caught, your age won't matter. You're eighteen in a matter of months. And as soon as *any* detective does the *smallest* amount of work, they're going to discover the connection here and realize that this was all *very* premeditated—"

I don't want to hear it.

Gaynor can keep her logic and her worries to herself. She's done nothing but try and dissuade me from this course of action since we left L.A. and I'll be damned if I tolerate any more talk of 'taking the higher road,' and 'letting the police figure it all out.' I throw back the rest of my coffee, my anger mounting as Gaynor continues to ramble on.

"…said the accidental death ruling could be overturned if we could provide any further evidence of—"

"Gaynor?"

"Yes?"

"Stop."

"I'm just saying! What kind of guardian would I be if I didn't try and play devil's advocate?"

"Enough. Theo Merchant is untouchable. You've already said so yourself. His parents are powerful and rich. He fucked up, drove recklessly, and killed Rachel. He *killed* her. The criminal justice system will not punish him, so I will. That's all there is to it. Now let's hit the road. It looks like it's going to rain."

Where Ruth is cold and emotionless, Gaynor is warm and sweet. She feels too much. I see her worry for me, plastered all over her kind face, and it cuts me to the quick. She looks stricken beyond belief, like there's so much more she wants to say, but she knows how futile it would be to try. So she doesn't.

The moment I get back into the car, a wave of exhaustion hits me with the force of a wrecking ball. Pain lances through my head, strobing right behind my temples. I have to screw my eyes shut against the light that was dull and grey a moment ago, but is now blisteringly bright. I can barely think around the *thrum, thrum, thrum* of my pulse rushing in my ears.

"You okay, sweetheart?" Gaynor asks softly.

I nod. "Just tired. And I have a *prodigious* headache. Jesus."

I hear Gaynor rifling around in the center console: The rustle of paper; the crinkle of plastic; the rattle of a pill bottle. "Here." She knocks the back of my hand with her own. "Take these."

Lord only knows how many Tylenol she passes me; she's always been a little heavy handed with her meds. Grateful, I toss them back, swallowing the pills dry. I slump back into my seat. "Damn, this one came out of nowhere," I say, wincing as the pounding inside my skull intensifies.

"Don't worry, sweetheart." Gaynor's voice sounds weirdly far away, but her tone is soothing. "The painkillers will kick in soon. Get some sleep. I'll wake you up when we get there."

* * *

Toussaint.

It's a stupid French family name or something.

I didn't even know how to say it when Rachel first showed me the pamphlet and informed me that she was applying. She had a grand old time teaching me how to pronounce it, skipping around the training room, repeating *'Too-SON, Too-SON,'* in a ridiculous French accent, making the 'N' at the end sound nasal and preposterous. She'd screamed and tried to kick my ass when I told her that it just sounded like Tucson. As in Tucson, Arizona. Apparently, she hadn't viewed the comparison as favorable.

I dream, and my dreams are memories, swimming together, full of laughter and utterly brilliant.

When Gaynor wakes me up, it's late. The sky is a purple, dusky bruise. A long, rutted out, insane-looking swathe of buckled tarmac stretches out in front of us. It's as if a huge earthquake has splintered the road apart, completely destroying it. This is, in fact, the only plausible explanation I can come up with to justify what I'm seeing as I clamber out of the passenger seat.

Alongside the road, a large, lop-sided sign reads:

Toussaint Academy Pick Up Point
EXTREME ROCKSLIDE DANGER!
EXTREME FLASH FLOODING DANGER!
EXTREME MUDSLIDE DANGER!
EXTREME CLIFF FACE DANGER!
Dial 55311 from call box for assistance.

"What the *hell*?" I'm still super groggy. My legs feel a little spongy. Weak. Gaynor blows hard down her nose as she assesses the fucked-up road, visibly marveling at the chaos of it.

"I could be wrong," she says, "but I think there might be some *extreme danger* up ahead."

I snort at the quip, kicking a chunk of broken tarmac out of the road. It tumbles off into the undergrowth, bouncing along the thick carpet of dried pine needles. "I think you might be right. Can you see a call box anywhere?"

"Over there." She points off to the left, where a small call box does indeed stand in the center of a cleared patch of dirt. It's painted red, but in the half-light, I didn't notice it. Gaynor sets off toward it. I follow after her, still dizzy and a little unsteady on my feet. "There are tire tracks everywhere," Gaynor observes. "No grass. Looks like this area is some kind of turning loop. Rachel never mentioned this to you?"

I squint back up the destroyed road, trying to make sense of the situation. "No. She didn't." It's cold, and the encroaching evening smells like smoke. The air feels too still, too full, too tense, and a strange prickling sensation climbs up the back of my neck. Somehow, I can tell that we're the only people for miles and miles and miles. I can *feel* it. The last of the sunlight disappears quickly in places like this. It'll be fully dark soon; fuck knows what kind of animals are lurking out there in the trees, waiting for the cover of night to commence stalking their prey.

Behind me, Gaynor starts talking and I nearly jump out of my skin. "Yes, yes, oh, good evening. Yes, I'm sorry. I know, we got here a little later than I was hoping." She titters politely. "Yes, that's right. Sorrell Voss. Well, no, ahh, actually *I'm* Gaynor Pettigrew, her guardian, but—yes. Yes. Oh! Oh right. Okay. Yes, I'm sure we can manage. See you soon."

She hangs up the phone, setting it back in its cradle inside the call box, and I raise my eyebrows, waiting on her to tell me what the hell's going on. She looks a little flustered when she turns and faces me. "She sounded nice. Ford. Principal Ford. She said we have to take the track that leads west from the call box, down the slope to the jetty. They're going to send someone to meet us."

"There's a jetty?"

Gaynor nods. "There's a lake down there, that way." She points. "You didn't see it. You were sleeping."

"Okaaay." This is all very unusual, but whatever. We've come this far. Gaynor helps me with my two bags, heaving them out of the trunk.

"Christ, child, what have you got in here, bricks?

"—got in here, bricks?" I finish the sentence along with her, knowing

perfectly well what she's going to say. Gaynor sticks her tongue out at me—very childish. "It's *books*, actually," I tell her.

"Ahhh. You brought your Shakespeare collection. The tragedies."

"Nope. It's fifteen copies of The Anarchist Cookbook."

"Sorrell!"

"What? They're all different editions. Some have updated information in them. Oh, and I also brought a book on poisonous plants and how to use them."

Poor Gaynor. She's white as a sheet. "You're going to put me in an early grave, child," she declares. "What's *that* going to look like, when the police show up to investigate a dead boy on campus—"

"Relax, relax. It's the Brontës I swear. It's just the Brontës."

She growls intelligibly—something about me not being funny at *all* —as she ambles off down the narrow single track that she found directly behind the call box.

Sure enough, after stumbling down the slope and tripping over tree roots in the twilight, the trail spits us out on the pebbly shore of a massive lake. The water is clear as glass and flat as a mirror, not a ripple in sight. It really is quite breathtaking. On the other side of the lake, the tree line is now a dark black silhouette against the fading sky. A single star flickers to the east, bright enough to be seen through the wispy clouds that whip astonishingly fast across the horizon.

"Would you look at that." Gaynor looks wistful as ever. "Beautiful, isn't it?"

"Yeah, I suppose it is." I no longer possess the part of my soul that used to recognize and appreciate beauty. It died a month ago. It makes sense to agree with Gaynor, when her words are laced with such awe, though. It'll go some way to convincing her that I'm not completely dead inside.

The jetty is little more than a small, wooden dock, painted white. It looks new. A large black crest has been painted on the sturdy slats, inside which a T and an A has been etched, presumably for Toussaint Academy. I expect a boat to come tearing across the lake or something, but after a solid forty minutes of waiting, growing colder, the night closing from all sides, something far more unexpected happens.

We hear it first—a high-pitched mechanical whine that is initially just a faint suggestion of sound, but as it gets closer...

"You've *got* to be kidding me." I stare up into the sky, shaking my head in disbelief. It's a fucking *sea plane.*

Gaynor's like a kid on Christmas morning. She whoops, clapping her hands together, bubbling over with excitement as the sleek little white aircraft touches down onto the water, buoyed by its skis, and casually parks at the jetty.

A dark-haired guy in his early thirties jumps out, his facial features blank, but...yep, the way he's holding his shoulders, so tense, his nostrils flaring a little—he is *not* stoked right now. "You kids were all supposed to be here by four at the latest," he grouses. "It's not safe to be taking off and landing out here in the dark."

"Sorry!" Gaynor grins from ear-to-ear, staring at the plane; the very last thing she looks is sorry. I don't think I've ever seen her this excited. "We had no idea about the road, and having to come down here, and—wow, I just—is that a *Piper PA 18 Super Cub?*"

The pilot gives her a dumbfounded look. He's nowhere near as surprised as me, though. "I didn't know you liked *planes?*"

"Good eye," the pilot says. "Yeah, it's a Super Cub. Unfortunately, we don't have time to hang around and chat about it. If you're going to Toussaint, you need to give me your bags and get in right now," he says to me. "I'm turning this thing around and heading back in the next fifteen seconds, with or without you. You getting in or what?"

SORRELL

GAYNOR IS A SHADOWY DOT, and then she is a blur, and then she's gone.

I wanted to walk her back up to the car, but Jeremy (which is apparently the sea plane's pilot's name) told me to get situated while he hurried her back up the slope toward the Subaru. He was back in no time at all, the plane was running, then speeding across the lake, and then we were climbing into the air in what felt like seconds.

"I am not a personal fucking *taxi*," he grumbles, as the plane banks heavily to the left. He skirts along the perimeter of the lake, the water a reflective black mirror below us. I say nothing. Jeremy is pissed, and Jeremy will stay pissed no matter what I tell him. A carpet of trees rolls onward into the night. In every direction, all I can see are trees and the dark, looming shapes of mountains in the distance.

We're in the air for all of ten minutes before Jeremy tells me to sit tight, and then he straightens out the plane, and we descend. We land on another lake—wait, the *same* lake? Surely it can't be?—and Jeremy pulls up alongside a much larger, more impressive looking dock, making the whole affair look easy.

"You tell Ford that I'm charging double for this one, you hear?" he tells me, as he grabs my bags and dumps them onto the dock.

"Uhhh. Should I…?" I point over my shoulder, into the darkness.

It's amazing just *how* dark it is when you head out of the city and there are no ambient lights to throw off some shadows. I have no idea which direction I'm supposed to head in if I want to find the school.

"No, no," Jeremy snaps. "Don't go wandering off. You'll only break your fucking neck. Just wait."

His attitude is shitty as hell, but kind of amusing. I like his generous usage of the word 'fuck.'

"He's also pretty hot, don't you think?" a voice in the back of my head comments. Rachel's voice. I laugh softly under my breath, a flood of sadness rising in me; that is *exactly* what she'd have whispered in my ear if she was here. And yeah, grumpy Jeremy is kind of hot. He ties off the plane like it's a boat and grabs my bags again, hurrying along the jetty toward solid ground. At the end of the dock, a golf cart is waiting for us. I consider asking Jeremy if I can drive, but I don't think his wicked temper could take the joke right now.

He fumes, muttering under his breath as he speeds up a hill and across a massive field. We turn a corner, the golf cart tipping precariously, and then—

Whoa.

The place looked impressive in Rachel's photos. Stately. But even in the dark, it is so much more than that. Toussaint Academy is *huge.* There is only one light on inside the building—a light in what looks like the entrance way, beneath a grand portico. The rest of the building, with its carved stone lintels, gables and parapets, is a Victorian masterpiece. Ivy chokes the eastern wing of the building, its tendrils clinging tightly to the stonework. The western wing is formed out of a colonnade, monolithic columns dotting a kind of porchway, seven, eight, nine…no *ten* monstrous cylinders of stone, rising seven floors, reaching all the way up to an elaborate iron cresting that runs the length of a fifty-foot-long parapet. A giant domed cupola sits in pride of place atop it all, it's beaten gold panels somehow bright and glorious even without any sunlight to bounce off of them.

"Oh my…*god,*" I breathe.

"Yeah, yeah, yeah. It's great. Come on. I have to get you signed in so I can go home." Jeremy has my bags again. He's halfway up the worn stone steps that lead to the entranceway before I've even gotten out of the golf cart.

Somehow, I have a clipboard in my hands a moment later. I'm signing my name into a registry. Gripping a flashlight between his teeth, carrying a bag in either hand, Jeremy guides me down a long, winding, darkened hallway, warning me not to touch anything, and then he's leading me up a flight of stairs. Another flight, and then another. I can't see much within the narrow beam of light thrown off by the flashlight, but I can feel how plush the carpet is underfoot. I can smell the beeswax, and the faintest hint of something floral and clean. The silence nearly crushes me.

Jeremy takes a right, hurrying along a wide hallway, gesturing for me to hurry up and follow. "Where is everyone?" I hiss.

"Where the hell do you think they are? They're sleeping."

"But it's early—"

"Hah! It's two in the fucking morning! Why do you think I'm so desperate for my bed?"

He's lying. He has to be. "But it was dusk earlier. It only went dark properly while we were waiting for you."

Jeremy stops abruptly and dumps my bags. "This is you. Rosewood 13. Breakfast is at six-thirty. Since you're on Rosewood, you go to the Rosewood room for roll call." He takes a breath, assessing me with very sharp, very blue eyes. "Dusk is subjective out here, princess. Sometimes it goes dark at four. Sometimes it doesn't ever get dark. Not properly. Depends on the season and the lights."

"Lights?"

Jeremy huffs. He obviously thinks I'm slow. "The *Northern* Lights? Aurora Borealis? We see them here sometimes. They've been crazy this year. I'm leaving now. Have you got everything?"

I nod.

"Awesome." Jeremy takes off at a jog, leaving me alone, standing outside a heavy dark wood door marked with a golden, shiny number thirteen.

SORRELL

I PASS OUT HARD, too tired to properly assess my surroundings.

In the morning, I wake to birdsong, and the sound of the frantic chirruping sets my teeth on edge. My new bed is a voluminous thing—a cloud, really, soft and enveloping. So warm and cozy that I hurl myself out of it as soon as I gather my senses, horrified that I could ever dream of being so comfortable in a place like this. Shafts of cold morning light spear into the room through a large picture frame window that looks out over the lake, where Jeremy landed in the Super Cub in the early hours of this morning. The plane is gone now. The only things gliding over the surface of the water now are a couple of very vocal Canada Geese.

"Shut the fuck up, assholes."

They do not shut the fuck up.

I quickly discover that I have an en suite bathroom, which is absolutely beautiful, all rose quartz, Italian marble and mirrors. Completely over the top. At Falcon House, I'd be lucky to make it to the very basic, very chipped, very run-down shower stalls before the hot water ran out in the mornings. Here, I have access to my own sunken tub? Ridiculous.

My bedroom is large enough to easily fit the hateful, extremely comfy king bed, as well as a nightstand and a chest of drawers on the other side of the space by the door. An antique-looking desk sits beneath a second window, with a plush wing-backed chair tucked underneath it. Shelves line the walls, ready and waiting for my books and all of the unnecessary accouterment Gaynor fabricated for me, that I might look like a normal student coming to finish out her final year of high school, away from her old friends and family.

It's absolutely beautiful, and I absolutely hate it.

I shower, gritting my teeth through a wave of nerves that show up out of nowhere, uninvited. They haven't dissipated by the time I dry my hair; they're still hanging around after I finish applying some mascara and lip gloss. They persist in harassing me as I get dressed.

Thank fuck this godforsaken place doesn't make its students wear a uniform.

I've never had to wear one before. Not at any of the elementary schools I was shuttled between as a child, when I bounced from one foster home to the next. Nor at the public middle school I attended for two years, before Ruth and Gaynor came and collected me one day, out of the blue, from the school gates when I was thirteen. The closest thing I've ever come to a uniform has been the black clothing Ruth demands be worn at Falcon House. Black shirt, black tank, black skirt, black pants, black underwear. Whatever. I'm given a clothing allowance once a month and permitted to buy anything I want, on the proviso that it's black and I don't claim more than a passing ownership over it.

This makes life easier for the few staff members hired to do the laundry and clean Falcon House. With fifteen young girls in residence, all ranging between thirteen and eighteen, making sure everyone's clothing is black ensures that everyone's wardrobe is easy to wash and no one fights over whose t-shirts or jeans are being picked out of the folded laundry hampers after wash day.

Of course, teenaged girls are bound to fight over that kind of thing anyway, but the residents of the house learn that arguing over petty shit is frowned upon and punished immediately. Scrap with another girl over an outfit and you'll quickly find yourself assigned a single pair of holey sweats and one faded t-shirt to last you the entire week.

You'll have to wash those items yourself every night after training if you didn't want to stink to high heaven.

I've never really had clothes of my own before, so I've never minded accepting whatever is left in the bins after everyone else has staked their claim. All I've ever cared about is having stuff that fits well and is comfortable to train in.

So, this…?

I stare at my reflection in the mirror of my new room, feeling a little out of sorts. My jeans are blue. My shirt is white. It's all new and good quality. I look… I think I look *good?* I didn't even think to inspect the clothes Gaynor placed in my bags for me. I've cared so little about that kind of thing that it just didn't matter. But now, I don't even recognize myself. My features are the same as ever. My mismatched eyes—one blue, the other green—always have and always will be the most striking thing about me. My skin is pale as hell. The bridge of my nose is smattered with a dusting of freckles, though—proof I did see *some* sun this summer. My hair is midnight black (the color of a raven's wing according to Ruth), straight as an arrow and almost down to my waist. My lips, a natural flushed red, look a little too big for my face, I've always thought. The black clothes I've worn for years have hidden the shape of my figure, but now, assessing myself in the mirror in my room, I have curves on show. Curves I haven't cared to notice before.

Aside from all of that…what do I look like? Do I look like a girl on a mission for vengeance? A girl desperately missing her best friend?

No.

I see a normal, soon-to-be-eighteen-year-old girl, wearing normal clothes, about to embark upon her first day at a new school.

What the *fuck?*

"Five-minute call! We need to be down at Rosewood by eight. Get these doors open and your asses downstairs, ladies!"

The voice on the other side of my new bedroom door is pleasant enough. Singsong and bright. The loud slap against the door is something else entirely, though. It brooks no argument. No matter how pampered and spoiled the people that I will be surrounding myself with over these coming weeks will be, I still find myself in a prison. I can't allow myself to forget that.

* * *

"Myra! Oh my god! Stop growing!. Did no one ever tell you that it's gross to be so tall?"

"Karla! Oh. My. GOD. Did you get your boobs done? You definitely got your boobs done. I fucking hate *you, girl. My parents won't let me get mine until I'm twenty-one."*

"Watch it! These are Minolos! Fuck, Leo. How did you get clumsier over break?"

I imagine this is exactly what it's like to show up for roll call as a prison inmate. The halls are shoulder-to-shoulder with strangers; I navigate my way through them, gritting my teeth. My heart's pounding, my palms slicked with a cold sweat as I forge a pathway through the sea of girls who all seem to know each other, meeting a series of blank gazes as their eyes skim over me. There are other girls my age hovering on the peripheries, standing in their bedroom doorways, nervously smoothing down their dresses and skirts like they feel hideously uncomfortable in their new clothes, too.

Two. Three. Four. I stop counting their nervous faces and keep my head down, mumbling quietly every time I nearly collide with someone who stops short in front of me.

I knew I wasn't going to be the only new girl at Toussaint. Sarai did some digging before she and Ruth decided that it would be smart to enroll me at the institute. They didn't want me to stick out like a sore thumb. Who are the school board and parents likely to look to when bad things start to happen within the walls of their precious school? Folks get suspicious of interlopers. But bizarrely there are twenty new students starting at Toussaint this year. Twenty new faces, with different stories, both guys and girls. Ruth figured that so many other fresh students would be an appropriate camouflage.

"Jesus. Looks like they took applications from the circus this year." The snide comment comes from a girl with bright red hair, loitering with three other girls at the mouth of the hallway that leads to the stairs. Her nose wrinkles as she looks me up and down. "I mean, wow. Her eyes are freaky as fuck."

Ahh, yes. The eyes. I've been expecting this. One of them is green, the other is blue. Big fucking deal. High schoolers will always find something to pick on their peers for though. I laugh derisively down my nose at the pettiness of this bitch's comment, mostly because I've seen myself in the mirror a million times and I know for a fact that my mismatched eyes are awesome. She can bag on them all she wants, but her bitterness won't make me look any less cool.

"She's probably a witch," the girl sneers.

"Oh yeah?" This comment is just *too* good. I can't pass up the opportunity to fire a retort back at her; she's left herself wide open. "I heard that most witches are actually *redheads*. You'd have been burnt at the stake for having hair that color three hundred years ago."

Their little group titters spitefully as I hit the stairs—I can't tell if the group is laughing at me or at the redhead now, but whatever. I don't give a fuck either way. I just can't wait to get out of here. My shoes ring out on the steps, my echoing footfall keeping time with the gallop of my heart.

This is temporary, Sorrell. Only temporary. You'll be back home before you know it.

Down on the ground floor, the polished marble, the fifteen-foot-high walls, and the stunning abstract paintings on the walls make the academy look more like an extravagant hotel than an institute of higher learning. At first glance, I think the flowers in the vases dotted all over the school's entranceway are fake, but the smell of lilies and gardenia flooding the back of my nose is something that cannot be imitated without reeking of chemicals.

Cut crystal chandeliers overhead cast a warm glow over the vast foyer, giving it an opulent feel that I can't say I've ever experienced first-hand before. Angry orphans with a history of violence don't often land themselves in places like this. Still with my head bowed, I navigate the madness of the lower level, making quick progress through the strum of chatter as I head for 'The Rosewood Room.' Ruth made sure I'd memorized the layout of the school before I left Falcon House. I know exactly where I need to be, and how many steps it will take for me to reach my destination. Unlike other schools I've attended, the classrooms here aren't numbered or organized by department. They're named after flowers or trees, and each one has its own theme.

Magnolia. Redwood. Bluebell. Gerbera. Pine.

I pass the doors to all of these rooms, ignoring the teenagers who spill inside, all amped up on the kind of excitement that comes with a new school year and the reuniting of friends. I have no friends here. If it were up to me, I wouldn't bother making any, but Ruth was very clear when I left the house. *"Fit in. Find your niche. If you ostracize yourself from the other girls there, you mark yourself as a target, Sorrell. People—especially teenagers—are very sensitive to the unknown. Make yourself one of them. Make them trust you. Make them* like *you. This whole plan depends on it. The community at Toussaint is tight knit, once the students get to know one another. You can't afford to have them hold you at arms' length.'*

This is wisdom, of course. It makes sense. But I've been a closed book for so many years that I don't really know how people make friends and forge allegiances in a place like this. I'm going to do it. I have to. But for now, all I want to do is find *'Rosewood'* and make myself as inconspicuous as I can. The classroom is bustling with life when I walk through the door. A couple of heads turn toward me, small frowns on the students' faces, but for the most part, no one pays me any heed. I sit down at the back of the room and take a notebook and a pen out of my bag, the cold sweat that coated my palms now making my skin feel clammy all over my body.

What the hell am I *doing* here? How the hell did I think I could do *this*?

One by one, the chairs surrounding me fill—polished girls with perfectly blow-dried hair and perfect make up. Clean-cut guys with broad shoulders and boy-next-door smiles, cuffing each other on the shoulders as they congratulate each other's numerous recent sporting victories.

I hunch down in my chair, trying to make myself small. If only I could just disappear…

The door opens one last time, admitting two new people into the room; the first is a dour looking man in his forties, wearing a neatly pressed white shirt and grey suit pants. No tie. No blazer. There's no mistaking that he holds a position of authority here, though. It radiates off of him, the same way Ruth's authority radiates off her. His hair is dark brown, but the full beard he's rocking is tinged a deep auburn. Black-rimmed glasses. His eyes are the color of a cold, overcast winter morning.

The student following directly behind him—

My pulse kicks into overdrive when I see his face.

Oh my god. Oh my god, oh my god, holy fucking shit.

Suddenly, it's difficult to breathe.

I remember very little from the night of the accident. Rachel and I had drunk a fair amount (my tolerance had been zero, it being the first time I'd ever experienced strong liquor) and the details of what transpired are hazy at best. I have one single memory of the boy with the coal-black hair walking toward me from that night—a single brief snapshot of him laughing, his face reflected in the rear-view mirror, as he sat in the driver's seat of the car. His handsome features—proud cheekbones, and strong jawline, full mouth and intriguing golden-chocolate eyes—all transformed by his broad smile. I remember thinking that he was the most beautiful guy I'd ever seen in my life. Everything is blank after that.

Theo Merchant's shoulders are broad. He's taller than most of the male students who just filed into Rosewood. He's also inked to hell and back. His long-sleeved grey shirt covers most of his skin, but I can make out the hint of intricate designs cuffing his wrists, extending out past his sleeves and climbing up his neck, peeking over the top of his shirt collar. There's something very magnetic about him, as he saunters through the desks toward the back of the room. All eyes follow him; it's as if *he* is the reason everybody came here, and now the seniors surrounding me are all patiently waiting for him to enact some sort of miracle that they came here to witness him perform. For some bizarre reason, I feel like I'm mirroring their reactions to him, too.

"Glad to see you all made it through the break," the guy at the front of the classroom announces. "We have at least five new faces here with us today." He casts an even look around at us, as Theo Merchant plants himself down into a chair two rows over from me, dumping his bag down onto the floor at his feet.

"I'm Mr. Garrett. I'll be taking some of you for Math. If I don't have you for Math, then you'll at least have me here during homeroom each morning. Aside from that, I'm not going to torture any of us by forcing you to introduce yourselves. You're old enough to conduct that kind of social nicety on your own time. Be nice to each other. Don't be dicks. If I find out any of you *are* being dicks, there's gonna be hell to pay. We good?"

The students around me chuckle. I crack an uncertain smile, faintly entertained that he'd use a curse word straight out of the gate. Sarai despises bad language. She's no fool. She knows we all swear like sailors, but heaven fucking help us if we curse in front of her. Even Ruth and Gaynor moderate their language so as to avoid her wrath.

Mr. Garrett takes roll call, and I'm surprised by the archaic method he uses to tally us. No smart pad. No keycard scanner. Toussaint boasts brand new laptops for its students, and there are online portals dotted all over the place, where emergencies or issues can be reported by students and teachers alike. There's a digital dashboard where I have to submit my work. I can also leave notices there for my yet-to-be-made friends, and open chat windows with any of my teachers. But Mr. Garret's going old school. In his hand, the ancient clipboard he's holding looks like it's about to fall apart. Its blue plastic is cracked all over the place, and the metal rivets on the back are bounded by an orange ring of rust.

Garrett reels off name after name, and the drone of his voice blends into the background hum of chatter, as I unashamedly stare *right* at Theo Merchant.

This bastard killed Rachel.

He may not have clamped his hands around her neck and snapped the bone on purpose, but his recklessness ensured that she didn't get out of the car and walk away that night. He was drunk. High. Obliterated. And now here he is, walking around like the second coming of Jesus Christ himself.

He grins at his friends as he unpacks his shit from his bag, muttering something under his breath to the blond guy with the chin dimple sitting to his right. He should be rotting behind bars for what he did. If I'd had my way, he would have been tried as an adult and sent to jail for a very long time. That didn't happen, though. He didn't even get sent to juvie. Not even for a fucking night.

His father stepped in and 'handled' the situation, and Theo Merchant was released from the police station less than three hours after the accident, never to suffer any further inconvenience from the whole affair thereafter. The whole thing is fucked is what it is. Fucking criminal. Money has always been able to buy guys like Theo their freedom, and the Merchants don't just have money. They have *old* money, and the reputation to go with it.

I hate him.

I fucking despise him.

I'm going to enjoy dismantling his life, one tiny piece at a t—

I go very, very still. Theo's stopped talking to the blond guy with the dimpled chin. He's whipped around...*and he's staring right at me.*

With a cold and creeping horror, I realize that he's not the only one; every single person in the room is staring at me.

"Sorrell Voss?" An irritated voice cuts through the fog that clouded my head, the sound of my name shocking me like I've just had a bucket of ice water dumped over my head. I snap my gaze to the front of the room, where Mr. Garrett is frowning at me, one eyebrow crooked higher than the other, waiting for me to respond.

"Shit," I hiss.

A ripple of laughter travels through the room.

I flush, hot and red.

Mr. Garrett raises both eyebrows now. "Daydreaming three seconds into your very first day on campus. Well, damn. I know this place isn't exactly a theme park, but I figured I might be able to hold your attention long enough to get through roll call. You *are* Sorrell Voss, I take it?"

I nod. "Yeah. I am. And...I'm here."

More laughter.

"Debatable, but I'll mark you present to avoid sparking a heated debate on existentialism." He marks the paper on his clipboard with a flourish, which entertains my new classmates even further.

"All right, all right. Settle. We've got a lot of information to get through and I have about five minutes to dump it all on you, so shut your yap holes. Justin, sit down, for fuck's sake. Let's keep this civilized. We're not marauding animals. You're gonna have to wait to kiss Hayley until you're out of my classroom." He takes a deep breath, dropping the clipboard down onto his desk with a clatter. "I can't believe that I have to say this to some of you again, but the gym's changing rooms are *not* co-ed!"

I'm immediately forgotten about as a loud groan goes up around me. At least five of my new classmates look genuinely frustrated by this reminder.

"Mr. Deakin decided to retire over break and won't be coming back. Some of you miserable bastards, yeah, you know who you are, forced him into early retirement. A substitute will be taking his English class, so..." He shrugs. "I dunno. I don't have a name. Figure it out. That'll be a nice surprise for you when you head to class."

Mr. Garrett talks and talks, spewing out announcement after announcement, sounding increasingly irritated as he goes through each of them. The guys and girls sitting around me react, groaning or laughing or booing, depending on the news, but I remain still in my seat, eyes locked on the whiteboard at the front of the room, not even daring to breathe.

I feel the pressure of those golden-brown eyes on me like a hand grabbing hold of the back of my neck. The weight doesn't shift; Theo Merchant does not look away.

SORRELL

"I'M TELLING YOU. He's not with her. He's *single*."

A girl standing near to her friend, two lockers down, laughs bitterly. "And? What am I supposed to do with that information exactly? Crack him over the back of the head with his lacrosse stick and drag him back to my room? I'm not even on his radar."

"*Put* yourself on his radar," the other girl insists.

I peek out of the corner of my eye, performing a quick assessment of them: both tall, waif-like skinny blondes. They're both wearing a fuck ton of makeup, and they're both wearing skirts barely long enough to cover their underwear. I see the curve of one of the girls' ass cheeks below the hem of the material as she shifts her weight from one foot to the other. They look like carbon copies of each other. I've encountered plenty of girls like them in the past—drones who finish each other's sentences, while impressively still failing to maintain a single logical thought in their collective hive minds.

"Panovich made it clear that Theo's off-limits this semester anyway. You should have heard him this morning, waxing lyrical about the importance of the school's varsity teams this year. How he'll be personally making sure that none of his athletes are distracted by *outside influences*."

The other girl snorts. I swear to god, I wouldn't be able to differentiate between the two of them if you stuck them in a line-up next to one another. "What's he gonna do?" she laughs. "Stand watch outside our bedrooms every night? He can't watch all of us all of the time. And you've fucking *saved* yourself for him, June. Your pussy's been gathering dust while the rest of us have been catching major dick all summer—"

If you leave children to listen in on adult conversations, they begin to think themselves very grown up. These girls sound like they're exactly that: children, playing grown-up. I laugh darkly under my breath as I take out an empty folder from my locker, slipping a brand-new notebook inside it.

"Excuse me? What the *fuck* do you think you're doing?"

I look up, and my mouth fights to curl into a smirk as I come face-to-face with Tweedle Dee and Tweedle Dumb. Neither of them looks very happy. Both of them have their arms across their chests, their tits straining against the too-tight material of their white shirts. I think… yeah, the one on the left with the beauty mark on her chin was on my floor this morning.

"Sorry? Can I help you?" I feign ignorance.

"No, you can't." The girl on the right has a sharp nose, a little hooked on the end. When she sneers down at me, her nostrils flare, and her whole face becomes angular, sharp and unattractive. Which is irrelevant anyway. It doesn't matter how expertly she tosses her hair over her shoulder, or how flawless her makeup is; one look at her and I can see just how ugly she is on the inside.

"You were eavesdropping," she accuses.

"You were *laughing*," Beauty mark adds to the charges being brought against me.

"You've been here five seconds and you've already pissed me off, Voss. Not smart." Hook nose shakes her head. "Not smart at all."

I close my locker door, taking my time to slide the folder into my bag. I make a point of giving these idiots an open-mouthed smile as I swing the bag over my shoulder. "Apologies. Do I know you?"

God, you could curdle milk with how smug these two bitches look right now. "No," Beauty Mark says. "But *we* know *you*. We know everything there is to know about you. Sorrell Voss. Seventeen. From Orange County. Mommy's a housewife. Daddy's a chemical engineer. You ran track last year and sucked at it from what I heard."

Holy fuck, if this isn't all extremely entertaining. These girls think that by gathering information about me, they somehow have power over me? Maybe that would be true, if every little piece of info they think they know about me wasn't a fucking lie. Except for the track thing, I guess. I did run track last year, and I did kinda suck at it.

I shrug. "You forgot my drug addiction. And the fact that I was the first fourteen-year-old at my school to get checked into rehab."

"*What*? Seriously?" Theo Merchant's biggest fan gapes at me.

"Uhh. Well. No." I lean in close, jerking my chin at them, signaling that I want to impart a secret. They lean in close too, unable to help themselves. "I actually got pregnant at the end of Freshman year. I mean, it was fine, but kind of hard to study when you have a newborn hanging off your hip, y'know?"

Their eyes double in size. The girl on the left has lost all motor function; her mouth flaps open and closed, while the one on the right takes a step back, as if teen pregnancy is catching. "Called it, Ash," the girl with the beauty mark sneers. "Didn't I say she looked like a slut?"

I could crush her trachea and end her life in a matter of seconds.

I could break her face so badly that she'd spend the next five years having reconstructive surgery and *still* look like a bag of hammered shit.

This knowledge warms immensely as I tip my head to one side, studying them. I point a finger at them in turn, laughing softly. "Y'know, I actually *do* think I know a little bit about you two. I address Beauty Mark first. "Margaret Elizabeth Johnson. You go by Beth. You're a Virgo. You tell everyone that you lost your virginity to Spencer Harris last year, but that's not true, is it? You lost your virginity to Lance Campbell when you were fourteen. Lance Campbell, your father's forty-seven-year-old business partner. Morbidly obese, right? One hairy dude. Your father bartered you off to him to settle a debt he owed him. Told you that you were such a good girl for helping him. And now when you fuck Lance..." I step in even closer, lowering my voice an octave. "Because you still fuck him, don't you,

Beth? Now when you fuck him, you do it because you like it. Because your daddy watches you on the cameras he's hidden in your bedroom, and the thought of his dick getting hard as he watches his fat slob of a friend pump his tiny little dick into you makes you all tingly, between your legs, doesn't it, *Beth*?"

My head snaps to one side when she hits me; the sound of her palm connecting with my cheek rings out like a gunshot in the hallway. Fifty people stop in their tracks, conversations halted, all turning to see what the fuck is going on. Beth is white as a sheet and vibrating with fury.

Of course I knew who she was from the moment I laid eyes on her. I've memorized the profiles of every single senior at Toussaint—profiles that were very comprehensive. Ruth was meticulous in her research. Always has been. The things that go on behind closed doors in some of these kids' homes is literally criminal, not to mention darkly depraved. The information I know about these kids could put quite a few people away for life and make the devil blush at the same goddamn time. I gave my new classmates nicknames when I first started analyzing their files to help me remember the sordid little details of their lives, though. Sometimes it's still easier to call them by those nicknames in my head.

"Lance *Campbell?"* Ashley hisses. Ashley Rainier, also seventeen. Has a penchant for beating her little sister. She's been in and out of therapy since she was eight because she can't stop eating her own hair. There's far more sinister shit going on with Ash, though. Far worse secrets I could weaponize to humiliate her if I chose to. I keep all of my stored facts about Ash hidden as she continues to stare at Beth. "That gross dude that was at your house on Christmas day?" she says. "What the fuck is she talking about?"

Beth's cheeks burn red as coals; the high color makes her look pretty in a way. From time to time, even our worst moments make us shine. "She's fucking lying. What the hell is wrong with you?" She shoves me, and I allow myself to be pushed back against the lockers. A loud clang rings out down the hall—the sound of my head bouncing off the metal door. "You're sick in the head," Beth spits.

"I don't know about that. My history seems pretty run of the mill in comparison to yours, wouldn't you say?"

I wouldn't be able to spout this line if she knew the truth. The skeletons in my closet are stacked so high and tight that it looks like a mass genocide took place in there. There's movement off to the right —a flurry of activity, heading towards us that tells me this little tête-a-tête is about to be broken up. I allow my eyes to become glossy and full of fear.

"Beth Johnson! Have you lost your mind?" A woman in a floral print dress charges toward us, parting the crowd of bystanders like Moses parting The Red Sea. Her skin is a warm brown, her hair a mass of tight curls. From the pictures I've seen of her on Toussaint's website, I know for a fact that Principal Ford's eyes are usually kind and soft, but right now they are far from it. "If you don't want to be expelled in the next three seconds, I highly recommend that you take your hands off that girl."

Beth shoots me a hard, hateful look but complies, giving me one last shove as she releases me.

"Beth!" Principal Ford blinks, shaking her head. Looks like her brain just can't compute what she's seeing. "I have no idea what's gone on but hear this right now. Whatever it is, it isn't going to fly. My office. Now." She turns to me, looking me quickly up and down. I can't decide if she's trying to remember my name, or is she checking me over for injuries.

"You're coming too, young lady. I will get to the bottom of this. You'll both sit in my office until I hear something that sounds like the truth."

Beth's cheeks flame, turning even redder. Her eyes are full of rage, but a pitiful shame resides there, too. She doesn't want to tell Principal Ford the truth. She doesn't want to even tell her what happened, because if she did, she'd have to tell her what I accused her of. And that? No. She's not going to do *that*.

"I was making fun of her," Beth blurts out.

Ford frowns. "And why would you do that?"

"Because I heard she was repeating her senior year."

Ford, slender and tall, makes a disapproving sound, folding her arms across her chest. "You're joking, right?"

Beth sets her jaw. "That's what I heard."

"Sorrell isn't repeating her senior year. And even if she was, why *would you pin her against a locker for it?"*

"Beth's boyfriend broke up with her," Ashley says, stepping forward. "She's had a really hard morning, and she just—"

Beth glowers at her best friend, and her message is clear: *shut the hell up. You're not helping.*

"I don't care if your boyfriend broke up with you, or your dog died, or a plane engine fell through your ceiling à la *Donnie Darko*. You do *not* physically assault another student because you're having a bad day!"

"I know. I'm sorry." Beth hangs her head, and the tips of her ears are scarlet.

"Is that what happened?" Principal Ford addresses me.

Hmm. Let's think about my options here. I could tell her the full story. It would be relatively easy to reveal what I know about Beth's fucked up home life. But...

But.

Information like this is a currency. Spend it now and its gone. Who knows what it could buy me in the future.

I nod, dragging up enough emotion to my face to appear embarrassed. "Yeah. She laughed at me. Called me stupid. Said she was going to tell everyone that I'd been held back."

Principal Ford rocks on her heels, sighing deeply. "Yes, well. It doesn't matter what she or anyone else says, does it? You know the truth, and that really is all that matters."

Humiliation isn't an easy emotion for me to emulate. After suffering through all that I did as a child, and then being thoroughly, ritually stripped of my ego by Ruth and Gaynor when I first arrived at Falcon House, I really don't care what other people think of me. This is all a manipulation, a front to build a story that people will believe about me. I try my best to force a tear out. Nothing triggers people's empathy response like a couple of fat, well-timed crocodile tears. "Yes, Principal Ford."

"Hush that now. You're fine to head on to your next class, Sorrell. If you have any problems settling in, my door is always open. And you," she says, wheeling on Beth. "You've scored yourself detention for a week, and you're banned from going to the Genesis Ball at the end of the month."

"Principal Ford!" both girls protest.

"I'm helping *organize* the ball," Beth says.

"Not anymore you're not. Go on. Get to class. And if I hear that you're bothering Sorrell again, so help me god if I don't ban you from every single social event of the coming year. Including your own graduation ceremony."

The two blondes wheel and stomp off down the hallway, bickering angrily between themselves as they flee. Principal Ford spends no more time coddling me. "Make some friends and fast," she tells me. "Those two are vipers. They'll make your life here miserable if you don't have a group of friends to protect you."

This place is even more prison-like than I thought.

I head down the hall, not really sure which way I'm supposed to be going, not really caring. The eyes of the entire school are on me as I hurry away from my locker. Mine are glued to my feet. Which is why I don't see him blocking my path, and I collide straight into his chest.

"Whoa! Jesus. Trying out for the football team, quarterback?"

Of course it's *him*. Just...seriously. Fuck my luck.

The first thing I notice is how tall he is; Theo Merchant towers over me. The second thing I notice is the weird blue tape wrapped around the tips of his index and the middle finger of his left hand. The spiderweb of fine, silvered scars that fan out across the back of the same hand, curving downward in a jagged line around the base of his thumb.

His hair—the color of coal, and midnight, and nightmares—is buzzed on the sides but a little longer on the top, swept back in that casual, artful way that boys seem to master without looking like they spent any time on their hair at all. His eyes are all honey and caramel, a brown so light that they look like burnished gold. His jawline is proud and strong, his cheekbones disgracefully high. His nose...damn. I've never given two shits about a guy's nose before, but Theo

Merchant's nose is as straight as an arrow and regal. There are three small freckles under his right eye that form an almost perfect equilateral triangle...

Fuck.

What am I doing? I'm staring, for god's sake. He cracks a cool smile at me, and hearts break all over the world. "You're not supposed to be here," he says.

Despite the warmth of their coloring, Theo's eyes have taken on a suddenly cold edge. In the back of my head, the alarm bells wail frantically, urging me to be on guard. I marshal my features, training my expression into a blank look as I meet those golden eyes. "In the hallway? I was just on my way to cl—"

His dark brows knit tight together. "At this *school*." Deep and resonant, the power of his voice hits me hard—a bass drum thumping in the cavity of my chest. The timbre of it fills me with dread.

'Take the wheel, Seb. She's got my dick in her fucking mouth.'

These are the words I remember Theo saying the night Rachel died. They've replayed in my head over and over again since that night. The sound of them looping on repeat have driven me to the point of nausea more than once. He speaks now, adding new words to my Theo Merchant memory bank, and my stomach rolls on cue.

"Excuse me?"

He huffs. "That would have been appropriate *before* you barreled into me."

Wow. This guy really is a prick. I master myself; Ruth will be disappointed in me if I don't stick to the plan, but everything inside me is screaming for me to hurl myself at this smug prick. *Hurt him. Maim him. Humiliate him. Kill him.* He deserves nothing better. Internally, I am a raging sea, a storm, a class ten hurricane that will rip him from his feet and tear the bastard limb from limb. Externally, I am as peaceful as a calm summer's day.

I give him the look that I've practiced so hard in the mirror—the doe-eyed, innocent, *'I'm so confused. Please help me,'* expression that turns even the most level-headed guys into morons. "Sorry. I'm new. I *am* enrolled, though. I'm not quite sure...what you mean?" I let out a nervous little laugh, looking down at the floor before quickly looking back up at him from beneath my own dark lashes.

Theo stares down at me blankly, unaffected by my coquettish little act. "I'm fully aware of your enrollment status. I'm fully aware of why you're here, and you can forget it. You're wasting your time. What, you thought I wouldn't remember you from the party?"

A jolt of adrenaline hits my veins, the burst of raw energy narrowing my focus to a pinpoint. Fuck. I barely saw him that night. I have no recollection of ever talking to him. I was in the car with him at the end of the night, but he'd been so fucked up…

He stares down at me, a god observing a pathetic little ant.

"Forget your little mission here. Leave now. Go home before anyone else gets hurt."

Theo doesn't even give me a chance to respond to this; the clicking of heels echoes down the hallway, the sound heading toward us, and Theo turns around, casually sauntering off toward a narrow staircase to the right.

"Miss Voss?" With her bright floral print dress and her colorful jewelry, Principal Ford is a vibrant pop of life against the cool pastels of Toussaint. I figured she'd left with Beth but apparently not. "Are you lost, Sorrell? This place can be a bit of a maze at first. Come on. Let me show you to your next class." She arrives next to me but rather than stopping, she swoops me up, wrapping one arm around my shoulder, and I'm carried along in her momentum as she bustles down the hall.

It takes me a moment to notice that the place is deserted—that the hallways cleared of all life the second that Theo Merchant showed up.

SORRELL

RATS CAN SENSE DANGER. Cockroaches. I mean, dogs and cats can, too. Horses are especially sensitive to people's emotions, as well as the weather. It's nothing special for complex organisms to perceive something or someone as a threat and react accordingly in order to preserve their own existence. People are a little more complicated. We're self-aware, and arrogant; we get sidetracked by our own egos.

Ahh, that storm's nothing. I can handle it.

I can take that guy. I'm way bigger than him.

I know what I'm doing, okay? I can make the damn jump!

Not one person stayed to linger in that hallway when Theo Merchant showed up. Down to a man, they fled the scene like rats fleeing a sinking ship, and I didn't notice because I was too busy reeling from the fact that the motherfucker *remembered me from the party.*

I'm fucked. I'm seriously fucking fucked.

The rest of the day speeds past in a blur of shuffling feet, and stuffy, airless classrooms, but I don't take any of it in. My racing thoughts make it impossible to focus on anything but this one devastating piece of information.

Theo knows who I am, and if he knows that, then what *else* does he know? At eight, once I'm done with dinner, eating alone at a table in the dining hall, slowly forking food into my mouth, tasting nothing but ash and silently screaming inside, I finally lock myself away in my room and call Ruth.

"Jesus, Sorrell. Stop this nonsense. So he remembers you from the party. It doesn't mean anything." She isn't remotely concerned when I'm done explaining my panic to her. "Stay the course. If you shit the bed now, all of this has been for nothing."

"I'm not shitting the bed," I hiss. "I'm *not* overreacting. He. Knows. Who. I. Am—"

"And what's he going to do about it? Burst into your room and point a finger at you, screaming that you came to Toussaint just to murder him in his sleep?"

"Uhh, *yes*?"

"You're being ridiculous. Get some sleep. Wait for me to contact you before you take any action against him. I'll tell you when the time's right."

"And in the meantime? What am I supposed to do?"

"Just go to school, Sorrell! Do your work. Keep your head down."

"Ruth, this—"

"Wouldn't Rachel have done this for you?"

This statement, well-honed and deadly sharp, stops me dead in my tracks. It's a cold and evil thing to say to me, but Ruth knows me well. Rachel would absolutely have come here to avenge me. She'd stay the course, no matter what. She'd be single-minded in her task until she'd accomplished her goal and Theo Merchant was dead.

I let out a tense, shaky breath. "All right. Fine. I'll move forward. But I'm telling you now, Ruth—"

The line goes dead.

I sit on the edge of my bed for a long time, clutching my cell phone in my hands, staring at a chip in the paintwork on the skirting board opposite me, unable to think straight. I figured Ruth would flip the fuck out when I told her what happened. I thought she'd send a car for me, immediately rethinking how we were going to deal with our

Merchant problem. In the very least, I thought she was going to turn the air blue with her cursing. But no. Nothing. She was irritated at *me*—that I'd worry over such a small, inconsequential turn of events.

I want to go home. Nothing about this situation makes sense to me right now. If Theo does know who I am and why I came here, then what's the point in staying? Once the element of surprise is lost, then there's no way to catch a mark off-guard. And who knows who he's talked to. If he's gone to any of the teachers, or even talked to his friends about me, and then something happens to him, I'm basically fucked. I'll be carted off in handcuffs before you can say *'premeditated murder.'* I was all bravado about going to prison yesterday with Gaynor, but I always planned to bail and disappear once Theo was dealt with. I never actually *intended* on going to prison…

A cold, tight knot forms in my stomach over the next few hours. I unpack the suitcase I brought with me from Falcon House, thrown off by the greys, reds, greens and blues of the skirts and dresses and tops that I carefully put away, feeling wrong that only one or two items of the clothes I've been given to wear are black. I make sure to put the photos of the fake family Gaynor had framed for me out on the nightstand. I arrange the little knickknacks and keepsakes Ruth said would be important to a regular high school senior around the room, feeling like a fucking fraud as I do it. These pointless little baubles mean nothing to me. I don't understand how they could be important to anyone. A threadbare, worn little stuffed rabbit. One half of a gold heart on a fine filigree chain. A stack of polaroid photos, and the camera to go along with them. A little box full of movie stubs, with names written on the backs in neat little black block letters:

Carla, Olivia and Spencer.

Wes and Carla.

Christina, Danny and Carla—Christina's b'day.

Ahmed—date.

Carla.

Carla.

Carla.

The names are all interchangeable, but not Carla's. Carla, my fake best friend, who Ruth and Gaynor agreed should have fake-died last year just like Rachel did. I don't know why they did that. Why, in this fabricated little world that they created for me, even my fictitious best friend had to be taken away from me. It doesn't seem fair. I've never begrudged the hand I was dealt in life. My childhood. Bolting from foster care the first chance I got. Living on the street. Having the ever-loving shit kicked out of me when I first joined Falcon House. I never resented any of it. Life is fucking hard; you're setting yourself up to be seriously disappointed if you expect it to be anything else. But I have to suffer even in my fake life? Ruth and Gaynor sent me here to accomplish a task, and to do that I have to become someone else. Would it have been so bad to let that someone else be happy? To have come from a happy place? To have lived a happy life, and have happy things to look forward to beyond their senior year? Where would the harm have been in that?

It's almost as if Ruth wants me to suffer. She's never been one to coddle—

BANG! BANG! BANG!

I drop the polaroid I'm holding—my face, photoshopped onto the body of a girl being hugged by two laughing friends—nearly jumping out of my skin at the loud hammering on my bedroom door.

What the fuck...

"Come on, New Girl! We gotta go!"

The little travel clock Gaynor bought me blinks at me from the windowsill; it's ten thirty. Curfew was at nine. Everyone should be in their own rooms now, studying or in bed. No way anyone should be out in the halls, banging on bedroom doors and yelling at the top of their lungs.

BANG! BANG!

"Come on, open up! We're gonna lose our window!"

"Fuck, Mel, just leave her," a different voice hisses. "What does it matter?"

"It matters because we've been waiting for this for three years," the other girl snipes back. "We're seniors now. We get to do this once. And you know the rules. *Everyone* has to come."

They're far from quiet. Their voices can probably be heard two floors down. I open the bedroom door, staring at the group of girls on the other side of it. None of them are dressed for bed. Their attire is certainly confusing, though. Dresses and short skirts. Low cut tops and push-up bras. A whole fuck load of makeup on their faces. But also thick, warm jackets, and furry suede boots, with thick rubber soles. They look like they're going clubbing but they have to navigate sub-artic conditions to get there.

The girl at the front of the group with shoulder-length wavy brown hair and bright blue eyeshadow sticks her hand out, grinning at me a little crazily. "Hey, I'm Mel. You are…?"

I take her hand and shake it, quirking an eyebrow at this motley crew. "Sorrell."

"Sorrell? Ohh, that's a pretty name. Okay, Sorrell. Nice to meet you. We're gonna need you to get dressed and ready in about sixty seconds if that's cool. We're in a hurry, and we forgot there was another newborn on our floor."

"Newborn?"

She waves me off, squeezing past me into my room. Wow. She's… she's really just making herself at home? Opening up my closet door, she begins riffling through the clothes I've just hung up in there, scrunching up her nose as she discards each item one by one.

"Newborns are new students. Sorry, I guess it's not a very friendly thing to call you. It's tradition, though. Jess?"

One of the other girls (who have all remained hovering respectfully in the doorway until now) steps forward. She's very short and slim. Waif-like. Her dark hair is cut into a pixie cut, and her button nose is slightly upturned at the end. She looks like her name should be Tinkerbelle.

"Do me a favor and run back to my room, will you?" Mel asks her. "The purple dress I tried on first is still on my bed. Can you grab it for me? And the curling wand in the bathroom too, please."

Jess grins, looking thrilled to have been tasked with this job. She takes off at a run, her boots stomping down the hallway, and I turn back to Mel, now half-submerged in my closet, throwing my hands up in the air.

"Well, it's lovely to meet you, too, but what the fuck are you *doing,* Mel?"

She laughs. "It's First Night, dumbass." The way she says dumbass makes it sound like an endearment.

"And I'm supposed to know what that is exactly?"

"Senior year commencement. First Night is *the* most legendary party of senior year."

"Apart from *Last* Night," another girl pipes up.

Mel pulls a face at her over my shoulder. "Well of course Last Night is a bigger party, Noelani. It's Last fucking Night."

I shake my head, unsuccessfully trying to dislodge the sounds of the bickering that ensues. "Woah, woah, woah. I'm sorry. It's super late, and I—I don't know any of you. I'm not going to any party right now."

"You have to," Mel says evenly. There's no threat or malice in her voice; she says this as if it's just obvious.

"I'm sorry, but—"

"If you don't, you'll be marked as an outsider. Someone who sees themselves as..." She cocks her head to one side, a small smile forming at the corners of her mouth. "...*Too good* for the rest of us. Do you think you're better than the other students at this school, Sorrell?"

I *am* an outsider. I won't be here long enough to change that, even if I do go to some stupid party. Do I consider myself better than them, though? There are plenty of reasons why I might: my insanely difficult childhood. The fact that I've had to work for every single advantage I've ever had in this life. The fact that all they've ever had to worry about is where their next designer dress is coming from....

No. None of that makes me feel like I'm better than them. Honestly, it only makes me jealous of them. Giving her a wan smile, I shake my head.

"All right then," Mel replies in answer. "Then we need to get you ready."

"Look, I'm sure everyone will understand. I'm tired, and I've barely unpacked, and—"

Mel straightens, crossing her arms in front of her chest. "They won't understand. They're elitist pricks with massive egos and *very* long memories, unlike some people I know." She laughs at this like it's the funniest thing she's ever heard. "If you don't come, you'll separate yourself from the rest of us. Once you're on the outside, there's no getting back in. No social clubs. There'll be no dates," she stresses. "Like, *none*. Any guy caught dating an outsider automatically gets kicked off the football team. The lacrosse team. Whatever team they're on…" She motions with her hands. "Booted. They get kicked out of their AP programs. Their clubs. Their friends all turn their backs on them. It's a fate worse than death."

"That's the dumbest shit I've ever heard. The teachers wouldn't allow that."

"Hah!" Mel throws her head back and laughs. She sounds positively amused. "Ahh, fuck. Of course. You're still under the impression that the *teachers* run this place. I hate to break it to you, Baby, but that just isn't the case here at Toussaint."

"Who runs it, then?"

She grins at me, wolfish, and I realize that I've just fallen straight into her trap. "Whoever wins the vote at tonight's party, of course," she says. "One guy. One girl. Together, they decide how we're going to live our lives for the next year. You wouldn't want to miss that now, would you?"

Dumb. So, so fucking dumb.

I should be packing up and getting the fuck out of here, not unpacking. Theo's little revelation in the hallway earlier is a massive spanner in the works, no matter what Ruth says. I promised her I'd stay the course though, so what choice do I have? It's not as if I can just walk myself out of here.

I have no idea what Mel means by this vote, but arguing with her seems futile, so I give in. When Jess returns with a purple sequin dress and a heavy make-up bag, brandishing a curling wand in her hand like it's an offensive weapon, I let Mel coerce me into getting changed. I sit very still while she curls my hair, and Noelani, a beautiful girl with almond shaped brown eyes, applies make-up to my face. They buzz around me like busy little worker bees around their hive, and they're finished with me in a mere matter of minutes. I stand in front of the mirror on the wall by the window, barely recognizing the girl staring back at me. She looks older than me. Less haunted. I suppose that has a lot to do with the full-cover foundation Noelani applied to the bruised shadows beneath my eyes, but still. The girl in the mirror looks healthy. Happy. I didn't even know my face looked like that when I smiled. There aren't many mirrors at Falcon House.

Mel stands back to admire her handiwork. "Perfect. Honestly, I'm impressed with myself, even if I do say so myself. Not everyone can work miracles under such duress."

Duress? She's the one who barged in here and demanded I let her poke and prod at me like I'm some kind of dress-up doll. If anyone's doing well under duress, it's fucking *me.*

She smiles benevolently, placing a hand on my shoulder. "Trust me, Sorrell. You're gonna be glad you came to this party tonight. You're gonna be really glad you let me work some magic on you first, too. I am literally your fairy godmother. Come on. We gotta go."

* * *

Seriously, Sorrell. Relax. Loosen up! What's the worst that can happen?

'Uhh, I could get drugged and assaulted and *die* like you?' I mutter under my breath, answering the sound of Rachel's voice in my head.

My best friend's taunting laughter rings in my ears as I traipse down the hillside toward the darkened forest, following behind a group of girls I do not know, heading into a situation that will more than likely blow up in my face.

Our breath kicks up in clouds of fog, billowing up into the night sky. The crisp winter air smells of wood smoke and is so cold that it burns my lungs and nostrils.

"Sorry? Did…you say something?" The tall, quiet girl walking closest to me blinks at me like an owl in the dark. Her name is Julia. Her lush, blonde hair hangs in a thick braid down her back, almost reaching her waist.

I shake my head, shoving my hands into the deep pockets of the winter coat Gaynor gave to me. I told her the thick Parka with the sheepskin lined hood was overkill, but she'd insisted I take it. I'm eternally grateful that I did now. "Just talking out loud," I say. "Bad habit."

"You know what they say…" Julia laughs a little uncomfortably. "Talking to yourself is the first—"

"No. Just. *Don't.*"

I'm all too aware that talking to myself is the first sign of insanity. Do I think that Rachel's voice in my head is real? Do I think I'm being haunted by her ghost or something? No. I know that I'm talking to myself when I carry out these conversations in my head. I just miss Rachel so damn much. I felt like I'd been ripped open and my heart had been cleaved out of me the day that she died. The sense of loss was too immense to comprehend. My mind coped with the hollow Rachel left behind the only way it knew how: it filled it up with her as best it could. Gave her some semblance of life, so that I might be able to have her with me still.

I won't stop talking to her in my head. Never. If I do that, I'll have well and truly lost her for good. And that? I just can't fucking handle that.

Poor Julia quails at the sharp tone of my voice. She tucks her chin into the collar of her jacket, so that just her eyes peer at me over the top of the material. "It's okay," she says, her words muffled. "My mom says that talking to herself is the only way she can have a sensible conversation most of the time. I get it." I can tell by the way her eyes crinkle at the corners that she's smiling, though she still looks nervous. "Anyway. I—I should catch up to Mel. My inhaler's in her purse, so…" She hurries up to the front of the group, leaving me to trail behind at the back.

Not wanting to risk another *oh-great-I'm-talking-to-myself-again* moment, I hum to keep Rachel's voice quiet—the same melody I was humming in the car yesterday with Gaynor. The rise and fall of the music streams through my mind easily, like flowing water over a riverbed, the sound of it beautiful and aching.

For the remainder of the walk, I'm alone. It's better this way. I'm lagging far enough behind that I could easily slip back to the school if I wanted to; the building looms out of the darkness, a gothic nightmare.

The vast lawns we have just crossed have been mown in opposite directions, giving the expanse of grass a striped appearance. I follow behind the other girls, listening to them chatter and giggle up ahead with a lead weight pulling at my chest. If everyone is expected to attend this party, choosing not to go *would* have been a mistake. I'd be drawing attention to myself, especially if I'd be ostracized the way Mel described. Blending in comes with a price, and Ruth told me I needed to blend in no matter what.

Mel leads us down a dirt track that winds down the hill, around a copse of towering trees, and out of sight of Toussaint. As soon as we skirt around the trees, the faint thump of music rises up to meet us. It's so dark now, away from the school, that I can barely see my hand in front of my face. Despite the dark, Mel seems to know exactly where she's going. I hurry to catch up with the group, grumbling unhappily to myself as I do so.

"Will Marcus be there?" Jessica asks up ahead.

Mel scoffs loudly. "What do *you* think? He'd never miss out on free booze. And you can bet your ass he'll be throwing his hat in the ring for Head Boy. The guy loves giving people shit. He'd never pass up the opportunity to have everyone fawning over him and licking his boots for the rest of the year."

Noelani makes a snorting sound; apparently, she agrees. "And what about Head Girl? Think Beth will get it?"

"Not if I have anything to do with it," Mel says.

"You know we'll all vote for you," Noelani replies.

"You'd better! Unless you wanna be running errands and shoveling Beth's shit until you graduate. I can't think of anything worse."

Urgh. Basic high school drama bullshit. This kind of divide never existed at Falcon House. It would never have been allowed to perpetuate. All internal grievances were settled on the mat, no matter how big or small, and the matter wasn't resolved until one of you was unconscious. You really had to mean it.

As we descend down into a small, enclosed valley, the source of the music comes into view: a large bonfire sends towering flames licking up toward the clear night sky. Crazy shadows careen in all directions as a crowd of people shift and cavort around the inferno, whooping and laughing at the top of their lungs. There are tables set up in the surrounding clearing, loaded high with food and drink.

I don't know what I was expecting, but it sure as hell wasn't this. The party isn't in the back room of a bar or a restaurant. Not at some rich kid's parents' house, like it was the night Rachel died. It isn't even in a *barn*. It's just a group of Toussaint's students, hanging around a fire in the middle of a clearing. It's freezing fucking cold, but as soon as we make it within twenty feet of that roaring bonfire, the girls begin to strip out of their coats and jackets, dumping them on top of a table already stacked high with winter gear.

Before I know it, I have a red solo cup in my hand and I'm glowering suspiciously at the noxious smelling liquid inside, wondering if it's spiked with the same shit Rach and I were given at that last party. I tip it out into the grass at my feet.

"Whoa, whoa, whoa! Don't waste that!" A drunk girl wearing a pink sequin tube top and white cut off jean-shorts snatches the cup out of my hand. There was barely anything left in it, but she tips back what remains and swallows it like it's manna from the gods. "This shit's expensive. And strong as fuck. The boys brought it as a gift. Why would you pour it out?"

I shrug, pulling the hood of my Parka up. "Not in the mood to get gang raped, I guess."

She narrows her eyes to slits, looking at me like I'm some kind of freak. "What the hell is wrong with you?"

"Ahh, y'know. A little childhood trauma here. Pinch of PTSD there. The usual..." I trail off as I walk away, smirking to myself. I feel so apart from these people. We're the same age, but we're different breeds. Different species entirely. While these motherfuckers were riding ponies and screaming at magicians, demanding more impressive tricks on their eighth birthdays, I was eating out of trash cans. When they were ten, they were going on vacations to The Hamptons and stuffing their faces on Maine's finest lobster. Meanwhile, I was kneeling in a filthy back alley, shooting Narcan up my foster-carer David's nose so he wouldn't fucking OD and die.

Apples.

Oranges.

I can never be like them.

Understand them.

Fuck, even tolerating them is going to be a challenge.

Ruth was crazy to think I could ever fit in here. I'm rubbed raw with contempt as I traverse the gathering, watching them flirt and laugh and tease each other, like they have nothing more important to worry about than impressing each other with theatrics at a dumb party. I despise them all.

On the other side of the fire, I catch sight of Beth and Ash, standing close together, whispering viciously. They've seen me, and from the looks of things they're really not happy that I've shown up here tonight.

You and me both, ladies. You and me fucking both.

Beth is wearing a pink feather boa, for god's sake. Ash, a fedora and heavy, elaborate electric blue eyeliner, swirling in elaborate designs around her eyes. Don't they realize how stupid they look?

I reach the edge of the crowd, content to walk my way back to the other side again, back where Mel and her clique are still standing, but when I turn around, I come face-to-face with the one person I would have loved *not* to bump into tonight.

His face is devoid of all expression as he stands in front of me. Shadows dance across his regal features, making him look ghoulish in the firelight. His full lips press together into an unimpressed line as he brings his solo cup up to his mouth and takes a sip of his drink. I say nothing. Do nothing. I just let him look at me. Though I'm wearing the Parka and my skin is basically covered down to my knees, I feel stripped bare by his gaze.

"I've been thinking, you know," he says. Another shiver traverses my spine, chasing up and then down, up and then down; I hate that a look like this from him could elicit any kind of physical reaction out of me, even if that reaction *is* repulsion. I find myself staring at the three dark freckles underneath his eye. I have to dig my fingernails into my palm to make myself stop. "Ahh, I'm sorry." I pout at him. "That's gotta hurt."

His flat smile curdles and turns sour. "Cute."

I try and slip past him, but he side-steps, blocking my path. "Girls like you think they're invincible. You think you're fucking untouchable."

I cock my head to one side. "That's funny. I literally said the same thing about you yesterday. And…girls like me? You know nothing about girls like me."

I attempt to move around him again. He mirrors my move again. "I know plenty."

"Oh really? Enlighten me." My tongue is slick with hatred. My throat throbs with it. "What do *you…*" I stab my finger into his chest. "Think you know about *me?* I'd love to hear it, Merchant."

He peers down at the point on his chest, right above his solar plexus, where my index finger just poked him. With his faded long-sleeved ACDC t-shirt and his ripped black jeans, his dark hair all mussed and so carefully messy, he looks like he's trying too hard not to be the person that he is—the rich, spoiled arrogant trust fund kid with the silver spoon shoved a mile up his ass.

"You think that just because you've suffered, we know nothing about suffering. You think that our pain pales in comparison to yours. Your pain is so much more important than ours. You, so holier-than-thou, with your fucking orphan kid doctrine, and your rules and your orders, with that white-hot vengeance burning in your veins."

It galls me that he's repeating the thoughts that were just clouding my mind out loud. It's even more galling that he does seem to know *something* about me. Once again, a tremor of panic sizzles in my gut. "And what do you know about my rules? My orders?" I spit the words out, forcing them past clenched teeth.

His dark eyes, almost black in the darkness, skip from my mouth, to my cheeks, to my own eyes, where they linger and burn. A sly smirk draws his mouth up on the left. "Oh, that would ruin the game. If you're intent on playing this thing out with me, we should at least make it fun, shouldn't we? But…why don't you help me out, Kid? When you report back tomorrow evening and relay all of the intel you've gathered about the situation here at Toussaint, will you do me a favor?"

"Why the fuck would I do *you* any favors?"

He ignores the question. "Ask her about Henry."

"Who the hell is Henry?"

Taking another sip of his drink, he shrugs. "That's for me to know and you to find out. Ask her, Sorrell." *He* slips around *me* now, heading back toward the fire, leaving me cold in his wake, and a spike of anger knifes me right between the ribs.

I follow after him. It's the wrong thing to do, but I can't help myself. "Ask *who*?" He doesn't answer, just keeps drinking casually from his cup, grinning broadly at people as he passes them by. The nonchalance is more than I can take. Grabbing him by the shoulder, I spin him around, and the dark liquor in his cup sloshes out, spattering down his shirt. He looks down at his chest again, now at the wet patch I've just caused, then slowly glances up at me with murder in his eyes.

"Who the fuck am I reporting back to, Theo? Who the fuck am I asking questions? Who the fuck do you think has—"

"*Ruth.*" The name fires out of his mouth, laced with venom—a cruel and raw sound that seems to cause him pain. "You know *that* name, don't you?" I reel back, both stung by his vitriol and stunned by that name on his lips. "Yeah, that's what I thought," he says coldly. "Why don't you ask your precious Ruth about Henry? And when she lies to you and tells you she has no idea what you're talking about? And tells you to do your job and stop asking stupid questions? Come find me. *I'll* tell you all about Henry then. Okay?" He breathes hard down his nose, nostrils flared, a dangerous light flickering in his eyes that has nothing to do with the fire.

"Hey, baby." Beth appears out of nowhere in a cloud of ridiculous pink feathers and cloying, sweet perfume. She runs her hand over Theo's chest, casting a look of abject disgust in my direction as she does so. She looks away from me and back up at him, fluttering fake eyelashes. "You haven't even said hello to me yet, babe. Where the hell have you been all night?"

He doesn't even look down at her. Tipping his cup back, he drains it, the muscles in his throat working as he swallows, knocking back the remainder of his liquor. With the cup now empty, he tosses it into the fire, never tearing his gaze away from me. No further words pass between us, but the look in his eyes speaks volumes: he's daring me to do as he's told me.

He clears his throat, turns and storms off into the throng of people without so much as a backward glance.

Beth wheels on me like an angry pit viper. "Stay the fuck away from Theo, bitch. He's *mine,* and everyone with half a brain cell here knows it. I don't know who the fuck told you that shit about Lance, but it's not true. And if you even think about releasing any kind of pictures, or video, or—or—or whatever, then so help me God—"

I laugh right in her face. "Beth, if I decide to do anything of the sort, then even God won't be able to help you. *Bitch.*" These petty games are beneath me. Engaging with the likes of her is demeaning on every possible level. I hate that I get drawn into it, but the sheer entitlement of the girl rubs me the wrong way.

Her face is a rictus of rage as she leans close to whisper to me, mirroring the very actions I took with her in the hallway this morning. "My father will never let that shit get out, you stupid little cunt. What, do you think he's just gonna sit by and let you spill something like that to the general public?" She wraps her hand around my forearm, tightening her grip, trying to dig her fingernails into my skin, but I'm wearing a thick jacket, for fuck's sake. "My father will sue you for every single penny your family is worth. He'll take everything. And I mean *everything.*"

With very measured, careful movements, I place my hand on top of hers and remove it from my arm, wrinkling my nose, as if I find touching her repugnant. It is not an act. "The beautiful thing about having nothing is that no one can take it away from you, Beth. When you have no things, or money, or reputation...you're free. I know that's a foreign concept to you, but it really is liberating. Your father can't destroy me, sweetheart. I *am* nothing. There's nothing to destroy."

She spits something after me as I walk away from her, but I can't even be bothered to listen. The show she just put on was pathetic, and I think she knows it. Theo Merchant is mine. Hah! The guy didn't even register her existence. If he wasn't responsible for my best friend's death and I hadn't been sent here to break him, I'd make a point of convincing the bastard to fall in love with me just to fuck with her.

"All right, guys. The moment you've all been waiting for has arrived!" Over on the other side of the bonfire, a tall guy with wavy brown hair stands on top of a stack of pallets, holding a bottle of tequila over his head. He takes a huge swig from the bottle and then sprays it from his mouth, sending an arc of fire leaping up from the blaze. Everyone goes quiet, turning as one to face him.

"Sorrell! Sorrell, Jesus Christ, girl. I've been looking for you all over the place." Mel's suddenly standing next to me. She places her hand in the small of my back, urging me forward. "Come on. You've gotta come with me."

The loud bass music that has been thumping out of the speakers, set up in the tree line, cuts out abruptly as Mel cajoles me back toward the girls from my floor. I allow myself to be pushed along, still hot with frustration over my interaction with Theo and the words that I exchanged with Beth.

"Take off your jacket, for crying out loud," Mel urges.

"It's cold," I say flatly. "I don't even want to be out here. I want to be standing out here in nothing but a tiny dress even less."

"It wasn't a suggestion." Mel sighs in frustration. "Look. We need to be noticed. We need one of us to be picked, okay? If we don't make an impression, we're *all* fucked."

Goddamnit. My patience for this horse shit is wearing paper thin. I swear, all I've done since that knock on my bedroom door is ask questions, and none of them have been answered to my satisfaction. "Picked for *what*? Head Girl?"

"You'll see. Fuck, just take the coat off! Please! I am literally begging you. They're not gonna pick *you*, I promise. Of all the people here—" She huffs out another sigh. "We just need to—"

"All right. As you're all aware, my name is Sebastian West!" the guy with the tequila bottle and the penchant for pyrotechnics calls out. "Eight years ago, my brother, Jared, created the inaugural First Night rituals, and those rituals have been carried forward ever since. Tonight, it is my greatest honor and privilege to continue what he started nearly a decade ago. We've all been waiting a long time for this, guys, so without further ado, let's get this show on the road."

I survey the senior students of Toussaint Academy, numb down to my core, amazed by the looks of excitement on all of their faces. I've heard about shit like this. College kids drinking each other's piss and swearing blood oaths while chugging beer naked and smashing their own hands in doors to prove their commitment to fraternities. I never thought for one second that this kind of neanderthal exhibition would take place in a fucking high school. Not even one so pretentious and over the top as Toussaint.

"First item on the agenda is guy's choice. Ladies! Form up! You all know about the selection. You've come here dressed in your finest, ready and willing to be judged."

"The fuck I *did*," I snap.

"Shh! Oh my god." Mel elbows me sharply in my side. "You know what? You're here," she hisses. "That's enough. You're not gonna get picked. Keep the ugly ass jacket for all I care. Just don't ruin this for the rest of us, okay? Stand there and keep your mouth shut." Through all of her corralling and jostling, she's been fairly sweet with me up until now. In fairness, I don't think she's truly angry at me. She looks more...worried. Which, I, in turn, find very worrying, too. What the *hell* is about to happen?

"Guys, form a line on the other side of the fire. Girls get to pick first as a group!"

The female contingent of the gathering dutifully line up, chattering nervously, all of them wearing conspiratorial smiles on their faces. Even Beth and Ash look eager as they bully their way to the front of the line that rims the fire, shoving their classmates out of their way.

"Two minutes. That's all you get!" Sebastian calls. "If you haven't come to a consensus by then, we'll draw lots and pick for you. You know the drill!"

How do all of these people know what the fuck is going on right now, and I am so utterly in the dark?

'I *think it's kind of exciting,*' Rachel's memory murmurs in my ear. Of course she would think that. Rachel was always so jealous of other kids' high school experiences. She always regretted the fact that she'd never played dumb high school games. Never got to chase down the Home Coming Queen title. Never got asked to Prom. She always felt like she'd missed out on so much. I'd been ecstatic to avoid the torture of such archaic teenaged popularity contests. She'd laughed at me for it and called me a stick in the mud.

"Lachlan Taylor," the girl next to me whisper-shouts.

"NO!" A chorus of shouts echo the same objection into the night.

"What the hell? No way are we picking, Lachlan. He's got a monobrow. And his father owns a chain of *grocery stores,*" Noelani mutters.

Lachlan's family owning a chain of grocery stores must be repulsive to the girls; a number of them nod in agreement, crinkling their noses.

"I vote Justin Rathers. He's jacked," Mel suggests. "I've heard that his dick is huge."

Ash rolls her eyes. "Why are we wasting our time with this? We all know who's gonna get picked."

"Right." Beth folds her arms across her chest, emphasizing her very considerable cleavage. "We need to hurry. If we don't choose fast, they're gonna choose for us, and I am *not* fucking Zack Richmond. His skin is disgusting. I've never seen that much acne on a dude before."

"Who says they're gonna pick *you?"* another girl demands.

"Yeah. What makes you think you're gonna get chosen?" someone to my left adds.

Beth rolls her eyes. "Get real. You really think a single one of them would select one of you over me? *Please."*

I blink, looking from Mel to Ash to Noelani. "I'm sorry? Someone has to *fuck* someone?"

Three girls down to my right, quiet Julia with the thick braid dips forward, shooting me a warning look, holding a finger to her lips. She wants *me* to be quiet, but I don't know why. None of this is making a lick of fucking sense, and I am just about reaching the end of my tether.

"Shut your mouth, Newborn," Ash hisses. "You're not even welcome here. No one asked you to come."

"I asked her to come," Mel fires back. "She has as much right to be here as anyone."

Ash looks like she's about to throw herself at Mel and start clawing at her face.

"Enough! SOMEONE TELL ME WHAT THE FUCK IS GOING ON!" Damn. I didn't mean to shout so loudly. On the other side of the fire, the guys, talking amongst themselves the same way we are, burst out into a hail of laughter.

"We have to pick one of them," Ash says tightly. "And then that guy picks one of us. Those two people fuck in front of the rest of us. It's just how it is. It's fun. It's hot. It's a rite of passage. Now we're running out of time. We need to pick someone, or they're gonna pick their grossest virgin to rail one of us and we won't be able to do a single thing about it."

"Umm, we could say…*no?*"

The girls look at me like I've lost my mind.

"That's it. I'm choosing for us," Beth declares. Before anyone can stop her, she steps forward and yells, "WE PICK THEO MERCHANT!"

A collective cry goes up amongst the girls, but it's weak, half-hearted at best. I get the feeling that Theo was going to be chosen no matter what. On the other side of the fire, a roar splinters the boy's group apart—it sounds nothing short of a victory cry.

"I'm fucking out of here." I step back, determined to peace out on this nonsense before it gets any more ridiculous, if that's even possible, but hands grab at me from all sides, holding me in place.

"You've got nothing to worry about, Sorrell," Mel says. "Like I said, no one knows you here. You've got no clout whatsoever and you look like a goddamn quaker dressed in that coat. Just stay the course. Let us handle this. It'll be over in a minute, and you can go hide back in your room."

It isn't as if I couldn't break free and bolt. On my worst day, that would be easy. But there's a pleading light in Mel's eyes. This is desperately important to her for some reason. It's important to everyone else here, and it seems as if I'll be making a lot of enemies if I bail.

I can't think of anything worse than watching Theo Merchant fuck one of these girls, though. My memory of the night Rachel died is so spotty and fractured that I can't even recall if she was *with* him or not, but I know in my gut that she was. She liked him. She flirted with him all night. Before things got really hazy and my recollection of that party starts to splinter, I remember her taking his hand and leading him up some stairs…

"Our boy Theo! Good choice, ladies! We all know how wet Merchant makes the lot of you." Raucous laughter fills the air as the boys begin to filter around the fire, joining us on our side of the blaze.

Sebastian still leads the gathering. Even without the pallets to stand on he seems like a giant amongst the sea of seniors. He stands in front of the line of girls, unbuttoning his black shirt, shucking it off and hanging it from a tree branch, out of the way. His chest is packed with muscle, his stomach a wall of ripped abs. If I saw him on the street, I'd think he was hot; there's no denying it. Right now, his cockiness as he struts up and down the line of girls makes me want to punch him in his throat.

The last guy to join us snatches the bottle of tequila out of Sebastian's hand and holds it to his lips. I watch the amber liquid drain from the glass as Theo chugs. He doesn't look particularly happy to find himself in this position, but he's still here. Still resigned to following through with this challenge.

"Careful, son!" Sebastian jeers. "You're gonna give yourself whiskey dick if you're not careful. Wouldn't wanna ruin the show for the rest of us now, would you?"

Theo grimaces at him, baring his teeth. "Fuck you, man. My dick'll be just fine."

"This is stupid," I mutter.

"*Shh.*" Jessica comes up behind me and places her hand in mine, lacing our fingers together. She holds onto me tight, squeezing. She's silent. She looks like she wants to speak now, but the time for that has passed, I think.

Theo begins to pace up and down the line, casually glancing at each girl as he goes. He stops in front of Mel, who visibly blushes under the scrutiny of his gaze. But he moves on. One by one, he works his way down the line. When he reaches me, he stops and glares at me dead in the eye. My heart surges like a piston.

No way am I screwing this monster.

No. Fucking. Way.

His eyes are twin burning coals as he lifts the bottle of tequila to his mouth again and drinks…

…and then continues down the line.

He assesses each girl in turn, but he doesn't stop again.

He starts over from the beginning of the line, looking at Ash, looking at Beth, looking at another three girls, and then Mel, and then Jessica, and then me…

He stops.

Runs me through with a look so burning and intense that I can feel the heat and the anger of it down to my bones.

He raises the bottle to his mouth once more and drinks. The light from the fire plays over the back of his hand, highlighting the web of faint scars that mark his skin there. His eyes stay locked on me as he swallows again and again. I feel the blood rushing to my cheeks. Theo Merchant isn't just some seventeen-year-old senior. No, he's far more than that. He's fire, and ice, and a maelstrom of chaos in between, and the way he's staring at me makes me feel like the ground is cracking apart around me and everyone else is falling away… disappearing… vanishing into the void.

I hate him.

He is a monster, and I can't look away. To look away would be to let him win.

He passes the bottle to me, and I take it without hesitation, draining the last few mouthfuls just to fuck with him. To spite him. To show him and everyone else here present that I'm not afraid of him. The liquor burns like hellfire itself as it races down my throat, setting fire to my stomach.

"Uhh…" Sebastian sounds confused. "Is this…uh, is she your choice, man?" he asks.

Theo's eyes spear me through, pinning me to the spot. If he so much as nods his head right now, I will knock this motherfucker out where he stands. I will not have his hands on me. I will not tolerate his—

Bitter laughter erupts from him, loud, full of disdain. "No, man. Don't be fucking stupid." He snatches the bottle from me, spins around and launches it into the fire.

"Then make up your mind!" Seb demands.

Theo runs his tongue over his teeth, looking down the line of girls again. He's looking at me again when he says, "None of them are hot enough to fuck. I'm out."

Beth takes a step forward, her mouth hanging open. "But..."

Theo's face is a mask of contempt as he turns to her. "But *what,* Johnson?"

The girl pales. As much as I detest her, I almost feel bad for her as she steps back in line. "Nothing."

"That's what I thought." Theo pivots, turning his back to the line-up. I watch him walk away. Black t-shirt, black hair, black jeans. The guy is made out of darkness. It's no surprise that he melts into the night, disappearing after only six or seven paces.

Sebastian looks like he's about to implode, looks like he has a thousand curse words dancing on the tip of his tongue, right behind his gritted teeth, but rather than reaming Theo out, he exhales sharply and plasters a mocking smile on his face. "Merchant wants to ruin our fun again. No surprises there. It's fine, though. It's fine. Whatever. If he can't be a man and get the job done, then I guess *I'll* just have to do it."

His statement elicits a variety of reactions, ranging from surprise and annoyance from some of Toussaint's students, to giddy excitement from a couple of the girls.

Seb steps forward and takes Theo's place. He doesn't waste time walking up and down the line like Theo did. He immediately takes Ash by the hand and tugs her forward. Ash's eyes go wide, shock rippling across her face as he pulls her to him.

Beth lets out a cold bark of laughter. "Yeah, Ashley! You're finally gonna get laid!"

"I—I can't!" Ash says. "I—" She looks back at Beth, shaking her head.

"You're gonna forfeit?" Sebastian asks.

"No! She's not forfeiting," Beth says.

Next to me, Jess sighs so quietly that only I can hear her. "If she forfeits..." she whispers. She doesn't finish the sentence, though.

"What? What happens if she forfeits?"

"They'll never let her live it down. She'll spend the rest of the year being mocked and ridiculed."

"So...that's what they're gonna do to Theo now?"

Jess shrugs noncommittally. "I guess?"

The light from the fire twists and shifts, casting ugly shadows across Sebastian's features as he narrows his eyes at Ashley. "What's it gonna be, Ash? Wanna have some fun, or are you chicken shit like Merchant?"

"I—I—" Ashley takes one last look at Beth, who guns her friend down with a murderous glare.

"You embarrass yourself and you embarrass me," Beth hisses. "It's just a dumb challenge. It doesn't mean anything."

Awkwardly, Ashley winds an arm around Sebastian's waist, smiling. "I'm no chicken shit. I'm down. But...got any more of that tequila?"

Sebastian's smile grows. He palms Ashley's ass through her short skirt, nuzzling his face into her neck. "Sure thing, baby. Follow me."

I can't imagine what the students at this wretched school could do to Ashley over the course of the next year that could possibly be worse than letting this smug bastard fuck her in front of everyone. Ashley probably has some idea, though, and she's willing to participate in this ritual rather than face the consequences.

Things unravel quickly. Seb hands Ash a new bottle of tequila, and she drinks, swallowing down four massive mouthfuls before handing it back to him. Dutch Courage. As soon as Seb has relieved her of the bottle, he passes it off to one of his friends and falls on Ash like a demon. His mouth crashes down onto hers, and a roar fills my ears. Toussaint's senior year class lose their ever-loving minds.

Ash melts into him like a good girl. As Sebastian's hands rove aggressively all over her body, she comes apart, curving into him, smiling against his open mouth as he flicks at her top lip with his tongue. Suddenly, she doesn't look so hesitant anymore.

A wave of nausea rolls over me.

This can't really be happening, can it?

Is this what happened to Rachel? Did Theo coerce her into some depraved sex act and let all of his asshole friends watch? Did they play the same kind of abhorrent game the night we went to that party? And could I have forgotten something like that, even if I had been drugged?

I can't say for sure.

More alcohol is passed from person to person, making its way around the crowd. I don't reject it this time. My insides feel as if they're boiling in acid. I think I'm going to throw up. As I accept bottle after bottle, taking a mouthful from each, the heat of the booze slowly increases, making me more and more numb the drunker I get.

By the fire, Sebastian strips Ash naked with rough hands. He says something to her, whispering into her ear, and she shoves him back, hands planted against his t-shirt, laughing. She shakes her head, and he shakes his, setting a firm look on her, leaning to speak into her ear again. She looks up at him, marshalling her face into a mock serious expression, then nods up and down slowly. I can't hear what she says, but...

Then she's pulling his shirt over his head. Then, she's unfastening the belt at his waist. Then, she's laughing, giddy and incredibly shy as she undoes his jeans and pulls them down over his hips.

"Jesus Christ. I'd heard rumors that he didn't wear underwear." Mel's eyes are huge in her head as she stares at Sebastian West's dick. I didn't hear her come and stand beside me. I didn't even notice when Jess let go of my hand; the girl's disappeared into thin air.

I try to keep my eyes trained on Mel's scandalous smirk but it's impossible.

Seb's cock stands proud and erect, hard as steel against the warm glow cast off from the fire. He trails his hand up Ash's arm, closing his grip around her bicep, drawing her to him, and she goes to him willingly. The girls all look on with jealousy burning bright in their fevered eyes, and a pinch of nausea rolls through me. I can't understand these people. I can't understand why they're all just standing here in their little factions, hungry to see more. Most importantly, I don't understand why *I* am still watching.

He kisses her, crushing her bare breasts up against his chest. Her skin looks like a painting, with the orange glow cast off from the fire dancing all over the backs of her legs and her buttocks. The muscles in Seb's arms flex as he wraps them around Ash's body—I hadn't noticed the tattoos flared across his shoulders and his back, but I see the black ink fanned across his skin as he spins her around, turning away from me and the other on-lookers, giving us his back.

Ash gasps, breathless, as he slides a hand between her legs, guiding them apart, and works his fingers there—

"Well, fuck me," Mel mutters, throwing back her drink. "Last guy who touched my pussy had no clue what he was doing. West doesn't seem to have any issues. I doubt Theo would have, either."

"Oh, I'm sure *he's* had plenty of practice." Spite drips from my every word.

Mel hums, shaking her head. "Theo? Hah!" She chews on her thumbnail, eyes glued to Sebastian's hand, still working between Ashley's legs. "Maybe. Maybe not. I think you'd be surprised."

"What does *that* mean?"

Sebastian slides his fingers into Ash, gradually pumping them in and out of her. The guys howl and yell obscenities at their friend, encouraging him, egging him on, and my need to vomit intensifies to a punishing level.

"Theo's never dated any of us," Mel says. "No matter how hard some of us have tried, he's never taken any of us out. Never flirted with any of us. Never even looked twice at any of us."

This news surprises me. I remember the sound of Rachel moaning in the back of the car, the night of the party we went to last year. I can't be certain what was happening between them, but it had sounded like things were getting hot and heavy. Maybe Theo Merchant has a 'don't-shit-where-you-eat policy? Maybe he just has high standards?

This thought nearly makes me laugh out loud. I can't imagine him having any standards at all. Bastard.

Sebastian's head tips back when Ash takes hold of his dick and begins pumping her hand up and down, working the thick length of him for everyone to see. His mouth falls open, and I watch his lips move, some small uttered curse tumbling out of his mouth, and the look of ecstasy on his face finally pushes me over the edge.

This place is so fucked.

Nothing seems like the truth. At every turn, it feels like I'm only being given half of the facts, and not just by Mel, but by Theo. By *Ruth.* Theo knew who *she* was, for fuck's sake. His demand that I should ask her about this Henry person is testament to the fact that there is more going on here than meets the eye, and there's no way I'm doing anything until I figure out what that is. "I have to go back." I hold the back of my hand to my mouth. "I can't—I can't fucking watch this. I feel sick."

Mel laughs softly. When I look at her, she's studying me, arching an eyebrow at me. "Are you a *prude,* babe? This is nothing. Haven't you ever watched porn?"

That's none of her damned business. I barely know her; I'm not going to tell her something so personal. "This is a little different than watching porn."

"Is it?" She smirks. "It's still sex. One version is on a screen. This version is just...right in front of you. I don't see the problem."

"This is...this is *ridiculous!*" My cheeks are too hot.

"Come on, then. If you're having such a terrible time, you need to make sure Sebastian's seen you properly one last time before you go." She takes me by the hand and tries to shove me forward. I've let her push and pull me around all night, though. I let her dress me up and paint my face. I allowed her to convince me to come down here against my better judgement. I'm done.

Wrenching my hand free, I dig my heels in, refusing to walk another step. "Fuck Sebastian!"

"I'm sure that can be arranged. Sebastian will screw around with anything that moves. Once he's done with Ash—"

"Oh my god. Look, just *stop!* I didn't come here for this! I didn't move all the way across the damn country just to jump feet first into some weird sex cult."

"No. You came here to finish your high school education, graduate and begin your life. We all did. But there's more to life than writing papers and maintaining your GPA, Voss. Don't you want to have a little *fun?*" She throws up her hands, laughing, and I can see it written all over her: she really believes what she's saying. There's really nothing wrong with this as far as she's concerned.

"Sebastian knows I was here," I say tiredly. "He saw me plenty of times. I'm going to fucking bed."

She doesn't try to stop me this time. As I turn and walk away, the crowd cheers, and I know why: Sebastian has Ash on her back, and he's inside her.

SORRELL

I DON'T like it here. The air is too clean, the sky too grey. The clouds hang too low, hovering just above the tree line, blotting out the mountains on the other side of the lake. I stare at the view out of the window, resenting the sheer greenery of it all, missing the mayhem of Los Angeles, while at the same time not seeing any of it at all.

Theo, standing by that fire.

Those dark, impenetrable eyes.

For fuck's sake, Voss. Get a grip of yourself.

I shake my head, erasing the images from last night's party from my mind. I am sick, and twisted, and broken. I've never despised anyone as much as I despise Theo, but both times when I've been in his presence, something bizarre takes place inside my body. The way my stomach rolls. The way my palms feel clammy. Fuck, the way my heart starts beating out of my chest like a frantic kick drum. I can't account for any of it. My reactions to him have nothing to do with how much I hate him. That's not what I'm experiencing when I'm in his presence, and it feels so fucking *wrong.*

I shouldn't be thinking about Theo like that. The only time I should even allow him to enter my thoughts is while I'm plotting his demise, but…

The cruel tilt of his mouth when he stood there, smirking at me.

The way the muscles in his throat worked as he drank from that tequila bottle...

The pressure of his hand on my arm, when he stopped me from walking away...

The smell of him, flooding my senses—mint and bergamot. The faintest hint of leather...

God *damn* it.

Lord have mercy, I am *so* fucked up.

Shaking my head, I hold my cell to my ear, listening to the purr of the ringtone, chewing on the inside of my cheek. I've been dreading this call, but it has to be made. I'm supposed to check in with Ruth every night at eight, but there's no way I can make it through an entire day with all of this shit playing on my mind. Theo told me to ask her about Henry. Though I don't want to give him the satisfaction of doing exactly as he ordered me to, I also need to know what the hell is going on here and I need to know *now*.

I came to Toussaint thinking that I held all of the cards, when the truth of the matter is that Ruth sent me into the lion's den, unarmed and ill-prepared. If there's any kind of connection between Theo and Ruth, then that is vital information that I have to know. If and when anything happens to him, I'm going to be the very first suspect on the police's list if there's absolutely anything at all in Theo's past to connect him to Ruth.

The phone rings out.

I hang up and call again, and this time the line doesn't even ring; it goes straight to voicemail.

Great. She's screening my calls now.

What does that mean? Does she know I've spoken with Theo again, and that I'm pissed as hell about the mission she's sent me on? She can't know. And yet something niggles in the back of my head, eating away at me. She sounded so weird on the phone last night. Abrupt and angry, even for her. Setting the phone down on my nightstand, I pack my bag for the day, grabbing the books I'll need for class.

'Better hurry up, Voss,' Fake Rachel singsongs in my ear. *"You're gonna be late."*

"I *know*," I bite back. "If I hadn't been thinking about what *you* would have told me to do last night, I would never have gone with those girls, and I wouldn't even be tired right now." I'm still stewing on thoughts of Ruth and Theo when I hurry out of my room... directly into the path of one of the girls from last night. Thank holy merciful fuck that it isn't Mel. It's the pretty blonde, Noelani. I didn't pay too much attention to her last night, but she looks like an old friend I used to have back in Los Angeles. Sun-bleached hair. Bright blue eyes. Almond-shaped eyes. Freckles across the bridge of her nose. It's uncanny, really. I find myself liking this girl, even though I know nothing about her. She smiles at me, giving me a friendly grin as I pull up short, stopping myself from running into her.

"Hey," she says. "You too, huh?"

"Me too?"

"Slept through your alarm? I swear I snoozed it once, and here I am, three seconds away from getting a demerit." Her tie-dye shirt is rumpled. Beneath her eyes, dark shadows lurk beneath poorly blended foundation. Now that I'm getting a closer look at her, she looks like she just rolled out of bed.

"I take it you stayed for the show last night?" I'm teasing her. At the same time, I'm also repulsed by the idea that she chose to stay and witness the display Sebastian and Ash put on.

She blinks at me a couple of times, as if she's trying to figure out what the hell I'm talking about, but then her expression darkens. She studies me with a look I can only call curious. "Yeah. Right. Last night. The party. You left right before everything kicked off, didn't you?" Her brow creases.

"Uh...well, I'd say everything was in full swing by the time I'd left, but I guess you could say that."

"You didn't get in trouble, though, did you?"

"What do you mean, trouble?"

"About fifteen minutes after you left, a bunch of security guards came down and cleared us all out. The whole thing got shut down. People bolted back to the school through the woods, but Principal Ford was waiting inside the main entrance when they came through the doors. I came in through the back with Mel and some of the others, but a whole bunch of people got caught."

"Fuck."

"Yeah. Fuck. Sebastian's raging. He thinks someone ratted us out to the night guards, but everyone was at the party. Apart from..." She trails off.

I've already seen where this is going, and I don't like it one bit. "Apart from me," I finish for her.

Noelani nods. "Yeah, well. I don't think Seb realizes that you'd already left. Mel, and Julia, and me…I think we're the only ones who *do* know."

"I didn't say anything to anyone. I came straight back here. Didn't see a soul. The place was in total darkness when I came in, too. There was no sign of Principal Ford.

Noelani looks me dead in the eye, her sandy brows banking together. "Really? It wasn't you?"

"I swear. I thought the whole thing was stupid. I didn't wanna get involved. I left. That was the end of it. I'd never go running to the guards to *report* a party, though. That's just fucking dumb."

She thinks about this for a moment; I can almost hear the gears in her head whirring. "Okay. Well…I believe you." She sounds surprised that she does. "But if Seb finds out that you left before shit kicked off, he's gonna figure it was you who went to Ford. Trust me. I wouldn't mention it to anyone if I were you."

* * *

The hallways are full of chatter and gossip as I make my way to *Rosewood.* I keep my head down, trying not to make eye contact with anyone. Thankfully, no one stops me to ask *my* version of events. I don't know why anyone would, but I'm grateful all the same.

Mr. Garrett is ten minutes late to *Rosewood.* There are still a handful of empty chairs when he bustles in through the door looking harried.

"Well, you morons sure know how to start the year on the right foot, don't you?" he says, casting a weary look around the room. He dumps his bag down onto his desk, then faces us, hands on his hips. "I hope you all had fun, 'cause there won't be any more shenanigans until graduation, I can tell you that much. Principal Ford's gonna have you guys on lockdown until you pack your shit up and move out of here and that's a *fact*."

"Sorry, what exactly are you talking about, Mr. Garrett?" a girl with hair almost as black as mine asks on the front row. She chews the end of her pen, grinning impishly.

"Don't give me that crap, Marnie. You were *all* down there at that party, and Principal Ford knows it. Just because she didn't catch all of you doesn't mean that you're in the clear. There'll be repercussions for what went down last night, and I promise you, you're not going to like them. No more common room. No more movie nights. No more taco Tuesday." He runs a hand over his head—he's done this a couple of hundred times already this morning, judging from how wild his hair is—and sighs. "Christ, why d'you have to ruin Taco Tuesday, you little punks? The food here's bad enough and now we can't even have *tacos*?"

I'd laugh out loud if I didn't think someone would notice.

"You're pretty much losing all of your privileges, and I have no sympathy for you. Now let's get this bullshit dealt with and get you out of here, so I don't have to look at any of your faces. Amber Yates?" He marks people off from his register, pausing and pulling faces as he goes, skipping over student's names who aren't in class. He doesn't read Theo's name out loud. Obviously, the missing students are in trouble and being dealt with somewhere, by someone with a little more authority than Mr. Garrett.

Fun.

My classes drag by. In each of them, the teacher berates us for being idiots. My chemistry professor, Dr. Farr, calls us all perverted little deviants, and suggests we might need intensive therapy to overcome our sex addictions. He then goes on a tirade about watching porn, and how easy access to pornography is the reason why we were all so fucked in the head.

I learn nothing new. I complete the work set for me, desperately bored, just waiting for eight o'clock to roll around so I can call Ruth at the allotted time. By dinnertime, I'm so antsy and on the edge of my seat that I consider skipping the meal altogether, but I missed breakfast and hardly picked over the salad I got for lunch, so…

The dining hall is pretty fucking awesome. Even I can admit that. It looks like the dining hall from Harry Potter—long wooden tables with benches on either side. Large chandeliers hang overhead, five of them in total, all cut crystal and candle sticks. I figure the candles are fake, the kind made of plastic with the little switches on the bottom to turn them off and on, but when the heavy, carved wooden doors open and close, admitting new students to dinner, an errant breeze sweeps through the hall, and the flames atop the candles gutter and strengthen. The little teardrop crystals set to swaying, scattering an explosion of rainbows over the walls. It's quite beautiful.

I sit by myself. I avoid talking to anyone. Even Noelani gives me a wide berth as we all sit down at the tables in the dining hall, shoveling down my Chicken Piccata. I give myself heartburn, eating so fast, but I want to be up in my room already. I need to plan out exactly what I'm going to say to Ruth, and that's going to take a minute.

'Should probably make a list,' Rachel advises. *'At least have some bullet points ready.'*

She's right. Ruth has a way of steamrolling you when she starts in on one of her rants. She'll walk all over me and I won't remember a single thing I wanted to say if I'm not prepared.

Grabbing my plate and cutlery, I make my way over to the busing station and place everything in an empty bin. I'm three seconds from the dining hall exit. Two seconds. One.

And then…

"Students of Toussaint, your attention please." Principal Ford's voice booms over a loudspeaker I didn't even realize was there, halting conversation across the dining hall and sending everyone's eyes upward, toward the ceiling, as if searching for some kind of omnipotent god.

"Ahh, shit. Here we go." At the closest table, Sebastian West drops his fork down onto his plate with a loud clatter.

"As you are all aware, an unsanctioned party took place last night on school grounds. The nature of this party was indecent and horrifying. Not

only were students engaging in sexual acts, but alcohol and narcotics were found on site, too. Many of the students we detained coming back into the building were so inebriated that they had to be confined in the recovery room in the nurse's office this morning."

"Locked in the nurse's office for a fucking *hangover*," Seb growls to his friends. "Are they that fucking stupid that they don't realize most of us are hungover every fucking day?"

"To say I am disappointed in the actions of our senior year would be an understatement. I'm shocked and appalled. Frankly, I have no words for what I'm feeling right now—"

"Then shut the fuck up?" I haven't noticed Beth sitting a table over from Seb until she mutters this. She looks tired. Her hair is tied back into a messy bun. Looking up, she makes eye contact with me and the pure hatred she sends my way is breathtaking.

Way to make enemies, Voss.

"As a result of last night's antics, three of Toussaint's pupils have been expelled and sent home to their parents. By the sheer grace of God, a number of you got lucky and have been issued with warnings. Please note that there is no three-strikes-and-you're-out policy at Toussaint Academy. If you step out of line again, you will *be expelled and asked to pack your belongings immediately.*

"As for the rest of you...you were clever enough to sneak back into the school undetected, but please know that you will not *be getting away with your involvement with this party. The entire senior year will be punished for this lack of decorum. Starting this evening, you will no longer have access to any common spaces on your floors or in the main part of the building after six p.m. There will be no more weekly social events. No more movie passes. No more television privileges. No Genesis Ball. After speaking with your parents and explaining the situation, none of you will be issued with passes to leave school grounds at the weekends under any circumstances—"*

A collective cry of dismay fills the dining hall, drowning out Principal Ford's voice. Everywhere I look, my new classmates are throwing down their napkins, slamming hands against the tables, red-faced, yelling at the speaker about the unfairness of this last ruling.

"They can't *do* that!"

"Fucking bullshit!"

"I have to be in Seattle for my coaching on the weekends. They can't stop me. My parents will never—"

Principal Ford must be a mind reader. *"I repeat: I have wasted my entire day calling and speaking to each and every one of your parents, and they have unanimously agreed to suspend all pass privileges for the foreseeable future. This punishment will be lifted as and when we deem it appropriate. Until that time, you will also be prohibited from using the library after five pm. Any homework or assignments you need to complete after this time must be done in your rooms. You are only allowed one other student of the same gender in your bedroom at any one time for study purposes. All students must be back in their own bedrooms by eight pm. A monitor will come to each floor every evening to make sure everyone is where they're supposed to be. You will be held accountable!"*

Uproar.

The dining hall descends into blind madness. On the other side of the room, one of the guys who was running around shirtless with Seb last night hurls his water glass at the wall, screaming something about injustice. He's quickly collared by Dr. Farr, who whisper-shouts admonishments at him as he frog-marches him out of the hall.

"Lastly," Principal Ford continues. *"We will be implementing a student enrichment program in the evenings, in the vain hope that it will engage your minds with more...healthy preoccupations. Once a week, students will be selected to teach a new skill or perform for their senior year classmates. Participation is mandatory. Again, a register will be taken. You will not pass your senior year if you do not attend—"*

I can't hear shit over the cries cycling around the room; for a moment, Principal Ford's words are drowned out by unified rage.

"—presence is required tonight in the auditorium. This is non-negotiable. Any student not marked present in the auditorium in just under thirty minutes will be automatically suspended without review. That is all there is to say on the matter."

"She can't fucking do this," Sebastian seethes. "My parents would *never* agree to this. This is unconstitutional or something."

I feel so outside of this. Ford's inane punishments do seem a little harsh, but they matter very little to me. For starters, I and can walk out of here any time I like. They'd have to physically restrain me, and

I'd like to see them even *try* and accomplish that. Secondly, I won't have to suffer under this new police state for long. A couple of weeks? Maybe a month? I'll be out of here, long gone, my task complete, and I'll never give this place a second thought.

But for now...

I glance down at my phone, checking the time. It's seven fifty-three. I have until eight-fifteen before I have to head to the auditorium, wherever the hell that is, and I still need to talk to Ruth.

The heavy door slams against the wall as I rush out into the hallway, holding the phone to my ear. It goes straight to voicemail. I try again when I hit the stairs up to my floor.

Straight to voicemail.

At my bedroom door.

Voicemail.

Frustration dances a dervish in my chest, provoking me to pace up and down the length of my room like a caged lion. *This is not good. This is not good. This is not good.* I watch the minutes tick by painfully slowly on the phone's display, waiting for the read-out to hit 8:00. The second it does, I try Ruth again, and for the fourth time, the call goes straight to voicemail.

"What the *fuck.*" I overshoot when I hurl the phone down; I aim for the bed, but it bounces off the edge of the mattress and hits the wall instead, making a worryingly loud *crack!* when it hits the bare stonework.

Please don't be broken. Please don't be broken. Please don't be broken.

Ahh, fuck. It's broken.

The screen is a spiderweb of fractures, so dense and interlaced that I can't even see the screensaver of my fake family that Gaynor saved on there as part of my backstory. That's no big deal, but...phew. I press the button on the side of the phone and it still brings up the facial ID. I can still unlock it. A couple of finger taps here and there reveals that the screen surprisingly *does* still work. Just very sporadically.

"Perfect," I grumble. "Just...seriously fucking *perfect.*"

SORRELL

I CONSIDER BRINGING a map of Toussaint with me, just to make sure I know where I'm going, but there are plenty of people still emerging from the dining hall, arguing and bickering furiously about Ford's P.A. announcement; they gripe and bitch about how unfair this all is, but clearly none of them dare disobey the principal's orders, because they dutifully stream north, down a drafty corridor, all gravitating in the same direction.

I'm expecting blue and silver curtaining—Toussaint's colors—to be draped on either side of the auditorium's stage. For the seats to be blue. For the carpet to be blue. In reality, it's red—blood-red crushed velvet. Deep crimson brocade-work. Maroon-colored seats with gold filagree and scrollwork. The place is painfully traditional, like an old timey movie-theater, though its luxury surpasses anything I've ever seen in one of those places.

The smell of honey and wood polish laces the air. A female teacher I haven't met yet stands at the top of the aisle, checking people off on the iPad in her hand. Not only does she ask for my name, but demands my student ID as well, which she then scrutinizes, eyes flicking from my picture on the plastic card to my face three times before she's satisfied that I am who I say I am.

"All right. Go and sit on row E," she tells me. "No talking. No texting. If we see you texting, your phone will be confiscated."

Hah. I can get some of the apps open on my phone, but texting is out of the question. I doubt I'll even be able to read a text now that my phone is busted, not that Ruth is making much of an effort to send many of those through. This teacher, whoever she is, doesn't need to worry about me fucking around with my phone. I flip the button on the side of it, silencing it, but I set it on my knee all the same, hoping against hope that it might light up with a call from Falcon House.

Why the hell is she avoiding me? Who is this Henry? And how does Theo even know Ruth's *name?* Ruth has a million different alter egos. Her driver's license will read Olivia Markham one day; she'll be Sarah Lothian the next. Her collection of passports have a variety of different names printed inside them. There is never a situation where she'll hand over a piece of identification with her real name on it. Even our mailman thinks her name is Valerie.

But Theo called her *Ruth.*

Somewhere on the other side of the auditorium, I can hear Beth laughing raucously. It's the kind of laughter that has always made the hairs on the back of my neck stand on end. Not real laughter. It's the sociopathic kind, a mimicry of humor that broken people will force out of their mouths to appear fun. Beth laughs and jokes and flirts with guys, vying for their attention, pouting and flipping her hair, looking down her nose at the other girls, daring them to challenge her popularity and beauty.

Inside, she's dying. She hates herself. She's so afraid that one day somebody will really *see* her. They'll take one look at her, and see past the hair, and the makeup, and the clothes, and the over-the-top, phony laugh, and they'll see the shy, insecure, frightened young woman who stands in front of the mirror each morning and practices that laugh so that it sounds and looks natural. She does it with tears streaming down her face.

There's a lot of hurt inside Beth Johnson. It spills out in the most vicious ways.

"Good. You're all here." Principal Ford stalks out onto the stage, the sound of the heels echoing dramatically through the cavernous space. She barely raises her voice above a normal conversational level, but her words carry perfectly; the acoustics in here are phenomenal. "I'm glad to see I won't be dismissing any more students from this establishment this evening," she says. Gone is the friendly smile she wore for me yesterday. There's a hardness to her eyes that makes me think of Ruth.

"I have no intention of rehashing what I've already said over the loudspeaker. And no, I will not be entertaining conversations with individuals, seeking to be excused from this punishment. I don't care what commitments or responsibilities you have that make you think you ought to be above the rules of this school, but it's this simple. You break the rules: you pay the price. Without exception."

A low rumble of descent rolls like a wave through the crowd; clearly a lot of the senior year were planning on approaching Ford privately to present their cases as to why *they* should be allowed to leave on the weekends or be out past curfew. They're not happy that this back-up plan is already being nipped in the bud.

"Don't worry. I won't be keeping you here for long. As part of our new student enrichment program, students are now being selected to share their gifts with the rest of the school year. Make no mistake. This *is* a punishment, and you are going to sit here every evening, for as often as I deem necessary, and you're going to pay attention to whoever steps up here on this stage. And if I call *you* to step up onto this stage to get something done, it'd better get done. Give me a show of hands so I can see that everyone here in the room has heard this with their own two ears and understood what I am saying."

A reluctant sea of hands raises across the auditorium.

Off to one side, bathed in shadows, both of my hands remain in my lap, stubbornly resisting the urge to rise. Over the years, I've become a people-pleaser. Making Ruth happy, giving her what she wanted, was a full-time task and felt like an uphill battle I would never win. It didn't matter how quickly or efficiently I carried out the tasks she assigned me; there was always something I could have done better. Ruth's cold grunt of approval was all I craved. It was the only reward that mattered to me. Here, in this foreign place, surrounded by people I don't know or care about, I care very little about making anyone happy, least of all Principal Ford.

The woman standing on the stage appears satisfied. "All right. Let's get on with this evening's performance, then. And just so you know, I won't be leaving. I'll be standing right by the exit at the back, so don't even think about trying to sneak out. If any of you even get up out of your seats, you'll find yourself in an unending detention that I promise you will be absolutely no fun at all." She turns to look off stage-right, jerking her head at whoever is waiting there in the wings.

Theo Merchant strolls out from beyond the heavy, crushed velvet curtains. Again, he wears another faded, over-sized long-sleeved black t-shirt and equally faded black jeans. I'm beginning to think his entire wardrobe solely consists of worn, threadbare clothes that used to be black but are now varying shades of dull, washed-out grey. His sneakers, on the other hand, are spotless and white, so bright under the single spotlight that snaps on overhead, that they glare against my retinas.

His dark hair is a tangle of disheveled waves. They tumble down into his face as he carries a large, black hard case across the stage and sets it down in front of a solitary chair that sits in the very middle of the rostrum.

The crowd mutters collectively as he unfastens the clasps of the case and opens it, silently hefting out a magnificent cello—the wood of the instrument is burnished black, sleek as hell, gleaming under the spotlights. It's beautiful. For some inexplicable reason, my pulse quickens when I see it.

I find that I'm holding my breath.

Why the hell am I holding my breath?

The susurrus ceases, plunging the space into tense silence as Theo sits on the chair and places the cello between his legs.

With the bow in one hand, Theo slides the fingers of the other deftly up and down the strings of the instrument, seemingly practicing a series of shapes and movements. Then he sits there, still as can be, head bowed, face hidden behind his hair, the horsehair of the bow hovering a fraction above the strings...and he waits.

The light washes him out, turning his bare arms and the slope of his tattooed neck alabaster white. I'm close enough to see his shoulders rise as he draws in a steady, even breath. And then he plays.

The sound begins as a single mournful, high-pitched note. It seems as though it will last forever. Theo draws the length of the bow to the left and swings it back to the right so smoothly that the note doesn't even quaver. Then he stops.

Waits.

Pauses.

My cheeks prickle as I watch him up there, his eyes still cast down, his focus fixed so intently upon the cello. My ears echo with the sound of the plaintive note he just played, the sweetness of it still vibrating along the edges of my bones. I'm as still as he is—still as a statue. Still as the flat, undisturbed surface of a bottomless lake. Still as a winter dawn after snow.

The moment stretches out, eating up the seconds that tick by, and the inexplicable need to *scream* rises up the back of my throat.

The second he moves again, drawing the bow back across the strings, a surge of heat floods my body in a wave of fire that makes my eyes prick and burn.

The sound he teases out of the cello is thunderous and intricate. The music climbs as he draws the bow back and forth, his left hand sweeping up and down the graceful neck of the instrument, transitioning from one note to the next with fluid practice, and no one makes a sound.

I—

I frown.

I recognize this music.

There's something so familiar about it. So haunting. I *know* it, I swear…

The veins on the backs of Theo's hands and forearms stand proud, testament to the effort that his performance requires, but the melody flows with such ease, such beauty, that you would think it cost him nothing at all.

Mesmerized, I sink into my seat, stunned by what I'm seeing.

How?

How can someone so vile be capable of *this?*

He's a murderer. Cold and callous.

He's made it plain as day that he doesn't give a shit about the world and everyone in it. But how can someone who cares so little be responsible for what's happening inside my body?

Within the hollow of my chest, my heart aches.

My ribcage is so tight, it's as though the bones have cinched around my lungs, preventing me from pulling down breath.

My hands, resting in my lap, have clenched into fists without me realizing it, and try as I might, no amount of coercion will force them to relax.

Well, well, well. He's quite something, isn't he?

Rachel's voice murmurs in my ear. Suddenly, I feel her presence so close that I'm afraid to turn my head. If I do, I won't find her sitting beside me in the dark. The spell will be broken, and the certainty that she is here with me in this godforsaken place, witnessing what I'm witnessing, will be broken. I can't bear the heartbreak of the thought.

Instead, I close my eyes.

If I reach out my hand for hers, I could take hers if I tried. In this very moment, she *is* here with me. The smell of her coconut body lotion hits the back of my nose. I can feel the pent-up energy of her, radiating from the seat next to me. For the first time in weeks, a peace washes over me, taking the tension out of my shoulders, erasing the frown from my brow. My hands finally relax, resting loosely against the tops of my thighs.

'*Christ. You should be seeing this,*' Rachel's voice whispers. *I know you don't want to hear it, but he's* magnificent.'

No. He's a monster.

He hurt you.

He took your life.

He's a fucking *liar*. We can't trust a word that comes out of his mouth.

Rachel's laughter rises with the swell of the music, and the sound of it makes my eyes prick even harder. *"Always taking things so seriously, Sorrell. He's just some guy, playing a cello. Look at him."*

"I won't."

"Shhh!"

Three rows back, someone hisses at me, startling me so badly that my eyes fly open. Shit. I hadn't realized I was talking out loud. I slouch down into the curve of the seat, willing the darkness to close in even tighter, to swallow me up. I need to be more careful. People really will start to think that I'm crazy if they hear me—

The thought dies, half formed, in my mind.

Up on the stage, Theo Merchant arches his body over the cello, sawing the bow at the strings. He plays like a creature possessed. The thick waves of his hair still hide his eyes, but I can see the line of his jaw perfectly well, and it's clenched, the muscles ticking as the music spills out of him.

It is sonorous and deep now—a raw vibration that floods the auditorium and doesn't even seem to come out of the cello anymore. It comes from within *me,* from the pit of my chest, from my soul, like it's the sound of the blood singing in my veins. I can't stand to watch, but it's impossible to look away.

This feels like an awakening, and Theo…Theo is something out of a dream. Half demon, half angel, he is a beautiful night terror, and I am haunted by the sight of him.

His teeth press into the flesh of his lower lip as the music reaches its crescendo, and his skin blanches bone white. If I could hate myself any more than I already do, then I would, because Theo Merchant is breathtaking, and I'm too awestruck by the vision of him playing up on that stage to deny it anymore.

It's inexplicable, this need in me. Powerful and strong.

I want things that I shouldn't want.

I want his body curved around *me.*

I want his hands on my skin.

I want his teeth biting *my* lip.

Oh.

Oh god, I—

I launch out of my seat, rushing back up the stairs toward the exit. I try to duck down, to avoid detection by any of the other students sitting in the audience, but I instantly regret it; bending double only intensifies the nausea rolling through me. Reaching the doors at the back of the auditorium, I fling them open, hurrying out into the lit hallway, and the sound of Theo's playing comes to a discordant end, the sustaining note that he was holding abruptly cutting off with a screech of his bow.

Fuck.

Fuck, fuck, fuck. He saw. He saw *me*.

"Miss Voss? Where do you think you're going?"

I spin around, clutching my stomach, to find Principal Ford stalking toward me. "I'm sorry. I—I think I'm going to—"

Her face creases with concern. "Good lord, you're sweating. What's wrong?"

"I'm gonna be sick." I grit my teeth against another tight pinch of pain in my stomach. My mouth fills with saliva. I want to swallow it, but my gag reflex is working overdrive, and I can't.

"I can see that. Let's get you to a bathroom." Principal Ford flusters around me, ushering me along; she rests a hand on my shoulder, the other in my lower back as she guides me quickly down the hall to the closest restroom. As soon as I'm in a stall, I sink to my knees and heave into the toilet bowl, retching and gasping as that fucking chicken piccata I wolfed down in the dining hall makes a reappearance. Principal Ford stands behind me, rubbing my back, and guilt slams into me out of nowhere. I should have raised my hand when she told us to before, back in the auditorium. She does care about her students. The only reason she's being so hard on us now is because she cares about us and our wellbeing. I can see that. And here I am, about to make her life infinitely harder. The woman shows me more compassion than I deserve.

"Shhh. It's okay, Sorrell. That's it. Get it all up. Gosh, you really are sick, aren't you?"

Tears stream down my face as I heave again and again, and I can't tell if it's because of the sting of the bile rushing up my throat, or because I'm actually crying; the catastrophic sense of shame I felt back there, watching Theo play, is certainly enough to turn me into a sobbing mess.

"Okay. Okay, sweetheart. That's it. Breathe. Take it easy and breathe now."

I stack my forearms on the toilet seat and rest my forehead against them, doing as I'm told. The foul taste of vomit coats my tongue, my mouth filling with saliva again. I spit into the toilet bowl, sniffing hard and then regretting it as a chunk of chicken that wedged itself up my nose comes loose and I nearly choke on it. Once I've spat *that* into the toilet, I drag down another ragged breath. "Urgh. *Fuck*."

"Fuck indeed," Principal Ford agrees. "I'll allow the language this time. I hate throwing up. I'm actually a sympathetic puker."

I wince at her; she's holding the back of her hand to her mouth, grimacing down at the toilet bowl like she's about to join me on her knees and add to the mess I've made.

"It's okay. You can..." I shudder, "...wait outside now. I'll be all right. I think...I'm done."

I can tell she wants to stay and take care of me, but she's also relieved that I'm letting her off the hook. "You're sure?"

I nod.

"Okay. I'll be right outside."

I give myself a minute to catch my breath, continuing to spit into the toilet, trying to clear the awful taste of half-digested food from my mouth.

From the stall next to me, I hear humming. It's the piece of music that Theo just played in the auditorium. The humming trails off, and a female voice full of humor says, *'Well* that *was a bit of an overreaction, don't you think?'*

I groan, letting my head thump back down onto my forearms. "Fuck off, Rachel."

SORRELL

I FIGURED I was going to have to convince Principal Ford that I wasn't throwing up because I was hungover, but she just waved a hand at me when I tried to explain myself to her on the way up to my room. "I know you weren't at the party, Sorrell. It's okay. Don't worry. You're not in any trouble. I just hope it's not food poisoning. The last thing I need is the entire senior year bed-bound because they can't stop purging their stomachs."

She knows I wasn't at the party. How does she *know* that? She says it like it's a straight fact. I was at the party. Under duress, fair enough, but I did go. I was there for at least an hour. It was a miracle I made it back up to the school before security went down there and broke it all up.

I'm too tired to worry much about Ford's statement at this point, though. I've pulled every muscle I have in my stomach from retching so hard and I feel disgusting.

"You're sure you don't want to see the nurse? I wouldn't be doing my job if I didn't make sure you got checked out." Principal Ford hovers in the doorway of my room, glancing back down the hallway every couple of seconds.

I know why she's so twitchy. Theo stopped playing when I bolted out of the auditorium, and since she left with me, god knows how many students ignored her warning and got the hell out of there while they could. I'm betting Sebastian's stolen Jeremy's Super Cub and is halfway to Seattle by now.

"I'm okay, I promise. I just get really bad cramps with my period sometimes. They can make me throw up if I don't take something quick enough."

She assesses me sympathetically, nodding. "Then get into bed and rest up. If you're still in pain tomorrow, go to the nurse's office first thing. I'm sure the nurse will have something to ease the cramps."

"I'm going to have a quick shower first. I think I have puke in my hair," I say sheepishly.

"Sounds like a good idea. All right, Sorrell. I'm going to have to leave you to it. If I don't get back to the rabble I left in the auditorium, the place will descend into pure chaos."

She goes.

While I'm in the shower, the sounds of the other girls from my floor returning reach me: doors opening and closing; muted conversations; laughter. I take my time, forcing myself to stand under the stream of punishingly hot water, waiting to feel like I am finally clean, but that feeling doesn't come. I scrub off one layer of skin after another until I'm raw and beet red, but the cloying, gross sense that I am dirty just will not go away.

Eventually, the water runs cold, and I get out.

I brush my teeth four times, determined to get rid of the disgusting taste in my mouth at least. There are no sounds out in the hallway anymore—the girls must all be in their beds by now. Opening my bathroom door, I let out a startled yelp when I see that I have a visitor.

Theo Merchant, sitting up on my bed, back resting against the headboard, comfortable as you like. At least he took his shoes off. His legs are crossed at the ankles, hands stacked on top of his stomach. When he sees me, he grabs something sitting on the bed next to him and holds it out to me: a hot water bottle.

"You've gotta be fucking *kidding* me."

He shrugs. "I've heard hot water bottles are *good* for period cramps." He says this argumentatively, like he thinks I'm objecting to the dumb hot water bottle and not the fact that *he is in my fucking bedroom.*

"You've got a lot of nerve," I growl.

Unfazed, he sets the hot water bottle down and begins to pick at his fingernails. "Careful. Better put those clothes down. You look like you're about to lose that towel."

I let out a frustrated snarl as I dump my clothes onto the chair behind the door. Once I've made sure my towel isn't about to fall down, I stalk across the room and slap at his feet, baring my teeth at him. "You have no right to be in here. You need to leave. Now."

He looks up at me, expression blank, and I see everything that his hair hid while he was up there, playing on that stage: the complex golden-amber-chocolate hue of his eyes; his high cheek bones; the regal line of his nose; the sharp curve of his cupid's bow, and the fullness of his mouth. Unlike yesterday, he's not quite clean-shaven. His jaw is darkened with the beginnings of stubble.

"You sure you want me to go?" he asks flatly. "Haven't you got me exactly where you want me?"

Heat climbs up the back of my throat. "What the hell are you talking about?"

"We both know why you were sent here. So, isn't me being here, alone, in your room, the perfect opportunity to do me in?"

So. Fucking. Casual. He doesn't seem fazed by the fact that I was sent here to do him harm. "Y'know. It's actually *insulting* that you'd come here, given the fact that you know I want you dead. If you don't consider me a threat, then you should really reconsider that tack, because—"

"You're perfectly capable of hurting me. Blah, Blah, Blah. I know, I know." He rolls his eyes. "I also know you're not going to hurt me in your own fucking bedroom. That would look a little suspicious, wouldn't it?"

He nestles back into my pillows, wriggling a little to make himself more comfortable.

"What. Do. You. Want?" It takes monumental effort to get the question out without screaming.

"I brought your shit up for you." He points behind me, where my bag and my cell phone sit on top of my desk.

Ahh. Crap. In my haste to leave the auditorium, I forgot all about my bag and phone. I hadn't even given it one thought…until now, obviously.

"You're welcome," Theo says.

"I'm not *thanking* you. You brought me back my stuff. Now you can leave. How…" I stare at him incredulously. "How did you even get *in* here?"

He looks back down at his hands. Distractedly, he picks at his thumb. "They don't lock us in at night, Voss. I walked out of my room, came down the stairs…" He pouts, as if the rest is obvious.

"Great. Well…if you don't mind, I need to get changed for bed. And no, before you even think about saying it, I will not get changed in front of you."

His eyes seem to glow amber as they flick toward me. "And why would I want you to get changed in front of me?"

I have no words. I look around the room, trying to find something to throw at him, and I grab the first thing that looks like it will hurt—the snow globe Gaynor gave me to flesh out my backstory. Inside the weighty globe, the winter scene of New York City's skyline is blotted out by tiny white flakes when I snatch it off the dresser and heft it over my head.

Theo's eyes round out. "Man. You choose violence real quick, don't you, Voss?"

I set my jaw. "You have no idea."

"You're gonna throw that thing at me, then?" He doesn't move. Doesn't flinch. If he had any sense, he'd be up on his feet and halfway out of the door by now.

"Yeah. I will. On the count of five."

Rage dances up my spine when he looks back down at his thumbnail.

"One…"

"Get changed in your walk-in," he commands.

"Why the hell would I get changed in the walk-in? I mean it, Theo. *Two!*"

The fucker smirks.

"Three!"

Nothing.

"Four! I swear to God, Theo. I'll hurl this thing right at you, and I have excellent aim. Do you wanna earn yourself a fucking head injury?"

This seems to do the trick. Sighing wearily, his eyes meet mine again as he slowly shifts himself to the end of the bed. "I definitely don't want *that*. Head injuries are the worst."

I glower at him as he gets up and crosses the room. I must look ridiculous, clinging to my towel with one hand while holding the snow globe above my head in the other, ready to launch it. I don't care if he laughs at me, though; I'll be ready to hurt him if he so much as looks sideways at me.

Which he does.

Stopping, his body angled toward the door, head bowed, he glances at me out of the corner of his eye, and it feels like the goddamn world grinds to a halt. "Have you ever been to New York?" he asks, jerking his chin up at the snow globe.

"What?"

"It's a simple question. Have you ever been to New York?"

"Why would I have a snow globe of New York if I hadn't?" I snap.

His mouth turns down. "I don't know. People collect those things. People give them as gifts. Where's your favorite place in the world?"

"What? That seems like a completely irrelevant question to be asking right now, considering the position we find ourselves in."

His shoulders shift, angling toward me a little. His head is still cast down, though, as if he's unwilling to turn and face me properly. "There are better positions we could be in, yes."

"Is that supposed to be innuendo?" I scoff. "You really think it's smart to come in here and try and flirt with me after what happened last night?"

He frowns quizzically. "And what happened last night?"

"You—you were going to pick me out of that line up by the bonfire!"

Genuine amusement plays across his face. "I don't think I was."

Fury bubbles in my blood, causing it to rush in an angry tide to my head. My temples begin to throb. "Don't pull that shit with me, Merchant. You stood in front of me, drinking that bottle of tequila. You—*you were fucking with me!*"

His expression is unreadable now. With careful, measured movements, he lifts a hand and reaches out with the tip of his index finger, making contact with the top of my shoulder. I mean to wheel away from the contact, revulsion tearing me apart from the inside, but…I don't move. Theo trails his fingertip across my skin—a featherlight touch, tracing his finger through the beads of water that still cling to my skin from my shower. "Maybe you should get your facts straight before you go accusing people of things."

"Oh, wonderful. Now we're using loaded comments."

"A loaded comment about *what*?" He is so, *so* fucking smug.

I'm so angry, I'm having a hard time restraining the maelstrom of feelings whipping around in my chest. He's baiting me. He wants me to say something about Rachel. I feel it. I know it. He wants to quip about me accusing him of causing Rach's death or something. I can't just come right out and say that, though. That would end this ruse between us. My purpose here would officially be laid bare once and for all.

Theo hums quietly, considering the pattern he's drawn on my shoulder with the droplets of water. "Okay. Well, I'll let you have a think on that then, Kid. Since you can't seem to figure it out right now."

My reaction is instantaneous. "Don't call me that. I'm not a kid. Get the fuck out of here, Theo. I'll fucking scream."

A cold, unfeeling expression settles over his features. I stare up at him, and the void expression looks so out of place there that it almost steals my breath from me. It's as if he's transformed into a completely different person. "I suppose you *did* reach five, didn't you?" His tone is all frost and spite.

"I did."

A horrible moment stretches out, where he pins me down with a fierce, hard gaze. The thumping at my temples turns into a relentless pounding; so quickly, it feels like my head's about to split open.

"What's wrong?" The words come out of his mouth, clipped and sharp.

"Your presence here is giving me the migraine from hell, that's what's wrong. Now ge—"

"Don't worry. I'm fucking gone."

He storms for the door and rips it open so hard that I think he's going to tear it straight off its hinges. He doesn't say another word as he disappears out into the hall. The door crashes closed behind him, the wood rattling in the frame...and the void he leaves behind is hollow as an abyss.

SORRELL

Two Weeks Later

Time passes strangely at Toussaint. A day turns into three, turns into a week, turns into two. I study. I shuttle back and forth from my classes, then back to my room. I spend more and more time with Noelani. A tentative sort of friendship develops between us, and I spend most of my lunch breaks with her, fantasizing about all of the things we can't wait to do once we get ourselves out of this hellhole.

With no internet and no television, the outside world doesn't exist for us here, suspended in our state of punishment; the only thing that keeps most of the girls on my floor sane is daydreaming about all of the fun shit they'll get into once Ford's weekend pass ban is lifted, which I, personally, am beginning to think will never actually happen.

I hear nothing from Ruth.

Nothing.

No phone calls. No texts. No check-ins whatsoever, which was very worrying at first. However, as the days pass by, my worry turns to anger. Ruth is the one who sent me here. She was the one who told me to face Theo and make him suffer the consequences of his actions. Then she told me not to do anything until she gave me the green light. Now she's abandoned me, without any guidance or reassurance over what I'm supposed to do? What the *fuck* is she playing at?

On day ten of radio silence from Falcon House, I make a decision. If Ruth doesn't want to pick up when I call her and doesn't even have the decency to fire off a quick message to me, then fuck it. I won't try and contact her, either. Why should I? She's keeping secrets. She's thrown me in at the deep end with all of this, and now refuses to even throw a lifeline in after me?

I'm supposed to await her instructions before I do anything to Theo, but the waiting is driving me crazy. How long does she expect me to stay here and just hang around, trapped in this bizarre little microcosm of humanity without any contact with the outside world? I'm a pretty patient person, but that patience has its limits. And having to see Theo every single day, to keep running into him in the hallways, to sit two rows away from him in class, to watch him fuck around with Sebastian outside the main entrance...it's more than I can bear. His outbursts of temper are random and spectacular. Every day, he seems to be brawling with someone new. I can't help but want to jump into these fights. Take him off guard. Slide a sharpened blade into his windpipe. Gut him where he stands.

It's Friday, our half day, when I finally break and say something about him to Noelani, who has recently asked me to call her Lani. The weather is uncharacteristically warm. We're sitting on the lawn outside Toussaint's main building, sunning ourselves in the weak afternoon light, when I catch sight of Theo's familiar mess of dark hair. He's sitting at the foot of a giant oak tree a hundred feet away, alone, scribbling in a notebook, and a frisson of anger bites at the back of my neck. This isn't the first time I've seen him sitting underneath the massive tree, leaning his back against its thick trunk. He's out there most days at ten-thirty, while the rest of us are shivering inside, grabbing a snack during our morning break. I know to expect him there now, but today, the sight of him lounging in the shade, his pen hurtling from one side of his notebook to the other, fingers wrapped in that ever-present blue tape, makes me want to fucking tear my hair out.

"Why does he *do* that?" I growl. "Every single day. He just sits there and writes and writes and writes. Doesn't he have any friends?"

Noelani looks over her shoulder at Theo, sees him and frowns. "Oh. Uhhh...yeah, he absolutely does. Theo's one of the most popular people here. You can't tell me you haven't noticed. Everyone falls over themselves to get in his good graces."

I have noticed that. I don't want to admit it, though. Admitting that people like him makes him seem less of a villain somehow. That's what folks always say about serial killers in TV documentaries, though, isn't it? He was so charming. So well liked. He had a ton of friends. Always stopped to help old ladies in the street. But behind closed doors, those psychos were butchering women they'd kidnapped and were wearing them like skin suits.

"What's with the tape?" I blurt out. It's been bugging me for weeks. *Weeks*. I wasn't about to ask *him* about it, though.

Noelani glances at me quizzically. "Huh?"

I hold up the index finger, middle finger and thumb on my left hand.

"Ohhhh, the *tape*." Noelani shrugs. "He uses it when he practices the cello, I guess. He used to want to be a concert cellist, but now..."

"What?"

"I think he's changed his mind now."

For some reason, this tiny little tidbit of information about him makes me irrationally angry. Furious, even. I bite the tip of my tongue, breathing hard down my nose. I don't care if he wanted to be a concert cellist one day, or that he's changed his damn mind now. I just want the bastard to disappear. "If he does have so many friends, then why is he always alone? Why is he just always...*there*."

Noelani looks away from Theo, glancing down at the grass we're sitting on. She plucks at it absentmindedly, stacking the torn blades into a little pile. "I suppose none of us have really noticed. He's always been his own guy. We just let him do his thing."

"We? *We?* Don't tell me *you* like him." I can't keep the disbelief from my voice.

Lani laughs. "Sure I do. He's not so bad once you get to know him."

"He seems pretty volatile to me." I have to be careful what I say here. I'll incriminate myself if I make my hatred for Theo Merchant too obvious. When he starts choking up blood one morning because I've poisoned his oatmeal, I don't need anyone pointing the finger at me.

"Volatile?" Lani asks. "What do you mean?"

"He shoved Sebastian into a locker and tried to choke him out three days ago," I say airily. "He punched Callum Fairley in the jaw before that. You can't have forgotten. You were standing right next to me when it happened. I'd hardly call those the actions of someone in possession of all their faculties."

These two separate events had both happened in the hallway, between classes, seemingly right in front of me. I'd been quietly seething, comfortable in my hatred of Theo, mad that he was there, right in front of me, as always, and then BOOM! Sebastian had muttered something, and Theo had launched at him, fists flying. The same thing had happened with Callum.

Lani's bright laughter fills the air again. She sinks back, lying down on the grass, cradling her head in her hands, using them as a pillow. "First of all, Sebastian is an asshole. He drives even his best friends to violence on the regular, case in point. We've all wanted to hurt him at one point or another. Callum..." She sighs. "Callum said something really shitty that he shouldn't have."

It sounds like she knows what Callum said to evoke such a startling reaction from Theo, but I'll be damned if I ask her for the details. I can't think of anything to say, so I just sit, staring at a patch of grass for a while. Noelani doesn't like long silences, I've learned, so it isn't too long before she's filling the void. "I guess he never used to be quite so...reserved," she says. "Theo. He was involved in an accident a little while ago. He changed after that. Now he prefers his own company, I suppose. A lot of the girls here are hoping he snaps out of his fugue soon and shows some interest in one of them."

I know exactly which accident she's referring to. Does it come as a shock that Theo changed after that night? After Rachel died? Maybe. I mean, maybe even evil fuckers who cause the deaths of teenaged girls get struck with a guilty conscience sometimes. I don't say that, though. Instead, I find myself fixating on her last statement.

"Let me guess. Beth Johnson's leading the charge on that one."

"Yeah. Beth's always had a thing for Theo. She chased him all through freshman and sophomore years."

"She saw sense junior year?"

"Haha no! He was taken sophomore year. Beth didn't exactly like it, but she kept her distance. Didn't wanna come off too desperate, I s'pose."

"He was taken last year? He was *dating* someone?" I don't know why this sounds so ridiculous. He's good looking. It makes sense that he'd be with someone.

Noelani pulls an odd face. "Yeah. But she…the girl he was with… she…I guess she died."

"You *guess* she died?" Acid spills from my words. It kills me to think that these people know about Rachel. It hurts beyond measure that they were aware of her existence, that they know Theo was in an "accident," and that they still treat him like he's some kind of god every day. It's an affront to Rachel's memory.

Noelani's expression flattens—it's as if she's biting back her reaction to my response very carefully. "She *did* die," she says. "It was really sad. We all really liked Rachel. Some days…it's almost as if she's still here. I forget that she's gone, y'know? It's…it really fucking hurts." She swallows thickly. The emotion in her voice triggers something deep within me that makes me want to hurt her, the way I'm hurting right now.

Rachel never mentioned Noelani to me. She never talked about any of the students here at Toussaint. As far as I was aware, she was terminally bored here and couldn't wait to escape. I had no idea she was involved with Theo like that. That they were actually *dating*. She never even mentioned his name. To think that all of these other people knew that part of her life better than I did makes me feel sick to my stomach.

Noelani allows another stretch of silence to span out between us, but eventually she says, "Anyway. Enough about Theo. I have to get to the library to finish my science report or I'm going to miss my window to get at the textbooks. You wanna come with?"

I consider her proposal: sitting in the old Toussaint library, the weight of an even deeper, more oppressive silence pressing down on me, pretending to study, and I just can't do it. "No, you go on ahead. I've finished my report. I'm so sick of being cooped up inside. I think the fresh air will do me some good."

"All right. If you're sure?"

"Yeah. I'll see you at dinner. We can study together tonight for a while as well."

"Okay." She gathers her things and heads off, striking out for the main building. I watch her go, wondering if I'm making a mistake by not going with her, but it really is a beautiful day. It's a lifetime since I've seen the sun, and the unexpected warmth of the day so late in the year has me feeling languid and loose, like my muscles are melting off my bones.

Taking off the light sweater I put on this morning, I wad it up, stuffing it under my head. Rachel and I used to do this on our summer breaks—lay out in the sunshine, telling each other stories and jokes until we were so drunk from the heat and dizzy from our laughter that we passed out.

I wake with a start some time later, shivering against a cool breeze that skates over my skin. The sun is gone. My arms and legs are bristled with goosebumps, and the grass that was warm and cushioned before now feels damp and sticky. Blinking up at the welter of clouds that have gathered while I was asleep, I see that it looks like it's about to rain.

Well, that didn't last long.

I fight off a wave of vertigo as I rise, and nearly have a fucking heart attack when I realize that Theo is sitting Indian style in the grass a few feet away. His battered notebook rests on top of one of his knees. He twirls a pen lazily around in his right hand, looking off into the distance, down the hill toward the valley where the First Night party took place.

"Jesus. For *fuck's* sake. What the hell are you doing?"

"Sitting," he answers, not looking at me.

"I can see that. Why are you sitting so close to *me?*"

"You looked cold." He nods to my legs, which have been covered with a plain black hoody.

I tear it off me, tossing it to him. "I don't need you performing random acts of kindness for me, asshole."

"Okay. Catch fucking pneumonia, then. See if I care." He takes the hoody, his notebook and his pen, and gets up. He's about to walk away, but my dumb mouth opens before I can gag myself.

"You really think covering my legs while I'm sleeping makes any difference to what you did?" Such a paltry action. If he thinks following me around and doing small little deeds like that will make me forgive him, he's got another thing coming.

He stops. Turns around. "I wasn't trying to earn your forgiveness, Voss."

"What then? You just love poking the bear or something? You wanna feel how much I hate you? How much I fucking *despise* you? Is that it?"

He gives me a flat, cold smile. "I don't give a shit if you hate me. Go ahead."

Infuriating. Absolutely *infuriating*. "Your arrogance knows no bounds. I don't need your fucking permission! You killed my best friend. I will hate you until the day I die, and I'll find a way to hate you long after that, too. I will never *not* fucking hate you. I—"

He drops to his knees in front of me. Moves so quickly that I don't have a hope of stopping him. Suddenly, his hands are in my hair, and his mouth…

Oh god.

His mouth…

His lips crash down on mine. He kisses me so roughly that I can't breathe, I can't move, react, think. What the hell is he *doing?* I press my hands flat against his chest, ready to shove him off me, brimming over with so much anger that I think it might kill me. But then…

What am *I* doing?

I don't push him away.

The smell of him hits me—bergamot. Mint. Fresh, cool winter air—and something happens inside me. A part of me cracks open. A sob slips out of my mouth and into his. The sound is so broken and pained, so animal-like and wounded, that my mind just goes...blank.

The press of his mouth grows gentler. His hands slide down to the tops of my arms, and he holds me carefully in place as he urges my mouth open. His breath comes hot against my face, quick and urgent, fanning over my cheeks, in and out, in and out, too fast. When his tongue dips past my lips to stroke against my tongue, I go rigid, paralyzed by a fear I cannot reckon with.

His lips...

God, the pressure of his mouth is exhilarating. I'm drawn to him so desperately, and I can't explain any of it. He is a curse and a plague, and I grow sicker at his hands every day. Ashamed as I am, afraid as I am, I find myself surrendering to the bastard, melting into him as if I've been traveling on an exhausting journey for years and I've finally found myself home.

My tongue works against his, tasting him, accepting him deeper into my own mouth, and a body-wide shudder runs through Theo. His breath catches somewhere between his lungs and his mouth, a sharp, insistent sound emanating from his throat, and his grip tightens on me. His warmth heats me. His hands steady me. The solidity of his presence anchors me back into a body I've felt like I was slipping away from for the longest time.

My head spins as Theo pulls me closer, so that our chests are flush, our stomachs, our hips, our—

Lord have mercy.

Our hips meet and I can feel him. He's hard against me, his erection straining against the front of his jeans, butting up against me between my legs, applying pressure to an area of my body I hadn't even realized could ache the way it's aching right now. What kind of insanity *is* this?

How can I need him this way, after everything that he's done?

The question brings me back to my senses, but also cuts me loose, unmooring me, cutting me adrift, out of my body again. I jerk back, pushing away from him, disgusted at myself for letting things get so far.

Theo's eyes are wide, his pupils blown out as he looks down at me. His face is flushed in a way that makes my toes curl in my shoes. "Hate me now?" he pants.

"YES!" I scramble back from him, away from the danger he represents. Dirt collects under my fingernails as I claw at the ground, using it to gain purchase and put some distance between us. Once I'm confident that he won't be able to lunge at me again, I scrub a hand at my mouth, trying to erase the feel of his lips. "Are you damaged in the head?"

The high color in his face dissipates right before my eyes. I watch as the arrogant, cold expression I'm so used to him wearing returns. "I must be if I wanna make out with *you*."

"Go fuck yourself," I spit. "Kissing someone without their permission is still sexual assault. I should report you to Ford!"

Theo sinks back onto his heels, watching me, the corner of his mouth curving up into a cruel smile. "Really, Voss? Sexual assault?" He laughs quietly. "Didn't feel like assault when you were sticking your tongue down my throat and moaning into my mouth like a sex-starved kitten. But we'll call it whatever you like."

"I didn't ask you to kiss me!"

"Didn't tell me not to, either. And when you pulled away, I didn't stop you. You were free to accept or reject me from the word go."

"Urgh! You're such..." I grope for the right words. *"You're such an ass!"*

"All day, every day," he agrees.

I can't fucking see straight. Getting to my feet, I sway, figuratively and literally unbalanced by what just took place. I've never reacted like that to someone before. It was visceral. Carnal. I've never wanted anything the way I wanted him in that moment.

He calls something after me, but my ears are ringing too loudly to hear whatever it is that he says. My heart hammers as I charge back toward the school. My blood boils. My jaw is locked. My hands are shaking, my shoulders tensed.

I'm not angry with Theo. I'm angry with myself.

He was right. I didn't stop him from kissing me.

I wanted it.

I wanted *him.*

It took every ounce of will power I possessed to tear myself away.

SORRELL

He's there when I eat breakfast. When I go to class. When I train exhaustively in Toussaint's brand-new gym, after every single torturous evening, stuck in the auditorium, watching student after student perform recitals, and sing, and dance, and read their stupid fucking poetry. He's there when I have dinner, and when I hang out in the library with Noelani. Worst of all, he's there when I close my eyes every night, running through my mind. When I fall asleep, I can't even escape him in my dreams. Night after night, I wake up drenched in sweat, unable to remember what's taken place in my sleep, but knowing on a very deep level that Theo Merchant has been hounding my every step there, too. I can still smell the scent of him. Feel his hands on my skin. Feel the press of his mouth on mine. More than once, I've sat bolt upright in bed, heart pounding, slick and wet between my legs, knowing that I've just *come,* for fuck's sake, and with no recollection of how it happened.

I hate him with every fiber of my being.

A month passes, and I hear nothing from Ruth. Three times, I try to make an escape from Toussaint, determined to flee this hellhole and make it back to Los Angeles, but every time my plans are thwarted, either by Principal Ford herself, or by the simple fact that we're in the middle of nowhere and I have no means of getting back to civilization. The school is still on lockdown.

Once a week, Jeremy arrives in the Super Cub, carrying perishables and other supplies for the school, but Principal Ford is always there to greet him, along with at least two other members of staff. I've tried to puzzle out a way to sneak into the back of that damned sea plane until I've given myself a migraine, but I'm yet to discover a way to accomplish that goal without being discovered.

I lie in bed at night, cursing the day I ever agreed to come here and do this. It seemed like the only way to obtain justice, but now I'm not so sure. Wouldn't it make more sense to report Theo to the cops? He was cleared of any wrongdoing after the accident, but surely they'd take another look at his involvement if I gave them a statement. A new statement. Since I have no real recollection of that night, it would have to be a *fabricated* statement, of course, but wouldn't lying to the police be better than being stuck here, seeing the motherfucker every day, having to face the idea that he's right there, within reach, and per Ruth's edict, I can't touch him?

Fuck.

I *know* Theo was responsible for what happened. Ruth told me I gave a detailed account of what happened after the accident, before all of my memories of that night disappeared on me.

As September turns into October, and Ford's punishment continues on, all I can do is go to class, do my assignments, try to avoid Merchant as best I can, and pray to god that the ban on weekend passes out of this godforsaken national park ends soon. The second Jeremy is allowed to start shuttling us back to civilization, I am fucking out of here and I am *not* coming back.

I begin to have hope that that day might come soon when Principal Ford steps up onto the stage one Friday night after we've all gathered in the auditorium for our nightly 'educational' punishment and addresses us. Sitting next to me, Noelani clutches my hand as we both listen.

"Firstly, I need to make an announcement. The Academy's internet service is being replaced. We're upgrading to a better system, since our satellite internet has been so patchy recently. That means your cells won't work, I'm afraid. Unfortunately, it also means the computers in the library will be out of commission for the next week. If you need to do research for an assignment, you're going to have to use some of the library's other resources. There are strange rectangular objects sitting on the many shelves in there. Crack one open, and you'll find that they're full of pages with writing inside. You might have noticed them. They're called books."

The entire senior year groans.

"Now that's out of the way..." Ford sighs. "As you're aware, every single one of you has come up here and shared a reading, or some poetry, or completed and shared an assignment, or performed, be that singing or playing an instrument. I had planned on extending this evening gathering for another month and making you all come up here and do something again, but honestly..." She shakes her head, puffing out her cheeks. "Honestly, I don't have the energy for it. This has been a punishment for me as much as it has been for you. So, starting tomorrow evening, you will no longer have to come here at eight. Your curfews are still in effect, though, and all other rules that were set in place still stand—"

A cry of excitement goes up around the auditorium none-the-less.

"Wait, wait, wait," Principal Ford says, addressing the students who have eagerly gotten to their feet and are making for the exit. "I said starting tomorrow. Sit back down. Tonight, instead of forcing one of you up here, I decided we'd watch a movie instead."

My fellow classmates' cheering grows louder. We have access to the movies and shows that people brought with them on hard drives, but without high-speed internet to download new stuff, we've all grown tired of what we had saved on our laptops. A new movie is welcome news. "Don't get too excited," Principal Ford warns. "Since you guys have made my life a living hell and I've had to waste so much of my own time babysitting your asses, I get to choose the movie, and I choose The Notebook."

The guys groan.

The girls cheer.

I've never seen The Notebook, but when Lani begins bouncing in her seat next to me, muttering something about Ryan Gosling and how sexy his beard is later in the story, I glean that it's some kind of epic romance. She's so excited that I can't help but smile.

Ford further surprises us when two of the kitchen staff appear with a catering trolley, stacked high with little red and white striped paper bags of popcorn. Lani's up and out of her seat before I can offer to go and grab us some. "Don't worry. I got you!" she calls over her shoulder, bolting down the aisle.

The moment that she leaves her seat, a screen unfurls from the ceiling, and Ford makes her way off stage. People are still out of their seats, squabbling over the popcorn, when the movie starts.

I've been so bored over the past few weeks that I'm immediately sucked into the story. When Lani returns and sits down next to me, I don't even spare her a sideways look; I take the bag of popcorn she offers and I munch on it, eyes glued on Ryan Gosling.

And then, over the buttery smell of the snack in my lap, I smell something else.

"I suppose I can see the attraction," Theo says, leaning in to whisper into my ear.

My popcorn flies out of my lap, toppling to the floor.

It's dark in the auditorium, so I can't see much of him—just the frayed collar of his long-sleeved t-shirt, and the swirling black ink creeping up his skin above it. Just the depth of his eyes, turned almost black in the dark. Just the swell of his bicep, as it rests on the arm of my chair, perilously close to brushing up against me. He smells like he was just out in the rain, fresh, and of fragrant pine.

"Don't tell me." He shoots me a cocky grin. "You're more of a Tom Hardy girl."

I lean away from him, until my spine digs into my other arm rest. "Where the hell is Noelani?"

Theo's fingers are wrapped in tape again. He must have been playing his cello before he came down here. Systematically, he rips it from his fingers, dropping the pieces to the floor. Once he's done, he looks back to the movie, popping a few pieces of popcorn into his mouth. The light cast off by the screen turns his eyes into reflective mirrors. I watch him eat—the muscles in his jaw and his throat working as he chews and swallows—morbidly fascinated by the sight.

I shiver involuntarily when he pops the end of his thumb into his mouth and sucks it clean. "Think I heard something about her going to sit at the back with Mel?" he says eventually.

"What the fuck? You told her not to come back and sit with me?"

He's unaffected by my tone. Shrugging, he pops another piece of popcorn into his mouth. Sucks his index finger this time. "I did nothing of the sort."

"Then get out of her seat so she can come back!"

"Noelani's her own person. If she wanted to go sit with Mel, who am I to stop her? I doubt me moving will entice her back."

"Theo!"

"Shh!" Principal Ford's head pops up from the front row. "I swear, if you guys keep fidgeting, I will turn this thing off and you can all sit here in silence while I watch it with headphones on my laptop. That what you want?"

The auditorium is quiet as the grave.

I glare at Theo, who shoves another piece of popcorn into his mouth, shrugging in an *ahh-well-what-are-you-gonna-do?* kind of way. I could legit scream.

I don't want to be the person who gets the movie turned off for everyone, so I can't say anything else. I can't get up and move, either. I'm stuck here, sitting next to him, a storm raging in my chest. He thinks he's so fucking smart. What can he possibly hope to achieve, coming to sit beside me?

The movie crawls onward, but I'm blind to it now. My focus is pinpointed on the heat rolling off Theo's body. I pull my elbows in, avoiding the armrests, but that makes very little difference. Theo's taller than most, and his huge frame barely fits in the chair to begin with. His arm brushes against mine every once in a while. Then his legs fall open and his knee rests against mine. The two points of contact where our bodies touch burn like nothing else. In my head, I'm screaming.

'He sure does smell good, though,' Rachel's voice points out. *'I bet it'd feel amazing if he had his arm around you. Imagine how* safe *it'd feel with your head resting on his chest, listening to his heartbeat....'*

What the fuck is she talking about? I can't imagine anything that would feel *less* safe. I try to blot out the thought of that—being held in the circle of Theo's arms, nestled up against him—but the idea is like an indelible stain on my soul. Now that I've thought it, I can't scrub it into non-existence. It lingers, pervading my thoughts until it's the only thing I can think about.

On the screen, Noah and Allie begin to fall in love, but all I can think about is Theo Merchant's proximity and how easy it would be to reach out and take his hand.

'Go on. Might as well. Never know. You might enjoy it,' Rachel urges mischievously.

Why, in the name of all things holy would she be urging me to take his hand? The Rachel I speak to in my head isn't real. She's a figment of *my* imagination. I don't want her to make these comments to me, so why the fuck won't she quit?

Shut. The hell. Up.

Time drags painfully slowly as the movie plays. Eventually, I grow so accustomed to Theo's knee resting against my leg that I jump every time he shifts in his seat, reminded that he's touching me.

After an hour or so, Theo discards his popcorn bag, placing it on the seat on the other side of him...and he casually places his hand on top of my thigh. The sight of the silvery interlacing scars that mar the back of his hand fills me with the perverse desire to reach out and touch them, to see what they feel like.

"What the fuck?" I mouth.

He shakes his head, cupping his other hand to his ear, making a show of not being able to hear me. All right. If he wants to be a dick about this, then fair enough. I'll be a dick about it, too.

I grab his hand, lift it off my leg, snag his pinkie finger, and wrench it backwards.

"*Arrrunghhhpphhh—*" He cuts off the strangled sound of pain as quickly as he can, but not quite quickly enough.

"All right. That's it. Last warning!" Ford snaps. "One more peep out of you and I am *done!*"

Theo tries to ease his finger out of my grip, but hell no...I'm not letting go. He'll need a pair of pliers to loosen the vice-like hold I have on him.

"Sorrell." His whisper is terse. "Let. *Go*. Sorrell."

Yeah, I don't think so. I tug his finger back a little further, delighting in the sound of his pain when he releases an agonized, deep groan.

Twisting in his seat, Theo grabs me by the back of the neck, pulling me close, so that I can feel his mouth move against my ear when he talks. "Do you want to know about Henry or not?"

A cruel, calculating trick. He hasn't mentioned the name Henry since he told me to ask Ruth about him, my first day here. My own stubbornness has prevented me from asking for more information. I originally chose to believe that Ruth would have told me about him if he was important in any way, or even *real* for that matter, but now I'm not so sure. Too many weeks have gone by without contact with Ruth or Falcon House that I don't know what I'm supposed to think anymore. So yeah. I guess I *do* want to know what Theo has to say about this mystery person.

I let his finger go.

Cold, hard flint flashes in his eyes. He shakes out his hand, flaring his nostrils, then leans in close to whisper in my ear again. "You're obstinate as fuck, you know that?"

I have to lean into him just as close in order to whisper in *his* ear. Heaven help me if the smell of him up this close doesn't make my head spin. I try not to breathe. "Just tell me."

The left side of Theo's face flares white, throwing the right into shadow as the scene on the projector screen goes from night to day. For a long second, he just looks at me, frowning...and then he holds up his pinkie finger.

"Kiss it better first."

I fight back the bark of laughter that rises to the back of my throat. "What are you, *five?* I'm not kissing your finger better, dumbass."

"No?" he arches a dark eyebrow coolly at me. "You don't wanna know about Henry, then?"

"Not if you're gonna make me coddle you like some kind of half-grown man-baby, no."

"Oh, rest assured, I am *fully* grown," he rumbles. There's something indecent about the way he says this—his tone, even though whispered, speaks of indecency.

A quick retort helps to erase that thought. "Even better. A *fully grown* man-baby. Wonderful."

Theo narrows his eyes. "Henry is another one of Ruth's pet projects."

What did he just say? Firstly, I'm offended by the implication that I am a pet fucking project. Secondly, he's wrong. He's just...he's fucking wrong. I shake my head. "Ruth doesn't foster boys. She only fosters girls. Girls like me."

A casual, slow smile spreads across Theo's tragically handsome face. "Seems there's a lot about your ol' pal Ruth that you don't know."

"Tell me," I spit.

Theo holds up his pinkie. "Like I said."

"God, you're pathetic." I take his wrist and hold it steady, quickly giving his little finger a brisk peck. The contact lasts less than a second, but my body reacts even so. I want to crawl out of my skin; I don't want this. I don't want to feel like this—

I'm getting used to Theo's icy smile, but this time it's a punch to the gut. There's a spark of heat to it that can't be denied. "You can do better than that, sweetheart."

"Urgh! What do you want from me?"

By god, I should *not* have asked.

Theo looks like a kid on Christmas morning, if that kid was a sadist and enjoyed causing others pain for his own enjoyment. "I'm so glad you asked. Let me show you." Fast as lightning, he sucks his pinkie into his mouth. It comes out glistening. A second later, he's rubbing the pad of it against my lips, running it over my bottom lip, wetting it, back and forth.

He bites down on his own lip as he watches what he's doing. Completely stunned, I have no idea what to do. I don't even really feel the pressure of his finger on my mouth. All I can see is how feral he appears, eyes so focused on his actions.

He looks like he wants to eat me.

He definitely looks like he wants to kiss me again.

It's all I can do to remain upright and breathe without passing out.

"Open for me, Voss," he murmurs.

NO!

In my head, I yell the word in his face. Slap him. Claw at him. Spit at him. I hit him so hard, I crack my own bones and split my own skin.

"Why? Why do you want this?"

He turns, angling to face me, making it very clear that I am the center of his attention. Briefly, his eyes dart up to meet mine. "'Cause this whole thing is *killing* me," he growls. "I want you. I wanna make you mine. I want your legs wrapped around my fucking head and your pussy wetting my mouth, just...like...this..." Theo's finger traces even slower across my bottom lip, leaving a trail of fire in its wake. "Because I want...*you*," he says breathlessly. "I wanna sink my dick so deep inside you that you scream. I can't stop fucking thinking about you, and your smile, and tits, and how sweet your cunt must taste. I want to hold you down while I rail the fucking shit out of you. I want to see the second when you fall apart." Never before have I witnessed the kind of intensity that's burning in his eyes at this very moment; it's utterly intoxicating. "Does that answer your question?"

I open my mouth.

It isn't even a conscious decision.

I just do it.

Somewhere in the back of my head, Rachel is whooping, cheering, giving me a mental high five. *'Finally! Atta girl. Make him squirm, Sorrell.'*

And yes, he *is* squirming.

A war rages within me, pulling me in four different directions: I want him; I hate him; I need him; I'm gonna kill him. If Ruth could see me now, she'd drop down dead on the spot. I could never disappoint her more than I am right now. But...I curl my tongue around his finger, savoring the taste of popcorn butter on his skin, exhaling heavily down my nose. In all the ways that this feels wrong, it also feels so right. Theo grunts, his teeth gouging harder into his bottom lip, turning his flesh white as he studies me at work.

"Jesus Christ," he groans.

"Shh!" The warning doesn't come from Ford this time. It comes

from further back in the auditorium. Clearly, some of the students really want to watch this movie. On the screen, the characters are arguing, but don't ask me why. All I know is that Theo's curling his finger in my mouth, digging it into my cheek, fish-hooking me as he pulls my face closer to his. His other hand closes around my throat, and I can't bear it anymore. I close my eyes. It was bad enough when I could feel his lips moving against my ear, but feeling them move against my mouth…

Fuck.

He removes his finger. "Good girl. It's about time you gave in. I was getting pretty sick of waiting."

"Screw you," I pant.

He laughs, sending a wave of hot breath skating over my cheeks. "You'd like that, wouldn't you? To screw me. Have you thought about what it would be like to have me inside you, Kid?"

I swallow thickly. "No."

"Look at me."

"Why?"

"'Cause I wanna know if you're any good at hiding your lies."

God, god, god, this is bad. This is really *bad*. "Go to hell."

His hand shifts, grabbing hold of me by my jaw this time. He gives my head a little shake. "*Open them,*" he snarls.

I do.

"Now. Tell me again. Tell me you haven't thought about me, the way I've been thinking about you."

"You are the furthest thing from my mind, Theodore. *Always*."

He clucks his tongue. "You need to practice that in the mirror some more."

Before I can curse at him again, his mouth crashes down on mine. I'm wound taut, my muscles bunched so tight that I must be about to shatter against him. His tongue slips past my teeth and I'm done for. I can't resist this any longer. He kisses me, working his hands into my hair, breathing heavily into my mouth as he explores every part of me with his tongue, and I let him. More than that, I kiss him back. I cling to him, giving him everything he wants and then some. I take what *I* want, and it's heaven. He tastes sweet and salty, addicting enough to make me whimper. For every move that he makes, I counter. This is far more than just a kiss. His hands work their way down, sliding over the sensitive skin of my neck, over my collar bone, and I match him, grabbing hold of him by his shirt, drawing him closer. His hands move down further, groping my breasts over my top, fingers pinching and rolling my nipples through the thin material of my bra and—

*Oh fuck. Oh god. Oh...*GOD!

—I slide my hands up the inside of his shirt, digging my fingernails into his stomach and his sides, relishing the feel of his hard-packed muscle. Theo lets out an animal sound, guttural and desperate, and I lose all sense of up and down. Right and wrong. The conflict that's been raging inside my head for weeks now comes to an abrupt cease-fire as I sit forward, as far the armrest will allow, curving myself into him.

"Do you have any idea how hard you're making me right now?"

The need in his voice is palpable. It travels between us, transferring from him to me, and I welcome it, because like this, locked together with the tip of his tongue flicking at my lips and his hands holding onto me tight enough to leave marks, the world has gone silent. I'm not in pain anymore. I'm not suffering. I find a kind of peace in this madness, even knowing that it's wrong, and somehow that makes what's happening even more addicting.

When did I become this weak? If I thought about it, could I pinpoint the moment when I lost this battle, or is it happening right now, in this moment, with his hand wrapped around my throat and his tongue in my mouth? God, I am the worst kind of creature alive.

Rachel is dead.

Rachel is dead.

Rachel is *dead.*

Repeating that phrase has kept me anchored and on track in the past, but the words mean nothing now. They're background noise. I can't hear them over the roaring in my head.

"Fuck, your mouth..." Theo groans. "I can't tell you what I wanna do to this sweet fucking mouth."

He kisses me again before I can pull away, or breathe, or even think.

I start to slide my hands out from beneath his t-shirt, unable to bear the feel of his skin, but he takes hold of my chin again, looking me dead in the eyes. "Put them back," he commands.

His tone brooks no argument; it's my nature to argue all the same. "Why should I?"

"If you're hands aren't on my chest and my stomach, I'll find somewhere else for them to be, Voss. And while the thought of you wrapping them around my dick sounds absolutely fucking perfect right now, I don't want either of us to get expelled."

"You wouldn't. You wouldn't *dare* get your dick out—"

He clenches his jaw, glowering at me, anger pouring out of him as he rips his hand away from my face and unfastens his jeans. I watch him do it, too surprised by his sudden display of fury to stop him. And then, and then...

Oh...holy *shit*.

I look back up at him, and my head spins at the primal, dominant expression he turns on me. "Don't tell me what I will or will not dare to do. You have no fucking idea. Look at it."

I keep my eyes trained on his face.

"Look at it, Voss."

Ford is going to overhear him any second now. She's going to lose her shit and stop the movie, and I'll be saved from this beautiful nightmare. Only she doesn't.

God help me, but I look down. Theo palms his cock in his right hand, slowly working his grip up and down his considerable length. He's hard, veins standing proud in the rigid shaft of his erection. He squeezes himself, harder than looks comfortable, and a bead of precum forms at the head of his dick.

An inferno burns inside me, scorching me from my stomach, up through my chest, blazing at the base of my throat, setting my cheeks on fire. The sight of him touching himself, working that hand up and down, makes my nipples peak. My breasts feel suddenly tight. Heavy. They ache as if they want to be touched, too. And between my legs... my pussy wants to be touched even more. I'm wetter than I've ever been in my entire life.

When Theo pauses, hand gripped around the top of his shaft, and he rubs that bead of precum all over the head of his dick with the pad of his thumb, I nearly spontaneously combust.

"What the hell is wrong with you?" I mutter.

"The hell is wrong with *you?*" he fires back. "You want this. I can fucking smell how bad you want it on you."

Shame rockets through me, all consuming. He can *smell* it on me? Jesus Christ.

"Sit there and watch, Kid. Look away, even for a second, and you'll regret it. That's a promise."

Theo leans back into his chair, releasing me, but his eyes never waver. They burn holes into me as he shifts his jeans down a little lower over his hips, giving him better access as he angles his hips up, making his cock jut out…

Oh my god.

Transfixed, I gasp down frantic gulps of air as he quickens his pace, shuttling his hand up and down his erection. Faster and faster. Harder and harder. It's the most primal, brazen, fascinating thing I've ever witnessed.

He pulls up his t-shirt, exposing the flat, muscled planes of his stomach. "This is 'cause of you," he hisses. "This is how crazy you make me. This is how badly you make me wanna *fuck*."

Quicker and quicker, he works his hand over himself, growing tenser by the second. His shoulders lock out. His legs. The muscles in his arms strain as he gets closer and closer.

It happens all at once: Theo's eyelids slam closed, his head tipping back, and he erupts, coming all over his hand and his bare stomach. Fuck! The sight of him, slick and wet, covered in his own come, is equally the hottest, most terrifying thing I've ever seen.

He releases a stuttering exhalation, his mouth falling open a fraction, and I feel like I might die.

He's beautiful and savage—so fucking sexy that I bite the inside of my cheek until I taste blood. I want him so badly that I can't see straight. "Fuck, Theo…"

He sits up, opening his eyes, and the raw desire that was there before he came hasn't disappeared; if anything, it's intensified. "The next time I do that, it's gonna be inside you, Voss. I'm gonna rub my come all over your pussy. I'm gonna feed it inside you with my fingers. You have my word." Without missing a beat, he reaches across me and grabs the little red and white bandana I used as a headband this morning—I discarded it and put it on top of my bag when I came into the auditorium earlier with Noelani, but now Theo uses it to wipe himself clean. Once he's done, he unzips my bag and shoves the wadded up material inside.

He puts himself away and does up his jeans. Then the bastard gets up out of his chair. "I'm coming to your room tomorrow night."

"You're not!" I hiss.

"I am. And I'm gonna fuck you. And you're gonna come all over my dick, and I am gonna lick you fucking clean. It's a date."

He walks away.

"Theo!"

He doesn't listen. Doesn't even look back.

Ford doesn't make a sound as he stalks up the aisle and lets himself out of the auditorium.

Goddamnit, I can't…I can't fucking *breathe.*

Go, go, go. You've gotta get the hell out of here.

It isn't Rachel's memory that tells me to follow suit and leave. It's a far more urgent, desperate voice in my head, screaming at me to bolt. My legs are unsteady as I make my way out of the auditorium. My vision feels weirdly blurry.

Out in the hallway, the air is cool, but I still feel like I'm burning up.

I'm going to pass out.

There's no way I'm going to make it back to my room.

Despite my doubts, I do make it, though.

The moment my bedroom door is closed behind me and I've dumped my bag on the floor, I lean my back against the solid wood and shove my right hand down the front of my pants. My fingertips immediately find my slick, aching heat, and the world ignites.

They're not my fingers.

In my mind, they're Theo's.

I rub tight circles over my clit, panting with frustration as the pressure builds between my legs.

Theo's hands, rough on my skin.

Theo's mouth, hot on my neck.

Theo's teeth, gouging into my flesh.

Theo's cock, pressing between my thighs, thrusting up violently inside me.

I cry out as I come, harder than I've ever come before.

The ground opens up beneath me, and I fall…

SORRELL

"You left in a hurry last night. Were you sick?" Noelani finds me the next morning as I'm leaving *Rosewood*. Concern is plastered across her face, and a wave of guilt rips through me. She's been such a good friend to me these past few weeks. It sucks to know that she was so worried about me, while I was back in my room, trying to satisfy an itch that refused to be scratched.

Yes, I was sick last night. Depraved. Desperate. Making myself come, standing there with my back pressed against the door, had not been enough. Not even close. I'd made myself come another two times, replaying the sight of Theo jerking off in the seat next to me over and over again, until I felt like my body was going to come apart.

And then after came the anger. The humiliation. The disgust.

I don't know who I am anymore—what kind of person I'm turning into—but I don't like it. I nearly flayed myself alive this morning in the shower, the water so hot it scalded, trying to wash myself to a point where I didn't feel dirty. I could shower a hundred times more and still not feel clean.

"Oh, I was fine," I lie, looping my arm through Noelani's. "I've just seen that movie a thousand times. I was bored."

Lie, lie, lie. I'm getting remarkably good at it.

"I know, right?" Noelani says, laughing. "What do you want? WHAT. DO. YOU. *WANT?*"

I get the feeling that she's reenacting a part of the movie that I clearly missed; I grin, laughing along with her, careful not to let my confusion show. "You were right about his beard, though. Ryan Gosling with facial hair should be illegal."

She sighs dreamily. "Shame none of the guys here look like that. It'd be a nice distraction from the boredom of being stuck at this godforsaken Academy."

I haven't really paid much attention to the guys here at Toussaint. Only one of them has caught and held my attention, and I want him dead now more than ever.

"I thought you might have fallen out with Theo, though," Noelani says. "First he dashes out, and then you right after. He told me he wanted to make friends with you. Bury the hatchet or something. I hope he didn't do anything to upset you."

"Oh no. He didn't do anything." *Unless you count flirting with me, kissing me, touching me, making himself come and then using my bandana to clean up his mess, of course.*

"Good. I'm glad. He can be pretty pigheaded when he wants to be. But he's a good guy, y'know. There's just been a lot going on here recently, I guess."

This pulls me up short. "A lot going on? What do you mean?"

Noelani's mouth opens, then immediately closes. "Oh, no, nothing really. Just with the lockdown and the punishments. Everyone's going a little stir crazy, aren't they? Hopefully Principal Ford will let us out of here soon and we can all burn off some steam. It's long overdue."

Her voice is a little too nonchalant. Why do I feel like she's not telling me something? I take a closer look at her out of the corner of my eye, but there's no sign of deception there. Only a bright smile that stretches from ear to ear.

"Ahh, my god. I can picture it now. Shopping. Coffee. Proper coffee. *Real* coffee. Urgh! And a trip to the movies. The Jump! I can't wait to go to The Jump with you!"

"What's The Jump?"

"Oh, it's just this place we like to hang out. It's kind of on the way back toward Seattle. If we ever get out early enough on a Friday, we could go on a road trip somewhere, too. Do you have your passport? Maybe we could go to Vancouver and—"

Pain explodes in the back of my head. It feels like a bomb going off inside my skull. It's so unexpected and out of the blue, that I drop to my knees, clutching my hands to the point of the pain, gasping, gasping, trying unsuccessfully to pull in a breath.

Something hard clatters to the ground beside me. My bag? My phone? I don't know. For a second, I can't see anything. My vision darkens, shadows creeping into my peripherals.

"Oh my god, Sorrell!" Noelani's anxious cry is loud and close. Her hands are on me, patting me down. The world around me sharpens back into focus and her terrified expression fills me with an inexplicable anxiety.

Thrum, thrum, thrum!

The pain in the back of my head isn't going away. It's getting worse. Arrrgh, it feels like my skull's splitting open!

"It's okay, it's okay. Shhh. Lean forward. Let me take a look."

I don't know what she wants. I don't need to lean forward. The pain isn't coming from the back of my head. It's coming from *inside* my head, and it—ahh, it fucking hurts!

"Not cool, Sebastian!" Noelani roars. I've never heard her shout before. She's not one to raise her voice at all. She sounds like she's about to go nuclear. "What the fuck were you *thinking?"*

I can see her properly now. She sits back on her heels in front of me, and when she lifts her hands to brush my hair out of my face, they're covered in blood. I shy away from her, my pulse racing.

She won't look at me. She's looking at someone behind me.

"I was thinking that I'm sick and tired of this bullshit," a male voice growls.

I put my hand out to steady myself, feeling dizzy, nausea rolling through me, but my hand hits something smooth and cylindrical. A can of coke? *What?* there's a huge dent in the bottom of the can, and the other end is pushed out, the metal bulging. It's hissing, the seal broken, a thin jet of soda fizzing out of it.

"I'm sick of everyone pretending. I'm sick of being punished because of *her*." The venom in the voice has me spinning around. Too fast. I nearly black out all over again. Five feet away, Sebastian folds his arms across his chest, his face a mask of anger.

"What the *fuck*?" I begin to piece together what's happened. The coke can, busted and leaking all over the floor. The splitting headache that now's settling in behind my eyes. *Sebastian threw the fucking can at my head, and he hit me right on target.* "What the hell are you talking about, Sebastian?"

He looks at me, disgusted, regarding me as if I'm something unpleasant that he just scraped off his shoe. His jaw works, like he's chewing on his words before spitting them at me. "*You*, Sorrell Voss. You're a fucking problem, and I'm sick of pretending like you're not."

"How the fuck am *I* a problem to you?" I gingerly place my palm against the back of my head and my hand comes away even bloodier than Noelani's. I can feel it now—the steady, hot stream of blood running from the open gash on the back of my skull, trickling through my hair and down the back of my neck. There's a lot of it. My stomach rolls.

Sebastian sees the slick crimson color of my hands and his face hardens further. He flares his nostrils. "Everyone's walking around, acting like they know nothing, but it's obvious," he spits.

"Obvious? What's fucking obvious? Nothing's obvious to me."

"*Seb*." A strange note laces Noelani's tone. I can't tell what it is, but it sounds like warning.

Sebastian rolls his eyes. A small crowd has gathered around us now to watch the exchange go down. Most of the other students skirt around us, however, heads down, clearly pretending that they haven't seen anything. Assholes. "I'm done with it, Lani," Seb sneers. "I'm fucking over it. This year was supposed to be fun for all of us and look what we've been doing."

"SEBASTIAN!"

The roar comes from the other end of the hall. The blood-soaked hairs on the back of my neck stand to attention at the sound of the pure rage held within it. A tall guy standing next to Noelani blanches, hiking his bag higher on his back. "Oh, fuck. I wasn't here," he mutters, and then takes off toward the English department.

"Sebastian West, you're fucking *dead!"* The crowd parts, forming a pathway, and Theo comes into view, hurtling down the hallway at a run. His hands are fists. His black long-sleeved shirt strains across his chest as he pitches up in front of us; he looks like he's about to destroy Sebastian, but he comes to me first, where I'm kneeling on the floor in a pool of my own blood; he ducks down so that we're at eye level.

"You okay?" he asks.

"I think so."

"Feel sick? Dizzy?"

"What do you think?!"

Theo bares his teeth. Leaning around me, he assesses the back of my head, parting my hair in a number of places and making furious sounds as he takes in the damage.

"Stay right fucking there," he snarls. "Don't you fucking move."

"I'm not going anywhere!" I snap back.

Done with the back of my head, Theo appears before me again. He cups my face in his hands and tilts my head back, frowning. "Not you. *Him,"* he says, jerking his own head toward Sebastian.

I hadn't noticed, but Sebastian's been inching away from the scene by the looks of things, trying to sneak off unnoticed.

"What, man?" he says airily. "I gotta get to class."

Theo squints even harder at me, looking into my eyes. *"Stay right fucking there, Seb."*

"What are you gonna do about it? Be the big man? Punch me or some shit? You forget, I'm captain of the wrestling team, asshole. I've been going easy on you. I could take you in a heartbeat."

Theo doesn't justify his claim with a reaction. He talks to me this time. "Pupils are responsive and equal. I don't think you have any real damage, beyond the cut."

"What are you, some kind of doctor now?" I appreciate the concern, I guess, but the fact that it's coming from Theo makes me want to scream. He's not supposed to be here, saving the day. I'm not supposed to want to fall into his arms and cry, just so I can have him hold me.

His thick, wavy hair falls into his face as he looks down at the coke can, his mouth pulling into a tight line. "Something like that," he murmurs. Without another word, he launches himself to his feet and rounds on his friend. In a flash, he has the other guy by the shirt and he's slamming him back against the wall.

"You're a dead man, motherfucker!" And then he really snaps. I watch in horror as Theo winds back and throws a fist at Sebastian West's handsome face. The punch connects, and Seb's head snaps back, making a loud crack as the back of *his* skull connects with the wall behind him.

'Ahh! FUCK!" Sebastian tries to loosen Theo's hold on his shirt now that he's pinning him down with one hand, but Theo won't let him. He hits him again, and again, and again, reigning down blows so fast that Seb barely has time to react between them. Eventually, he shakes off his shock and starts hitting back, though.

Reeling back, Seb launches a right hook at Theo and lands it; the sound of his fist connecting with Theo's jaw cracks and reverberates off the hallway walls—it seems loud enough to wake the dead. Theo's head whips around. He staggers back, but he doesn't lose his footing. If anything, the blow serves less as a warning and only makes Theo madder.

Seb sees it. I see it. Noelani sees it: the moment when Theo decides to murder Sebastian West right where he stands. Noelani covers her mouth. Sebastian holds his hands up in protest—he's apparently realized that being captain of the wrestling team won't help him any here —and starts to back away.

I know anger. I've lived with it coiled around my bones for as long as I can remember. It's been a stalwart companion, dogging my every move ever since Rachel died. But I've never been witness to the kind of condensed, magnified hatred that lives in Theo's beautiful eyes now. The sight of it makes me tremble.

"Theo. D—Dude. Be reasonable," Sebastian stammers.

"Reasonable?" Theo's face twists. "*Reasonable?* You're fucking kidding me, right?"

"I didn't mean any harm."

"Your actions suggest otherwise." Theo has him trapped; he's backed Sebastian into a corner, and his only escape route now is through Theo. Which simply isn't an option. Theo towers over him, blocking his path...and then proceeds to beat the shit out of him.

"Theo! Oh my god! *Stop!*" Noelani's loud shriek threatens to rip my head apart, but Theo doesn't hear her. Can't. He's disappeared into another world. I can see it in his vacant eyes.

Noelani pulls me to my feet; she squeezes my arm so hard, her fingernails gouge my skin through the sleeve of my sweatshirt. "Say something, Sorrell. Stop him. He'll listen to you!"

Sebastian's face is a bloody, pulpy mess. He slides down the wall, sagging to the floor, but Theo doesn't stop hitting him. I try, and try, and try again, but I can't look away. This is brutality at its cruelest. A horror show that would give most people nightmares. But to me, it's a symphony. A bloody, breathtaking ballet. Theo Merchant is about to kill this guy for hurting *me*. He has no right to take these actions in my defense, but his fury is stirring something within me that's been slumbering for a long time. Some strange sensation that makes me want to crow from the rooftops. It feels dark, and twisted, and wrong on so many levels, but seeing Theo like this, at his most vicious, is like seeing his soul laid bare.

And it's fucking breathtaking.

"Stop him!" Noelani urges again. "He's gonna kill him!"

Oh, God. I shouldn't be enjoying this. I step forward, breath catching in my throat as I yell, *"THEODORE WILLIAM MERCHANT!"*

The words fire down the hall like a gunshot. Theo stiffens, still as a statue, one bloodied fist raised behind his head. Slowly, it lowers to his side.

No one speaks a word.

On the floor, Sebastian whimpers, covering his face with his hands; it's a miracle that he's still conscious; by rights, he should have passed out somewhere between Theo's tenth and fifteenth hit.

I'm impossibly dizzy, but I manage to weave over to where Theo looms over Seb, his back still turned to me. His shoulders inch up around his ears, tension radiating from him like smoke. It wouldn't take much for him to snap and start kicking the crap out of his friend again. I place my hand on his shoulder and like magic the tension drains from him; he sags, his muscles relaxing, as if my touch has given him permission to release the rage that was devouring him. Far from calm, though, Theo glares down at Seb, his hair wild and unkempt. "Tell her why you did it," he demands.

Seb coughs, blood dribbling down his chin. "What do you expect me to say?"

"Tell her," Theo repeats, tone promising more violence if he doesn't comply.

Seb laughs, sighing heavily. "Fine. You want me to play nice. I'll play fucking nice. Ridiculous…"

A low, threatening rumble issues from Theo's throat.

"All right. All right! Fuck." He looks up at me through rapidly swelling eyelids. "I threw the can at you because it's obvious. You're the one who ran back to Ford and told her about the party."

"I did not!"

"Bullshit. You left early, before security showed up. You're the only one who wasn't punished—"

"What are you talking about? I haven't been able to leave. I've had curfew, the same as everyone else!"

"You're the only one who wasn't called up onto that stage," Seb spits. "Out of thirty-four students, you're the only one Ford didn't make come up on stage to dance or sing like some kind of performing fucking monkey. Explain *that*."

"I—" Oh. Oh my god. The world comes to a standstill. He's right. How did I miss that? *I wasn't called up to do anything*. Somehow, I just assumed that that punishment didn't apply to me, and it really didn't. How can I have been so blind to this? How can the thought not even have occurred to me? I sputter, trying to find some logical reason for this, but no words come to mind. "I—I can't explain it. I don't know why Ford didn't call on me. But I wasn't the one who told her what was happening down by the lake. Why the fuck would I tell them?"

"You made it pretty clear that you were disgusted with all of us that night. You stood there in that ridiculous fucking coat, judging us all. And when your boyfriend here decided to bail—"

"He's not my fucking boyfriend! Jesus fucking Chr—" I break off, unable to handle the heat building inside me. My head is swimming. The flow has slowed, I think, but I can still feel the trickle of blood down the back of my neck. I can't fucking deal with this. I can't handle any of it. I should already be back at Falcon House by now. Theo should be behind bars, or humiliated, or worse. And now Sebastian Fucking West is calling him my *boyfriend*?

Theo looks stricken as he reaches out, trying to take me by the hand.

I slap him away, snarling as I turn on him. "No! You don't get to touch me. You don't get to protect me. Don't pretend like I fucking mean something to you!"

He looks ravaged, torn inside out by my words, but I have no sympathy for this devil. He's played with me. Toyed with my emotions. Turned me inside out with this fucked up game that he's playing. "You can keep your stupid information about Henry. I don't care what you know. It doesn't matter anymore. Just stay away. And you…" I turn my rage back to Sebastian. "I didn't fucking turn you in to Ford. I couldn't give a shit about you, or him, or anyone else in this godforsaken place. Come at me again and I'll tear your fucking throat out."

I storm away from them, snatching up my bag from the ground as I go.

"Make sure she gets to the nurse's office, Lani," Theo says softly behind me.

"I don't need anyone to take me," I snipe back. Lani looks devastated by this. Guilt rakes its claws over me—this isn't her fault. She's been nothing but sweet and kind to me—but I'll scream blue murder if I have to spend another second with another one of these people right now.

I'll get myself to see the nurse.

I'll get myself back to my room, and I'll get my shit packed up all by myself.

And then, so help me god, come hell or high water, I am getting my ass back to Falcon House.

SORRELL

I NEED STITCHES. Four of them. The nurse threatens to shave around the gash, but when I bare my teeth at her and tell her she'd better not dare, she backs off and agrees to sew me up if I promise to keep the wound clean.

She's no help when it comes to sending me back to Seattle.

Neither is Ford.

The principal barely blinks at me when I charge into her office and start making my demands. "I'm afraid it's not that easy, Miss Voss. There are procedures and protocols here when a student wishes to leave Toussaint. I have to file paperwork. I have to speak to your guardian—"

"I want to leave, Principal Ford. You can't fucking keep me here."

Ford gives me a measured look. She sets down the pen in her hand, whatever note she was taking on the legal pad in front of her now forgotten about. "Okay. Okay. All right. Calm down. We'll get this sorted—"

"Good. Then tell Jeremy that I'll be going with him on the plane when he lands here this afternoon."

"That's not possible, Miss Voss."

"You just said—"

"I know what I said, but Jeremy is on vacation. A replacement pilot is flying in, but he isn't insured to carry passengers. He can't take you. Jeremy won't be coming back here until next Wednesday."

"Next Wednesday isn't going to work. I need to get out of here today. You *can't* keep me here," I repeat.

"I'm not keeping you here," she says calmly. "You *are* free to go. I've asked the charter company to organize another plane, but their schedules are planned a week out, and they won't change it on a dime just for us. I've already tried—"

"Then try harder."

She laughs softly, shaking her head, her exasperation clear. "Believe me, if I thought calling them again would make a difference, then I would. You're more than welcome to call them yourself directly if you wish." She points to the phone on her desk. "The number's right there."

She doesn't think that I'll call her bluff? She has got me *all* wrong. I stalk around her desk and snatch up the phone's receiver, plucking the Post-It note marked 'CNP Private Air Tours,' from the front of a binder resting on top of a stack of paperwork.

I make the call. I half expect that it won't connect, that Ford's playing some kind of trick on me, but it does. Someone picks up on the fourth ring. I explain that I need to be picked up from the Academy, but the agent on the other end of the line isn't helpful at all.

"I understand your predicament, Miss, but there's nothing I can do. My hands are tied. We're running on a skeleton staff right now and we just don't have the pilots. And since your principal informed us the school didn't require transportation for their students to travel back and forth to the city for a while, we took the opportunity to service a number of our aircraft. Even if we did have an insured pilot who could make the trip, three of our planes are currently in pieces on the shop floor—"

I hang up. Principal Ford's apologetic smile makes me want to trash her fucking office.

"Wednesday isn't that far away, Sorrell. Just five days. Might I suggest that you use that time to really think about the choice that you're making. What Sebastian did was reprehensible, and trust me, he will suffer the consequences of his actions. But if there's any chance that you might change your mind—"

"There isn't."

She closes her eyes, taking a deep breath. "If there is a chance that you might, then I urge you to consider all of your options. Toussaint isn't a prison. It's a highly regarded educational institution, and you could learn a lot here if you just..."

I turn on Principal Ford. "I'll call a taxi."

She splays her hands, nodding to the phone again. "Feel free to try. You saw the road for yourself, though. It's impassable. There isn't a taxi company on this earth that would risk their cars by coming up here. Not for all the money in the world. Uber. Lyft." She shakes her head. "The terrain's too dangerous. And even if it wasn't, you can't call any of those rider share services without cell reception."

"I can use the WIFI to order one," I spit. But before she can say anything to counter that, I remember the announcement she made earlier over the P.A. system. The Academy's internet will be down for the next week as well. Holy fucking shit, the universe is conspiring against me right now. I swear, I'm about to go nuclear.

"Just take a deep breath, Sorrell. I know this isn't ideal, but—"

The tail end of Principal Ford's sentence is cut off by her office door as I slam it closed behind me.

SORRELL

I USED to be afraid of the dark. When I was little, I'd cry myself to sleep every night, petrified of the monsters that lurked in the shadows, waiting to sneak out of their hiding places to come and hurt me when I lowered my guard.

I was seven when I learned that the worst monsters, the ones capable of hurting you the most, didn't bother to hide themselves in the dark. They were the people who promised to care for you and provide for you in one breath, while in another raising a fist to you. They were the ones who'd touch you in places you begged not to be touched. The ones who'd fill your head full of lies, make you believe that they were good, only to hurt you in ways you could never have even imagined.

I didn't fear the dark after I learned that lesson.

I sit in the dark now, relishing the velvety quality of the silence that comes with it. My room is a tomb. Beyond the door that separates me from the rest of Toussaint, all of the other bedrooms stand empty; the girls on my floor have all gone down to the common room to play pool, and talk, and watch movies. Ford, in all her benevolent glory, decided to unlock the common room doors for us after all.

Noelani knocked around eight, begging me to come down and join them if I felt well enough. I didn't answer.

My head feels fine now. Ish. It only hurts when I touch the gash left there, courtesy of Sebastian, whom Noelani informed me through the door has been confined to his room pending a review of today's 'incident' by the school's administrative board.

Lani probably thought I'd feel more comfortable if I knew Sebastian wasn't going to be down there, but his presence matters little to me. I couldn't give a shit about him. I was serious when I told him that I'd tear out his throat before. I'll do far worse if he tries to hurt me again. I know how to deal with assholes like him.

It's close to ten when another knock comes at my door.

I've been waiting for it. Dreading it. Knowing that it's coming.

"Go away, Theo."

"Open the door, Kid. I wanna talk to you."

"I think I've made it very clear that I don't want to talk to *you*."

"I'm not leaving until we have a conversation."

"Then I hope you enjoy loitering in hallways."

"I can out-stubborn you," he tells me.

Hah. I doubt that very much. Rachel always claimed I was the most stubborn person she'd ever met, and she knew Ruth, so that was really saying something.

"Just fuck off. I've said everything I want to say to you."

"Oh really?" I can imagine the cocky uptick of his mouth. The mental image I've conjured of him leaning against my bedroom door, sweeping a hand through that messy hair of his, makes me see red. I breathe through my rising temper and release it, pulling the duvet up over my head. The down feather comforter won't totally block out the sound of his voice, but it will certainly muffle it to the point that I might not be able to make out his words.

"Don't you want to make me take responsibility for what happened to Rachel?" he says.

I throw the covers off, laying very, very still on the mattress. Damn. I heard him say *that*. He has absolutely manipulated me with promises of information about this mysterious Henry guy, but this manipulation has a foul taste to it that I won't be able to rid myself for days. "Like you'd ever do that," I snarl.

"I've never been one to shirk responsibility when I've done something wrong," he says quietly.

The gall of this guy. The fucking stones he has, to come here and say something like that to me. I get up and cross the bedroom, my blood boiling. When I open the door, he's standing exactly how I pictured him, propped up against the wall, hands in his pockets. The ghost of a bruise blooms on his jaw, angry and purple; the three freckles underneath his eye stand out, extraordinarily dark against his skin in the dim lighting of the hallway, too. His hair is swept back out of his face. There's no cocky, self-assured smirk. Wearing a white long-sleeved t-shirt and ripped blue jeans that hang low on his hips, the sight of him evokes a weird, overwhelming rushing sensation through my body. For some reason, his feet are bare.

I square off against him. "Where the fuck are your shoes?"

He huffs out a laugh. "That's your first question? Where the fuck are my shoes?"

"What kind of person roams around the school in the middle of the night with nothing on their feet?" I hiss. It's stupid to be upset about something so bizarre and unimportant, but the sight of his bare feet has done something to me that I don't like and attacking him for it seems like the only logical thing to do.

"I'm only one floor up, Kid," he tells me. "Carpet's pretty soft. Didn't think I was gonna cut myself up on broken glass or anything. Though I guess you never know. Someone might hurl a *bottle* of Coke at you next time. They do say it tastes better."

"I'm not in the mood to spar with you. Say whatever it is you've come here to say. I have to pack."

"You think I killed Rachel," he states. "That's why you came here. To punish me."

I glare at him flatly. If he wants to get down to brass tacks, then so be it. Finally. I'll have this conversation with him at last. "Yes. That's exactly why I came here. Because I wanted you to suffer, the way that she suffered."

"How did Rachel die, Voss?" he asks. So calm. So composed. The question jars me.

"You know how she died. You were there. You were the *reason* she died."

"We've established that. But how did she die? How was I responsible?" He doesn't deny that her death was his fault. Doesn't imply that I'm wrong in this belief. What kind of shit is he trying to pull with this line of questioning then?

"She was in the car. You were driving."

He angles his head slightly, dark brows knitting together. "Was I?"

"Look, I don't have the patience for this bullshit. You were driving. Rachel was in the passenger seat. You were drunk. Something...something ran out into the road and you hit it. Rachel was ejected from the car."

"Was she wearing her seat belt?"

"I—I don't know. How the hell am I supposed to know that?"

"Where were you when all this happened?"

"I was there! I was with you!"

He nods, as if taking all of this in. "You were in the backseat then?"

"Where else would I have been?!"

"And you weren't hurt when the car crashed? You walked away unscathed?"

"God, what the fuck are you doing, Theo? You think you're gonna undermine me by playing twenty questions? I was there," I say firmly. "I know what happened. I know what I saw."

He stands there, unmoving, watching me warily as I scream at him. "All right, then."

"All right then? What the fuck is '*all right, then'* supposed to mean?"

"I'm sorry. I'm deeply sorry for killing her. I never meant for that to happen. I hate what happened to her just as much as you do, believe me."

"So you *do* admit it, then? You admit that you killed her? That it's your fault that she's gone?" My emotions claw at the back of my throat, my voice thick with it. My eyes burn with unshed tears. I didn't think I'd feel this way when he finally took ownership for what he did. I figured I'd feel vindicated. Victorious. Not this…this…painful sense of loss and panic that has ahold of me now.

A harrowed, bleak look flickers across Theo's face. He's the picture of devastation. "It *is* my fault that she's gone. I'd do anything in my power to change that…"

"YOU *CAN'T* CHANGE THAT!" I roar. "SHE'S FUCKING DEAD!"

He rocks back. It's as if I've hit him a hundred times harder than Sebastian did earlier, and the force of the blow has shaken him to his core. "I realize that," he says quietly.

"And now, of all the people in this entire school, you're chasing after *me*. Her best friend. Someone who hates you more than anything else in the entire fucking world. You've got some fucking nerve."

"I can't help how I feel," he whispers.

"And you think that just showing up here, owning up to what you did, and saying you're sorry for it will make it all better? That I can just forgive you for what you've done, and I'll fall into bed with you like none of it matters anymore? What kind of person do you think I am?"

His eyes are full of pain, the complexities of the tawny, rich browns and golds shifting and twisting together as he watches me steadily. He inhales deeply as he says, "I think that you're a human being. That you can't help how you feel any more than I can."

A lump aches at the base of my throat. Why can't I swallow? Why are my eyes burning so badly, so full of tears? Why do I want to go to him so badly, when I need to be as far away from him as possible? "It doesn't matter, Theo. None of this matters. I should never have come here. It was a mistake. I can't make anything better, staying here. Hurting you won't help. And being around you is a fucking *punishment*—"

"You can leave, but it won't change anything. I promise you, it won't," he says. "You won't just stop caring about me."

"Why do I even give a shit about you in the first place?" I could scream the words. Yell them into his face. It would feel like a release. The question comes out as a whisper, though, full of pain and a desperate longing that I feel down to the roots of my soul. I can't understand it.

Theo looks so torn. His jaw is set, his eyes hard, but his brows pinched together over the bridge of his nose. His hands clench, as if he's at war, ready to fight again. Fight me? Fight himself? Who the fuck knows. He runs his tongue over his teeth, narrowing his eyes at me. "I don't have all of the answers. I only know what I know. That I want you. And you want me. Everything else pales in comparison to that."

My heart physically *hurts*. "Just go."

Slowly, he shakes his head. "I can't do that. I can't leave you now. You know I can't."

"I'm not asking you. I'm *telling* you. I want you to go!"

His voice is soft and full of agony when he says, "If you want me to go so badly, then why are you crying?"

A sob bursts out of my mouth right on cue. I haven't noticed that my tears have overflowed and are streaking down my cheeks. The outline of Theo's face swims as my eyes flood, these strange, unwelcome emotions swelling in my chest to the point that they overwhelm me.

"Fuck. Come here." Theo shoves away from the door jamb, taking his hands out of his pockets. He attempts to draw me to him, but I push him back, stopping him. "Jesus, Voss. Just stop fucking fighting me! I'm not going to hurt you!"

Something inside me breaks. Just shatters into a million pieces. I've been doing my best for so long, trying to hold myself together, but there are limits to what I'm capable of. This is my threshold. I've reached the point where I physically can't keep all of this tamped down anymore, and so it comes spilling out. My strength leaves me. My fury and my anger depart in a rush, leaving behind only confusion and the need for Theo's arms around me.

I let him hold me. He pulls me to him, crushing me against his chest, and the storm inside me quiets. This is bitter medicine; it's unfair that it takes *this* for me to feel better. Anyone else. Literally *anyone* else in the world would have been better than Theo, and yet it's him who calms my racing heart and soothes the panic in my veins. In his arms, I feel anchored down, safe in a way I don't think I've ever felt before, and the relief that comes with that? It's *everything*.

I bury my face into his t-shirt, breathing in the scent of him. Mint and bergamot. Winter rain and the promise of snow. So familiar now that it stirs something inside of me, kindling it to life. Theo's muscled chest flexes beneath my hands as he tightens his hold on me, lifting me from the ground. I don't object. Not even when he dips down and picks me up properly, cradling me in his arms like a child, and carries me into my bedroom. I lace my arms around the back of his neck and cling onto him for dear life, sobbing into his shirt, letting it all go, as bit by bit all of the hurt and the suffering I've endured and carried with me recently finally cracks, comes loose and falls away.

Theo sits on the edge of my bed and holds me. Doesn't say anything. Doesn't rush me into recovering myself. He gently rocks me, back and forth, occasionally resting his cheek against the top of my head. After a while the air in his lungs starts to vibrate, resonant, filled with bass, and he begins to hum.

It's the piece of music he played in the auditorium. The same piece of music I was humming in the car the day Gaynor dropped me off at Toussaint. I don't know how I know it, but I do. I'm suddenly overcome with frustration. So sick and tired of feeling sad, and angry, and guilty. I want to feel something else, *anything* else, for just five fucking minutes.

Theo stops humming when I lift my head from his chest. "If you're going to start yelling at me again—" he starts. But I cut him off with my mouth.

Cupping the back of his neck with my hand, I pull his head closer so I can kiss him harder, and the warmth of his skin against my palm sears me to the bone. I've wanted to touch him for so long. Needed to touch him. I brace my other hand against his chest, and I feel his pulse quicken in time with mine as I urge his lips open and drive my tongue into his mouth.

He groans, desperate and urgent, huffing heavily down his nose, kissing me back, and I'm swept away on a tidal wave of relief. *He's* kissed *me* before. He's made plenty of moves on me, but I've never been the one to try and kiss him. The thought that he might reject me was terrifying, but I need not have worried. Theo's reaction is engulfing. His hands rove over my back, down my arms, up to cup my face. He digs his fingers into my hair, roughly pulling my hair back. He falls on me, tearing his mouth away from mine to leave a trail of burning kisses down the column of my throat, and my stomach tightens. My thighs clench together, a heat building between my legs, and I know precisely how far this is going to go if I don't stop it now.

I should. But...I can't.

"Voss. Fuck, Voss, you're fucking killing me," Theo gasps. "I want your pussy. I want you riding my goddamn face. I fucking *need* it."

Heat slams into me—a burning hot poker burning right at my core. The desperation in his tone matches the urgency I feel, raking its claws down my spine. Normally, I'd cringe away from such a graphic statement. Boys have talked dirty to me before, but I've always found it embarrassing. Nothing about what Theo just said was embarrassing, though. I already know how good he is with that tongue. No one kisses like that and *doesn't* know how to go down on a girl. And I want him to make me come like that so badly, I really fucking do.

For a second, I'm dizzy; Theo shifts, getting to his feet, but not for long—just enough time to twist me around so that we're chest-to-chest, and for his hands to guide my legs around his waist. Then he sits back down on the bed and kisses me again.

I can't tell if there are fireworks going off inside my head or if it's lightning bolts. It shouldn't matter but it does—one of those options is used to celebrate momentous occasions; the other causes natural disasters and kills people. Either way, the raw energy roiling around in my brain is too much to bear as Theo's tongue explores my mouth, and he nips and teases at my lips with his teeth. His hands roam down, over my shirt, until he's cupping both of my breasts in his palms. He is not gentle when he starts to knead them, rolling and pinching my hardened nipples through the fabric of my top and the thin lace bra I'm wearing.

"I'm gonna fill your holes," he says. "I want my dick in your mouth. Your pussy. Your ass. I want to make you fucking scream. I've needed to hear my name on your lips for so fucking long..."

Grabbing me by the hips, he jerks me down, rocking up *his* hips, and I can feel him, solid, rubbing up against me through his jeans. His cock is as hard as reinforced steel. When he rolls his hips beneath me, grinding himself up to meet me, the sensation is mind-blowing. Amazing. Everything I've ever imagined it could be.

I angle my hips back again, waiting for him to shift, and then when he does, I angle myself back down at the same time, so that we're both moving in concert, both applying pressure at the same time. Theo loses his goddamn mind. His fingers dig into my ass cheeks as he rocks me back and forth against his dick.

"I'm going to fuck you so damn hard," he grits out through his teeth. "I'm gonna hold you down and make you come again and again and again. You're gonna be begging me to stop."

I won't. I'll never want him to stop. I scramble with the material of his shirt, fisting it and dragging it up his body, determined to have him naked in the next five seconds. Theo places a hand around my wrist, shaking his head, though. "No. No time."

Okay. Fair enough. I can get on board with that. Theo pivots, dumping me onto my back on top of the bed. I wrestle with the button on his jeans—thank god he isn't wearing a fucking belt—while he wrestles with mine. His hands work quicker than mine. I gasp when he jerks my pants down over my hips, and then tears them down my legs. My panties go with my PJ shorts. With a feral, animal smile on his face, Theo drops down between my legs and pushes them further apart, propping himself up on his elbows.

A deeply satisfied growl of appreciation works up his throat as he inspects me. "Holy fuck, Kid. Goddamnit, you're beautiful. You have the prettiest cunt I've ever fucking seen." My cheeks burn hot and bright. He reaches out and, using the tips of his index and his middle fingers, he parts me, his breath stuttering out of him as he explores a part of my body nobody has ever investigated this thoroughly before.

"So. Fucking. Wet," he hisses. "You're ready for me."

I let my head fall back against the duvet, screwing my eyes shut. My skin prickles like there's an electrical current running over it. My nipples and breasts ache so badly they hurt. I need him to touch me properly. I need his fingers on my clit, his tongue...something. I need to feel his cock thrusting inside me before I lose my fucking mind. I've never experienced anything like this before. If I don't have him, I think I might die.

"Please. Please!" I never thought I'd beg. Not for this. Not with him. But here I am...

"It's all right, Kid. I'm gonna give you what you need. It's okay. Shh." Theo laps at me, the tip of his tongue probing in between the wetness of me, finding and stroking the taut bundle of nerves at the apex of my thighs, and every muscle in my body seizes. My legs lock out. My spine curves away from the bed. I'd scream if I had any air in my lungs. Starbursts of light feather across the dark void behind my eyelids, lighting up my head.

I act without thinking, driving my hands into Theo's hair. I've known what this would feel like—the shape of his head cradled between my legs. My sweat-soaked dreams have given me glimpses, even if I can't remember them. The reality of it is just as heady, just as deviant. He runs the flat of his tongue over me, from my entrance all the way up to my clit again, and my thighs spasm, closing around his head. I realize what I'm doing and lower them, mild embarrassment tugging at me, but Theo tuts into the inside of my leg.

"No, Voss. Clamp 'em tight. I wanna feel how bad you want this. And there are worse ways to die. If I go with my face buried in your pussy, it'll be with a smile on my face."

Oh.

My.

Fuck.

I oblige him, clenching my thighs around his head, pushing him down on me. I need more, more, more. I want to be laid bare before him, all of me on show for him, for him to peruse and inspect me at his leisure. I want him to use me. I want to surrender all control over this nightmare. For the first time in months, I want to feel anything but sad. I want to feel *good.*

Theo flicks his tongue over my center again. Flames of heat strengthen in my gut, traveling up into my chest, burning there. The band of tension across the backs of my shoulders, ever-present, never relenting, finally releases, and my body sinks even deeper into the bed. I let out a startled gasp when I feel a new pressure—Theo's fingers, dipping into my opening. I am the center point of a brilliantly burning star when he slips them inside me and begins to curl them against a firm part of my insides that I didn't even know existed. Coupled with the sensation of his tongue languorously working over my clit, I nearly come apart right then and there.

"Oh my god. Holy shit, that feels... that..."

"Good?" Theo murmurs.

"Fuck, yes. Good. Really fucking good."

Merchant rumbles his pleasure into my pussy, and he sounds for all the world like a very pleased predatory cat. Not the domesticated kind. A *lion*.

He pauses what he's doing with his mouth to say, "I meant it. I want you riding my face. You're going to give me what I need. Not tonight. Not tomorrow. But when you're good and ready, I'm gonna make sure it happens."

Thank god he's granting me a little time. I'm really not ready. I can't imagine spinning him over and taking charge like that. I want to. It would be empowering as hell to sit on his face and grind myself against his mouth, finding the point of friction that felt best and then claiming it for myself while he used the wet heat of his tongue to please me. For now, having him go down on me like this is just about all I can manage.

Still, I jerk when he quickens the pace with his fingers, stroking them inside me, creating the most delicious kind of pressure against my interior wall. His tongue presses harder, the tip of it flicking faster and faster, and a rush of warmth floods me.

"Mmm. Fuck, you taste so good," Theo pants. "You're so fucking wet for me. I'm going to lick you clean."

"Yes. God, yes!" I push his head down again, forcing him between my legs, increasing the pressure of his mouth all by myself, telling him I want more. That I need it. He chuckles darkly as he indulges my none-too-gentle request.

Faster. Quicker. Harder. Theo licks and sucks at me, driving his fingers inside me, massaging that point inside me with renewed intent, and I burn even hotter. Brighter.

"Oh! Oh...*shit!*" He sucks my clit, sweeping tight circles around it, and all is lost.

Theo knows that I'm close. He must. Changing pace altogether, he fucks me with his fingers, curling them slightly into me, plunging them into me faster and faster until—

"Fuck! Shit, Theo! Oh my god! Oh my god, oh my god, oh my god!"

It hits like a nuclear bomb.

My back arches so violently that I topple over to one side, my legs begging to straighten as the orgasm charges through me, but Theo wraps his arms around my thighs, hooking them around his head as he continues to lick and suck.

I scream.

I can't help it.

The sound is raw and hoarse, searing at my throat.

I'm no longer the center of a fiery star; I am a supernova, shattering into a trillion pieces, bursting out into space. The explosion within me can't be contained. I feel as if I'm coming apart on a molecular level, splintering, breaking, falling.

"Oh my god, stop, stop, stop!"

Theo does stop...but only for long enough to shove his already unfastened jeans down over his hips. I open my eyes, watching him do it, too stunned to speak. My breath comes in short, sharp blasts, made staccato by the echoes of my climax still rippling through me. He looks down at me as he crawls up my body, leonine, his eyes full of a frightening hunger. "You ready for me, Kid?" he demands.

"Yes." The word is just a shape on my mouth. I try to give it sound, but nothing comes out. I give him a brief, desperate nod just in case he didn't catch it, but—

Theo drives his hips forward, sinking himself deep inside me. I gasp, grabbing hold of him, trying to steady myself against the feel of him thrusting inside me. The move wasn't gentle or tender. It was a declaration. A claiming. He fills me so deeply that my body fights to stretch to accommodate the girth of him. It doesn't hurt. I just feel...complete.

Theo stills, supporting himself over me, hands planted on either side of my head. Our eyes lock, and for a second we just stare at each other, trying to come to terms with the bewildering feeling of *rightness* between us, where our two bodies have come together and now join us. I *know* he feels it, too. It's right there, written in his expression of wonder. His pupils—blown to all hell—look like twin black holes.

"Goddamnit," he growls. "You fit me like a glove. You feel fucking incredible."

I have no words. Can't comprehend the first thing I want to say in return. A primal part of my brain has taken over, rendering my speech centers redundant. Instead of answering him, I wrap my legs around his waist, holding him tighter, pulling him even deeper. Theo's lips part. His eyes widen. Feline satisfaction courses through me at the sight of him coming undone.

"Voss," he rasps hoarsely. "Don't move."

It would be very satisfying indeed to ignore his plea and rock against him, to feel his erect cock grow even harder inside me as I make him spill. But I'm selfish. I want more. If I push him over the edge too quickly, then this moment will be over. So rather than roll my hips as my body is begging me to do, I clench him from the inside, tightening myself around him. I'm not sure that he'll feel it. I've never tried to do it before. From the way his eyes round out, a deep, strangled blast of air leaving his lungs, I'd say that he feels it.

"Cruel," he mutters. "You're fucking cruel."

"So what if I am?" I whisper.

He bares his teeth, quickly closing a hand around my throat. His fingers gouge into my skin...but not hard enough to mark. I can still breathe, just about. Theo obviously knows exactly how much of his weight to lean against me to make my head spin a little. "Cruel girls? Girls who misbehave? They get punished," he promises.

I clench again, pulsing around him, and he hisses through his teeth.

I give him an open-mouthed smile. "How?"

Theo takes advantage of my open mouth and hooks his fingers inside my cheek again, just like he did last night in the auditorium. I can taste myself on him, the smell of my arousal coating his skin. I moan, unable to keep the sound at bay. He leans down, eyes full of fire, and says, "They get throat-fucked, sweetheart. They get bent over and have their assholes stretched out."

"I don't...do...that." It's difficult to get the words out.

He cocks his head to one side, narrowing his eyes. I'll be damned if his cock doesn't twitch inside me. "Don't you?"

I shake my head.

"You sure? 'Cause I think you're a *good* girl. I think you do what I tell you to do."

Fucking hell. The feminist in me revolts at his words. But the subservient part of me, a side of me I didn't know existed until now, glows with pleasure. I *do* want to obey him. I want to be his good girl. The idea of him putting me over his knee and teasing my asshole makes my cheeks flush to the point where I feel like my own blood is giving me sub-dermal second-degree burns. I've never even thought about that before...

With one hand around my throat, and the fingers of his other hand fish-hooking me, Theo's leaning a considerable amount of weight on me. Still not all of his weight, though. His core strength must be ridiculous if he's holding himself off me with his stomach muscles alone. I'd kill to rip his shirt off right now. I want to see his skin, see his ink, study every line of his chest and his abs, but when I go to try and grab his shirt by the hem again, Theo releases me and grabs me by both wrists, using one hand to pin them over my head.

"I don't recall giving you permission to touch me."

"I don't recall giving you permission to touch *me*," I counter. My voice is rough. I'd blame it on the way he was choking me, but it would be a lie. It's pure need. I hear it. Theo does, too. He smiles a savage smile, stroking his fingers down my cheek, my neck, over my own shirt. He palms my breast again, kneading and squeezing it until I cry out.

"Do I need permission to touch you?" he asks.

"I—"

"Do I *have* your permission? Can I touch you wherever I like? Whenever I like? However I like?"

Only a fool would say yes.

I am that fool.

I nod.

Theo glows at my response. "That's an *extremely* good girl. I'll let you know when you can see me naked, Voss. Until then..."

I'd object at the injustice of his double standard, but I'm lost for words when he jerks his hips back and slams himself into me. *Hard.*

"This is what you get for moving when I told you not to."

I wait for another punishing thrust, but when Theo rocks back and dips his hips forward again, he only slides an inch of himself inside me—again and again, short little thrusts, inserting just the tip of his cock. I had no idea my body could need anything as much as I need him to push all the way inside me again.

"Fuck! Theo! Oh my god, please! Fucking—"

My teeth crack together when he slams himself home again. All the way to the hilt.

"THEO!"

I brace for another powerful thrust, but no. He goes back to the short, teasing little strokes that make me want to rip out my own hair.

I try to pull him further into me, but Theo's far stronger than I am —and so is his will. "Patience. Ride it out with me. You got this."

I'd love to be able to contain myself. My self-control and dignity have flown out of the window, though. I need him—my body is on fire —and I will do anything I can to claim what I need. I writhe beneath him, wrestling with him, urgently trying to rock my hips up to meet him, to take more of him, to steal more than he's trying to give me.

He buries his head into my neck and nips aggressively at my skin, the unexpected pressure of his teeth causing me to drag down a sharp breath. "Do I need to tie you down, Kid? Or should I just stop fucking you until you can behave yourself?"

"No! No, please, no. Don't stop!" That would be a fate worse than death. I shudder as I marshal myself, attempting to calm the racing of my heart and the pounding rhythm of my blood. I'm aching for him though, and that ache is threatening to consume me from the inside out. It's so fucking difficult to relax my body and let this happen.

Somehow, I release the tension in my back and my legs, though. Theo smiles down at me, all satisfaction and...the faintest hint of pride.

"There. Perfect," he breathes. Brushing his lips over my forehead, my temple, along the line of my jaw, he peppers feather-light kisses against my mouth, and I can *feel* his smile now. It makes my soul burn to experience the shape of it there and to know that it's all for me.

He begins that grueling pattern again, dipping himself inside me, the tip of his cock just reaching deep enough to *almost* answer the demand thrumming around my body. And again, just as I'm about to lose my fucking mind, he surges forward, burying himself so deep that my eyes go wide and all common sense abandons me.

"Please!." I've never whimpered for anyone before. Never begged them to relieve me like this. My shame is a whisper, drowned out by the roaring current of electricity channeling between us, though. I'm so delirious that I pay it no heed. "Please. Please. *Please!*"

Theo is relentless. There's no mercy in him. He leans back, his golden-brown eyes locking onto mine, and his grim look of determination tells me that begging is futile. He's set his mind to this task, decided how he's going to make me purr, and no amount of pleading will change that. Again, and again, he repeats his actions, and with each repetition, I feel a little more of myself whittled away, my consciousness plummeting into the depths of insanity.

"Fuck. Oh my god. Please!"

He slams himself in deep once more, and an impossible heat kindles between my thighs. "FUCK, THEO! I CAN'T—OH MY GOD, I'M GOING TO—" I lock up, my blood a raging inferno in my veins, fire licking at my insides...but I don't come. I almost burst into tears when he starts rocking himself into me again, not enough, too shallow, rubbing against the spot inside me that wants more.

"Shh. It's okay. It's coming. It's coming," he murmurs breathlessly. "I've got you, Kid. It's coming now, I promise."

Theo Merchant doesn't break his promises. At least not this one. When he drives himself into me for the last time, the explosion of sensation that tears through me leaves me incoherent and screaming. It overcomes me all at once, detonating everywhere, in what feels like every cell of my body. I can't breathe. My vision sways and for one heart-stopping moment, goes black. I don't even fucking care. I gasp, arching off the bed, an unimaginable ecstasy coursing through me, crashing down on me as Theo pumps himself into me.

He lets out a tight groan, shaking against me, and I feel him emptying inside me. The knowledge that he's coming does something to me that I've never experienced before. I cling onto him, desperate to be as close as possible, and this time he gives in and lets it happen. He collapses against me, blowing hard, his heart thundering in his chest so fiercely that I can feel the rapid-fire beat of it against my breasts, through both of our shirts.

"God, Kid," he whispers breathlessly. "You're gonna be the death of me one of these days."

A strange thing to say right now. But hell, my brain isn't working properly, either. My mind is filled with a high-pitched ringing sound and not much else. We lay tangled together for a long moment, and gradually both our racing hearts slow. Theo breathes into my hair and my neck, *his* hair tickling my nose, and the smell of mint and winter air bathes my senses. He draws small, light circles on my collar bone with shaking fingers, and I stay as still as possible, concentrating on this moment and this moment alone.

I know what's to come.

Any second now, the guilt will arrive. It'll show up gun's blazing, staggering me with the force of its power, and I will hate myself. Nothing on heaven or earth will allow me to forgive myself for this act of betrayal. In letting this happen, I've doomed myself to a lifetime of misery. Rachel—

Rachel.

The mere thought of her name sets the wheels in motion.

"You need to go," I whisper into Theo's hair.

"Sorrell—"

"No, Theo. Please." My voice is choked with tears. "Just go."

SORRELL

I WAKE TO A POUNDING HEADACHE. I can't see the wound on the back of my head no matter how creatively I angle my makeup compact and the mirror on the medicine cabinet in the bathroom. I can feel it, though, and the two-inch long gash is swollen and hurts like a motherfucker to touch. I shower and get ready for class, wincing at the brilliant shafts of sunlight that lance through Toussaint's stained-glass windows as I make my way to *Rosewood*—typical that the one day the weather picks up around here is the one day that heavy cloud cover would actually be a blessing instead of a curse.

Everyone is talking about Sebastian hurling that stupid soda can at my head. I hear them whispering about it as I sit at my desk, rummaging in my bag for a notepad and pen. I've barely given the incident in the hallway any thought myself—I've been too preoccupied with what happened in my room last night to think of anything else—but it seems as though the rest of the school hasn't been thinking of anything else.

"Are you okay?" Ashley asks, sitting down in the seat next to mine. "I heard about Seb. I know he feels terrible about it."

I laugh bitterly, cutting her a dour sidelong look. "Does he? Really?"

"Yeah. He does. I saw him this morning at breakfast and he was pale as a ghost. He was just so pissed about being stuck here, and the party being ruined, and—"

"And he hurled a projectile at me to make himself feel better?"

Ashley frowns at me like I'm being difficult. "You don't understand what it's like here sometimes. You're..." She huffs, frown growing deeper as she appears to search for the appropriate word. "You're new. We've been stuck here a long time. Sometimes it feels like we're never gonna get the hell out of here. Resentment builds."

"I'm sorry, why are you even talking to me right now? I wasn't under the impression that we were friends." I called her bestie out on some pretty dark shit, my first day here. She saw how disgusted I was with the shit that was going down at the First Night party. She—

Goddamnit.

My head hurts too much for this.

I slam a black ball point pen down onto my desk. "Look, Ashley. Tensions run high. I get it. This is also high school, and no matter how excellent a person's breeding and how wealthy their parents are, I know that doesn't stop them from being dicks and acting like children. I didn't snitch about the party. I don't know why Ford didn't call me up to perform in the auditorium, but I promise you, I was not the cause of the sanctions Ford placed on us. I was as bound and restricted by them as everybody else. Now please go back to your own seat. I have a banging headache and I can barely see. I just wanna be left alone."

She looks like she wants to argue, but when she opens her mouth, nothing comes out. She shakes her head in what appears to be frustration, then grabs her bag from under the desk and moves back to her usual spot by the door on the other side of the room.

I make it through home room without anyone else bothering me.

History, English and Biology speed past in a blur.

I don't even know why I attend the classes. I'm leaving on Wednesday, and I have no reason to put myself through any of this. But when I thought about hiding in my room and waiting out the rest of my time at Toussaint, I felt so claustrophobic and panicky that this seemed like my only other real option.

I tell myself it's the boredom and the close quarters until I almost believe it. I pretend like my room didn't smell of Theo when I woke up this morning. I refuse to acknowledge the fact that my bedsheets are still rumpled because we had sex in them last night, and—

"Ahh! There you are. I've been looking all over for you. What the hell is *that?*" Lani plants herself down in the seat opposite me in the dining hall, eyeing the mess I've made of my sloppy joe. The sandwich is a mountain of mush in the middle of my tray, and my plastic fork is sticking out of the top of it like a flagpole.

"Inedible," I answer morosely.

"I see that. Here. Eat this." She slaps a chocolate cake bar, still in its wrapper, down on the table beside my tray.

I slide it back to her. "It's okay. You don't have to do that. I'm just not hungry."

She shoves it back. "Bullshit. I know the look of a girl who needs chocolate. Are you upset about yesterday?"

I take the chocolate cake bar and open it, shoving it into my mouth and biting off the end. Sugar explodes across my tongue, and for a hot second, I *do* feel better. "I don't give a shit about yesterday," I mumble around the mouthful of cake.

Noelani gives me a reproachful look. "I'm your friend. You know you can tell me if you are. I'm not gonna think badly of you for it. You're only human. And Seb's a dick. What he did was—"

I swallow. "Seriously. It's fine. Aside from being pissed off about the massive lump on the back of my head, I'm really fine. I couldn't give a shit about Sebastian. Honestly, I have other, more pressing matters on my mind right now."

She takes a bite of her egg salad sandwich, raising her eyebrows. "Such as?"

For a moment, I consider brushing off her question and making an excuse for my black mood. But the earnest look in her eyes, and the genuine concern in her tone has me letting out a deep sigh. "I need to go to see the nurse."

She pales, dumping her sandwich down onto her tray. "Shit, Sorrell. Your head's bad, isn't it? Do you have a concussion? We can't fuck around with stuff like that. It's super important that we get you to a proper hospital if you're having any weird symptoms—"

"No, no, my head's fine. I promise. It's not that."

She stares at me, eyes wide. "Then what?"

Urgh, man, this is going to suck. I take a deep breath and slump back into my chair, pinching the bridge of my nose between my thumb and my index finger. "Well. I hate to admit this, but...I kinda need the morning after pill."

* * *

"I thought you hated him," Lani says, sitting beside me outside the nurse's office. She hasn't stopped chewing her nails since I told her what took place last night. She's didn't seem shocked at all when I told her about Theo. If anything, she seemed excited. I can only attribute her obsessive nail-chewing to sympathetic nerves—I *do* have to walk into this office in a second and tell the nurse that I fucked someone without protection last night.

"I hate him plenty," I growl, letting my head fall back unti—actually, ow. No. Tipping my head back to that angle is really painful. I straighten in my seat, sighing heavily at the ridiculousness of this situation. Next to me, Lani twists in her seat so that she's fully facing me, her entire being humming with fraught energy. "Are you guys dating now? Did he tell you he was in love with you? Does it feel really..." She shakes her head. "I don't know. Really *right* or something?"

I pull a face at her. "No, of course not. It doesn't feel really right. It feels really *wrong*. I'm not dating him. I'd buy Theo Merchant a one-way ticket straight to hell if I could. And why would he profess his undying love for me, Lani? The guy barely freaking knows me."

Disappointment replaces her sunny expression. "I don't know. I just thought...you can't deny there's been some tension between you two. After he beat the shit out of Sebastian, and...I mean, you *slept* with him last night, Sorrell! Why would you sleep with him if you hated him so much?"

I puff out my cheeks, glancing at the clock on the wall. It's almost two-fifty. The nurse's office closes at four. Still plenty of time to see her, but she has other appointments. If they run over, she won't be able to fit me in. And I can't not see her. *Today*. I absolutely did not come to Toussaint to destroy Theo's life, only to get knocked up by him instead. That's just fucking madness. "A moment of madness," I tell Lani, echoing my thoughts out loud. "My life has been nothing but madness ever since I got here."

I can tell she doesn't like this response. She stares at the floor, chewing on whatever she just ripped off her thumb, her knees bouncing up and down, up and down. "So you don't feel anything for him? Nothing at all?" she asks.

"Oh, I feel plenty for him and none of it's good. Look, I know you're trying to be sweet and you're just looking out for me, but you don't need to wait with me. If there's something you need to do, I can always meet you later. It's really no problem."

Her eyes are double their normal size and full of hurt when she says, "Dude. I would never abandon you at a time like this. What kind of friend would I be if I let you do this by yourself?"

The kind of friend I need right now? I know saying something like this out loud to her will only hurt her feelings more. And she's right in a way—ever since I lost Rachel, I haven't had a friend to lean on. I've gotten so used to taking care of myself and dealing with my problems alone, that it does feel nice to have someone support me through this. I just wish she'd stop talking about Theo, what Theo did, what I feel for Theo, for, like, five seconds. I'm having a hard enough time ejecting the bastard from my head as it is.

"I had to get a Plan B from here last year," Lani confesses out of the blue. "It wasn't so bad. They didn't ask too many questions."

I have to say, I'm surprised to hear this. I just assumed that Lani was a virgin. She's so sweet and shy that it never occurred to me that she might be sexually active. I round on her, looking at her through a new lens. "Who did *you* sleep with?" I demand.

She blushes. "Oh, he isn't here anymore. He graduated last year. His name was Clay. It was a mistake, but…it was still fun," she says, grinning wickedly.

"Lani!" I slap a hand to my chest, feigning shock. "Who *are* you? I'd never have had you pegged as such a wanton—"

The door to the nurse's office swings open and a young girl clutching a rag to her mouth scurries out with tears in her eyes. She sobs when she sees me and Lani, then bolts down the hall.

"What the—?"

"Miss Voss?" Nurse Riley's mousy brown hair is braided into pigtails today; there are little pink plastic flowers attached to her hair ties. She looks like she's going to try and give me a lollipop. She won't be grinning at me so broadly when she realizes why I've come to see her—promiscuous teenagers without a lick of common sense don't deserve candy at the end of their visits. For now, she beams at me. "Come on in, sweetheart," she says.

"Do you want me to come in with you?" Lani asks.

"You know the rules. Only the patient can come into the office," Nurse Riley says. "But don't worry, Lani. I'll have Sorrell back to you in a shake of a rabbit's tail."

I follow the nurse inside and sit down on the exam table as she directs me. Nurse Riley hums as she heads to the tall filing cabinet in the corner of the room and opens it up. She flicks through a row of files, finds mine—it's *massive*—and then takes it out, sets it down on her desk, and begins tapping into her computer.

"Why is my file so big?" I ask, breaking the awkward silence.

"Hmm? Oh!" Nurse Riley turns that million-megawatt smile on me. "Yeah, it is big, isn't it! When a new student arrives at Toussaint, we have to gather all of their medical records from their previous doctors. We need hardcopies of everything on file, y'know. The weather's so bad up here that the system goes down all the time. If you have an emergency while we're stuck in the middle of a power outage, we still need a fully comprehensive record of your medical history to hand. Wouldn't do to give you medication that you're allergic to now, would it?"

"I suppose not."

"And I remember, getting all of your records was a bit of a nightmare," she laughs, wagging a finger at me. "You moved around a lot when you were little, didn't you?"

I just stare at her. "I was in the foster care system."

Her smile dims. "Oh, yeah. That's right. I remember now. Sorry."

"It's okay."

"So, what brings you in today?" She swiftly changes the subject. "That head bothering you some?"

"No. That's not it." And I was right. Indeed, her smile vanishes altogether when I explain the reason for my visit.

* * *

I leave, not only after taking a Plan B pill in front of Nurse Riley, but with a prescription for the pill, which I politely declined but she insisted I take. I'd have to fill it off-site, she informed me, but she wouldn't feel comfortable issuing the emergency birth control to me without ensuring I had measures in place that would prevent me from requiring it again in the future. It didn't matter to her that I was leaving in a matter of days. She was firm, wasn't budging, and I needed that Plan B. So I took the prescription, and she gave me a fucking Tootsie Roll on my way out of the door.

Four hours later, I'm so nauseous and miserable from the meds that even getting out of bed feels like a monumental task. This is why I yell, "Go away!" instead of answering the door when someone knocks, after eight.

The person does not go away.

The person, who is Theo, lets himself into my room with no trouble whatsoever, even though the damned door was locked.

I throw myself back into my freshly changed bedsheets, groaning theatrically. "Urgh! This is like some kind of bad joke that keeps repeating itself, dude. I hide in my room. You show up at my door. I tell you to go to hell and you ignore me. Aren't you *bored* of all of this?"

Entering, Theo doesn't bother to look at me at first. He spends a moment surveying every other element of the room *except* me—the fake pictures of my fake family on top of the dresser; the concert tickets and movie stubs tucked into the frame of the mirror; the Polaroids that Gaynor expertly mocked up, depicting me with a crew of smiling friends I don't know; the little stuffed teddy bear on the bedside table; the earrings, necklaces and bracelets draped over the jewelry tree that I've never worn. All of it false. All of it a lie.

Dressed head to heel in black, his dark hair tumbling into his savagely beautiful face, Theo looks like a haunted wraith as he peruses the fiction that Gaynor curated for me, observing each little detail with a fierce intensity. He picks up a gilded silver photo frame of a younger me, photoshopped next to a pretty middle-aged woman with open, clear blue eyes and long dark hair a similar shade to mine, and a tall, intelligent looking man wearing glasses, whose nose bears the same gentle upturn as mine at the end. Gaynor did a great job of finding images that I would blend into all right.

"Tell me about them," Theo says.

I almost choke on laughter. He knows why I came here. He knows all about Ruth and Falcon House. Why bother indulging this nonsense? I groan, throwing an arm over my face, wanting to block him and the rest of this bullshit out. "Last night doesn't change anything, y'know."

He's quiet for a moment. The bed dips next to me; he's taken a seat, uninvited. What a surprise. "Doesn't it?" he asks softly.

"*No.*" The word comes out hard. "It doesn't change a thing for me."

"Has it occurred to you that it might change things for me?"

That really is rich. I lower my arm, propping myself up on my elbows. The room sways, my head pounding, nausea cycling around my gut, but the effects of the contraceptive I swallowed in Nurse Riley's office are secondary to my spiking temper. "Oh? What has it changed for you, Theo? Have you decided that Rachel meant nothing to you now? That you're in love with me instead? *You don't fucking know me,*" I spit.

He remains calm in the face of my fury. His expression is difficult to read, really, but for the life of me I think I see a brief moment of sadness chase across his features. "How can I? You don't even know yourself."

"I know myself perfectly," I counter. "I know that you took the most important thing in the world from me. Do you even feel bad about what happened, Theo? Do you regret any of it? Do you even *miss* her?"

In the blink of an eye, Theo's face becomes a mask of rage so tumultuous and powerful that it almost matches my own. "Of course I fucking miss her!" he snaps. "I miss her every fucking day. I miss her more than you can possibly imagine. You don't have the market cornered on grief, y'know. God, you can be such a spoiled little brat sometimes."

This accusation is a slap in the face. It stings like hell. My face grows hot, my blood rising to my cheeks. I'm so outraged that I want to strike back, to bite him, to scratch his eyes out, to cut his skin so viciously that I hit bone, but I don't have the words to hurt him as effectively as he's hurt me—I've been completely robbed of the ability to speak. It's a shame Theo hasn't. He leans toward me, his lips pressed into a flat line, and for the first time I see real, true pain in his gold-threaded eyes. I'm stunned by the weight of his gaze on my skin.

"Rachel was precious to me. You'll never fucking know what she meant to me. You walk around this place with your nose in the air, acting like such a fucking victim, but you're not the only one who's suffered through all of this. Do you really think you're the only one who wakes up in the middle of the night, feeling like they can't breathe? Do you think you're the only one who's been fucking crushed by this? I can't even look at myself in the mirror. You can hate me to the very depths of your soul, until you feel like it's eating you alive, but I can guarantee you right now that you will never hate me as much as I hate myself. Now tell me about the people in that fucking photo, Sorrell!"

I blink at him, wrecked by the words he just lashed at me…and utterly confused by his last command. "What the hell are you talking about? I don't know a thing about them! They're not real!"

He sets his jaw. "Yes, they are."

"It's a stock photo! They're just models Gaynor found online. She downloaded a picture of a family having lunch on a beach and replaced the girl in the image with me. Why is that so difficult for you to understand?"

Theo's hands turn into fists. "You're so goddamn stubborn," he hisses.

"If I annoy you so fucking much…if you loved Rachel so much…" I gasp, fighting to speak. When did I start *crying*? I hiccup, trying to rein in the wash of emotion sweeping over me, but it's no good. It's too much for me. Bigger than me. More powerful than I can contend with. "If you loved her so much, then why are you even here?" I grit out. "How could you sleep with me last night?"

If Rachel meant so much to me, then how could *I* sleep with *him* last night? The question burns a blazing trail through my mind, obliterating every other thought. This is the crux of it—this question right here, the true source of my anger. I hate Theo but...Rachel was my friend. I've fought like hell to ignore what I feel—this undeniable attraction I have toward Theo. I've railed against it day and night, trying to push it away, to reject it out of hand, but it doesn't matter what I do. I still feel it, every waking moment of every day, and I can't escape it. What I feel for him goes beyond simple attraction. There are plenty of other hot guys at Toussaint, but they don't plague my thoughts and keep me from sleep. I don't think about them twenty-four seven. I don't crave or need them the way I crave and need Theo. What I feel for him goes well beyond attraction. It's a pull in the pit of my belly. A hunger I don't have a name for. A desperation and an urgency for him that makes no sense and scares me half to death every time I try and face it.

Theo is the living embodiment of frustration when he says, "Rachel's gone, Sorrell. I had to accept that a long time ago. *You* are here." He seems to struggle with what to say next. "*You* are alive. *You* are in my life. God forgive me, but I can't help it if I love you, too."

This is too much to bear. "You don't love me. You don't know the meaning of the fucking word."

He laughs a bitter laugh. "I know the meaning of it intimately."

"Then how can you sit there and tell me that you loved her and in the same breath tell me that you love *me?* It isn't possible. I don't want to hear it!"

"That's the problem, isn't it? You just don't wanna face the truth."

"Get the fuck out of my room before I start screaming."

I think he's going to fight me on this. When *hasn't* he fought me when I've told him to do something? But Theo gets up from the bed. Cold moonlight, pouring in through the huge picture window by the bed, paints his pale skin a deathly silver as he regards me. "You know it's true. And you feel it, too. Deny it all you li—"

"Oh, believe me. I fucking will. You're delusional." Even as I say this, I'm torn apart by the urge to run my hands through his hair, to sweep his unruly locks out of his face. I want to feel the thickness of it, and to twine the waves of it through my fingers. I want to crawl into his lap and cry into his chest; it's as if the circle of his arms is the only safe place left on Earth. Such a cruel and bitter lie.

The guilt is unbearable.

I want to run from the hateful things he's saying to me, but I can't. The truth of it all destroys me, though Theo hasn't voiced the one truth that hurts me the most. I dodge around the thought, trying not to let it take shape in my mind, but the knowledge has a mind of its own. And it wants to be heard.

I was *jealous.*

Listening to him talk of his grief, and how deeply he loved Rachel, made me want to crawl out of my fucking skin. It made the vicious nausea from the Plan B riot until it was all I could think about. He *loved* Rachel. It's an irrefutable fact. I saw it on his face and heard it in his voice. And hearing him say that hurt. I've never known shame this bitter.

Theo moves to the end of the bed, and some wretched, terrible part of me suddenly doesn't want him to go. How can I feel this way, so conflicted and torn, when my path should be so clear? God, I just want to curl into a ball and stop breathing. If that would take this confusion and pain away, then I'd gladly surrender myself to oblivion.

"Lani told me about the Plan B. Don't be mad at her," he says, cutting me off sharply when I sit bolt upright in the bed. "She's just worried about you. She just wants to help. I only came here to see if you were all right."

My eyes prick, welling with a fresh influx of tears. I don't know why it matters that Theo knows about the pill I took. He was there last night. He fucked me. He came inside me, and he knows we stupidly didn't use any protection. It's obvious that something would need to be done in order to mitigate any disastrous consequences because of what we did. But the embarrassment of him learning about me taking something from Lani just…it fucking guts me for some reason. I throw my hands in the air, letting them fall down into my lap —a show of pure resignation. "Great. I'm so glad you did. As you can see, I'm perfectly fine. You can leave now that you've eased your conscience."

His eyes are full of steel and annoyance. "My conscience is clear. I wouldn't have cared if you hadn't taken it."

"Oh, please, Theo! What guy screws a girl and doesn't want to make sure he's not gonna be paying child support for—"

"Enough," he says quietly. "I told you. I wouldn't have cared. I know that shit has crappy side effects sometimes, so I came to make sure you were okay."

I don't know what to make of this statement. I truly don't. "Well. I'm not throwing my guts up if that's what you mean," I say bitterly. "But am I okay?" I shake my head, desperately clinging on to what little sanity I have left. "No. I can't say that I'm *okay*."

For a second, I think he's going to come to me. The tortured look on his face indicates that he will. And for that split-second, his comforting embrace is all I want in the world. He drags his hands back through his hair, blowing a strained breath out of his nose. And then he looks at me. "I know. I'm really sorry."

When the door closes behind him, I collapse into my pillows and I sob.

SORRELL

WEDNESDAY ARRIVES. I cling to the knowledge that I'll be leaving Toussaint in a matter of hours like I'm drowning in a raging river and that information is the only thing keeping my head above water. I refuse to see Lani. She knocks on my door before she goes to class, but I don't answer. I sit beside my packed bag, staring dead-eyed at the wall in front of me, ignoring her soft pleas through the door, focusing my attention down to one narrow point.

I'm leaving.

I'm finally leaving.

I'm getting the fuck out of here.

It's not that I'm angry with Lani. She's sweet and kind; I know that she was only trying to help. She shouldn't have told Theo about my trip to the nurse's office, but she did it with the best of intentions. That isn't the reason why I won't see her. I just detest goodbyes. Making a friend here was a fool's errand. Friends are weakness. I learned that the moment Rachel died. I had no business forging a relationship with Noelani, knowing what I came here to do and that I wouldn't be staying long, but...some small part of me had craved the companionship. I'd been weak. Loneliness is a disease that will kill your spirit quicker than most, and I hadn't had the energy to fight it. I don't want to escape this hellhole in tears, regretting the loss of another friend. I don't think my heart could take it.

At noon, Principal Ford comes to fetch me. She doesn't say much as she escorts me out of the school and across the lawn to the waiting golf cart, but it's hard to miss the disapproval radiating off her.

When we arrive at the dock, she helps me grab my bags off the back of the cart. At precisely twelve-twenty, the Super Cub approaches, swooping low over the lake, the sound of its engines whirring in the cool midday air, fracturing the quiet. Once the plane has landed, sending rippling waves slapping against the dock, I grab my bags in both hands, ready to climb aboard, not wanting to waste another second, but then the door opens out and I see the figure there, waiting to step onto the jetty.

Ruth.

She wears blue jeans and an over-sized cream-colored sweater. Tan boots. Her hair is neatly swept back into a French braid. Her appearance is a far cry from the tight black tank tops and black tights she usually wears to work out in. She looks like a mother, on her way to go grocery shopping or to pick up her kid from school. Her blue eyes are actually warm when they land on me.

"Hello, Sorrell," she says, smiling.

I have to stop myself from dropping my bags and flying at her.

I haven't heard a fucking *word* from her, and now she shows up here, looking like some kind of Stepford Wife, smiling at me like she's done nothing wrong? I had planned on tearing her a new one the second I walked through the doors of Falcon House, but I suppose here, in front of Principal Ford is as good a place as any.

"Don't *'Hello, Sorrell'* me," I say icily. "Where the hell have you been?"

She steps onto the jetty, adopting her no-nonsense expression as she comes to me and pulls me into a hug. "I'm sorry. I've been busy."

"Busy?" I shove her away. "You've been lying to me. Who the hell is Henry?"

Her eyelids shutter. She's momentarily surprised but gathers herself quickly. "Where did you hear that name?" She asks the question evenly, but I'm familiar with every minuscule shift in Ruth's mood and demeanor; she's annoyed.

"Where do you think I heard it? Theo fucking Merchant told me I needed to ask you about him, right after he got done telling me that..." I glance sidelong at Principal Ford, not wanting her to overhear any of this. I might be done with Toussaint, but that doesn't mean that it's safe to spill information about this whole sordid mess in front of her. I don't have much choice, though. "After he got done telling me that he knows all about you, and Falcon House, and the fact that I came here because of Rachel."

Ruth's quiet calm doesn't slip, but her eyes flash with irritation. "Did he now? Well, that certainly messes with our plans a little, doesn't it?"

"You'd know all of this if you'd bothered to pick up your cell or return any of the fifteen hundred messages I left for you," I hiss. "What the fuck was so important that you couldn't get back to me?"

"I told you," she clips out. "I've been busy. Now why are you leaving Toussaint?" She jerks her head at Ford. "I've had a series of long, berating voicemails from this one, telling me that you've decided not to continue on with your education here. Do you have any idea what it cost to get you enrolled here in the first place?"

"None of that matters anymore—"

Ruth smiles sweetly but it's all for show. "Like hell it doesn't. You need to get back to that school and finish what you started. One way or another, Sorrell. One way or another."

I look the woman in the eyes, trying to figure out what the hell is going on. She reacted very poorly when I brought up Henry; she looked like she'd seen a ghost. Now she's acting really fucking weird. This whole thing is weird.

"It's pointless, Ruth. Theo's a fucking mess. He's sorry for what happened to Rachel. There's—I just—I don't want to be here anymore!"

She glances at Ford. "Would you mind giving us a moment, please?"

"Of course." Principal Ford heads back toward the golf cart, as if none of the conversation she's already heard has been the least bit troubling. As soon as she's out of earshot, Ruth hisses, "You wanted revenge for what he did. You wanted to see this thing through. Don't you want that anymore?"

"No!" My response is out before I can even think about the question. I'm surprised to find that it's the truth. Coming here with revenge on my mind was the worst possible thing I could have done. I've suffered every day for it. It's consumed me, poisoned me, and I didn't even follow through with it anyway. Something far worse happened.

Panic seizes me, rattling my bones. "Please. Can we just go back to L.A.? We can sort this out from there. I just…I can't *be* here anymore."

"I don't care if you want to leave here. I really don't. You wanna get on this plane and head back to L.A.? Fine. But is that really what you want?"

"I—" I screw my eyes shut. "There's no moving on from this. I can't just return to my life like nothing happened. There's still so much left up in the air. There are still so many secrets, I know there are."

"Then you know what you have to do," Ruth says, grim. She looks so strange in her blue jeans and sweater, her hair all done up so nicely, that it's hard to hear these words coming out of her mouth. "Stay and figure everything out. This is your chance for some closure. You won't find any back at Falcon House. That's not something I can give to you. You need to figure it out for yourself."

I've never liked the idea of disappointing Ruth. And that's how she sounds: disappointed. That same old need to please her settles over me, and I feel that necessity leap to life within me—to do whatever it takes to win her approval. Stay here. Spar with Theo. Tolerate this shit. Handle it somehow and make my peace with everything that happened to Rachel. But for the first time since I met her, my need to please her is overruled by my anger. She left me to deal with this alone.

She was *busy*?

Fuck that.

This woman's heart is shielded by a twenty-foot-high wall, a meter thick, and none of her wards have ever penetrated it. The only emotion she's ever publicly displayed has been anger. Never kindness. Never sadness. Never empathy, or happiness. She's the coldest, most clinical person I've ever encountered. And, for once, I needed more from her. I was desperate for some kindness, and all she can say is, "*I was* busy?"

Rachel deserved more than that. *I* deserve more.

I take a step back from her. "I'm just an inconvenience to you, aren't I?"

"Sorrell. Don't be ridiculous. You know that you're important to me."

"Why am I important? Why do I matter to you? What happens to me if I leave this place, huh? Am I out on my ass, the second I return to Falcon House? What does my life look like after I get on this plane?"

Ruth's eyes bore into me with a frank harshness that cuts me to the quick. She shrugs. "You know how it is. You've been with us for a long time. You're practically an adult now. It's time for you to figure things out for yourself. Falcon House is a sanctuary for girls who are too young to make their own way in the world. Girls who have nowhere else to be—"

"You mean girls who still bring in a government check every week, right? I'm eighteen soon. Aged out of the system. This cash cow has ceased to be financially beneficial, am I right?"

She shakes her head, and there it is again, even worse than before—her disappointment is a living, breathing thing, a monster lurking behind those unfeeling blue eyes. She could turn a heart to stone with that look of hers.

"You know how it is, Sorrell." That's all she can say: a statement that bears repeating in her mind. She thinks I should have expected this. I should have seen it coming. I've been so blinded by what happened to Rachel that I really didn't. I've been the golden child in Ruth's house for so long that I never considered I might fall from grace.

"Stay here, Sorrell. Figure out all of the mysteries that are plaguing you. Get the closure you need over what happened with Rachel. Make that boy pay for what he did if you need to. Forgive him if you need to. Forget he ever existed if you need to. Don't come back to Los Angeles until you're ready for what comes next. Once you are, *then* get on the plane. Come back to us and we'll help get you set up somewhere—"

"Fuck you. Seriously. Just…fuck you."

Rachel saw this coming, I think. She always said we were a commodity to Ruth. I was so fucking naïve. I turn from her and do the only thing I can right now; I make a beeline for Principal Ford. She doesn't even seem surprised by the hollowed out look on my face.

"Guess I might just be finishing up the semester after all," I tell her.

"Oh. I see. Well, I can't say I'm sorry to hear it. We're lucky to have you at Toussaint—"

"Why?" I rock my head to one side, glaring at her. "Why are *you* lucky to have me, Principal Ford? I can't think of a single reason why you'd want me at your academy. I'm hardly the smartest student. You're just as bad as her, cashing another check for my scholarship, aren't you?"

Principal Ford watches me evenly, letting me rant. I have a thousand and one other accusations I'd love to hurl at her, but I'm so tired all of a sudden, so exhausted and stunned by what's just happened, that I completely run out of steam. Fifteen minutes ago, I'd never thought I'd find myself thinking this, but right now all I want to do is to go back to my room and hide. Amazing how everything can change in the blink of an eye.

"I don't think that was very necessary," Ford says stiffly.

"You're right. I'm sorry. I'm just gonna go back up to the school."

"Are you sure you don't want to say goodbye to your aunt?"

Yeah. Right. I forgot. In this fiction we've created, Ruth is my aunt. I wonder what I'm going to have to tell Ford in the coming weeks. Ruth won't be coming back here ever again. I'll have to fake kill her off or something. Good thing I'm so practiced at lying these days. "No," I reply. "I've said everything I need to say to her."

I walk away, heading back to the car. I'm about to get in, when a figure comes tearing around the stand of trees, running full tilt down the slope toward the lake.

Oh.

Fucking.

Great.

I didn't tell him I was leaving. Lord knows how Theo discovered that I was going back to California, but he clearly found out somehow and he does not look happy about it. He races down toward the jetty, heading right for me. His brows are banked together, his eyes cold and furious. He jabs a blue-taped finger at the golf cart and snarls at me. "Take it back up to the academy, Kid."

I *was* going to get into the golf cart. Now, I'm not so sure that I want to. I'm not in the habit of obeying this asshole's orders. I hurl my bags onto the back of it, but I refrain from climbing in and starting it up. I round on Theo, marshalling my emotions—I'm so angry that I could cry. "Why are you even here?"

He doesn't even stop to talk to me. He skirts around the golf cart, right past me, and storms down the jetty toward the principal…and my "aunt" Ruth.

Oh, *shit*.

I follow after him, a riot of nerves making my stomach twist all over again. "What the *hell* do you think you're doing?" I hiss.

Theo doesn't hear me, or just ignores me. Either way, he doesn't answer my question. "I mean it. Take the cart and go."

"Who the fuck died and made *you* god?" I grab him by the arm, wrenching him around. I don't think he was expecting me to do this, because I very nearly succeed at stopping him in his tracks. He wrenches his arm free, letting out a ragged breath, and—

Oh god. The look on his face…

Why does he look like that?

"Take the cart and go, Voss."

"I will not! I'm a fucking human being!. I'm not a mindless piece of meat, to be ordered around. My dad was a drunk and an addict, and he died in a pool of his own puke when I was five years old. I've managed without a father ever since then. I'm not holding auditions for a new one now!"

He draws deep—a ragged, painful breath. "Fuck, Sorrell. Please. Just...*please*. I'm literally begging you."

My mind reels. I can't even begin to unravel what's going on right now. I feel like I will officially lose my shit if I don't get some answers soon. I've never seen anyone look so desperate, though. Theo's is unrecognizable. There are dark circles beneath his eyes. His skin is wan and pale. His lips seem bloodless, and such a terrible pain shines out of his eyes that I can't bear to feel it cast in my direction.

"If I get back into that cart, you're going to tell me what the fuck is going on," I say. Not a request. Not a plea. A statement. The time for begging for information is over, and I will have the answers I need or there'll be hell to pay.

Theo looks utterly defeated...but he nods. "All right. We'll talk tonight."

"Great." Going against every instinct I possess, I get into the cart. I do not leave, though. I wait. A rotting, festering sinking unpleasantness settles in my gut; it takes all of my will power not to throw up into my own lap. I watch as Theo stalks across the jetty, to where Principal Ford and Ruth look to be locked in a heated discussion. Are they arguing? As soon as Theo arrives, he rounds on Ruth and *rages*. I can't hear what he says. I can't understand the strange series of emotions that pass over my mentor's face—sadness; confusion; irritation; frustration. I understand the last look that settles on her, though. Pure anger. Out of nowhere, she lashes out at Theo, striking him hard across the face.

I cover my mouth with my hands, watching in disbelief as Theo goes for her; he looks like he's about to hit her back, for fuck's sake. But he doesn't. He reins himself in, both his hands balled up at his sides. Principal Ford steps between them, holding her hands up in a placating gesture that doesn't seem to calm either Theo or Ruth down. The principal speaks, her mouth moving a mile a minute, and Theo looks away, back out across the lake, clenching his jaw. He looks wound tight enough to explode.

Without saying another word, he spins on his heel and charges back up the jetty. He doesn't look at me as he charges along the edge of the lake and disappears, not back up toward the academy, but toward the dense forest to our right.

I hardly register Principal Ford getting back into the golf. A heavy, oppressive silence chokes in the air. Ford opens her mouth, but I slowly shake my head. “Don’t. Please. Just…don’t. I can’t stomach any more lies right now. Just take me back up.”

SORRELL

I CURL INTO A BALL, listening to the rain hammer against the window. On the other side of the glass, the world is a streaky grey, gunmetal mess. The green of the lawn and the copse of trees in the distance is drab, the details of the landscape reduced to muddy smudges.

I unravel in my cocoon of blankets, quietly coming apart.

I don't even rehash the events of this afternoon in my head. What would be the point? I wouldn't even know where to begin. Where would I start, if I wanted to make sense of any of this? If I could just *find* a starting point, the beginning of the thread, and work my way forward from there, I might have a fighting chance of muddling through, but everything is so tangled together that doing so is simply impossible.

So I lie in my blankets, nursing a pounding headache, that cursed piece of music haunting my thoughts, doing my best not to think at all.

Just after seven, there's a knock at my door. It's Lani. She wears a pitying look that stokes my anger into a burning inferno. It could destroy the world, this rage I have inside me. I know I shouldn't direct it at Lani, but the very last thing I need right now is her fucking sympathy. "If you've come here to try and make me feel better, or talk it out, or braid my hair or some shit, you can forget it," I say, blocking the entrance to my room with my body.

She nods, as if she understands perfectly what I'm going through and how I'm feeling right now. "I know. I haven't, I promise. Actually…Theo sent me."

"Wonderful. Let me guess. He's breaking his promise and not coming to have a conversation with me, right?"

"No. He wanted to make sure you still wanted to see him first. I take it that you do?"

"Damn right I do."

"Good. Then he asked me to let you know that he'll be waiting for you in his room. You can go and see him whenever you like. He said he'd wait up for you, so if it gets late—"

"Which is his room?"

Lani looks confused for a moment. And then, "Oh, right. You haven't been there before?"

"No."

She laughs a weird little laugh that makes my headache intensify to annoying levels. "It's up one floor. On the east side of the building. He's in two-fifty-eight."

"Thanks." I grab the comfortable sweatshirt that's hanging on the back of my door, and I step out into the hallway.

"You're going right now?" Lani squeaks.

"Might as well get this over with."

"Okay. Well, I'm going to be finishing up a couple of assignments for a while. If you get done and you want to talk…" She trails off, a soft, kind light in her eyes, and the heat burning at the back of my neck ebbs a little. I'm treating her like shit right now. I hate this ugly, angry side of me. It's turning me into a dick, causing me to lash out at the one person who's done nothing but be there for me since I arrived at Toussaint. I fight to bring down the wall I've erected between us, nodding stiffly.

"Okay. Thanks, Lani. I might just do that."

* * *

Theo opens his door to me when I knock, immediately stepping back, letting me inside. He retreats into his room, heading over to sit down at his desk, swiveling in his office chair so that he's facing me. He gestures to his bed, indicating that I should sit myself there.

For some reason, I expected his room to be much grander than mine. Bigger. The space is about the same size, though—big enough for his bed, his desk, a chest of drawers and a nightstand. It feels a lot smaller in here because of his cello, which takes up a huge chunk of his real estate next to the window.

It smells of him so strongly in here—winter cold, and snow, and mint. The air is so thick with the dizzying smell of him that my head spins for a second, my body reacting in the strangest of ways. My heart aches in a way I don't know what to do with.

His walls are bare, except for a corkboard above his desk, which is covered with photos—Theo with a couple who I presume are his parents; Theo with Sebastian and Callum; Theo with Lani, and Ashley, and Beth. There are a number of empty spots, though. Spaces, rectangular in shape, where it looks like some photos have been taken down.

A hand closes around my windpipe when I realize which photos those spaces likely held: images of Theo and Rachel together, laughing, kissing, pulling goofy faces. Did he take them down after she died? Or has he taken them down tonight, for my benefit, because he doesn't want me to see them together? Bile rises, hot, up the back of my throat, and I have to look away from the board.

"You want anything?" Theo asks softly.

I turn my attention to him and my pulse quickens. His hair is so dark it's black as jet, wet, as if he's just gotten out of the shower. It's brushed back, out of his face, making this one of the rare occasions when I can see his entire face without obstruction. Even the three-freckle triangle just above his cheekbone. His eyes are serious, the brown like liquid chocolate, the golden flecks threading his irises even brighter than usual. His cheeks are flushed, which makes a change from earlier this afternoon, when he was so ashen it looked like he was going to pass out. I try not to be distracted by the fact that the white long-sleeved tee he's wearing isn't five sizes too big for once, and the material pulls taut across his chest and his arms, emphasizing how muscled his frame is beneath it.

Feet bare, dark grey sweatpants low on his hips, he's the most devastatingly attractive person I've ever laid eyes on. Even now, amidst all of this confusion and obfuscation, my stomach still fills with butterflies at the sight of him.

Curse him, and curse my own stupidity.

"Sorrell?"

"Hmm?"

"Do you want anything?" he repeats, his voice low.

I smirk, feeling just a little mad, just a little reckless. "Not unless you have any tequila."

He laughs silently, but the sight of his smile, so easy, lighting up his face a little, tears a hole in my chest and rips my damn heart out. "Funny you should say that." He reaches down and opens the bottom drawer in his desk, taking out a bottle of Don Julio and two shot glasses. "I don't have any lime. Or salt," he admits.

"That's okay." I doubt alcohol will make the thumping pressure at my temples any better, but I'm willing to chance it; I get the feeling I'm going to need a drink once we get into this.

Theo pours two shots and offers me one, keeping one for himself. He holds his out as I sit down on the edge of his perfectly made bed, and I clink the glass he's given me with his.

"Cheers," he whispers.

"Cheers."

The amber liquid sears a pathway down my esophagus, and I swallow down the urge to gag, shaking my head to ward off the burn.

Setting his glass down, Theo takes mine from me and refills it. We do another shot, and the harshness of the tequila isn't so bad the second time around. I'm so on edge that I'd accept a third one from him if he poured it, but when he takes my glass from me this time, he sets it down on his desk along with his and pushes them off to one side. Probably for the best.

From there, he just looks at me, eyes searching my face, his brow pinched into worry lines. Doesn't say a word.

"Okay then. Here we are," *I* say, because one of us has to say something. "Where do you plan on starting? 'Cause I have a lot of questions."

Theo's frown deepens, carving deep grooves into his forehead. He sits forward, blowing out a deep breath, scrubbing his hands over his face. "I don't know. I'm not sure where to start. Honestly, I don't know if this is even a good idea. It's probably isn't. It *definitely* isn't."

"You'd better not change your mind and spin me some bullshit now, Theodore William Merchant."

He glances at me out of the corner of his eye, a little amusement replacing his troubled expression. "Full name treatment, huh? Some things never change."

"What's *that* supposed to mean?"

He laughs again, shaking his head. "Nothing. Just stop looking so pissed off for one second and just relax, okay? I need a moment to figure this out."

I'm not feeling very benevolent. Or patient. I give him a beat to collect himself, though, because he really does look like he's thinking deeply, trying to find the solution to a very complex problem. Eventually, he says, "There's only one way to do this."

"And that is?"

"I need to rip off the Band-Aid."

"Sounds like a great idea. Get on with it." I swear if he keeps me waiting any longer, I'm going to have a nervous breakdown.

Reluctantly, Theo gets up from his chair. He's going to come lie on the bed with me? He's going to pull me to him? What the hell is he *doing?*

"I hope you're ready for this," he whispers. *And takes off his t-shirt.* The white fabric falls to the ground, and Theo brushes a hand through his hair, sweeping it back out of the way again. He stands before me, naked from the waist up, and my breath seizes in my lungs. He's a thing of beauty.

His chest is a wall of muscle, his abs sculpted flawlessly. Twin grooves dip over his hips, forming a deep vee that disappears below the waistband of his sweatpants. His skin, smooth and bearing the remnants of a tan, is so fucking perfect that I can't help but want to reach out and touch him.

Spanning his chest, rising up his neck, the ink I've only caught glimpses of until now fans out across his pecs, intricate and intriguing. An elaborate sun has been etched into the very center of his chest, spears of linework bursting from its center, creating its rays. Amongst those, wildflowers, and roses, and bees, and hummingbirds all slot together to create the most detailed, stunning piece of art I've ever seen on a person's body. The tops of his shoulders are inked, too—on the left, a compass, the arrow pointing north. On the right, another design that looks almost like a compass too, though this one is surrounded by what look like...runes? And then down his chest, below the sun, down the left-hand side of his ribcage, delicate script work—

I halt my inspection of him, looking up at him, trying to make sense of what I'm seeing.

Names.

Girls' names.

Four of them.

The last of which reads: *Rachel.*

"What the hell is this?"

"Sorrell."

"No, Theo. What the hell *is* this? You think you're going to make me despise you any less by showing me a list of your past conquest's names tattooed onto your body? What the fuck?"

"*Sorrell,*" he says pleadingly.

"You should have made the script a little smaller, asshole. You're gonna run out of room before you finish freshman year of college."

I go to grab my bag, but I didn't bring one. I snatch up my sweatshirt and put it on, angrily thrusting my arms into it, wrenching it on over my head. I'm not cold, but I need to *do* something. I—I need to get the fuck away from him. This doesn't make any sense.

Theo grabs my wrist as I head for the door. "You said you wanted the truth, so let me tell you the fucking truth!"

I wheel on him, ripping free of his grip, my heart kicking against the cage of my ribs. It feels as though it's trying to bust its way out of me. "I was an idiot to come here, thinking you'd do the right thing. Give me an honest answer to my questions. But no. You're still playing fucking games with me, aren't you? You're still...you're trying to *hurt* me!"

Devastation leaves a bleak trail across Theo's face. He clasps his hands around the back of his neck, lacing his fingers together there. "I'm not playing games," he whispers.

"Then why do you have Rachel's name tattooed on your fucking ribs?"

"Because I loved her," he answers quickly.

"And...*Amelia*?" I sputter.

"I loved her," he repeats.

"And Catherine?"

He just looks at me. He doesn't feel the need to say anything at all now.

I hold the back of my hand to my mouth, trying to keep back the sob building in my throat, but it's useless. It escapes me anyway, loud and awful. I can't understand this. I can't wrap my head around what I'm seeing.

"Why?" I whisper. "Why is *my* name at the very *top* of your list?"

"Sorrell. If you'll just let me explain..."

I bolt for the door, unable to bear it a second longer. The confusion. The panic. The untenable agony, tearing me apart. It feels like death itself, roaring through my veins, channeling a pathway to the center of my chest, where it will wrap itself around my heart like barbed wire and fucking kill me.

I have to get away.

In the hallway.

Running toward the stairs.

Tripping, stumbling, falling.

Pain flashing through my knees.

Another hallway.

Another set of stairs.

"SORRELL, WAIT!"

I run.

I run so hard, I don't even feel myself break.

SORRELL

I'M SOAKED down to the skin.

My legs ache. My thighs burn. My lungs scream. I'm covered in mud.

I race down the hillside, barely able to keep myself upright. Some horrendous fear roars at the back of my mind, warning that if I stop running, a truly horrific fate will befall me, and I can't reason myself out of that fear's grasp. I feel as though I'm trapped inside an hourglass, sinking into the sand, which pours from one end to the other, too fast, and I'm scrambling at the sides of the glass, trying to keep myself from disappearing, to stop myself from being swallowed by the narrow gap, to stop myself from being unmade.

My skull is splintering apart.

I tear through the trees, careening blindly onward, not thinking about where I'm heading. It's dark, and I'm freezing, and I can't see where the fuck I'm going, but I don't stop running. Eventually, I hit a road. I keep running.

I'm more scared than I have ever been in my life and I don't know why.

I just keep running.

The night stretches on forever in front of me. I roll my ankles. I fall and get back up again. My hands are slick with blood, my palms torn open.

After an eternity, lights flare into the darkness from behind me, casting twin pillars of yellow-white onto the ground, illuminating the blacktop and making a shadow out of me. I stop dead, exhaustion sinking into my bones, and bend over, resting my hands on my sodden jeans, coughing and choking the wickedly cold air down, trying to catch my breath.

A car door slams behind me.

Wait.

A car door?

It hits me all of a sudden: I'm on a road. A fucking *road.* Not the destroyed road that Gaynor and I gawped at a couple of months ago. This road is whole, in one piece, perfectly fine to drive on.

"Sorrell, you're gonna break your neck, hurtling down here like that. Please, can you get into the car and talk to me?"

Theo's deadly calm does something to me that I can't explain. The fear and the panic blink out, abandoning me to my exhaustion, and suddenly it's all I can do to remain standing on my own two feet. When I feel his hand on my shoulder, I turn and collapse into him, letting out a strangled sob as I bury my face into his chest. He's put his t-shirt back on now, concealing the names on his ribcage, but it's as if I can feel them burning there beneath my hands, and I feel so lost and turned around that I can do nothing but cry.

He picks me up, sweeping me into his arms. He carries me back to the car—a sleek black Mustang—and gently places me into the passenger seat, clipping me into my seat. I'm in a daze as he gets in and starts to drive. Not back up the mountain, I realize. But down.

"Where are we going?" I ask stiffly.

"Somewhere special," he answers.

And I'm too tired to ask any more questions.

I'm *outraged* when Theo drives past a bus stop.

A fucking bus stop.

My anger is a living, breathing thing.

There weren't supposed to be any other roads leading to the Academy, just the one solitary, destroyed road that I saw when I arrived at

Toussaint. It was unnavigable, the sign had said. Impossible to pass through, Principal Ford had said. But here we are, speeding down a perfectly good road, *streetlights* whipping past the car windows as Theo burns into the night.

I chew the inside of my cheek until I taste blood, refusing to open my mouth, because I know what will happen if I do. I'll start screaming, cursing, throwing fists, and I can't see how that will help anything right now.

I'm livid by the time Theo makes a left hand turn and we enter a small town—a fucking *town!*—driving past a painted sign that reads, '*You are now entering Sumner, WA. Population 1287. Please drive carefully.*'

A pharmacy. A general store. A post office. A real estate agent. A liquor store. We pass each of these businesses, the only car out on the potholed road in the rain, and I seethe in astonished silence. Another half a mile up the road, Theo pulls into a parking lot. A diner—*Patty's*—sits on the other side of the lot, still open, it's lights blazing out into the darkness.

Theo kills the engine. He looks down at his hands, picking at his fingernails for a second, then says, "Come on. They have great coffee here. You really like it."

* * *

I stare down at Theo's phone, blinking at the image on the screen.

It's not fucking possible.

I'm there in the photograph, locked in the circle of Theo's arms. He's kissing my cheek, and I'm wincing, pretending to hate it. But I'm not. I can tell that I'm not. I'm *loving* it.

"Here we go. One black coffee. One coffee with creamer. One sugar." The tall waitress with the matching dimples sets down two cups, one for me and one for Theo, beaming nervously at us. She didn't take an order from us when we came in. Her whole face lit up when she saw us enter, but Theo shook his head at her in warning and she nodded, turning back to the cash register. He guided me over to a booth by the window and sat me down on the bench, operating my limbs for me like I was an inert robot, and then sat down on the bench opposite me, clearing his throat. He'd given me his phone then. Told me to look through the camera roll.

I still haven't managed to process the pictures I've flicked through.

Me in a yellow summer dress, standing in front of the Space Needle, arms held aloft in the air. Me asleep in Theo's arms, nestled in a welter of sheets. Me on a couch, hair tied up in a messy bun, a cupcake in my hand, cheeks full, frosting on the tip of my nose, grinning like a little kid. Me in Central Park, hair wet from the rain, clutching hold of the snow globe that's currently sitting on the chest of drawers back in my bedroom at the academy. Theo and I kissing. Theo and I kissing in a million different images, in different poses, in different places, surrounded by snow, and in the rain, and washed in sunlight.

Theo, and me, and Lani, and Ashley, and Sebastian, the girls wearing bikinis, the boys wearing boardshorts. In this image, there's only one name inked into Theo's ribs, and its mine.

"Let me know if I can get you kids anything else," the waitress says quietly. Theo thanks her, and she retreats back behind the counter, giving us some space.

"What is this?" I whisper.

"That's us," Theo answers simply.

"You're lying."

"I'm not."

"These are all photoshopped."

"They're not."

I set his phone onto the table in front of me. "Do you think I'm stupid, Merchant? Gaynor photoshopped me into all of those photos back in my room just fine. *They* look real. Do you really think I don't know when I'm looking at fake photos?"

He takes a steady breath and reaches for his phone. He quickly flicks through the images and finds the one he's looking for. After a long moment, staring down at the screen, he bites down on his bottom lip, sliding it towards me.

I'm lying in a hospital bed. My eyes are closed. I'm wearing a hospital gown, and my head is wrapped in thick bandages. I'm hooked up to too many monitors and machines to count.

"Gaynor was your nurse," he says. "She was on the night shift most of the time, which was when you'd wake up the most. You remember the accident sometimes. Most of the time...you don't."

I push his phone away. "What are you *talking* about?"

"It was summer break and we'd gone to stay at West's friend's place in L.A. There was a party in the hills. I was supposed to drive us all home, but I'd had too much to drink. You'd only had one beer, so you offered to take us back instead. Sebastian and Ashley were fooling around in the back of the car. I was fucking around with them too, being an idiot, but I passed out halfway back to the place. There was oil on the road. You tried to slow down in a corner and ended up going through the guardrail into oncoming traffic."

He rushes through this with zero inflection in his voice, quickly, as if he's rattling off a list. As if it's a story he's told many times before.

But it's not true.

I'd remember if it was true.

"I'm *from* Los Angeles," I tell him.

"You're from *here*," he says. "From Sumner. So am I. We grew up next-door to one another, Sorrell. I've known you my whole fucking life."

And *that*, ladies and gentlemen, is right about where I black out.

* * *

I don't remember how I end up back in my room. I wake up in my bed somehow, though. I'm out of my soaking wet clothes and in sweats and a t-shirt, shivering beneath my covers. Theo sits in the chair beside my bed, staring out of the window. He sighs when he realizes I'm awake.

"Sorry," he says tightly. "I tried to ease you into it slow, but...I guess it wasn't slow enough."

I remember everything he told me back at the diner. I wish I didn't, but his words are emblazoned in my mind, cycling around on repeat. "Why are you doing this?" I whisper. "What are you getting out of this? Is it some attempt to assuage your guilt over Rachel?"

"Rachel—" Theo flares his nostrils, looking back out of the

window. A vein pulses in his temple, signaling a flare of frustration that looks very real. "I don't know how to do this without triggering you again," he says.

"Triggering me?"

"You passed out back at the diner. You pass out a lot."

"No, I don't."

"Yeah, you—you fucking *do*," he says, laughing bitterly. "We've been through this before, okay, and it never goes fucking well, so just..." He throws his hands up, letting them fall back into his lap. A deep breath seems to even him out a little. "We were all wearing our seatbelts that night, thank God. The car didn't hit any other vehicles, just the guardrail. The driver's side airbag didn't deploy, though. You hit your head on the steering wheel. We all managed to get out of the car, but you were stuck. I couldn't drag you out from the passenger side." He chokes out a laugh. "And your window was stubborn as fuck and *refused* to shatter." He looks down at his hands. At the jagged scars there—the faint, silvery lines that crosshatch his skin.

"I put my fist through it," he says matter-of-factly. "The safety glass wasn't supposed to be sharp, but...I guess they were wrong about that, weren't they? Sebastian and Ashley waited by the median for the ambulance. I didn't wanna move you that far, though, so I stayed with you in the road. The car's engine caught light. It didn't explode like in the movies, but...it was bad. Traffic was bad, bumper to bumper, and those fucking idiots wouldn't pull over for the emergency services further down the road. It took thirty minutes for them to reach us. If they'd gotten there sooner, I don't know..." His eyes shine too brightly. "Maybe shit wouldn't have been so bad. But you didn't even have any open wounds. There was no blood. They said I didn't make it worse by moving you, but..."

"Stop," I rasp.

"If I'd left you in the car, maybe they could have stabilized your neck properly. You were fine for a day or so. But then you got compression. Your brain swelled up to the point that they had to cut a giant fucking hole in your skull. They didn't think you were gonna make it. You had three separate contusions on your brain. Your surgeon said the largest one was catastrophic. Said you wouldn't even make it through that second night. But there was another surgeon. This fucking...*cowboy*." He shakes his head. "She swore she could fix you, and she did. Kind of. She was reckless as hell...but you survived. You were in a coma for eighteen—" He stops talking. I'm horrified by the tears that streak down his cheeks.

This isn't fucking happening.

Dashing those tears away with the backs of his hands, he finally looks back at me. "Eighteen...days," he finishes. "You were a fucking miracle. After making it through the swelling, and the bleeds, and the surgery, the other doctors said there was no way you were waking up after an eighteen-day coma. And if you did, you'd be a vegetable for the rest of your life. But you woke up. And you were fine. You could see. Speak. Move. Walk. It was the best day of my fucking life."

"You are *sick*." I try to get away. My arms are like lead when I attempt to throw the covers back. It's as if I'm moving through thick, cloying mud, and my body won't respond to me. Theo jumps up from the chair and sits next to me, taking hold of my hand.

"What about this doesn't feel true to you?" he demands. "Logically, *why* would I make something like this up?"

"Because! I don't know! I—if any of this was true, then why wouldn't I remember it? If I woke up after all of that and I was fine, why wouldn't I remember?"

"They said it was amnesia at first. Short-term memory loss. Common after that kind of head injury. But after a couple of weeks, you lost more and more of yourself. They began to suspect it was something more complicated. I was the last thing you remembered. I'm usually the thing you remember first too, though," he admits.

I inch back into the pillows, somehow finding the strength to remove my hand from his. *"Liar."*

"I wish I was fucking lying." Theo's always been so distant. Withdrawn. Cold. Harsh. I've never seen him like this. Wrecked. Broken. So full of hurt.

"If..." There are so many ways to argue myself out of this. So many 'ifs.' I can't contain them all in my head at once. "If you're not lying to me, then why do I think I'm from Los Angeles? Why...why do I remember being in foster care there?"

He breathes evenly, shoulders tense, as he says. "You were never in foster care. Your parents—"

I jerk back, stunned. "My *parents*?"

"The people in all of your picture frames," he says gravely.

"Your father died in a motorcycle accident when you were eleven. Your mom died from cancer when you were thirteen."

"Jesus Christ!"

"I know. Fuck! Too fast. This is all too fast. I'm screwing this up."

I have—*had* parents? I can't process this. I just can't. My brain short circuits when I attempt to understand what Theo's just told me, so I don't even try. "You still haven't explained why I have these other memories..."

"In a lot of cases, head traumas are a complete mystery. The brain is still an unknown universe, still being explored. Very little about it makes sense. A person can have their skull split wide open, it can look like there's no logical chance of survival, but that person makes a full recovery. Then, there are people who get a tiny bump on the head and lose everything. Their motor functions. Their ability to speak. Their memory. Their entire sense of self. The brain always wants to heal itself, though. And it's very adept at filling in the gaps. If the mind perceives that it's in danger and its surroundings don't make sense, it'll do whatever it can to *make* sense of its surroundings. Your mind's still recovering from the accident, so it's filling in the blanks, giving you a background and a history, a sense of self, so that you can survive. Eventually, the swelling in your brain will right itself and you'll start to remember."

He sounds so confident. Not a shadow of a doubt in his voice. The shadow of uncertainty in his eyes tells a different story. They make me think that there's more to this fantastical, absolutely *insane* story of his, and that I really won't like it when he eventually surrenders the information that he's sitting on.

I close my eyes for a second, breathing.

In... Out...

In... Out...

A shaky sort of calm settles over me, but I know as soon as I start talking again, that calm will abandon me. I relish it for a moment, attempting to piece my thoughts together into some sort of structure that makes *any* sense. And then I say, "All right. Say I believe any of this, then, what...I've been wandering around like this, thinking I grew up in foster care, that I don't know you or anyone else from my past? For *weeks?*"

Theo sits back in the chair, his eyes drifting up to look at the ceiling. "It's been a little longer than that, I'm afraid."

I suddenly feel very sick. "*Months*?"

He doesn't say anything.

"Theo! For fuck's sake! Tell me I haven't been floating around in a fake, fantasy world for months!"

Reluctantly, he lowers his chocolate-gold eyes, his gaze finding mine and holding it. "It's been nearly two years since the accident."

Bile rises up the back of my throat. I think I'm going to be sick. "And Rachel? Rachel's been gone all that time, and I—" I want to say the words, I really do, but I can't get them out. My throat is aching, full of fire, closing up. I can't swallow. Can't breathe. Can't process any of this. My best friend has been gone for nearly two years, and I've been treading water, thinking... I don't *know* what I've been thinking. I'm so fucking confused, my head feels like it's about to splinter open.

My rising panic intensifies when Theo's eyes shutter, as if he just stepped through a mental door, through a gateway, to a place where I cannot follow after him. "What is it? Whatever it is, you might as well just say it now. You've already turned the world on its head. Just...for God's sake, I can't take any more of this! Spit it out!"

"Fine," he blurts. "Rachel hasn't been dead since the accident."

Hope soars within me for one beautiful moment. She *didn't* die? Oh my god. Oh my *god*—

"You *were* Rachel." I can tell this admission is difficult; the words look like they bring razor blades up the back of his throat with them. "Just like you were Amelia. Just like you were Catherine."

"No. No, that's not possible. I *remember* her."

"When you began to lose yourself after you woke up from the coma, you started telling people your name was Amelia. You had a whole life as Amelia. A history. A past. I stayed with you at the hospital for as long as I could. I tried to remind you of who you were before the accident, and our life together. The one we'd been planning for so long. You were Amelia for three months. You were so different from the person I'd fallen in love with, but you were also the same, at your core. Your favorite color was still green. Your favorite ice cream flavor was salted caramel. You were still kind, and brave, and sarcastic, and defensive. You still looked at me like I was the only thing that mattered in the world. All of our history was erased, though. Every special moment we'd ever experienced together, just..." He snaps his fingers. "*Gone.* One day, I just..." He clenches his jaw. "I lost it. I was just so frustrated and I—I screamed at you. It startled you so much that you *did* remember for a second. And then...you just stared at the table and didn't say anything. You stared into space for three days after that. When you started talking again, Amelia was gone. You were Catherine."

I've never known horror like this.

I can't even comprehend how I'm supposed to listen to this and believe any of it. If I could, I'd get up out of this bed and run for the door, but I know my legs wouldn't carry me. I wouldn't make it three steps before I sank to the floor and burst into tears.

"How long...*supposedly*...was I Catherine for?" I whisper numbly.

"Seven miserable fucking months," Theo replies. "You hated me. You were angry. Depressive. You'd break out of the hospital and get fucked up with strangers. Drink too much. Take drugs. You were still you, though, underneath all of the anger and the pain. I could still see you in there. So I stayed. I tried to help you remember. I tried to be more patient that time. More understanding. But Catherine..." He laughs shakily. "Well, she nearly fucking killed me if I'm being honest. In the end, you nearly overdosed at a party. The EMTs took you to a hospital down in Seattle. They pumped your stomach and dosed you with Narcan, and by the time I'd driven down there to get you, you weren't Catherine anymore. You were suddenly Rachel."

I don't...

No.

I screw my eyes shut.

That's not right.

It can't be.

"They think that trauma causes these shifts. Stress. Your mind's been through so much that whenever it encounters a really difficult experience or it can't quite handle its surroundings, it just..." He makes a flicking motion with his hand. "Your old doctor, Doctor Perez, explained that it's kind of like changing the channels on a television. The viewer doesn't like the show that's playing, so they see what's on the other side."

"And I'm the viewer in all of this?"

"Your subconscious," Theo says. "The animal part of your brain that detects danger has been so triggered since the accident that your subconscious is trapped in this fight or flight cycle. And it takes flight every time things get hard. And you become someone else. And I—" His voice cracks. He stops short.

He looks more angry than upset, but I feel like I should comfort him somehow. Still, the furious cyclone of emotion in my gut that tells me I should despise him persists. How am I supposed to make him feel better if I want to make him suffer for what he did? If what he's saying is true, then why can't I shake this terrible fury that seems so set on poisoning me?

"You should get some rest," Theo murmurs. "I'd say right now qualifies as one of those times when things get hard. If I push any further..." He rakes his hands back through his thick waves, letting out a defeated chuckle that contains no humor whatsoever. "Who am I kidding? It's probably too fucking late already. God…just seriously. Fuck my life." He gets up from the chair, groaning as he puts his sneakers back on. I hadn't even realized he'd taken them off. From the looks of them, the rain soaked them all the way through. He shivers, grimacing as he shoves his feet into them and begins fastening his laces.

"Don't," I whisper.

His head snaps up. "What?"

"Don't go. I still hate you. I think you're the literal worst. But…I don't want you to go," I admit.

"I can't answer any more questions. I can't tell you any more than I already have. Not right now—"

"I don't want to know anything else. Not yet. I just...please? Stay?"

"You want me to sleep with you? Here?" Something catches in Theo's throat. "After all of this?"

I'm so fucking tired. So frayed around the edges. I've exhausted myself, trying to keep pace with the information as Theo relayed it to me, but processing each little detail has cost me something, and it's more than just energy. It feels like, whatever it is that I've lost, I won't be getting it back. "I feel like I might just slip away if you go," I confess. "Please. Just stay with me. Lie next to me? Hold my hand?"

This version of Theo is unrecognizable. He's nothing like the guy that I met here on my first day of Toussaint. He looks...happy.

My head is throbbing so violently that I can't think straight, anyway. If this is some ploy to trick me into forgiving him, then fuck —it'll be easily disproved, won't it? I'm heading straight to see Principal Ford in the morning. One conversation with her will confirm or refute Theo's claims. If he's lying to me about this, I will cut the bastard's throat. It would be such an evil, terrible lie to tell, and he'd deserve everything I did to him for it.

I already know the truth, though.

There really is no point in Theo lying about something as outlandish as this. Where would it get him in the long run? So that means he's telling the truth.

I just don't understand any of it. None of this will make sense, at least until the morning.

Theo approaches the bed slowly. The mattress dips as he pulls back the covers and gets in beside me, fully dressed. I don't ask him to strip. We aren't here to fuck; this isn't about that. I just want to feel safe, and to have the warmth of another body next to mine. And honestly, I'm scared. If all of this is true, then I might not even wake up myself tomorrow, and that thought is terrifying. I can't stand to even think about it. I don't want to lose myself. But if I do, then at least this way I'll wake up in Theo Merchant's arms.

THEO

THREE YEARS AGO

"Fighting? Seriously? You're so *predictable*. Why not spice things up a little? Join the chess club. Get into robotics. Shake up the status quo. I can't believe my big brother turned out to be a jock. It's so...*cliché*."

Noelani tries to steal a blueberry from me. I slide my plate out of her reach, jamming a piece of toast into my mouth as I get up from the table. "I play the *cello*, Lani. Isn't that dorky enough for you?"

Across the kitchen, by the fridge, Lorelei talks to one of the gardeners about edging the lawn or some shit. The poor bastard's trying to tell my mother something about his schedule, but the woman, in all of her stubbornness, is refusing to accept whatever he's trying to tell her.

"We have a contract, Sam. You come here twice a week and take care of whatever needs taking care of. You get paid very handsomely for it, too, remember? I have a garden party next week—"

"I know, Mrs. Merchant. I know. But our contract allows *me* vacation time, too, and I told you about this trip three mo—"

"No, no. No." Lorelei tucks her dark wavy hair behind her ears—a sure sign she's getting frustrated. She sighs deeply. "I'm talking, Sam. Please don't interrupt me when I'm talking. It's very rude. Now, you know I need the garden to be absolutely perfect for this party. I need the lawns taken care of. I can't have the edging looking like shit, okay? I just can't. Now that someone will be living next door again, I—"

I'm used to tuning my mother out. She can go on and on for hours. I feel sorry for Sam, our long-suffering gardener, though. I'm surprised he didn't quit years ago. Snatching up my bag, I pocket the keys to the Mustang and shove my chair back under the table.

Lani looks up at me with dark chocolate eyes—eyes like our mom's. Like *mine*—and gives me a cheesy, shit-eating grin. "If you're not gonna eat your fruit, then why can't I have it?"

"'Cause I'm a dick." Grinning, I give her the plate with the remnants of my breakfast on it. "Want a ride?"

She looks up at me, mock horrified, like she might fall off her chair. "Absolutely not! It's my first day at a new school. The last thing I need is for any of my new classmates to figure out that I'm related to the notorious Theo Merchant."

I stick my tongue out at her. "Probably the only way you *will* make any friends, little bug. Once people find out you're related to me, they'll be all over you like flies on shit."

"Theo!" Lorelei calls across the kitchen. She's annoyed—sick of dealing with idiots today. "No, thank you. No cursing. She's fourteen-years-old—"

"She's heard you say far worse," I volley back.

"I'm her mother. I'm allowed to swear in front of her. Don't do that, please."

I frown at her. "Hold up. Did you just say someone's moving into the Voss's place?"

"Yes, baby. Some woman who knew Sorrell's mother. She's the executor of her estate. She won't be staying long. Just enough time to see Sorrell settled in up at Toussaint. Then she'll be heading back to… lord knows. Wherever she's coming from."

"Wait. Sorrell's enrolling at *Toussaint?*"

"Yes. Today. She'll be *boarding*," Lorelei says, disgusted. "I suppose it's not as though she can take up residence in the house by herself, though. She isn't eighteen yet. It's a crime that that beautiful place was left to a child. It should have been sold. We would have bought it. Expanded the gardens—"

"Sorrell's enrolling at Toussaint *today*?" I repeat.

"Yes, Theo. For crying out loud, keep up! That uncle from New York who took her in after Hilary died finally decided she was old enough to come back by herself. She and that executor woman got back late last night, which is why I need this garden party to be a success so that—" She rounds on Sam again, wittering on about how important this party is to her and how she can*not* be shown up in front of James Voss's orphaned daughter and some nobody from the middle of bum fuck nowhere.

I'm already gone. Out of the kitchen. Down the hall. Out the front door.

Sorrell's coming to Toussaint.

Sorrell and I used to make mud pies in the Voss's back yard when we were little. Hilary Voss was way less neurotic than my mother. She never gave a shit about us making a mess. She used to let us finger-paint on the walls of the formal living room in their beautiful old brickwork mansion, and Lorelei would have conniptions about it. I remember even saying to her, at seven years old, "What does it matter? It's not *your* house." She'd threatened to shove a bar of soap in my mouth for sassing her over that. But I'd learned two things very quickly because of the conversation that ensued afterwards: my mother, as hardworking and as kind as she could be, had a chip on her shoulder heavier than an Acme anvil. And she was so jealous of Hilary Voss, it made her sick.

Hilary was married to James, for starters. James and my mother had dated back in high school for years. Lorelei had spent a lot of her formative teenaged years in the Voss's house, and that formal living room was her favorite room in the entire place. It was sacred ground, as far as she was concerned. Lorelei hadn't gone away to college. She'd been given her sizable inheritance from my grandparents early—my grandparents, who told Lorelei that it was uncouth for a woman of means to work or bother with higher education. So Lorelei had stayed at home and waited for James. Except, James came back from college after graduation with a stranger on his arm. And the Voss's Victorian heirloom engagement ring was nestled quite snuggly on the third finger of that stranger's left hand.

Lorelei had gone digging and found out everything she needed to know about the future Mrs. Hilary Voss. She wasn't from working class stock. No, it was far worse than that. Her parents were hippies and had raised Hilary on a commune down in California, in the Anza Borrego desert, just outside San Diego. Hilary had gotten herself a degree in humanitarian law and planned on using it to help the vulnerable and weak.

My mother had scoffed at that. Told me that Hilary Voss had a savior complex and thought she was better than everyone else in the neighborhood, just because she took the occasional pro bono case. Lorelei had gone into mourning when James died. She was less upset when Hilary had passed.

Sorrell, on the other hand, had understandably been heartbroken, and it had broken *me* that I couldn't be there for her. She'd moved to New York to be with her uncle. We'd kept in touch through email. Once a week. Twice a week. It was all well and good at first, but after a while, we both became so immersed in our own lives that things just kind of...fell off. But I'm going to get to see her again, though? *Today*? After a year and a half, waiting for the light to go on in her darkened bedroom window across the way? Fuck *yes.*

I contemplate knocking on the Voss's door to see if Sorrell's there. We always used to ride the bus to middle school together, back before either of us had a license. It would be the most normal thing in the world to ask her if she wanted a ride, but a weird sense of awkwardness stops me from crossing their lawn and ringing their doorbell. It's as if there's a hand on my shoulder, holding me back.

A lot has changed in the past few years. *A lot*. Maybe Sorrell won't even recognize me. We were kids when she left, barely thirteen. I've grown nearly two feet since then. Even I can see the changes in myself when I look in the mirror: I'm broader. Thanks to all of the exercise and gym time I've been getting, being on the lacrosse team, I'm not the gangly, disproportionate boy I used to be. She left me a nerd, and now I'm...something else, I guess. There's every chance that bossy little Sorrell Voss, who's opinion has always meant more to me than anyone else's, might not like the man I'm becoming.

Jesus. She won't like me at all if she finds out how long I sat outside her house, debating whether or not I should go see her, for fuck's sake. I get into the Mustang, calling myself a pussy, berating myself as I enter the forest, snaking through the switchbacks that lead up to Toussaint. For fifteen minutes, I harass myself like this, driving faster and faster, anticipation building to crazy levels inside me. I get to see Sorrell today. Voss is fucking *home*.

It strikes me as funny, as I hit the halfway marker to the academy, that today will be Sorrell's first day *ever* at Toussaint. I can't stop laughing.

Callum and Seb wait for me by my usual spot in the parking lot. They're wearing their Toussaint Academy lacrosse team shirts; the moment I lay eyes on them and I see their perfectly styled hair and their crisp white Adidas sneakers, I realize that Lani was right—I *have* become a jock. I hang out with jocks. I play a fucking *sport*.

Callum's on me as soon as I kill the Mustang's engine. "Well? Did the old man kick your ass?"

I slam the car door. "Why would he kick my ass?"

"'Cause you nearly got suspended for three weeks! I'm amazed you're even allowed to step foot on school property."

Hah. I only got involved in that fight because Callum's big mouth got him into shit with Jonah, the one person at Toussaint you don't want to antagonize, and he needed his friends to drag his ass back out of it. I got one hit in, *one* good hit, and Jonah went down like a sack of shit. Naturally, I was the only one of the three of us Principal Ford saw throwing hands. Callum and Seb had bolted. I'd stayed, knuckles smarting, skin split open and bleeding. I hadn't bothered to take off after my friends. Some sick part of me had *wanted* the punishment.

"I can go home if you want me to," I say mockingly, snaking an arm around the back of Callum's neck. He struggles against the headlock I put him in, escaping after he jams his elbow into my side, forcing me to let him go.

Seb groans, leaning his weight against the side of the car. "Don't do that to me, Merchant. If you're gonna bail, at least take me with you. I don't think I can stand another second of this asshole acting like the big man. Anyone would think *he* was the one who knocked Jonah out. If I have to hear about the sound Jonah's head made when it cracked off the ground one more fucking time, I'm gonna officially lose my shit.

"You're jealous," Callum proclaims. "You just wish it had been you who'd knocked him out. Instead, you just stood there with your thumb stuck up your ass."

"Fuck. When did we start squabbling like girls?" I'm bored of their bullshit already and the day hasn't even started yet. To avoid suspension, I'd had to apologize to Jonah in front of his fucking parents. I'm really *not* sorry for knocking the tool out; feigning sincerity as I apologized for my actions had been really fucking difficult. I'm beginning to think I should have just taken the suspension and chilled at home for a couple of weeks. At least there, I wouldn't have to listen to my friends bickering like eight-year-olds. I'd have missed too many games, though. Missing out on games means no scholarship, and since Lorelei is insisting I go to a west coast school and won't pay for me to study music at Juilliard, then I'm really going to need that scholarship.

The bell rings. "Come on." I grab both of my friends by their shoulders, urging them up the steps, into the building. "We got about three minutes before we're in shit."

They allow themselves to be steered toward the entrance, but they continue with their chatter as they go. Relentless. They're fucking *relentless*. "Marcus is throwing the First Night party tonight. He told me he'd break my nose if I even thought about gatecrashing," Sebastian says. Marcus, Seb's brother, has been planning this First Night party for his senior year since he enrolled at Toussaint. As Juniors, we're definitely not invited. I couldn't give a shit about Marcus' dumb party, but Sebastian would love nothing more than to attend. Dude worships the ground his brother walks on. Idolizes him at every turn, even though he's a cocksucker of the highest order. Crashing this First

Night bullshit has been on Seb's agenda since he found out about Marcus' plans two years ago.

"We need dates," Callum says, as we push through the double doors, walking into Toussaint's main hallway. "I heard they were gonna be getting into some freaky sex shit. Be pretty fucked if we rocked up to the party and didn't have anyone to partner up with."

I tune all of their chatter out.

I'm not going to any party.

I brushed Callum's comment off earlier, but I *am* in serious shit with my father over the Jonah incident. I don't board at Toussaint like these punks. Why the hell would I, when I live so close? There's no way I'll be allowed out of the house past dark for the next few weeks. And even if I was allowed, I wouldn't bother testing my father's patience by attending what already sounds to be a shit show in the making.

"What about you, Merchant?"

Sebastian is looking at me expectantly. "Sorry. I spaced. What about me?"

He shakes his head, then repeats his question nice and slow, obviously unhappy about having to do so. "Who…are you…going…to ask…to the party?"

"Sorry, boys. It's my parents' anniversary. They're gonna be out all night. I'm on Lani duty."

"Your folks are loaded, Merch. They can afford a babysitter. You are *not* missing this party," Sebastian states.

"Take it up with my father. I'll shoot you his contact info."

This shuts him up. Sebastian's just as big as me. He's packed on a heap of muscle over the past year and a half. Doesn't matter how tall he gets, or how much muscle he packs on, though—he'll always be scared of my dad. Paul Merchant is a slim man. Physically unimposing. Reserved. Quiet. But you do not fuck with him. He's a serious man. He commands respect and gets it. My father only has to glance sideways at Seb with the hint of a frown on his face to make my friend quail. It's hilarious to watch him squirm, poor bastard.

"No need to get sassy," Seb mutters. "Why don't you just ask your old bestie to come as your date? I heard Little Miss Sunshine is back from the East Coast—"

I shove Sebastian ahead of me, through the classroom door. Callum follows behind. Once we're all seated—me in front of Seb, Callum at the desk directly to my right, I address Seb with more manners than he deserves. "First, to repeat myself, I'm not going to the party. Second, don't call her that."

"Why not?" He laughs nastily. "Wasn't she always just *the sunniest?*" His tone stinks. Sorrell walked around with a thundercloud over her head and a scowl on her face, which made her look like she was about to throat-punch the closest person to her and then set fire to the building. Her eyeliner, even at thirteen, was always aggressively thick. She refused to take shit from anyone. I adored every angry little detail of her.

Other people didn't find her hostility quite so charming.

But it was more than that for Seb. He couldn't understand why I wanted to spend so much time with a girl. One I was just friends with, especially. He moved to Sumner to attend the middle school partnered with Toussaint, packed off to board up here when he was only eight. He and I met at junior lacrosse practice and became fast friends. He wanted to hang out all of the time, wanted to do 'dumb guy shit.' Sorrell's presence had irked him even back then. He's been running amok ever since she left; I'm sure he's just hating that she's back now.

As if reading my mind, my friend jabs me in the back. "Just remember," Sebastian says. "This is the start of junior year. We don't have time for distractions. Not even from *friends*. The team matters more than anything else."

I don't always want to throttle Seb. Just most of the time. The dude's so fucking petty. I give him what I hope translates to an understanding smile. "Of course, dude. No distractions. No old best friends. No *parties*..."

"Parties are different. A party's just one night. A way to blow off steam. We're nearly seventeen, Theo. It makes sense that we'd wanna fuck around with girls and get wasted. Sorrell Voss is bad news, dude. She's needy as fuck. She'll eat up all of your time. Your classwork will suffer. You'll lose your spot on the team."

I laugh. I have to. "The sun will explode in the sky. Crops will fail across the planet. A new ice age will grip the earth, and all of humanity will die. Voss isn't the fucking Anti-Christ, Seb."

"Isn't she?" he grumbles.

I choose to overlook the comment. "I'm perfectly capable of hanging out with my friend and taking care of my—" My jaw nearly hits the floor, "*—shit!*"

The girl standing in the classroom doorway bears a passing resemblance to my childhood friend. But it can't be Sorrell, can it? I feel like I just got sucker punched in the gut. She's...

Fuck.

Her thick, wavy black hair cascades all the way to her waist. Her cheekbones are razor sharp, her cheeks rosy, her color high. Her eyes, the left a verdant green, the right a startling ice blue, are brighter than ever. I'm run through and speared to my fucking seat when her gaze travels across the room and lands on me. What the fuck *happened* to her? I thought *I'd* changed, but the girl I grew up next door to is completely unrecognizable. She's turned into a goddamn smoke show.

"Oh, great." Sebastian slaps his notebook down onto his desk. "Now she's hot. That is just... fucking...*great*."

His complaints go unheard. I can't stop staring at her. I feel like I'm trying to catch my balance, teetering on the edge of a precipice. Wobbling. Fighting to keep my footing. Every single moment I've ever spent with this girl flickers through my mind at once, blurring and blending together. The laughter. The teasing. The arguments. The petty bickering. Watching movies on the couch together, her head resting in my lap. Throwing scrunched up pieces of paper at each other in the library. Jumping into the lake. Riding bikes around town. Every Christmas. Every birthday. Every spring, summer, winter, fall.

A lifetime I'd forgotten about.

Until now.

Sorrell heads in my direction, weaving through the desks, a small, casual smirk playing over her full lips; when she arrives in front of me, my heart gives a hard, desperate thump, as if it'll never beat correctly again now that she's here.

"Well, look who it is. Theodore William Merchant," she says. Her voice is deeper than it was before. Raspier. More than that, it's fucking *sexy*. A weird panic sinks its teeth into me. What the *fuck* am I supposed to do with this knot of fire that's kindled to life behind my sternum? It takes far longer than it should for me to smile back up at her and speak, and even then I can only manage two words.

"Hello, Kid"

SORRELL

NOW

The cadence of his breath feels familiar.

As far as I'm aware, I've never woken up in Theo's bed before, but if the absolutely insane story he spun to me last night is to be believed, then I probably have. Many times. I will admit that feeling his chest pressed up against my back, his body curved around mine, his arms wound tight around me…all of that feels…fuck, it feels good. How can that be possible? And how can *anything* he told me last night be possible?

I lay in the cradle of his body, listening to the slow draw and pull of him inhaling and exhaling in his sleep, terror mounting inside me.

I remember Rachel. Her laugh. Her smile. How badly she annoyed the shit out of me whenever we fought. We shared whispered secrets in the dark. I try to recall what her hand felt like in mine, as we ran across the train tracks behind Falcon House, whooping and screaming, and it comes to me so easily that I know without a shadow of a doubt that she *was* real.

But then, there are the holes.

What color were her eyes?

Was she taller than me, or was I taller than her?

Did she have *any* family?

The night of the accident, where was she sitting in that car?

Where was *I* sitting?

What exactly happened?

Jesus fucking Christ.

I gulp down a frightened breath, screwing my eyes shut tight. What the hell is *wrong* with me?

At my back, Theo stirs. I feel the moment his consciousness returns to him, and the moment when his body stiffens with tension afterward. His weariness radiates off of him so powerfully that I can almost taste the sour, metallic tang of it on my tongue.

Tick. Tick. Tick.

The little analogue alarm clock on the nightstand marks the seconds that pass with no consideration for how badly I want time to stand still. As soon as Theo says something, I'll have to face whatever comes next. The peace will be shattered, and there will be questions, followed by more stories far too fantastical to be believed, and all of that is beyond me.

At last, Theo pulls in a long breath, his frame relaxing into the bed, the rigidity that locked up his body falling away like it never even existed.

I should say something. I have to say something. Theo gets there before I can, though. "Sleep some more, Voss. You're still tired." He pauses. His hand, resting on my side, shifts, his fingers working slow, reassuring circles over me, where my shirt has ridden up in the night, exposing a sliver of bare skin. "It's okay." His warm breath stirs my hair. "You're still here. You're still you."

Three hours later, he isn't behind me when I wake. I can tell immediately—the cold, empty space behind me makes me shiver. I feel violently, unbearably alone, until I realize that he's sitting in the chair by the window.

His eyes are beautiful, wolfish, alert, and wild, watching me with an intensity sharp enough to cut.

His hair is a mess, the dark waves ruffled and springing all over the place. Those three freckles, arranged in a near perfect triangle beneath his right eye, stand out starkly against his washed-out skin. In the cool morning light filtering through the window, he sits shirtless, chin propped up on his elbow, wearing nothing but his boxers, looking like he hasn't slept in millennia. The tattoos marking his chest, his neck, his side and his arms are extensive; I haven't really acknowledged just *how* inked he is.

He blinks at me, not saying anything, waiting for me to speak, perhaps, but I just lay on my side, looking at him the same way he's looking at me, trying to make sense of how I'm feeling right now.

After a long moment where we do nothing but stare at each other, he murmurs, "Stop doing that."

"What?"

"Looking at me like you *want* me. I'm trying to give you some space. I'd love nothing more than to climb back in that bed and fuck the living shit out of you, but you couldn't handle it right now."

"I couldn't?"'

His head rocks from left to right. "Not the way *I* wanna fuck you. I'm too stressed out to be gentle."

A flash of heat ignites in my stomach, unexpected, making me suck in a breath. My mind is a tangle of emotions and feelings right now. I found out I had parents last night, only to discover that they're now both dead in the same conversation, for fuck's sake. There are a million other things I should be thinking about, but as always when I'm around him, Theo absorbs my mental bandwidth like a black hole absorbs light.

I want him. I want him to fuck me roughly, the way he just implied he would. I want bruises on my body, and teeth marks on my skin, and I want him to put them there—

"Stop," he says, his voice a warning. "I can read you like a book, Voss, and those impure thoughts you're having right now? They're making my dick hard."

"I'm rather enjoying them."

"No. You're too scared to face what's going on so you're *hiding* behind them."

Rude! How dare he call me out on my avoidance tactics. I gun him down with a spiteful glare, but eventually, the steady, even liquid depths of his gaze makes me look away. I pull myself up so that I'm leaning against the pillows. My head thrums. "They're the reason why you're always wearing long sleeved shirts, then?" I say.

"Hmm?" The rough quality of his voice makes the hairs on the back of my neck stand to attention.

"The tattoos." I eye the intricate designs on his arms: wings, fanning out over the back of his left tricep. A ship, and a book, and a crest. His left arm is a maze of ink—patterns and blocks of text that I can't discern properly from where I lay on the bed. The sun in the center of his chest is beautiful. Down his side, I can only see *'Sorrell'* and the beginning of *'Amelia'* beneath it, because of the way he's sitting in the chair, but the knowledge that the other names exist there, one after the other, evidence of my impermanence in the world, makes me avert my gaze. "Are...are some of the other tattoos related to me?" I ask.

His eyes become distant. "They're *all* about you, Sorrell. Every last one." He glances over his shoulder, out of the window, frowning at the grey world beyond the glass. He doesn't just have a couple of tattoos. He has so many that they blend into one another, one merging into the next. It's hard to even imagine unravelling them. "All apart from this one." He taps a little four-leaf clover on his right arm. "That one was for someone else."

"What do they all mean?"

Theo shakes his head. "They're just tattoos. They're not going anywhere. There are other, more important questions you wanna ask."

There are. There are a million and one questions I want answers to, but I don't even know where to begin. I throw my arms over my face and blot out the world, trying to calm my racing pulse, already knowing that my attempts to hide will be futile. There *is* no hiding from this.

"You wanna know who else knows about all of this," Theo says softly. "The accident. Your memory loss. Your...personality shifts."

My stomach drops. I do want to know that, and Theo knows that's the case because we've done this before. He's had to explain this before. How many times have we been through this exactly?

"Tell me," I whisper.

"Sebastian knows. Ashley. Beth."

"What?"

"You're surprised?"

"They hate me. And yet they never said anything?"

"They don't hate you." He sounds so sure of himself that I almost believe him. Almost.

"Come on, Theo. I've spent enough time around all three of them to know that isn't true. They can't stand the sight of me. Sebastian threw a can of fucking Coke at my head."

"He did that 'cause he hates *me* right now, not you. You and Ashley used to be close once. Beth..." Theo blows out his cheeks, shaking his head. "You and Beth used to be thick as thieves. She confided some stuff in you years ago. Dark shit. Something about some guy called Lance? Ash told me you busted that shit out in the hallway when you got here this time around. Scared the crap out of Beth. Guess she figured you'd never remember..."

Damn. I did lay into her about fucking her father's friend. About her dad watching her screw him on some cameras in her bedroom. That information *had* seemed to come to me out of the blue, but I'd *known* in my head that I'd read it somewhere. That it was information Ruth had armed me with to help survive here. Now none of that is true. Beth confided that in me because we were friends once upon a time? God, this just gets more and more complicated...

"She was weird with you for a long time before the accident, though. She wanted..." He trails off, grimacing a little uncomfortably.

"She wanted *you*. She was jealous." I finish for him.

He shrugs, brushing it off. "Beth just wants what she can't have. She couldn't have me, and she resented you for it. She's still kept her mouth shut and hasn't told anyone else about the accident, though."

"Why would she do *that*?"

"Money."

"You're *paying* her to keep quiet?"

He just looks at me blankly. Slowly shakes his head. "Not me, Kid."

"Then who?"

He stares down at his hands, cracking his knuckles one at a time. Doesn't say a word.

I sit up straight, frustration tugging insistently at my nerves. "Let me guess. You can't tell me that. Not yet. I'm not ready."

Sighing, he lets his head fall back against the chair. "We're already going way too fast here. You need time to wrap your head around this shit. We rush this and god knows what'll happen. You'll turn into Meredith, or Jennifer, or Natalie, and we'll have to start all over again. I don't want that."

My eyes prick so painfully, it makes my throat ache. My emotions churn around in my chest like cement in a mixer. I can't tell if I want to scream or cry or laugh at the absurdity of it all. "What difference does it even make? I can't remember who I was before this shift. Who fucking cares if I shift again?"

He rockets out of the chair, dragging his hands back through his unkempt hair. "I fucking do! 'Cause when you woke up this time, you weren't some made up creation. You didn't give us some unfamiliar name. You woke up and said your name was Sorrell Voss. Your real name. You were *you*. Really you. All of you, not just pieces of you. *Your* personality traits. *Your* temper. *Your* sense of humor. Everything about you is you again, Sorrell. The only thing missing is your memory."

I'm too stunned to speak. The anger and desperation in his voice has cut me down to the quick. He falls to his knees at the side of the bed, cupping my face in his hands, looking at me so deeply that I can feel his gaze reaching down into my fucking soul. "This is the closest I've come to getting you back. I'm not letting you go ever again. You just need to remember everything, okay?"

* * *

It turns out that Seb, Ashley and Beth aren't the only ones who know about my strange predicament. Noelani knows. Noelani, who is also Theo's *sister*, which, just...my mind can't even begin to comprehend *that*. I told her that I *fucked* him, for crying out loud. I didn't go into great detail, but still...

Principal Ford is also in on this whole fiasco and has been since the very beginning. As soon as Theo tells me this, I demand to be taken to see the woman, determined on giving her a piece of my mind, but the moment Theo drops me off at her office and I plant myself down in the worn leather seat opposite her at her desk, I can't find the right words to say.

We stare at each other.

After a ludicrous amount of time has passed, she clears her throat and leans back in her high-backed chair. The leather creaks. "I can see that you're angry," she says.

"I don't think angry comes close to what I'm feeling."

"And I understand that. I can understand how—"

"Oh, I'm glad *you* understand. I'm glad *you* have such clarity right now, because I have to say..." I laugh bitterly. "*I* really don't understand any of this. Yesterday, I woke up knowing myself. I knew exactly who I was. I knew that my best friend died, and I was so...so fucking angry, and I wanted to exact revenge on the person who caused her death. Today, I wake up to someone telling me that I'm someone entirely different. That...that he's like my fucking *soul mate*—"

She bristles, folding her hands on her stomach.

"Oh, don't get all bent out of shape about me cursing. I think I'm entitled to say fuck right now, don't you?"

Her brow creases. She doesn't look happy, but she inclines her head.

"I don't...I don't even know for a fact that anything Theo's told me is true! I have no evidence for...for *any* of it!"

Principal Ford sighs heavily, brows raising, eyes wide. "Yes, well, Theo knows better than to do what he did. He shouldn't have even been at Toussaint this time around, but—"

I jerk as if she's struck me. "What do you mean, *this time around?*"

Another deep, frustrated sigh. "This isn't the first time we've done this, Sorrell. Against my best judgement, this is the *third* time we've attempted to trigger your past memories and bring you back to yourse—"

"THIRD TIME!"

She swallows thickly. "The first time was only a couple of months after the accident. It was too soon. You weren't even physically healed from what happened, and who you were at the time...god. Catherine was very angry. Very troubled. Theo pushed you...*her*...so hard, and it ended in disaster. You had to go back to Falcon House and start all over again. Amazingly, you managed to complete your junior year there. I don't even know how that was possible. You'd lost every scrap of your past and what made you you that time, but you remembered everything you'd been learning perfectly. You picked up assignments you were halfway through when you were injured and finished them like it was completely normal. Without even missing a step."

I don't remember any of that. None of it. I definitely don't remember being Catherine.

"Then we staged a new school semester here with your old classmates during the summer break," Principal Ford continues. "You weren't Catherine by that point, thank god. You were Rachel. We had two months to try and coerce you back to health, and it looked like it was going to happen for a moment there. You did start remembering bits and pieces from before the accident. You remembered Theo most of all, which obviously made it impossible for him to take a step back and let things take their course, to just see what would happen. He insisted that we tell you the truth. And when we did, it was all too much. You slipped again. We were all *so* thrilled when you said that you were Sorrell. But it quickly became clear that while you recalled your name and your personality traits seemed to be very similar to the old you, you had no idea what was going on. You were convinced Rachel was a separate entity, that she had died, and that it was all Theo's fault. You can imagine how hard that was for him—"

So it's true, then.

Principal Ford keeps talking.

I watch her mouth move, but it's as if I'm falling down a deep, bottomless well, tumbling further and further away from her as this news sinks in. I can't hear her. Can't process.

All of it is true?

Some small part of me has been clinging onto the possibility that Theo's revelations last night were all some cruel lie. A joke on his part, designed to make me question my own sanity. That would have been preferrable to this. I would have just hated Theo even more—that would have been so, so easy. But no. Now I have to align myself with the fact that my entire existence is akin to navigating quicksand; the ground might shift out from under my feet at any moment, and I might just...cease to be.

"Sorrell?"

My head whips up.

Principal Ford smiles apologetically. "I know that this must all feel like some huge act of betrayal to you. We've kept things from you and lied to you repeatedly. I apologize for keeping you here, for the subterfuge with the old access road and the sea plane, I do. This whole..." She gestures, hands up, to the school around us, "...façade is more than a social experiment, though. Some of your doctors believe that having you here, in a setting that holds so many memories for you, is the one thing that's most likely to bring you back to yourself. This academic year is a little different, I'll admit. Aside from three or four of your old friends, most of the students you're studying alongside now are brand new to Toussaint. Last year's junior year have all transferred to another location to complete their senior year, at great inconvenience and expense to a lot of people. We thought keeping only Seb and the girls here might help trigger you in some way. That having a few familiar faces amongst a sea of strangers could potentially jar you back to reality. We were going to give it at least three more months before we changed tactics or introduced new, additional measures, but..." She looks so defeated. "Your connection to Theo has once again made that impossible. He was warned a thousand times—"

"Will you excuse me, please?" There's no two ways about it: I'm puking. The sheer lengths so many people have gone to, to try and fix me...I can't even begin to wrap my head around any of it. It's incomprehensible. Yep. Definitely going to puke. I bolt from the chair and fly out of Ford's office, racing down the hallway. It isn't until I'm on my knees, bowed over a toilet, that I realize Theo has followed me; he must have been waiting for me outside Ford's office.

Luck would have it that the first bathroom I came across was a disabled restroom—much larger than most. There's plenty of room for the both of us in here. He doesn't say anything. He sits himself down on the floor beside the toilet, hiking his knees up, resting his elbows on them, letting his head hang as I hurl.

I don't want to throw up in front of him. I don't want him to see me like this. It turns out that he's seen me in far worse states, though.

I'm wracked with cold sweats when I push away from the toilet bowl and lean my back against the bathroom wall. I can't remember the last time I felt this bad. But that's the whole point of this nightmare, isn't it? I can't fucking remember *anything*.

I drive the heels of my palms into my eye sockets, trying to push back the urge to cry. I am so done with crying. It isn't going to get me anywhere. When I feel like I've mastered myself, I lower my hands and look at Theo.

"You're still here," I say quietly.

"I am," he whispers.

"I was awful to you. I've hated you. I *told* you that I hated you. To your face."

He picks at his fingernails, chewing ruefully on his bottom lip. His face is unreadable, blank, as if none of this can touch him anymore. "Yeah, you *did* say that. You asked me if I wanted to *feel* how much you hated me."

"And you said yes." My voice cracks on the last word.

He smiles, finally displaying a flicker of sadness. "I did."

"Why? How could you want that after..." I'm hopeless. I thought I was safe from my tears, but all I did was delay them.

"Because having you hate me was *something*, Kid," he says. "It would have been enough. I would feel it, and know that underneath all of that anger, you once *loved* me so much fucking more." His voice catches again, belying a deep well of emotion, choking him just beneath his all-too-calm exterior.

"I've put you through hell, Theo..."

"You were *in* hell," he answers quickly. "The moment that car struck the guardrail you've been in hell. I just—" He breathes. Composes himself. And out of nowhere, his façade fractures, and he looks at me with so much love in his eyes—a love so deep and impossible that I know he must have had to fight this feeling every single day that I've been around him. A love as big as this takes a monumental effort to hide. "I did the only thing I could think of. I followed. I went down into hell with you. I was *never* going to leave you there, in darkness, alone."

THEO

THREE YEARS AGO

I hate this fucking song.

I've *always* hated it.

I'm going to kill whoever keeps playing it on repeat. Kieran's never thrown a party before and you can tell. The dude needs some fucking pointers. Pointer number one: don't allow everyone access to the sound system. Hire a DJ. Make a fucking playlist. At least confiscate the iPad connected to your shitty speakers so that this bullshit doesn't happen.

The sound of *'I'm Blue'* by Eiffel 65 kicks in again, and I grind my teeth together, downing the rest of my beer. The last thing I need is an empty cup right now. I'm crossing the roiling crowd of Juniors dancing in Kieran's trashed living room, when Seb swoops down the stairs and grabs me by the arm.

"I just fucked Sawyer Smith in the ass on Dave Littlemore's desk."

Dave, Mr. Littlemore—Kieran's District Attorney father—will have a fit if he finds out about that. Seb doesn't look too concerned, though. He looks like the cat who just busted in a cheerleader's backdoor.

"Congratulations," I say, rolling my eyes. More beer. I need more fucking beer for this. I didn't even want to come to this, but I'd bailed on Seb's brothers dumb First Night party at the beginning of the month, so I hadn't really had much of a choice. Heading for the kitchen, I shove my way through swaying, sweaty bodies.

"What's your deal, man? You always said Sawyer had the best ass at Toussaint. Six months ago, you told me you wanted to fuck her so bad you thought your balls were gonna explode."

I huff under my breath. "Oh yeah? And if I did say that, then what kind of friend does that make *you?*"

"That makes me quality control, asshole. Can't have you dipping that precious Merchant wick into potentially spoiled goods."

"I'd say she's definitely spoiled goods now that *you've* had your dick in her ass." I grab the tap to the keg and start filling up my solo cup.

"Ahhhh, come on. We're brothers. Brothers share. You'll be pleased to know that I didn't completely ruin that tight little asshole. Give her a week and she'll be good to go."

"You're disgusting." I chug half the beer and go right back to refilling it. Somewhere at this raging dumpster fire of a party, Sorrell Voss is dancing with Ashley and Beth. It's been three weeks since she returned from New York, and things have been…*strange*.

I can't stop looking at her.

I can't stop thinking about her.

I. Want. To. Fuck. Her. Senseless.

I never thought about her before, not like this. So why the hell am I doing so now?

Could have something to do with the fact that she's fucking beautiful, the annoying voice in the back of my head suggests. *Or the fact that her tits look incredible, and you want to bury your face between those, long, gorgeous, tanned legs of hers and suffocate yourself in her cunt.*

My cheeks flare red hot at the graphic thought, unable to contain the rush of heat that fires directly to my cock. I have been thinking about that a lot. My best friend. I've been obsessing over what my best friend's pussy tastes like. I'm fucking *broken* or something. I used to tease her for eating her own hair when she was five, for fuck's sake.

Seb jostles me, shoving me out of the way so he can refill his own drink. "Look. All I'm saying—"

"I know perfectly well what you're saying. And have at it, dude. You want to go around fucking half the academy then be my guest. Doesn't mean I have to." The kitchen is a mess. A group of kids are gathered around the marble island, playing drinking games. One by one, they draw little folded slips of paper from a glass bowl, pulling either a truth or a dare. One of the girls squeals when she discovers that she's been dared to flash everyone in the room. She pretends she doesn't want to, that she's shy, but the huge shit-eating grin on her face as she lifts up her shirt and jumps up and down, making her tits bounce, says she's perfectly fine with it. More than fine.

Momentarily distracted, Seb gapes at the chick, and I attempt to make my exit. The captain of the lacrosse team has other plans. His hand clamps around the top of my arm like a vice.

"I'm getting pretty sick of you manhandling me." I pepper my tone with a hint of malice.

"Come on. You love it," he retorts.

I'm about to demonstrate to him just how much I *don't* love it when Ashley and Beth enter the kitchen, clinging onto each other, laughing like witches. They're holding each other up; fuck knows how much they've already had to drink.

Sorrell is notably missing.

"I'd definitely hit that, too," Seb says, pointing his beer at Ash. "And Beth's been begging for your cock since summer. I have no idea why you haven't fucked her, man. She looks fucking filthy. I can see her eating ass like a champ. I bet she'd stick that pretty little tongue of hers so far past your sphincter you'd find religion."

"Please remind me why we're friends again," I growl.

"Because I make you less boring, Merchant. And, loathe as I am to admit this, you're an attractive dude. I'm not saying you're hotter than *me*, but still. There are those of us out here wanting to get our dicks sucked, and your whole, 'abstinence makes me interesting' bullshit is making the rest of us look bad. All of these chicks are holding out for you. The moment you fuck just one of *them,* the others will settle for the rest of *us.* It's really only fair, asshole. Come on. Catch and release."

"Don't blame your inability to get laid on the fact that I don't want to fuck everything that moves, West."

"I just got done fucking Sawyer Smith. I *just* told you that."

"Then stop worrying about what I'm doing with my dick and go *clean* yours."

"Goddamn it. You are impossible to talk to," Seb mutters, slamming his beer down onto the counter next to me. "I'm gonna go find Callum. He's way more fun that you right now. I *never* thought I'd utter those words, Merchant."

I laugh to myself as the bastard struts off, out of the kitchen and into the surging swell of bodies, dancing in the hallway.

This beer isn't cutting it.

Not even close.

I drain the cup one more time (because where's the sense in wasting perfectly good, watered down, piss-weak beer?) and then I go rifling in the cupboards for a rocks glass. A glass that an actual adult might drink from. I find one eventually, at the back of a cupboard, set back on the highest shelf. The glass is cut crystal, beautiful and probably very expensive. Kieran's dad would go mad if he knew what I'm about to do, but he has no idea that Kieran's even having a party tonight. Kieran's nice enough but not so smart. He's gone about this all wrong. His parents are staying at a hotel less than an hour away to celebrate their twentieth wedding anniversary. I can't even begin to list all of the reasons why they might return home early, but there are a million and one of them, starting with, "We just wanted to sleep in our own bed." They're gonna get a shock when they realize there are a bunch of rutting teenagers wriggling around beneath their one thousand thread count Egyptian cotton sheets.

It takes a while to find the whiskey, but I persist because I know that there *is* whiskey.

A man like Kieran's father doesn't come home from a job like his and soothe his frayed nerves with a glass of fucking sweet tea. He also doesn't lock his expensive shit in the liquor cabinet, where his wayward, asshole kid will inevitably get at it. No, he hides it in plain sight. Well, kind of. District Attorney Littlemore's Scotch collection is in the laundry of all places, in a cupboard, hidden behind a stack of freshly folded towels. I don't think this is the permanent location of his stash. Clearly, he figured that laundry was the one thing his son *wasn't* going to do while he was away and hid his liquor store in here for the time being.

I pour myself three fingers from the bottle of Balvennie and slip back into the kitchen, nursing the rocks glass like it's the Holy Grail itself.

I stand apart from the crowd.

I watch the truth or dare game play out, bored to my back teeth, counting down the minutes to midnight—once the clock strikes twelve, I am fucking *out of here*. I do my best not to think about Sorrell. Trying not to think about her is like trying not to be bound by the laws of nature, though. Try not to blink. Try not to breathe.

It's impossible.

The ceiling fan overhead is dusty.

The whiskey sears my throat, scorching a pathway down to my stomach. I begin to feel comfortably numb.

There's a dental appointment reminder card on the fridge for Kieran, for tomorrow morning at nine am. No way the fucker's making *that*.

I finish my drink and help myself to another heavy pour, returning to my spot in the kitchen, leaning against the counter. By the time I'm halfway through my second glass, I'm feeling looser, a little less annoyed by the antics of my school friends. But only marginally. My heart seizes, clenching like a tight fist in the center of my chest, when Sorrell finally makes an appearance, dragged along behind Ashley as the girl with the bright blonde hair tugs her through the melee into the kitchen.

Sorrell's eyes—mismatched and beautiful—are wild with energy. Her thick black hair flows in artful waves over her bare shoulders. The dress she's wearing is tight and black, and—Jesus fucking H Christ—leaves nothing to the imagination. The fabric clings to her curves, accentuating her tits and her hips and her ass in a way that makes me want to groan out loud like some sex-starved caveman. I groan internally instead, training my expression into a blank façade, forcing my features to obey me and remain unaffected, but inside I am a raging inferno.

Sorrell never used to wear dresses, let alone tight, figure-hugging ones. Her favorite Nirvana t-shirt, and her ripped jeans, and her battered sneakers are missing tonight. She's allowed Ashley to apply a little eyeliner and mascara. Her lips are painted a vivid, wicked red. She's always been beautiful, without a shadow of a doubt, but tonight, standing in this overly fancy, boujee kitchen, every other girl in the room pales in comparison to her. They look drab and sallow—wilting dandelions, made utterly ordinary next to the delicate beauty of an orchid.

In short, she's fucking breathtaking.

Her mismatched eyes meet mine, her attention snagging on me as her gaze passes over the room, and the wide, open-mouthed smile she wears fades to something *more* as her focus narrows on me. Ashley says something to her, but she's too busy staring at me to answer. After a second, Ashley nudges her with an elbow, and Sorrell jerks, her gaze returning to her friend.

I'm basking in the sun one second, warmed down to my bones by the heat of her attention, and then cast into a frigid wasteland the next, robbed of the only thing capable of sustaining me. Ashley Rainer is the worst.

Speaking of Ashley, she tries to pour herself a drink from the mess of alcohol on the kitchen island, but one of the guys overseeing the game tells her she has to pay the tax first. In other words, do one of the dares first. She plucks a piece of folded paper from the bowl and opens it. The dare is lame. Show the most embarrassing photo on your cell phone or some shit. Ashley passes her phone around the group, a topless photo of herself displayed on the screen. The girl is *not* embarrassed by the shot. She looks pretty fucking smug about it, actually. Sorrell rolls her eyes at her friend, laughing along with the rest of the group when Ashley throws her drink back like it's a fucking shooter.

Sorrell doesn't look as stoked to be playing their dumb game when they tell her to stick her hand into the bowl of dares, though.

Gingerly, she selects a piece of paper and unfolds it, setting it down on the island.

Ashley reads it out loud for everyone to hear. "Who is the hottest person in the room right now?"

Blanching, Sorrell turns the color of a freshly bleached sheet. "I thought these were supposed to be dares?"

God.

She's so fucking stunning.

I can't take my eyes off her.

The guys in charge of the game—two idiots from the football team —jostle and roughhouse, bickering about something, but I pay them no heed. They earn my attention when one of them calls Sorrell '*Wolf Girl*,' though. She's always been sensitive about her eyes. Has always hated people commenting or remarking on them. I think her eyes are fucking mesmerizing, but Voss has never liked people pointing out the one thing about her that so blatantly marks her as different. I make a mental note to knock this guy's front fucking teeth out later.

Sorrell doesn't flinch away from the old nickname that's followed her since middle school tonight. She accepts a Jell-O shot and throws it back, smiling as she points a finger across the kitchen and says, "*Him*."

A random dude I've never seen before points at himself and says, "*Me?*"

"No. Behind you." A tiny, teasing smile pulls at the corners of Voss' mouth.

Everyone turns and looks. They realize pretty quickly what I've already realized: she is talking about *me*.

"Goddamnit, Merchant. I thought for sure she was gonna say it was me. Why don't you find somewhere else to skulk, you bastard?" one of the guys from the football team grouses. A Seattle Mariners ball cap hits the cabinet door next to my head—I'm fairly sure it was supposed to hit me in the face. I ignore the slight. My eyes are locked on Sorrell.

The house could be on fire.

I could be seconds from getting smoked by a car.

I could be moments away from walking off the edge of a cliff.

I still wouldn't be able to look away from her.

She is the loveliest thing I've ever witnessed.

Taking a slow sip from my whiskey, I relish the heat that flares behind my ribcage, but it's not from the alcohol this time. It's from the knowledge that something has shifted between Voss and me now. Ever since she came back, things have been weird between us. A taut tension has festered away, where before it didn't. The ease that used to exist between us was the kind of comfortability that exists between siblings. The electricity that's snapped and burned at us over the past couple of weeks has been very, *very* different. I've known it. She's known it. I told myself that I've been giving her time to settle back into life at Sumner, letting her get used to Toussaint. I've kept my mouth shut, afraid that if I say anything or make a move, I'll ruin the friendship.

Sorrell has just been brave for the both of us, and holy *fuck* is my dick hard right now.

I smile slowly at her over the rim of my glass, and it's a mistake, because I see the fire in her eyes, the way she sucks her bottom lip into her mouth, wetting it, and the primal part of my brain screams to life.

Charge her.

Grab her.

Take her.

Claim her.

She's mine.

Mine.

Mine.

MINE.

Fuck, I have to get out of here before I do something highly fucking illegal. Slowly, I turn and walk out of the kitchen, the sound of my pulse slamming in my ears, drowning out the thumping bassline of the music in the hall.

I've made it halfway to the stairs when a hand lands on my shoulder, spinning me around.

Sorrell's cheeks are flushed crimson. She's breathing so rapidly, it looks like her tits are going to spill over the top of her tight dress any second. God, her skin is fucking perfect. Flawless. The color of fresh poured cream and alabaster. Her eyes dance with electricity, so fucking strange and wonderful. She's never looked at me like this before.

Never.

She sounds winded when she says my name. "*Theo—*"

I slam her back against the wall, taking her face in my hands. Pinning her, I bring my mouth down on hers, crushing her lips with my own. She tastes like summer, and strawberries, and lime. The wet heat of her mouth makes my head fucking spin. Sweeping my tongue past her lips, she opens to me, letting me inside, and I can't stop the possessive growl that climbs the back of my throat. She kisses me back, her tongue stroking mine, her breath fanning my face with short, sharp, frantic bursts of air as she winds her arms around my neck. Her heart slams in her chest, her pulse charging just beneath her skin as she curves herself into me, and my brain short fucking circuits.

Holy.

Fucking.

Shit.

I have to have her.

I need her more than I've ever needed anything in my entire life.

I'll fucking *die* without her.

Ripping her mouth away from mine, she looks up at me, lips swollen, her pupils blown, and for once the vibrant jade coloring of her left eye and the ocean blue of her right is swallowed by bottomless black. She looks so turned around that I want to scoop her into my arms and hold her to me and protect her for fucking ever.

"Is it just me?" she whispers breathlessly, "or have we been waiting for this moment for a very long time?"

I run my fingers over her lips, possessive, fascinated by the intensity of this pull in my gut. "I've been so fucking *blind*," I answer.

"This feels like coming home," she pants.

"You are home. *My* home. Fuck."

"Gross! Merchant and Voss are eating each other," a female voice cat-calls. Nasty tone. Spiteful. Beth, naturally. She was always the most dominant member of Sorrell, Ashley and Beth's little friend group. She worked hard to be the prettiest, the funniest, the cleverest, the most popular with the boys. Voss never tried at all. Ever since Sorrell came back from New York, Beth's been a total cunt to her. She's even more threatened by her now, because Voss *still* isn't trying, and she is everything that Beth will never be.

I study the lines of Sorrell's face—a face I know so well, and yet it feels like I'm seeing it for the very first time, with new eyes. The smattering of freckles on the bridge of her nose. Her dark brows. Her pouty, full lips, the top slightly fuller than the bottom. Her canines have always been a little pointier than most. It's a silly, unimportant little detail about her that most people wouldn't notice, but alongside those remarkable eyes of hers, the combination does make her look a little wolfish. I used to tease her about her feral appearance, but I would never dream of teasing her for it now. She looks fierce. Defiant. Unique and incredible. She's stolen my fucking breath away.

She blushes, turning her face into my hand, attempting to hide from me inside my own palm. "Do not look at me like you're already in love with me, Theo Merchant. My heart can't take you looking at me like that yet." She shakes her head, digging a knuckle into my ribs, as if we're still just friends. Like the world isn't a whole new plane of existence now. "I need some time to prepare before I can handle you looking at me like that."

I pepper her forehead, and her temples, and her cheekbones with slow, lazy feather-light kisses. "All right. Fine. I'll stop. But let me know when you're ready for it, Voss. 'Cause I'm so gonna be waiting."

SORRELL

I'VE NEVER HAD REOCCURRING nightmares until now.

They're waking nightmares, vivid in detail and merciless in their persistence. For ten days straight, I stir from my sleep, exhausted even though I sleep like the dead. And then there is Theo, waiting for me. He says nothing. Grim-faced and pale as Death himself, he escorts me from my floor to class, to the next class, to the dining hall. At lunch, he sits opposite me, eating his food in silence, eyes cast down at his meal in front of him.

He becomes my dark-haired prince of déjà vu. Slowly, I *know* things about him. Perhaps I've always known these small details that present themselves to me, but each one feels like some kind of colossal revelation. The tiny scar on his right pinkie knuckle, from when I snapped one of the wheels off his GI Joe truck and he punched the doorjamb when we were eight. The quirky little cowlick above his right temple that makes his hair stick up at a weird angle when he doesn't tuck it behind his ear. The mole at the base of his neck that I still haven't seen properly, hidden behind his hair. The way he taps the end of his pencil between his teeth when he's thinking about something. The four-leaf clover tattoo on his right arm, in memory of his grandfather, who…who *died*…

Oh god.

When I think about this tattoo, a wave of emotion slams into me, a deep, pervasive melancholy, and I know that it didn't just destroy Theo when his grandfather passed. It destroyed *me*, too. I knew his grandfather. Loved him. I mourned him when he passed.

After another discussion with Principal Ford, I agreed to stay here at Toussaint to see if any of my memories return to me, and little by little, painfully slowly, the plan seems to be working. That doesn't mean that I'm happy to be stuck here, in this dusty old boarding school. I am a ghost, walking the hallways, feeling disconnected from my body in a way I can't describe. It isn't as if the other students can't see me. I'm not invisible. But some of them see me in a way that I will never be able to see myself, because *they* actually know me, and I do not. Such an unsettling thought.

On day eleven of my self-imposed incarceration at Toussaint, I finally look up at Theo and ask him a question; I just can't go on wondering any more. "Did you take my virginity?"

Theo spits out a mouthful of tomato soup.

On the end of the table, Lani, who's been gradually creeping closer to us over the past week, determined to come and sit with us but chased away by her brother at every turn, nearly knocks over her can of Diet Coke. She catches it in the nick of time and sets it right. "Jesus," she hisses. "I do *not* wanna be around for this conversation."

Theo wipes his mouth with the back of his hand. "You shouldn't be eavesdropping on our conversations anyway."

"Psssh! I haven't been! You two have barely said a word to each other in over a week!" Lani collects her bag, slings its strap over her shoulder, picks up her half-eaten lunch and faces me. "I swear to god, he's not normally this boring," she says. "Time was you couldn't shut the loser up. All he ever wanted to do was talk to you. Or about you. It drove us all insane at home."

"Noelani," Theo growls. "Kindly fuck off and leave us alone."

"I'm just trying to help," she snaps back. "I don't want you to fuck this up for the third…wait, is this the *fourth* time?"

"*Lani*." This time, it's me who speaks. "It's okay. He's not fucking anything up. He's just…giving me space."

Theo shoots me a surprised look. Did he really think I'd say something different? Give him shit? Make him feel bad for his silent companionship over the past week? He frowns at me as I address Lani. "I'm...processing. Trying to understand. Trying to figure out if I should even be here or not. I mean, I have no reason to stay here now."

"You do still need to graduate," Theo reminds me.

"So do you," I retort.

"No, he doesn't," Lani says, laughing. Her smile fades when she sees the murderous look on Theo's face.

"What?" I look back and forth between the two of them, my gaze landing on Theo. "What's she talking about."

"I already graduated. A while ago," Theo says stiffly. He sets his spoon back down in his bowl with a clatter.

"Our mother insisted," Lani says sheepishly. "You were back in the hospital. Lorelei said that she wouldn't pay for Theo's scholarship if he didn't finish his senior year—"

I feel sick to my stomach. "Oh my god, why aren't you in college? What are you *doing* here?" I already know the answer to this question. Theo just looks at me pointedly.

"We always said we'd do college together," he says quietly.

"You need to stay here and finish out the year," Lani says. "I haven't graduated yet, either. Personally, I'm thrilled by the idea of being a freshman at college with you both."

"You should be so lucky," Theo mutters.

"Likewise!" Lani fires back. "Anyway. I really *am* leaving. Sounds like you guys are about to take a journey down memory lane that I have no desire to join you on." She wrinkles her nose. "Seriously. Gross."

"*Child,*" Theo tosses over his shoulder after her. He goes back to staring at his soup once she's out of earshot.

I lean back in my chair, assessing him quietly. His hair falls into his face, obscuring his expression, so it's hard to get a read on him. I get the distinct impression that he's feeling a little uncomfortable, though.

"You wanna talk about the graduation thing or the virginity thing?" he asks.

"The virginity thing." If I think too hard about the fact that Theo is currently repeating his senior year even though he's already graduated, because of *me,* I think I might have a nervous breakdown.

"Are you trying to ask me if..." He sighs, looking up at me. Frustration lingers in his eyes. "If you were *you* when you lost your virginity? Or if I slept with another version of you. One with no memory of me."

My stomach twists itself into a tight knot. I hadn't been thinking of it in those terms, but now that he puts it that way, I suppose it's a salient question. Theo sees my answer on my face. "Can you come to my room tonight? This isn't a topic of conversation I wanna discuss now, with half the dining hall watching us."

* * *

I show up at eight on the dot, just like he told me to. Theo Merchant might look like he got dressed in the dark most days, but holy fuck does he make it look good. His hair is wet, tucked behind his ears. He smells fresh. Clean. He didn't shave tonight, while he evidently was showering, and a smattering of dark scruff marks his jaw. In a fitted black t-shirt and blue jeans, he looks ridiculously sexy. A *'he-could-have-any-girl-he-wants'* level of sexy that makes my toes curl against the plush rug beneath my feet, as he stalks across his room and plants himself on the edge of his bed.

He *could* have any girl he wanted, but somehow Theo chose me. He's chosen me again, and again, and again, even though it's cost him so much.

Clear-eyed, he holds out a hand to me. "I want you next to me," he says. A command. One I won't dispute. No matter how alien it feels to me, I know I'm safe when I'm in his arms. It's an irrevocable fact that my body knows on a cellular level, even if my mind and my memories don't.

Accepting his hand, I sit in his lap. Going by his surprised intake of breath, he wasn't expecting me to make myself comfortable by planting myself right there, curling myself around him, but I want to be buried in him. I want to drown in the scent of him, bask in the warmth of him, and feel secure in the cage of his arms as they crush me to his chest. I *need* it more than I knew I possibly could.

Tucking my head under his chin, Theo folds me into his arms, holding me close, exactly how I want him to. Curled up against him, my body fits perfectly here, as if it was made to snap into place against him. His warm breath stirs my hair. The *thrum, thrum, thrum* of his heart counts out a steady, comforting beat against my ear drum.

"You always fought me when I wanted to hold you like this," he says. The bass swell of his voice sounds huge with my ear pressed up against his ribcage. Like when he draws the bow of his cello across the lowest note and sustains it perfectly, making the very air in *my* lungs vibrate.

C2.

Somehow, out of nowhere, I know that, with the way Theo tunes his cello, the lowest note he can play is C2.

"Why did I fight you?" I whisper.

He mulls on this for a moment. I think that's what he's doing; I can't see his face. After a while, he says, "You were always so determined to be independent. Strong. Fierce. Like you didn't need me to make you feel safe. You didn't want me to think that you were weak. But after a while, you'd relent and give in, and I'd stroke your hair and hum whatever I'd been working on to you, and you'd fall asleep."

A shockwave of unidentifiable emotion courses through my veins, warm and sad and beautiful. Yet again, I'm hit with the sneaking suspicion that even though my brain can't draw on memories of the events that Theo's talking about, my body somehow remembers and deeply longs for those days, when life was as simple as climbing into his arms and passing out to the sound of him humming.

"Will you do that tonight?" I'm a little scared of his response. He hasn't slept in the same room as me since the night he told me about the accident. A part of me is terrified that, somehow, after all the shit he's tolerated, he's finally had enough.

"I can't."

Oh, shit, he *has* had enough. "Why not?"

"I have nothing to hum for you. I haven't…written anything new since…"

"Since?"

He clears his throat, kisses my temple, and then rests his cheek against my forehead. He doesn't answer the question for a while. I get the impression he's revisiting memories that aren't particularly pleasant. "I haven't written anything new since the piece I played in the auditorium," he finally confesses. "It was a requiem. *Your* requiem."

My heart skips a little, my nerves getting the better of me. "And what, exactly, is a requiem?"

He exhales steadily. Absently, he slides a hand up the back of my shirt and starts drawing circles over my side. The action is familiar and proprietary. It makes me feel a little less anxious about whatever he's going to say next. "It's a piece of music written for masses for the dead. For...*funerals*," he whispers. "When you went into that coma after the last big surgery, they said there was no way you were waking up. Categorically no way. I spent a lot of time in the chapel at the hospital. I don't believe in any of that shit. It was quiet. Peaceful. The only place I could hear myself think. There was this priest there most days. Father Simmons. I used to bring the cello to the hospital with me. I hoped the sound of it'd wake you up, so he already knew I played. He said it would be cathartic to write you a piece of music, like...like a way to say goodbye," he says awkwardly. "I had no plans on saying goodbye, but I wrote the piece anyway. It saved me. Occupied me while I was sitting there with you in that room, waiting for you to wake up. Once I'd finished, I played it for you over and over again. And then one day, while I was playing...your hand twitched."

I close my eyes against the mental picture that he's painting, hating every second of it. The pain in his voice is raw. Real. He sat by my bedside in that hospital every day for weeks, being told that I was going to die. I can't even imagine...

"After that, you seemed to respond whenever I played that specific piece of music," he murmurs into my hair. "So I kept fucking playing it. I didn't stop. About a week later, against all the odds, you woke up."

He stayed. For me. Here at Toussaint, even after he graduated. He stayed at the hospital with me. He didn't give up hope that I'd make it back to him, against all the odds. He wrote a piece of music for me that was supposed to help me pass and instead he used it to bring me back to life. I knew that music before I came back here with Gaynor. I've known it for months and months. It has been a constant melody, playing in the back of my mind, haunting and soothing me for as long as I can remember. He wrote me the song of my soul.

"I could hum something else to you if you like?" he offers. "Something I didn't write."

"Don't you dare," I whisper. "I want my requiem. I never want to hear anything else."

"You don't think it's morbid?"

I shake my head. "I think it's beautiful."

He's quiet for a while, thinking. "I played it for you again. That night in the auditorium. I thought maybe...it would bring you back a second time. Wake you up again, in a way. When you ran out of there, I hoped..."

That I'd remembered him. That the music had brought me back to myself properly at last. This boy is determined to make me cry. I won't be able to help myself if he carries on like this.

"I knew it meant something to me," I say. "I knew...it was important. And watching you play up there on that stage...you were the most amazing thing I'd ever seen. I felt like I was losing my mind. I had this strong, inexplicable feeling that..." I shake my head. "None of it made any sense."

"Do...you still have those feelings?" Theo whispers.

"Yes," I admit, whispering back.

He kisses me on the temple again, pressing his lips to my skin for a long second. I can tell that he's relieved. "Do they make more sense to you now?" he asks.

I go very still while I consider this question. "Not much of anything makes sense at the moment. But how I feel about you? I know that it feels...*right*."

He laughs gently.

"What?"

"Does that mean I don't have to sleep with one eye open anymore? There's nothing weirder than waiting for your amnesiac girlfriend to burst in and slit your throat in the middle of the night because she can't remember she's in love with you and she thinks you murdered her imaginary best friend."

"No, those feelings are gone now. I don't hate you anymore."

"That's a relief." He snorts, but the way he pulls me tighter to him, holding onto me like he's afraid I'm going to slip through his fingers, lets me know that this whole thing has been no joking matter to him. It's been hard. It's been fucking brutal.

The guilt that descends upon me might just eat me alive.

"Sorry," he says. "Sometimes it's easier to make fun of a shitty situation, y'know?"

I can't hold it against him. I have no recollection of the trauma we've both been through. Theo's lived and retained every second of it. He had to deal with me when I was Catherine, and that alone sounds like the stuff of nightmares. "It's okay. I get it. And...*I'm* sorry," I say. "I'll never be able to make any of this up to you. I don't even know where to start—"

"Don't." He squeezes me. "You don't *owe* me anything. Let's throw this thing in reverse. You asked me a question at lunch?"

"The virginity thing?" It doesn't even seem important anymore.

"Mmhmm."

"It's okay. We don't have to—"

"It was before the accident. You were you. I was your first."

"And I was yours?" He's quiet. Too quiet. I push away from him, laughing, a little scandalized. Looking up at him, I slap his chest playfully. "Were you a raging man-whore before I moved back from New York? I'm *shocked!*"

"No! Fuck! *No!*" He can't keep the grin off his face, though. He's self-conscious. I can see it in his eyes, and it's the most adorable thing I've ever seen. "I slept with one person before you. One time. She was..." he cringes, "...a Swedish exchange student."

A bark of laughter explodes from my chest. "You're lying!"

"I'm not." His eyes crinkle at the corners.

"You are fucking *lying!*"

"I swear to god I'm not. I told you about her in an email when you were living with your uncle. Any idea what her name was?" he prompts. He's started doing this—asking me random questions about little things, to see if I'll remember.

"Uhhh..." I wrack my brain. I have no specific recall of the email he sent me, so I guess instead. "Helga?"

He sobers a little. "Annika. She was two years older than me. And she had *so* much pubic hair."

"Oh my god. Stop. I can't. I can't."

"It was a terrible experience all around. I never...it never *counted* to me," he says, becoming very serious now. "I was too young to know what I was doing, and it didn't mean anything. When you and I slept together for the first time? We'd waited forever. I mean..." He raises his eyebrows, pulling a face. "*Forever,*" he emphasizes. "We teased the shit out of each other. Made each other come every chance we got. But the actual act of sex? We both wanted it to mean something. And it did. We were in New York. We'd gone to see your uncle before he died. It was also my birthday. We went to this amazing sushi restaurant for dinner."

I remember. Not the trip that he's recounting, but the time when he stood in my bedroom doorway, a matter of weeks ago. He'd asked me a question, while I threatened to hurl a snow globe at his head.

"Have you ever been to New York?"

"What?"

"It's a simple question. Have you ever been to New York?"

"Why would I have a snow globe of New York if I hadn't?"

His mouth had turned down. *"I don't know. People collect those things. People give them as gifts. Where's your favorite place in the world?"*

I hadn't been able to answer him then, and I still can't now. A profound sense of loss swamps me, making my chest ache. "*You* bought me that snow globe. The one in my room," I say.

Theo, about to continue his story, stops short. His shoulders sagging a little. "You said the skyline reminded you of Christmas and how you'd look out of the window and daydream about coming to see me for the holida—"

"Stop!"

Theo freezes, immediately anxious. "What? Is it your head? Is it hurting?"

"No, no, I'm okay. I just—" I don't know how to explain myself. I have to try, though. "I changed my mind. I don't want you to tell me this. I want the chance to remember. It sounds like it was...special..."

Theo's eyes shine brightly. His cheeks are a little red, his color high. "It was more than that. It was everything."

"That settles it. I don't want to hear about it second hand. I want to get back there and relive it for myself. Those memories are still up here, I'm sure they are." I tap the side of my head. "I'm gonna get them back. I'm gonna work my ass off until I remember every second of our life together before the accident."

Cautiously, I reach up and do something I've been dying to do for weeks; I use the tip of my finger to lightly trace a line between the freckles that make up the triangle underneath Theo's eye. He laughs softly, closing his eyes as I do it. He looks so at peace. I almost expect him to start purring like a cat.

"Have I done this before?" I whisper.

He nods *very* slowly. "You have." Eyes opening, he gingerly reaches up a hand and strokes his fingers along *my* cheekbone, down my cheek, carefully, as if I might break. I'd put money on that—that he *does* think I'm going to break. How awful that must be, to be holding your breath, waiting for the person you love to splinter apart and not be themselves anymore. To watch them become someone else, over and over and over again.

"I mean it," I tell him. "I'm gonna figure this out. I'm going to get my memories back. We've got time. And I'm not going anywhere."

He smiles a smile that says he knows better. "You promise?"

This is a promise that I can't make. Shouldn't make. There are no guarantees here. But I find myself making it anyway. "I promise."

He brushes his lips gently over mine, and all the world goes quiet. "I've decided," he whispers against my mouth, "that it doesn't matter either way. I've thought about it long and hard over the past couple of weeks, and it doesn't matter. If you get your memories back, then that'll be amazing. If you don't..." He pauses, stealing another featherlight kiss. "It'll be okay. I've discovered recently that I can be endlessly patient when the need arises. If I have to wait for you to fall in love with me all over again, then that's okay with me. I can do that. I'll cherish the past we shared for the both of us, and we can look to the future instead. Because we still have a fuckload of firsts to look forward to, Kid."

My heart breaks to hear him talk like this. Our history sounds beautiful. It must have been, for a guy like him to have walked through fire to try and save me. I hate the thought of abandoning something that must have been incredibly important to me, too. But I do like the sound of us making new memories together. Ones that will be mine and don't belong to another version of me. "Oh yeah?" I smile up to him, twirling a curl of his hair around my fingers. "And what kind of firsts might *they* be?"

"Well." His smile is wickedly suggestive; I melt at the sight of it. "We've never been together here before."

I look around his bedroom. "Seriously? We haven't?"

"I didn't board here before. I only moved into the academy this year. I wanted to be closer to you. So yeah. If I were to strip you naked and fuck the shit out of you in *this* room, it would be a completely new experience for the both of us."

I want Theo.

I need him.

I'm drawn to him so desperately that I can barely breathe when I'm around him. I've already had him inside me, and it was the highlight of my entire fucking life. Hearing him talk about fucking me shouldn't make me blush, but it does. I duck my head. Theo tuts, mirroring me, moving so that he's occupying my line of sight all over again. "You can't hide from me. I'd have thought you'd figured that out by now," he says. His left hand moves to my t-shirt. His fingers trail over my stomach at first, but they quickly travel upward, the light contact making me break out in goosebumps as he heads north. Within seconds, he's tracing a pathway upward toward the swell of my breasts; he hisses when he realizes that I'm not wearing a bra. *I* hiss when he locates my nipple and begins to draw lazy circles around and around it, causing it to peak and stiffen. A wolfish hunger settles over him when he flicks it, making me squirm in his lap. "It's been hell, sleeping upstairs, knowing that you're down here. So close. I've made myself come every night, imagining all of the depraved shit I could be doing to you."

"Shit. Theo—"

"Do you want me? You only have to say the word," he rumbles.

"Yes. God, yes! It's been nearly two weeks since...since the last time." Lord have mercy, why is this so hard to say this to him? To fucking *think*. "I figured that maybe I wasn't...the *same* or...something. That I was better before? I suppose I figured that you haven't wanted me because I'm so diff—"

Theo's mouth collides with mine. The air in my lungs is heavy as lead; there's no pushing it out of me. No pulling fresh air in. My muscles lock, rigid and unresponsive. I can't fucking move. My blood roars in my ears when Theo cups my face, holding me steady as he parts my lips and slides his tongue past my teeth.

He tastes like mint, and sugar, and cold mountain air. A current fires to life in my veins, crackling, spitting, biting at my nerve endings, jumpstarting me to life. A second later, I'm clawing at him, winding my fingers through his hair, kissing him back, desperate to be closer to him, to feel every part of him crushed against my body, to have his hands on my skin, under my shirt, his palms on my naked breasts, his fingers gouging into my skin.

Fuck.

Fuck.

FUCK!

If I don't calm down, I'm going to start hyperventilating. Theo pulls back a little, grinning. He laughs against my lips, nipping and biting at them, teasing me, still cupping my face in his hands. "I wanted to give *you* some time. I wanted to make sure you wanted *me*. Seems as though we've both been waiting on the other person to give us the green light."

"The lights are green. Oh my god, the lights are always green. Please fucking touch me. I'm losing my mind."

He rips at my clothes. I'm topless first. My pants are gone shortly after. I scrabble at his shirt, tearing it off over his head. My hands shake as I unfasten his belt, but Theo doesn't rush me. He kneels up on the bed, hands by his sides, watching me, his gaze searing into my flesh. I finally manage to get the damned belt undone, then his pants. I drag them down his legs, sighing against my will when his cock springs free and I realize that he hasn't been wearing any underwear.

His dick is perfect. It's length. It's girth—it looks good enough to fucking eat. So fucking hard and standing to attention. A silver scar runs from the head of his cock downward, a centimeter long, and I already somehow know that this is from when he was seven, when he had an emergency circumcision after he fell off his bike. His balls are pulled up tight beneath his shaft, heavy and swollen. I want to touch him so badly, but when I go to wrap my hand around him, he grabs my wrist and shakes his head.

"Not yet. You don't get to touch me until I've had my fill of *you* first."

I nearly whimper, like a spoiled little brat who can't get her way. I want to feel him heavy in my palm. I want to feel the smooth, silken texture of his skin as I shuttle my hand up and down his length. It's wholly unfair that he won't let me have what I want.

Theo lifts my hand and places it against his chest. He takes my other hand and places it there, too, so that my palms are braced against his pecs. His skin, his warmth, his muscle—fuck! I practically purr like an alley cat in heat when I start to explore the curves and lines of his torso. My palms are on fire. I gouge my nails into him, on either side of the burning sun that has been inked onto his body. It's a thing of elaborate beauty. *He* is beautiful, in the same way that panthers, and sharks, and other sharp-toothed predators are beautiful. There *is* a danger to him. He could destroy me if he wanted to. He could rip out my heart and grind it to dust. He could sweep me away from myself, send me hurtling off a cliff face, so that I tumble, and spin, and never stop falling.

Without a shadow of a doubt, this guy could bring me to my knees and keep me there indefinitely, using me for whatever twisted pleasure he saw fit, and I would never complain. I would accept each new deviance gladly, without complaint, and then beg him for more.

"How far do you wanna take this?" Theo asks, running his thumb along the edge of my jaw. "You want me gentle, or do you want me raw?"

"How r—raw?" I stammer.

"That's for you to find out. You can take the easy option. Back down. Or you can be brave. It's up to you."

Holy shit. His voice is husky, made of velvet. His words caress my skin, soft as silk, turning me to liquid fire. My stomach flips, need building between my legs. My pussy clenches, anticipating his touch, the rigid hardness of him pushing up inside me, and a wave of need whips my breath away.

"I can be brave. I'll follow your lead." I rush the words out before I can change my mind. *"Please!"*

Swiftly, he throws me back onto the bed, pinning my arms over my head with one strong hand. With a knee, he shoves my legs apart, settling himself between them, and then he falls on me. His mouth finds my nipple and the world ignites.

"Fuck! Ahhh! Holy shit, Theo!"

He works me with his tongue first, swirling the tip of it around the hardened bud, wetting my areola, licking and laving at the swell of flesh. I watch him, heart thumping right out of my chest, mesmerized by the sight of him. My pulse pounds between my legs. Every time he sweeps the flat of his tongue over me, another piece of my sanity chips away.

"Shit. Ahhh shit. Oh my god, I want you so fucking bad!"

He looks up at me, still dipped over my body, and when our eyes make contact over my breasts, I nearly fucking scream.

He is *so* hot. His halo of dark hair. The ink creeping up his neck. The sheer perfection of his body, lithe muscle shifting beneath smooth skin. There are no words to describe the intensity of my need for him. We're trapped by this eye contact, locked together, our desire pouring out of us, feeding into each other.

"You can have me when I say so, Kid. Not a second earlier. Now lie still and let me make you feel good."

I feel more than good. I feel fucking *desperate*.

Theo takes my nipple into his mouth again, sucking on it, and my eyes roll back into my head. I moan, arching away from the bed, trying to lean into the perfect heat of his mouth and the rough-edged spike of pain that fires from both of my nipples directly to my clit when he grazes me with his teeth.

"You like that," he rumbles. "Good girl. You like a little pain."

I do. I do. I do. *"Ahhh!"* He bites harder, and I clench my teeth together, grappling with the beautiful agony. I gasp when he grabs my breast with his free hand digging his fingers into my skin, holding me in place while he sucks and bites and flicks me with his tongue. Just when I'm on the verge of crying out, he switches to the other breast, the other nipple, and repeats his ministrations on that one. Peaked and hard enough to cut glass, my nipples are so sensitive that every time he makes contact, my head reels out of control.

"Mmm." He hums against my skin, sending delicious vibrations of pleasure firing down my body; they gather at the apex of my thighs, driving me wild.

"I could do this all goddamn day," Theo growls. "You have the most amazing tits. Your nipples are perfection. I'd lock us in this room and just suck on them for the rest of time if I thought I could get away with it."

That would be the most divine kind of torture.

I arch up away from the bed again, my spine curving off the mattress. I want him to bite me again. I'm dying to feel that frisson of pain shooting down to my pussy. Theo tuts, reprimanding me. "I told you to lie still."

"I'm— I'm trying," I pant.

"You can't have everything you want, when you want it." He releases my hands. "I'm in charge of the pleasure you receive right now. I get to give it. I get to take it away." He lets go of my breast and traces his fingertips down, over the hollow dip of my stomach, leaving a trail of fire in his wake. I moan when he inches them down further still, the muscles in my legs jumping when he starts to stroke the inside of my legs. So, so fucking close. He gets so close to touching my pussy, but then he changes course at the very last moment, leaving me vibrating with nervous energy.

I *need* him to touch me. His slow, featherlight contact is going to make me lose my mind. My hips buck up off the bed, but Theo shakes his head, grabbing me and pushing me back down. "Rude, Voss. Very, very rude. Wait."

God, he's trying to kill me. He's legitimately going to be the death of me if he doesn't give me what I need and soon. *"Theo!"*

The wicked son of a bitch smirks at me cruelly, his dark eyes sparking with dominance. "Your tits are mine. Your cunt is mine. Your ass is mine. Your orgasms are mine. I'll touch you when and how I please. I'll let you come when I say you're ready. Yes?"

He cups his hand over my pussy, applying a firm pressure, and while he's not touching my clit or fucking me directly, the act of him doing that, cupping my sex, has me seeing stars. It ignites the heavy ache building there, amplifying the demands my body is making. When he removes his hand, drawing a line down my center with his index finger, I damn near come apart.

Theo grunts disapprovingly. "*Yes,* Voss? I need you to say it."

"Yes! YES!"

"Good." He runs his finger along me again, but this time he parts me, rubbing, quickly finding my clit. He groans, and my eyelids shutter closed. "Fuck," he whispers. "So hot. So fucking wet. So fucking sexy. You have no idea what you do to me."

I know what he's doing to me, and it's borderline cruelty at this point. If I thought begging again would help, I'd do it. I'd tell him anything right now if only he would slam himself inside me and answer this feverish call in my blood.

"I'm going to eat your pussy until you scream," Theo promises. "And then I'm going to fuck that pretty little mouth with my cock. And then…" He probes me, sliding a finger inside me, barely entering me, just enough for me to suck in a startled breath. "Then I'm going to fuck you here. And here." His finger slides back, running through my slick heat, until he reaches my ass.

I open my eyes.

Theo stares down at me, his expression intense. His eyes lock with mine as he teases his finger over my asshole, where he rubs me gently, apparently waiting for me to react.

Have we done this before? Is this another one of those new firsts for us that Theo was just talking about, or is this ground we've already trodden?

Fuck.

I bite down on my bottom lip as he carefully pushes his finger a little deeper, and a shockwave of heat rolls through me from my feet to the crown of my head.

"Feel good?" Theo asks roughly.

I surprise myself by nodding.

"I'm gonna make it feel *really* good, Kid. Don't worry." He falls down between my legs and I cry out, a strangled animal sound slipping free from me as Theo starts working my clit with his tongue.

Holy...

Fuck!

His mouth is so fucking hot. The feel of him laving and licking at me almost sends me over the edge in two short seconds, but then he eases back a little, the pressure he's applying lessening as he taunts me with the very tip of his tongue.

Since he's no longer restraining me, I wind my fingers into his hair, cradling his head, gripped by the need to pull him down onto me, to make him give me the same level of pressure he just took away from me. I refrain somehow. Sliding his fingers inside me, Theo pumps them in and out of me, wickedly slow, until my whole body begins to quake. A building wall of pleasure kindles in the pit of my stomach, in my chest, between my legs—I can't tell *where* it's building; I feel it everywhere, all at once, eating me alive, consuming me from my core to my extremities. The roaring inside my ears grows to a deafening pitch, but I manage to keep myself still.

I shake. Tremble. I can't fucking stop. Theo groans into my pussy, sucking on my clit, and—and—

"Oh shit. Oh fuck, you're gonna make me come!"

Quickly, Theo lifts my legs, pushing my knees up to my chest, and yanks my hips, angling me so that I'm even more exposed and every part of me is available to him. He drives his face into my pussy, feasting on me, fucking me with his fingers faster than before. With his free hand, he teases my asshole again, rubbing my slickness all over me, and then—

Oh my god.

He has a finger inside me there, too.

I stiffen, overwhelmed by the sensation, the oxygen frozen in my lungs. I'd scream if I could, but I can't. He licks and sucks on my clit, working his fingers inside me. The building pleasure evolves into a raging furnace, biting at my nerve endings.

I—

Stars.

The room is an explosion of *stars*.

A crescendo of ecstasy detonates through my body. I cling onto his head, wildly rocking my hips up to meet him, shamelessly grinding my pussy against his mouth.

Now I scream.

"THEO! FUCK! OH…MY…*FUCK!*"

I've never experienced this before. I can't see, hear, think, breathe. All I can do is rock against his mouth as I come.

An age passes before I return to my body, limp and languid, my insides molten.

When Theo sits back, gently sliding his fingers out of me, the look of satisfaction he wears is so glorious that I'm nearly brought to tears.

His mouth is wet, lips glistening, his chest heaving. "I fucking *felt* that," he growls. "You were fucking perfect."

The air that wouldn't come to me while I was gripped in my orgasm floods me, making me dizzy. I've barely caught my breath when Theo climbs up my body and kneels, one leg on either side of my head.

"Open," he commands.

He is so fucking sexy, towering over me, his cheeks high with color. He is a storm personified, treacherous and deadly. I have no option but to obey him.

I open my mouth.

"Stick out your tongue."

Breathing hard down my nose, I stick out my tongue.

Theo's eyes shutter as he takes his cock in his hand and slowly rubs the tip across the flat of my tongue. He tastes clean, of soap, and of something else too, musky and slightly sweet. He silently mouths the word, *"Fuck,"* as he rolls his hips forward, sliding himself into my mouth. He's so hard. So big. I can barely breathe around him.

I've wanted this. In bed at night, tangled in my sheets, frustrated and alone, this is what I've thought about. Theo rocks himself deeper, pushing himself further down my throat, and my eyes start to water. He catches his bottom lip between his teeth as he draws himself out and then back again, setting a pace that's manageable for me—just about—as he makes good on his promise and fucks my mouth.

"Jesus Christ, Voss. Your mouth. Your fucking mouth." The muscles in Theo's shoulders, arms and across his chest tense, locking as he watches me suck.

His erection grows even harder as he guides himself into my mouth, holding himself at the base of his cock. I run my hands up his legs, gripping his thighs, doing my best to swirl my tongue around the length of him, but it's all I can do to keep regulating my inhalations as he quickens his pace.

"Fuck. Holy shit, you're gonna make me blow like this," he says, voice rough.

I reach between his legs, cupping his balls, and Theo falls forward, bracing himself against the wall behind us as he continues to rock himself past my lips.

"Yes. Fuck yes. Just like that. Good girl."

His balls tighten in my hand, and I get the feeling that if he keeps going like this, he *is* going to come. Tears streak from the corners of my eyes, over my temples and into my hair. Open mouthed and fierce as hell, the look on Theo's face makes another wave of heat rock my core. He's loving this, and it's *my* mouth making him feel this way. A strange sense of pride washes over me. I tip my head back, allowing him deeper, sacrificing my breath, and Theo's legs begin to tremble.

"Shit. Oh god, Sorrell. That feels… that feels fucking incredible. You take my cock so well. You're such a good…fucking…girl!"

Another three seconds and his whole body is shaking.

"Fuck, stop, stop, stop!" He jerks back, withdrawing from me, his cock making a wet popping sound as he frees himself from my mouth. He sinks back onto his heels, his chest heaving. "I can't," he pants. "It's too good. I have to fucking have you."

I nearly pass out when he thrusts into me. The feel of him, so goddamn hard, throbbing, is too, too much. "Theo! Jesus! Please!" It's all I can get out before he starts driving himself into me at a punishing pace.

I think he originally planned on holding back, on drawing this out, but he can't. I can see it in his eyes. Leaning forward, he wraps a hand around my throat, cutting off my oxygen again.

"You're mine," he hisses. "*Mine.*"

"Yes!"

He's thrusts himself into me, again and again and again.

"You're gonna come for me, Sorrell. Come all over my cock. Right. Fucking. Now!"

I clench, riding out the swelling sensation of bliss coursing through my veins. He's going to tip me over the edge. He's… oh my god, *ohmygodohmygodohmygod!*

"That's it. Come. Come. Fucking come!"

My mind goes blank.

A high-pitched ringing fills my ears.

I bow away from the bed, my back arching to painful degrees. Theo holds me by the hips, releasing my throat, slamming himself home so hard and so fast, coming with me.

"Theo!"

He roars with his release, head thrown back, the veins in his neck standing proud, and the sheer sight of him coming undone like this makes me feel like I'm levitating out of my body again. He is fucking magnificent. He is…he is a fucking *god.*

Eventually, his head rocks forward, his body loosening. His fingers still gouge into my skin at my hips, possessive and unrelenting, though. His eyes find mine, and a flood of emotion saws into me, so alien and unknown that it feels like it's going to suffocate me. Inexplicably, a lump forms in my throat. My eyes burn, my vision swimming.

What the hell was that? How the fuck did he just make me come that hard? *Twice?* And…and what the hell am I *feeling* right now? A welter of emotions twist around my bones, making knots of my insides. I'm overwhelmed, so brought to my knees, confused by the sheer power of this thing between us, that I can't for one second comprehend how the hell I'm going to handle the sheer magnitude of *us*.

Theo leans forward, lying onto the bed next to me, turning me at the same time so that he can stay inside of me. He cups my face in his hands, stroking his fingers over my cheeks. The heat of his skin against mine soothes me. The scent of him, all wild mint and winter rain, grounds me. It feels so right, to be tangled up in him like this, our bodies connected, our hearts slamming in our chests. "Sorrell," he whispers. "What did I do? Why are you crying?"

If I answer him, then I might just end up telling him the truth, and I can't. I cannot tell Theo Merchant that he doesn't need to be patient. He doesn't need to wait for me to fall in love with him again. I *am* in love with him. I don't understand where this feeling, this *knowledge*, has come from, but it is a force so massive that it can't be turned away. This tremendous love I feel for him in this moment has always been inside me, lying dormant, biding its time, waiting to rise to the surface, and now that it's here, it's too big for me to contain and I'm overflowing with it.

I feel so fucking stupid, but I am small in the face of this. I cry into his chest, great heaving sobs wracking my body. "Nothing. You haven't done anything," I choke out.

"Shhh. It's okay. It's okay. I've got you. Just breathe." Theo holds me, running his hands over my hair, quieting me.

The words burn on my tongue, begging to be set free, but I can't.

I just *can't*.

THEO

I'M NERVOUS AS SHIT.

I stare at the notice tacked to the board, my breath hitching erratically. This could either be a good thing, or a really, really bad thing, and my emotions have been tossed around, put through the wringer and shredded so many damned times at this point that I can't figure out which way I'm leaning. I used to be able to trust my gut when it came to this kind of stuff, but that was before. Before the version of Sorrell that called herself Catherine nearly put me in an early fucking grave.

I run a hand through my hair, gnawing on the inside of my cheek.

SENIOR YEAR RESTRICTIONS NOW LIFTED. EVENING PASSES DURING THE WEEK TO SUMNER PERMITTED, PROVIDING 9PM CURFEW STRICTLY OBSERVED.
CELL RECEPTION/INTERNET ACCESS NOW RESTORED ACROSS THE ACADEMY.

BE ADVISED: ANY INFRACTION OR FLOUTING OF THE RULES WILL RESULT IN IMMEDIATE SUSPENSION AND REVIEW OF ENROLLMENT BY THE BOARD.

DON'T MESS THIS UP.

"I suppose now that Sorrell knows the truth, Ford and the others don't really need to shutter us away," my sister muses, standing next to me. Ever the light-footed little punk, she's snuck up on me. I haven't given two shits about being here, in the same year as her, until now. I've had way bigger fish to fry. But now that Sorrell does indeed know the truth, my baby sister's presence has begun to grate a touch. I love her, sure, but I could do without sharing a friend group with her.

"Don't you dare tell anyone that Sorrell was the reason Ford found ways to lock us down here," I grumble. "It's bad enough that Seb and Ash and Beth know. If any of the other students find out, they're gonna take it out on Sorrell, and—"

Lani elbows me sharply in the ribs. "Do I look like an idiot?"

I look her up and down out of the corner of my eye, smirking at the pink knee-high socks she's wearing. "That's a matter of perspective."

She sticks her tongue out. "Asshole. All I'm saying is, now that she knows *most* of the truth—"

"What do you mean, *most* of the truth?"

Lani's left eyebrow hikes halfway up her forehead. "You know exactly what I'm talking about. Now that she's armed with *most* of the truth, we're free to go back to our regular lives. That means you can take her into town, back to Patty's. Back to The Jump. Maybe being back at all of the places we used to hang out will jog her memories some."

"She's already starting to remember some stuff."

"Right. But the odd detail here and there isn't really progress, Theo. It'll take ten years for her to recover fully if we don't try and push things a little."

I growl, anger flaring in my gut. "It doesn't matter if she gets everything back. She's fine just the way she is."

"You've changed your tune. A couple of weeks ago, you were desperate for her to get it all back at once. Now, you're...what? Just willing to accept that she might never fully recover?"

I meant what I said to Sorrell yesterday, in my room. It used to be vital to me that she remember every single encounter we've ever shared up until recently. Things have been good, though. Better than good. In the past, pushing Sorrell to remember has been the very thing that's made her slip away. I won't risk losing who she is now simply because I'm selfish and I want her to remember us. "Yeah, well, I'm entitled to change my mind. We just have to accept that this is the way things are. Sorrell might not get her memories back. There's no point beating a dead horse."

My sister, always so full of opinions and advice, is conspicuously quiet. She gives me a weary look. "What? If you've got something to say, you might as well say it now instead of in a couple of hours, when you can't bite your tongue any longer."

"There is a way for her to remember, though, isn't there? And you seem to be making a lot of decisions on other people's behalf. We've been here before, and it hasn't ended well in the past. If you'll recall—"

"*I'm* not the one with the memory problems, Lani. Just keep those thoughts to yourself, okay?" I hate that she's right. I am making decisions for Sorrell. There *are* things I haven't told her, but that doesn't mean it's okay for my little sister to stick her nose in where it's not wanted.

"Walking on thin ice," Lani says in a sing-song voice.

"Just quit it. If I can keep Sorrell from seeing this for a couple of days," I say, ripping the notice from the board, "that will give me some more time to figure out how to talk to her about...*everything*."

"Hah! Good luck with that. These things are posted all over the academy. Seb and Callum are rallying the troops. They've planned a hangout down in Sumner for tonight already. Half the academy's talking about it."

I groan, pinching the bridge of my nose. Great. Of course Seb's chomping at the bit already. What a fucking shocker that he immediately wants to party as soon as we're given our freedom back. He and I haven't spoken since he hurt Sorrell. The guy's lucky he can still eat solid food. If I'd had my way, he'd already have been shipped off, out of Toussaint, but it's too late for him to head off to college this year now, and the factors that have kept him here in the first place are still at play. Beth and Ashley, too.

"Look. If I were you, I'd talk to her before anyone else can," Lani warns. "I mean, maybe she's happy staying here at the Academy for the time being. She might not even *want* to go into town."

I huff, clinging to that hope a little more desperately than I'd like to admit. "Yeah, you're right. This has been a lot for her already. Maybe she *won't* wanna go."

* * *

"Are you kidding me? I absolutely want to go!"

Sorrell's eyes dance with excitement. In her short little black skirt and strappy top, her long dark hair tied back into braids, she looks like a cute little manga character. I always used to love when she dressed like this. Throwing her arms around my neck, she laughs with what sounds like sheer relief. "Do you have any idea how hard I've tried to escape this place? I've been cooped up here for months. So have you. We all have. I can't *wait* to get out of here. We can go have dinner somewhere. Watch a movie or something. Wait." She leans back, her brows pinching together, the bridge of her nose wrinkling cutely. "Is there anywhere to go have dinner? Is there a movie theater? Oh god, I just want to do something *normal* for once."

I have to laugh. Despite the worry that's using my bones as toothpicks, I can't help myself. "Yes, there are restaurants in Sumner. The movie theater's tiny and smells like stale popcorn. They never have the newest releases playing but—"

"I don't care. I really don't!" she crows. "I wanna go. With you. Just the two of us."

Relief floods me, beating back some of my concerns, but not all of them. There's still so much that can go wrong if we spend time in Sumner. I risked it when I took Sorrell to Patty's, the night I told her the truth, because I figured I had nothing to lose. It was two in the morning, so I knew the place would be dead. I thought she'd immediately slip away, too shocked by the truth to handle the enormity of it all, and I'd be taking her back to the hospital anyway. But that isn't what happened. She'd coped with it, as much as any person could, and now I'm left fearful that being out in society will just be too fucking much, all at once.

I smile through my apprehension, plastering a broad grin on my face for her. She doesn't deserve to suffer the weight of all the worst-case scenarios bouncing around inside my head. Not when she seems so goddamn happy.

"Alright then. Dinner and a movie it is." I can deal with dinner and a movie. I think she can, too. So long as we steer clear of Seb and his crew, we should be fine. And who am I to deny her a little normalcy? I'd be a stone-cold fucking liar if I said I didn't crave that with her as well.

* * *

My heart does that weird backflipping thing when Sorrell steps out of her bedroom and closes the door behind her. She's dressed in skintight black jeans and a low-cut top that shows off her tits in the most distracting way. Her lips are painted blood red, and the pop of color draws my attention to her mouth—a mouth I still fantasize about doing very filthy things to. I have to scrub the mental image of her lips wrapped around my cock before I can even bend down to kiss her. Her hair is a waterfall of black waves, lush and thick, just begging for me to mess it up. I know she spent a long time blow drying and styling it for our date, however, so I settle for cupping her face in my hands, my thumbs stroking the line of her cheekbones as I kiss her gently.

"You are the most exquisite thing I've ever fucking seen," I murmur against her mouth. "I wanna get you all dirty."

"Yeah?"

"I want you covered in my sweat and come. Fuck dinner. We're staying here."

"You're going to get red on you," she says breathlessly.

"What, you don't think I could pull it off?" Flicking my tongue against her lips, I growl, desperate to kiss her more deeply, to sweep my tongue over hers, to explore and devour every inch of her. If I were to give into my darkest desires right now, I'd open that door behind her and shove her back into her room. I'd have her on her hands and knees with her ass in the air, and I'd be buried up to my balls in her pussy. But this date is important to her.

As far as she knows, we've never been on an actual date before. All of the concerts we went to together, all of the movies we've seen, all of the weekend trips we've taken, all of the times I've badly cooked for her, or she's badly cooked for me… Those experiences are lost to her. She needs to experience just how amazing those moments are way more than I need to fuck her, so I rein in the heat building between us, pulling back to survey her beautiful face. "Seriously. You look incredible. Sumner, population 1287, isn't gonna know what's hit it."

She bounces on the balls of her feet like an adorable little kid. I haven't seen her do this in far too long. "You clean up pretty nice yourself, y'know." She eyes the dark blue button-down shirt and jeans I picked out for this evening with some amusement. "Don't take this the wrong way, but I really did think every single item of clothing you owned was threadbare and ancient."

"Yeah, well." I give her a small smile. "Clothes shopping hasn't been a very high priority on my to-do list, the past couple of years."

A flash of what looks like guilt passes over her features. Her grin dims a fraction. "I suppose not. You've been hanging out in ICUs and running around after that amnesiac with the multiple personality disorder, haven't you?"

Ahhh shit. I'm such an asshole. I didn't mean to spoil her good mood. I certainly didn't mean to make her feel bad. "You don't have a multiple personality disorder, Kid. And there was literally no place on Earth I would rather have been. And anyway, I was just using that shit as an excuse not to go shopping."

She chuckles a little, her smile returning. "You hate it that much, huh?"

"So much. It's the fucking *worst*. But I bought this shit online, so…"

"I'm honored that you'd go to such great lengths to look good for me."

"You should be," I say, nipping at her bottom lip. "You...really... fucking...should...be..." My hands roam downward, cupping her tits over her top, and that fire starts building again. My dick's already hard as hell. When her breathing quickens, her chest rising, her back arching, body curving into me, I can't bite back the groan that slips out of my mouth. I want her so fucking bad. God, what I wouldn't give to just strip her naked and bury my face in her bare chest. I'd make it last an eternity this time. I'd have her slick with sweat, begging for another orgasm quicker than you can say—

"Holy fuck, we have to go right now or I'm seriously going to fuck the living shit out of you." I shake my head, stepping away from her.

Sorrell's pupils are blown, her cheeks flushed. By the look on her face, she was just imagining all of the dirty shit we'd get up to if we let this fire burn a little brighter between us, too. She laughs, and the sound makes my chest ache with joy. Her eyes travel down my body, settling just below my waistband. "You'd better hope that your hard-on settles down by the time we reach town, or you're gonna be getting some strange looks, baby."

Baby.

It's a trite term of affection, one that would have made my skin crawl and my teeth itch a long time ago, but I used to *love* when Sorrell called me that. This is the first time she's called me baby since the accident, and the sound of that word on her lips makes a lump form in the base of my throat.

"Sorry. Was that—was that dumb?" Anxiety clouds her eyes. "I don't know why I said that. It just...came out."

"No. It wasn't dumb. That's...what you always used to call me," I tell her slowly. "Before."

I can't tell if that makes her happy or if it freaks her out. She just nods, taking my hand. "Okay then. Let's go, baby. I'm fucking starving."

SORRELL

It's bitterly cold outside. Overhead, a sea of stars bristles above us in the expanse of velvet black, distant pinpricks of light that I find myself appreciating for the first time since I arrived at Toussaint. The night is close and dense like a shroud. It presses in from all sides, clinging to us as we make our way down to the parking lot.

Yeah, that's right.

There's a goddamn parking lot. It's nearly half a mile away from the academy, located on the other side of the hill behind the school's gym. With the lockdown in place and weekend passes revoked, none of Toussaint's students were permitted to venture over there. It's a miracle that no one ever mentioned it in passing, but…then again, why would they? Frankly, I feel stupid when I first see it.

Down the grassy slope leading away from the hillside, the small lot is half empty now, with half of the senior year either in Seattle or down in Sumner, there are still plenty of vehicles sitting in the numerous numbered spots. Had I have known about it, I probably would have stolen a car in order to escape weeks ago. I would have hot-wired one of the older models and bailed as soon as I could have. Only, I probably can't hot wire a car. I just thought that I could.

Theo is quiet as he drives us into town. The silence is comfortable, though, and I relish it as we cut through the dark, winding our way to an unknown destination that Theo insisted on keeping a secret. A part of me is disappointed when we sail straight down the lit-up main street, heading to the very outskirts of Sumner.

Pulling into a tiny restaurant's parking lot, I grin when I see the name of the place: *The Golden Palace.* "Chinese food? Chinese food is my favorite!"

Concentrating on the rearview mirror as he parks the car, Theo spares me a sheepish sidelong look, and realization hits me like a lightning bolt.

"Urgh. You already knew that, didn't you?" I say.

"I might have already known that," he admits. "It might look kinda seedy, but the food here is incredible."

"Have we been here before?" It seems like a stupid question. Sumner isn't very big, by all accounts, and there can't be that many restaurants. We *must* have eaten here before the accident. For some reason, I want to know, though. For sure.

"We have," Theo confirms.

"And I like it?"

Theo kills the car's engine. He smirks devilishly. "Why don't we go find out?"

I can't wait. Theo jumps out of the car and runs around to the passenger side, rushing to open my door for me. This gentlemanly side to him is a far cry from the guy I first met at Toussaint. He smirks at me, more handsome than ever, but his expression changes as I climb out of the Mustang. Pain flashes across his face. I slam the car door, rounding on him. He shakes out his hand, wincing.

"Oh my god, are you all right?"

"Yeah, it just spasms sometimes. The nerve damage gets triggered by the cold."

"You have *nerve damage?"*

"Ah. Yeahhh, kind of. I can do most things, and it won't bother me, but playing can hurt a lot. The tape helps a little. Makes my fingertips burn a little less. Looks crazy, but…whoa. What's up? You okay?"

"You aren't going to be a concert cellist anymore." Lani told me that, the day on the grass when I quizzed her about why he was always alone. I remember feeling super upset and uncomfortable about her comment. Now I understand why.

Theo looks a little uncomfortable. "No, I'm not."

"Because of *me*."

He throws his arm around my shoulder, drawing me to him. Slamming the passenger side door, he kisses me on the top of my head. "It was an accident, Kid. Accidents happen to people all over the world, all of the time. You didn't crash the car because you were drunk, or tired, or..." He shrugs. "It just wasn't your fault. I smashed that window because I needed you out of all that twisted metal. I'd do it again, and again, and again..."

"Your whole career—"

He takes me by the chin, forcing me to look up at him. His expression is the most serious I've ever seen it. "I'm going to be a doctor instead," he says. "Your accident made me obsessive about the human brain. It's fascinating to me. I want to research these kinds of head injuries and figure out how to help repair them. I'll never be able to operate, but I'm excited to have a whole new career path to look forward to. One that I find interesting as hell. So no, I won't be a concert cellist. But I will still play for myself, and for *you*, because I love it. Plus my mother's much happier that I'll have a job that pays eight times what I would ever have made with music, and she gets to tell everyone her son is going to be a doctor, so it's all working out for the best."

I feel terrible. Absolutely terrible. Is there a single aspect of Theo's life that the accident didn't destroy? It doesn't matter what he says. If I hadn't been driving that night, the car would never have hit the guard rail. I wouldn't have such a fucked-up brain, and he would be at Juilliard right now, halfway to accomplishing dreams he's had since he was a kid.

"Don't. Don't look like that, Kid. Life has a weird way of giving us what we need, not what we want. And I promise you that I'm okay. I'm happy."

"Did I *need* the traumatic head injury?" I ask, laughing a little grumpily.

"Maybe. Who knows?" Theo looks down at me with such surety,

with so much love in his eyes, that it's hard to feel sorry for myself, or for him, or for anyone else who's been affected by this shit show. "The lessons we've both learned from this experience have molded us. They're shaping us as we speak. They've definitely shown me how fucking miraculous and strong we both can be. I was angry about your injury *and* my hand for the longest time, but all that anger did was twist me up inside. I choose to see the positive now. I *know* that everything's gonna be okay."

I don't have the right to discount or discard Theo's words. Not after everything he's tolerated in order to stand by my side through this. So I nod, leaning my forehead against his chest. "Okay. All right. You're gonna look really hot in a lab coat, *Dr.* Merchant."

"Oh, believe me, I know!"

"Ahhh! So *arrogant!*" I jab him playfully in his ribs; I'm not expecting the reaction this provokes.

"Stop! Oh my god, STOP! I can't breathe!" he gasps.

I step back, mouth hanging open.

Theo *is* arrogant as hell. He can knock out a guy's front teeth with one right hook. He smashed a car window and dragged me out of a wreck before the car literally went up in flames.

He is also *ticklish?*

He holds up a finger, cocking his head to one side, still wearing a shit eating grin. "No. Don't you say a word. We don't talk about this, Voss."

"I had no idea you were so *sensitive.*"

"I swear to god, I will spank you so hard you'll have a handprint on your ass for a week if you tell anyone—"

"What if I *like* being spanked?"

"Get inside this restaurant before you get me into trouble," he growls.

Inside, the delicious scent of orange chicken and Mongolian beef hits me square in the nose. I nearly sink to my knees and start weeping tears of joy. "Oh my god. *Oh my god!*" I moan.

"Okay, now you're just fucking with me. You'd better stop that or you're gonna make my dick hard again."

"Promises, promises."

Theo's warning look, dominant and possessive, makes my toes curl inside my shoes. "I don't need to make promises on that front, Voss. You already know it's true. I'll fuck you right here in the bathrooms if you don't behave yourself."

I'm tempted to take him up on this threat, but my stomach growls, reminding me that we should at least sample some of the amazing-smelling food here first, before we get banned for life and they tell us never to come back.

The Golden Palace is packed, couples seated at the booths and tables across the restaurant floor. The air hums with chatter. We're seated in the only available booth by the window, and when the host removes a 'reserved' sign from the table, I realize that Theo must have called ahead and booked this specific spot for us ahead of time. He looks a little red-faced as he slides into the booth opposite me, making a show of picking up the menu and studying it intensely.

"Is this *our* table, Theo?" I ask coyly.

"What do you mean?"

"Is this *our* table. Is this booth special for us?"

He shrugs nonchalantly, trying to play it off. "Quit asking questions and check out the menu, Kid." I didn't know Theo Merchant was capable of blushing. It's endearing as hell that he's doing so now. I want to tease him for it so bad, but I think any further ribbing might just make him explode with embarrassment, so I hold my tongue.

We place our orders—some of that Mongolian beef I smelled when we came in, and special fried rice. Some spring rolls, and chicken and mushrooms in oyster sauce—and the waitress doesn't even flinch when Theo orders us two beers.

As soon as she leaves, I lean across the table and whisper to him. "She didn't ID you?"

Theo becomes the embodiment of awkwardness. He shifts in his seat, then picks up his chopsticks and taps them nervously against his water glass.

"What? What is it?"

"Uhhh..."

"What?"

"Well..."

"Theo!"

"We had fake IDs for this place years ago. They stopped asking us a long time ago. And besides…" He squirms in his seat., looking like he wants to run and hide.

I just stare at him.

"We're *almost* old enough to drink anyway."

I nearly spit out my water. *"What?!"*

"Well, yeah. We both turned eighteen six months before the accident. And that was…" He raises his eyebrows, waiting for me to do the math.

"Oh…my *god.*" Shock slams into me, sinking its teeth deep.

He nods. "Yeahhhh. We both turn twenty-one in a couple of months."

What. The. Actual. FUCK. "I've been hanging out at a high school all this time and, I'm…" I can't even wrap my head around this. "I'm *twenty* years old? Fucking TWENTY?" No amount of cursing can express the horror I'm feeling right now.

Theo's bemusement mirrors this sentiment. "We are *not* the coolest. I've kinda been waiting for you to put two and two together about that, but…" He trails off.

"And Sebastian? Beth? *Ash?* They're all…"

He nods, sighing. "Yep. Well, Beth's still nineteen, but her birthday's coming up. She's planning a rager."

"Why the hell aren't *they* in college?" The lights suddenly feel too bright, the room too loud. I am not processing this news very gracefully. I mean, I *should* have been able to figure this out for myself. He told me how long it's been since the accident. Principal Ford also told me how many times they've attempted this high school experiment with me since I lost my memory. I just…I didn't even think about the fact that I've been aging throughout this entire process. There are so many aspects to this mess that I've just skipped over, too focused on the fact that I might just wake up one day and be someone fucking new. That one fact has taken precedence over everything else. I am the biggest moron on the face of the planet.

"They're gonna go, though. Seb and the girls. Eventually," Theo tells me. There's a tight quality to his tone that does not make me feel good. Doesn't make me feel good at all.

"They stayed because of *me?* To help with this whole charade?" I don't even attempt to mask my incredulity.

"They wanted to help."

"Bullshit." The word flies out of my mouth. "None of them like me very much. And even if they did at one point, there's only so long a normal person puts their life on hold for someone who...who might never recover from something like...like *this.*"

"You'd be surprised."

I can tell there's something he's not telling me. Something he doesn't think I should know. I'll be damned if I'm going to let him get away with hiding anything from me right now, though. "If you don't explain right this instant, I'm going to lose my mind. In public. And it will not be pretty."

"Here we go, guys. Two large Tsingtao beers. Your food'll be right out." The waitress places our beers down in front of us, beaming beatifically. She seems oblivious to the fact that I'm glaring at Theo like I'm about to go nuclear. "I know you probably hear this a lot," she says, "but it's so great to see you back in here, Sorrell. You're looking good. We're all just so glad to hear that you're doing better."

I snap my head around, ready to fire some dismissive retort at the waitress, desperate to send her away, but the moment I see the genuine happiness on her face, my ire fades and dies. "Thank you, that's really sweet. I appreciate that, uh..." I look for a nametag but apparently those aren't a thing at The Golden Palace.

The girl looks confused for a moment, and then realization dawns on her. "Oh. It's Rachel. My name's Rachel. I'm sorry, sometimes it's just so easy to forget..."

The sound of that name is like a bell, tolling within my soul. It shakes my very foundation, setting me even further off balance.

Her name is Rachel? How well did I know her before? She's young. Maybe just a little older than me. Is she the reason why I woke up and decided to call myself that name one day? A sharp, piercing pain forms behind my eyes.

"Thanks, Rach," Theo says quietly.

"Sure, Merch. Let me know if you guys need anything else." She goes, and the look on Theo's face speaks a thousand words.

"I know. I'm sorry. This is all…a lot. I know there's a metric shit ton of stuff we still need to go over, but perhaps we can just eat and watch the movie. We'll get through all of your questions, I promise."

I am so tired of this. Like, fucking exhausted. What am I supposed to do, though? Cause a scene and ruin dinner? I know I promised one, but out of nowhere, I'm so bone weary and drained by this whole affair that it's all I can do to nod.

Thus far, Theo's kept his promises, and if he says we're going to get through everything, I am just going to have to trust that he will keep that promise, too.

We eat, and the food is just as delicious as it smelled. It takes a long time to shake off the shock of learning that I'm old as fuck now, and my boyfriend and all of my old frenemies have chosen to stay in fucking high school for as long as they have. Another beer helps me shake off my mood. By the time Theo picks up the check and we leave, I'm feeling a tiny, tiny bit better though. Less freaked out, if that's even possible. I mean, of all the revelations I've been hit with of late, these most recent ones don't even tip the balance on the fucked-up scales.

Outside in the car, Theo sits quietly for a second, staring down at his hands. "Do you still want to go to the movies?" he asks softly. "Because…" He lets out a shaky breath. "My delightful little sister thinks that I'm making decisions for you. I know how difficult this whole thing is. I'm…" He cracks his thumb knuckles. "I'm just trying to do what's right, but I get that keeping things from you, or feeding them to you piecemeal is…maybe not the best. And the thing is, Sebastian's organized a party at The Jump, and—"

I cut him off. "The Jump?" Why does that sound familiar? Ah, yeah. It comes back to me almost immediately. Lani talked about The Jump a while ago, when we were fantasizing about getting away from Toussaint. She'd said it was far away, though, on the way back to Seattle. Surprise, surprise, it's a lot closer than she made out.

"It's a bar. We used to go there," Theo clarifies. "They used to have underaged hours for kids from Toussaint, but now that *some* of us are practically legal, at least..."

I don't even consider it. "I want to go." Going to the movies with him does sound good, but there's so much going on inside my head right now. I won't be able to focus on what's happening on the screen. I'll just sit there, and all of this shit will fester away in my head, and I'll wind up fucking screaming at the top of my lungs for no reason or something. I need noise. I need life. I need to be somewhere so crowded and chaotic that I won't even be able to hear myself think, even if I want to.

"All right then," Theo says, sounding more than a little resigned. "The Jump it is."

SORRELL

I BRACE as I shove the door open to The Jump, hoping like hell that this doesn't blow up in my face. Behind me, Sorrell vibrates with a pent-up energy that feels somewhat dangerous. I've been waiting for her to put two and two together and realize that she's not eighteen anymore, but when that didn't happen, buying her a beer over dinner seemed like a good way to bring it up. That hadn't exactly gone to plan. After that, hiding the fact that half of the Academy were hanging out here tonight then seemed like a piss-poor strategy. I chose to eat on the outskirts of town in the hopes that we'd steer clear of Seb and the others, but maybe Lani is right. Maybe pulling the strings and coercing Sorrell into doing what I think is best for her really *isn't* what's good for her. I could barely even taste dinner over the tang of my own selfishness. I had no choice but to let her make up her own mind about it.

Condensation runs down the windows of The Jump. The place is slammed, bodies crushed up against bodies, people shoving at one another to get to the bar. Music thumps through crackling speakers, making it impossible to differentiate between the beat and the wobbling bass. I've never been in love with this place. It smells like sweat and old beer. The bar staff are dicks. It was the only place in town that would allow us to hang out though, so the students of Toussaint quickly adopted it as their stomping ground.

I take Sorrell's hand, placing her in front of me so that I can try and protect her from getting pushed around as we forge a path through the crowd. I growl at a guy in a trucker cap that nearly spills his drink on her when he turns from the bar, flashing my teeth at him like some sort of rabid dog. Sorrell tugs on my hand and pulls me away before I can say something shitty to him that could potentially end in a fight.

In the back, by the pool tables, it's a little quieter, though not by much. This is where we find the better part of Toussaint's senior year, gathered around Sebastian, who is holding court like the arrogant, jumped up piece of shit that he is. His face is still a fucking mess, courtesy of yours truly. He stands on a chair with a pool cue in one hand and a beer in the other, mid-way through some bawdy story that he is no doubt the star of. When he lays eyes on me, he stops talking, surprise evident.

"Well, look who it is! If it's not the Prince of Toussaint himself, deigning to come slum it with the commoners."

I roll my eyes. "Shut up, Seb. Why don't you get down off your soap box and go grab me a beer?"

There will be no make up deep and meaningful between us. There never is. He does something to piss me off. I beat the crap out of him. We don't talk for a couple of days. I give him shit and make him buy me a beer. The end. Our friendship has been tenuous at best, these last few years. I still owe him a lot. He did agree to stay here and help with this situation, even though he resented Sorrell even more for it. He did it for me. Mostly.

It's going to take a cold day in hell before I forgive him for the soda can incident though, and he knows it. I doubt it'll ever happen. But if keeping the peace tonight means that Sorrell can relax and enjoy herself for a while, then I'll bite the bullet and make it happen.

Seb eyes me, his gaze skittering to my left, where Sorrell stands, glowering at him defiantly. He laughs harshly, jumping down from the chair. "Your wish is my command, Your Highness." He sketches a dramatic mock bow, and then darts off toward the bar, leaving his audience hanging.

Noelani appears out of the throng, a bottle of Bud Lite in her hand. She sways a little too much for my liking as she throws her arms around my neck, pulling me into a hug. "Big brother! You're here! And you brought Sorrell! Hey, girl." She lets go of me and hugs Sorrell, grinning impishly. "I knew he'd bring you," she tells her conspiratorially. "My brother's a very simple creature. You just have to plant a few seeds of doubt in his mind and give it some time. Eventually his conscience gets the better of him."

"You're drunk," I tell her.

"Awww, is big bad Theo Merchant mad that his sister is having a good time and drinking beer?" She tries to pinch my cheek, but I swat her hand away.

"No. I'm mad that you're drinking *bad* beer. You could at least develop some taste."

"Ahh, go eat a dick, buddy. Hey, Sorrell, wanna play pool? If I close one eye and do thissss," she slurs, sticking out her tongue, "I think I could hit the balls."

Sorrell laughs, giving me a backward shrug as Lani drags her over to a free table. Even though she's left me, I make sure I keep her in my line of sight, very aware of what's going on around her. She looks fucking phenomenal tonight. She always does. But I'm not blind. I can see the way that guy with the trucker cap is still staring at her, and I do not like it one bit. The moment it looks like he's heading in her direction, I'll head over there and rip the fucker's drooling tongue right out of his goddamn head.

"Whoa, son. Calm down. I can feel the rage pouring off you from the other side of the bar." Sebastian shoves a beer at me. "Here. I bought one for your girl too, but I'm not dumb enough to try and give it to her. Figured you'd break three of my fingers or something."

"Four," I snap, taking a mouthful out of the other beer that he hands to me—the one intended for Sorrell.

"Come on, man," Seb chides. "You don't trust me? You really think I'd be stupid enough to spike her drink?"

"There are a lot of things I didn't think you'd be stupid enough to do, but I've been wrong before."

"I s'pose that's fair." He's quiet for a moment. "Look, man. I know it doesn't count for much, but I do regret what went down the other day."

"Use more words," I command.

He has the audacity to look put out. "Okay. Fine. I'm very sorry for throwing that coke can at your girlfriend."

Taking another sip, I narrow my eyes at him. *"More."*

"Fuck. You're such an asshole. Fine. At your girlfriend, who already has a major head injury, and who isn't at fault for my shitty temperament."

"Better." I thrust the other beer back at him, nodding in Sorrell's direction. "Now go give her the beer and repeat what you just said to me, only with way more sincerity and a healthy dose of contrition."

"Seriously?"

"Seriously."

* * *

SORRELL

I'm nearly done with the beer by the time Seb stops apologizing. I'm not feeling super forgiving, but now armed with the knowledge that he stayed here to help me, I guess I'm a little more lenient than I would normally be.

"I'm not saying what you did was okay, but I understand. A little. If we could avoid any projectiles aimed at my head in future, that would be great."

"Got it. Got it. Loud and clear." Seb nods enthusiastically. I think he's borderline drunk. "I'll keep all soda and other beverages to myself in the future, yeah. Apart from that beer. That beer is yours, princess. Enjoy!"

"Princess?"

He cackles like a wasted hyena. "Yeah. You're with His Highness, so that makes you royalty, too."

"If you say so." I don't think I'm ever going to like Sebastian. It's a wonder that I ever did. That thought occurs to me, as he's turning his back to me, making ready to walk away. "Hey, Seb?"

He twists around theatrically. "Yes, Princess?"

"Were we ever…*friends?*"

A brief frown flickers across his brow, and then he says, "Would a friend ever throw a can of coke at your head?"

"Yeah. That's what I thought. So then…why…?"

He understands my meaning; out of nowhere he seems to sober up a little. "Look. Were we ever besties? No. We were not. But. BUT!" He holds up a finger. "Theodore Merchant is a good dude. And while I didn't get it at first, I *came* to understand it after a while."

"Understand what?"

"You two. Together. When I thought you were just some little high school fantasy of his…that you two would just fuck around for a while and then break up…I didn't like it. I didn't get why he wanted to waste time with his friends on some temporary pussy, when he could just stick his dick anywhere he wanted and then we could get on with our shit."

"Charming," I say dryly.

"Right. But then…I saw you two together. I watched it all happen. You weren't just some hole for him to fuck—"

"You really have a way with words, you know that?"

He snickers. "You were…like…god, this is so lame, but you were his true fucking north. That's why he got those stupid fucking tattoos on his shoulders. Compasses. Compi? Whatever. And he…he was yours. I don't think I believed in love before you two. Watching you together was like…witnessing two planets, orbiting each other. Sheeewww sheeewww sheeewww." He mimics two objects spinning around each other with a finger on each hand. "Everyone saw it. Everyone knew. Even Beth. She'd never admit it, but she did. You two were meant to fucking be. Fated. Destined. Whatever you want to call it. And when you got hurt…" He blows out a monumental breath. "Fuck, that sucked. Have you ever seen those YouTube videos of the dogs when their owners die, and they lay on their graves and just fucking pine for them until they die, too? That's what it was like. He was still locked in your orbit, and you were like sheeeeeewwwwwww! Kablam!" He mimes one of his imaginary planets shooting off out of its orbit and then exploding.

"Dark, man," he says. "That was *really* fucking dark."

Hammered though he may be, Sebastian's rudimentary description of what happened after the accident breaks something inside of me.

"Oh shit. Why do you look like you're about to cry? Please don't cry. He'll fucking kill me. It was the dog, wasn't it? I shouldn't have brought up the dog. Don't watch that shit. It is deeply depressing. Here. Let me get you a napkin."

"It's fine, Seb. It's fine. I'm not going to cry. Just...stop. Seriously, I'm fine." I am not fine, though. I'm hanging on by a thread, barely keeping it together.

"It won't always feel like this. Things will be better once you get the surgery out of the way. Then you'll have all of your memories back and you won't ever have to worry about the whole, '*Who-am-I gonna-be-today? Do-I-love-Theo-or-do-I-want-him-dead?*' bit."

"I'm sorry, *what?*"

"Yeah. He said it was risky, but I'm sure you're sick of all this—"

My hand tightens around my beer glass. "*What* surgery, Sebastian?"

His mouth opens. Words are about to come out, but then a spark of confusion flashes in his unfocused eyes. A look of realization follows promptly after. "Oh shit. You don't—" He wags a finger at me. "You do *not* know about the surgery." Looking over his shoulder, he scans the crowd. "Uhhhh, Theo?"

"Sebastian!"

"THEO!"

He's there, then—my dark prince, pushing his way toward us through the melee. His face is stormy, anger and concern warring for dominance over his features. He looks to me first, and then narrows his eyes, glaring at Seb. "What did you do?" he demands.

"He let slip about my *surgery*," I say stiffly. "A surgery I know nothing about."

Theo's shoulders sag. The anger that was visibly building in him falls away when he looks at me. "Oh, *fuck*."

"Yeah. *'Oh fuck,'* sounds about right. Now would you care to explain what the hell he's talking about before I lose my shit?"

SORRELL

"It isn't safe."

I clench my jaw so hard that I think my teeth might crack. I couldn't give a shit about my teeth, though. I glower at Theo, hoping with every fiber of my being that my face accurately portrays just how furious I am right now.

The night air shivers with snow. Huge fat flakes eddy down from the heavy midnight sky, the largest I've ever seen. They catch in Theo's disheveled black waves and across the tops of his shoulders as he paces up and down outside the entrance to the academy. Toussaint is deserted and dark as a tomb, all its students having all fled with their weekend passes in hand. Sitting on the bottom step of the stone stairs, I pull my Parka around me tighter, too mad to even think straight.

"It's an unproven procedure. They've only attempted it a couple of times over the past few years and each experiment ended in disaster. Total loss of motor function. Speech centers destroyed. *Extreme* seizures," he says, counting off a litany of side effects on his fingers. "Dizziness. Headaches. Pulmonary disfunction. Cranial nerve injuries—"

"Theo."

"One girl went *blind*—"

"Theo, stop."

He stops and turns to face me. Tense as a bowstring, he drags his hands back through his hair, flaring his nostrils as he blasts a breath down his nose. "This isn't one you'd walk away from. You've defied the odds so many times, Kid. Risking this would just be asking for trouble."

I have to fight the urge to scream at him. Miraculously, I manage to hold myself in check until I'm calm enough to speak. "Don't you think that this sounds like something I should decide? Did it ever occur to you that, I don't know, maybe giving me all of the information and letting me come to my own conclusion would be the best way to handle this?"

"I was going to do all of that, Kid. I was. The right time just hasn't presented itself to talk to you about it. And you're *fine* right now—"

"I AM *NOT* FINE!" My shout echoes across Toussaint's snow-dusted lawns, echoing through the thickness of the night like a shotgun blast. I get to my feet, a ball of white-hot rage swelling behind my ribs. "I am about as far from fine as I could be, Theo. I have no idea who I am. I'm—I'm not *permanent!* Anything could make me slip again. *Anything*! I feel like I'm barely here most of the time—"

"You're *you*, Sorrell. You're doing great! You're starting to remember little things all the time—"

"I am missing an entire lifetime, Theo! It's mine and I fucking want it back! I want to remember our first kiss. I want to remember the first time you told me that you loved me. The first time we had sex. I want to remember *my parents*, Theo."

"You'll get it all back. In time, there's a decent chance—"

"What kind of chance? Exactly? I want a number."

Theo's jaw works overtime. "It isn't that easy to quantify."

"But it's small, isn't it? Like an impossibly small chance that I'll get *all* of my memories back?"

He looks down at his feet, crossing his arms over his chest. "Yes," he admits reluctantly.

"And the surgery? What are my chances if I have the surgery?"

"You can't base a decision like this on which option has the least shitty odds, Sorrell. They're both bad options, except one of them might leave you fucking dead."

"They both might leave me dead," I grit out. "Don't you think that's what it feels like for me? This constant uncertainty? The thought that I might go to sleep and wake up a completely different fucking person tomorrow morning? Don't you think that would be like dying to *this* version of me?"

"It's not the same and you know it."

"Do you wanna deal with another Catherine? Or someone even worse? What if I turn into a complete fucking psychopath?"

"That's very unlikely."

"JUST TELL ME WHAT MY ODDS ARE, THEO!"

His eyes snap up to meet mine, and a world of hurt exists within his gaze. He looks tortured beyond belief when he says, "Twenty-seven percent. There's a twenty-seven percent chance that, if you make it through the surgery, you *could* get your memories back."

"Twenty-seven percent's not bad."

"You're not listening. If you make it through the surgery. *If*. There's a fifty-fifty chance you *die* on that table. Fifty-fifty. It's a fucking coin toss at best. It's unethical that they'd even *offer* the surgery—"

"I like those odds." Even as I say this, fear creeps its way into my mind, rattling me to my core. They're terrible odds. There's nothing to like about them at all. Still… "Isn't it worth the risk? To get everything back? To get *me* back?"

I know I've struck a chord with this question. Theo glares at me, anger bubbling out of him, his eyes fucking alive with it. "I lost you to Amelia. I lost her to Catherine. I lost Rachel to you. I cannot lose *you* because you fucking *died*."

"You don't even know that I'm gonna die!"

"For fuck's sake, Sorrell, I do!"

"How?"

"Because that's what happened to Henry!" he roars.

SORRELL

The Henry DeKosky Center for Neurological Study.

I stare at the brass plaque on the wall of the grand brick building with bile rising up the back of my throat. "When did they change the name?" I ask quietly, turning to Theo. After three days of bitter arguments, he agreed to fly back to Los Angeles with me, on the proviso that this be an exploratory trip only, where I ask questions and gather more information. Theo runs his tongue over his teeth, studying the plaque, too.

"Couple of months ago, I think. His father's a politician. Donated a lot of money to the hospital while Henry was a patient here. I'm sure they renamed the place to keep him happy. He was understandably upset when his son died."

I know this building. I recognized it the second the Uber pulled into the parking lot. But of course I know it as Falcon House.

Theo places an arm around my shoulders, pulling me into an embrace. "You're sure you want to do this?" he whispers into my hair. "It's not too late. We can always go back."

I shake my head. It's way too late to go back. I can't do this anymore. Knowing the truth is one thing but try telling that to my brain. I still live in a world where I'm convinced Rachel was a real person. A separate person. I still have all of these memories of a horrific childhood that make no sense, whilst having absolutely no memories of my mother and father, who loved and cared for me deeply. I don't want to live a lie anymore. I want my life back, every single detail of it in sharp focus.

Taking a deep breath, I pull back from Theo's hug. I'm still so mad at him for keeping this from me, but I understand why he didn't say anything. I know how scary this is for him. I also know what it's costing him to come back here with me. This place holds unimaginable nightmares for him—I've already nearly died here twice already, and he was sitting by my side both times it happened. It was probably unfair of me to ask him to come, but I'm weak and I needed him. The prospect of coming here alone, without his support, nearly broke me clean in two.

"Sorrell! Oh my goodness, what a surprise!"

I look up and tears spring to my eyes. Gaynor stands in the sliding glass doors, her mascara clumpy and smudged as ever. She's wearing pale blue scrubs this morning. I get the feeling she's *always* worn them, only I wasn't paying attention somehow. The huge oatmeal colored cable knit cardigan she's wearing over her nurse's scrub top is full of holes, the sleeves are far too long.

"Cool cardigan." I stifle a laugh.

"Thanks. I knitted it myself."

"Really? I'd never have known."

"All right. All right. Good to see you haven't lost that wicked tongue of yours." She hugs me, and her embrace is so comforting that I nearly break down and sob. She smiles at me, holding my face and rubbing her thumbs over my cheeks, regarding me with what can only be called motherly affection. "It's very good to see you, sweetheart. And you…" Her expression becomes even softer when she turns to Theo. "It's a gift to see you again, dear boy."

"Whoa, now. Who do you like better here, me or him?" I rub my nose with the back of my hand to hide the fact that I'm sniffling.

"Oh, definitely him," she tells me winking conspiratorially. "I told you he was handsome, didn't I? If I were twenty years younger—"

"Sorrell would definitely have some competition." He draws her into a hug.

I pretend to be offended, but I'm secretly enjoying how cute he's being around her. It occurs to me, as we head inside, that Theo knows Gaynor far better than I ever did. They spent a lot of time together after the accident, when I was hanging onto life by little more than a thread. She must have comforted him when things were hard. Must have tried to make things more manageable for him.

The inside of Falcon House—or the Henry DeKosky Center—is nothing like I remember it. The faint tang of bleach hangs in the air. Everything is sterile and white, and different. My heart skips a beat when we walk past an open door and I see the huge, open space on the other side, though. A gym. A training room, to be precise. This is the space where I trained so hard before I left for Toussaint. On a little metal plaque mounted to the door, is the word 'PHYSIO-THERAPY.'

"Ahh yes. The old torture chamber," Gaynor says. "You worked your ass off in there."

Behind Gaynor, another familiar face appears, heading toward us down the hallway, and my chest tightens. It's Ruth. "Oh good. Sorrell. You made it." She gives me a curt, professional smile.

She doesn't wear nurse's scrubs. She wears a tailored white button-down shirt and a pair of dove grey suit pants, under a pressed white lab coat with the name Doctor Ruth Brighton embroidered over the pocket and the center's logo.

Doctor Brighton. Ruth. The woman who I always wanted to please. The woman who I thought had saved me and taken me in off the streets. Turns out she did save me, but not in the way I had convinced myself she did. Dr. Brighton—god, I can't get used to not thinking of her as Ruth—is the doctor who performed my last surgery. The cowboy, Theo had called her. She pulled off what everyone else in her field claimed was impossible: she dragged me back into the land of the living, and now she wants to save me a second time.

She's as stern as I remember back on the dock at Toussaint. Twin lines form a deep eleven between her brows. Her eyes are sharp and assessing, clinical and cold. She holds a hand out to me in greeting, and it feels beyond weird to shake it.

"I hope the flight wasn't too taxing," she says. "Cabin pressure has been known to worsen some patients' headaches. That's why Nurse Richards drove you to Washington back in September. But I understand that the drive might have been a daunting prospect, given who you'd have had to spend all that time with this time around." She turns an icy, pointed look on Theo—it takes me a moment to put two and two together and realize that she's throwing shade. "I'm glad to see that you're here, supporting Sorrell's decision to go ahead with this surgery, Mr. Merchant."

"Oh, I'm not. I only came to make sure you don't downplay the risks involved in this butcher's procedure. I'm gonna do everything in my power to talk her out of it."

"What a surprise." Her lips press together in what amounts to be the unfriendliest smile of all time. "I'm allowing your presence here because it's important that Sorrell has access to her support system, but let me make this clear to you, Theo. If you insult me, my staff, or any of—"

"Might I remind you," Theo says, interrupting her. "That the last time we were in each other's presence, *you* were the one who physically assaulted *me*."

"That's because you had just implied that I wanted to *murder* your girlfriend just to get my name in a medical journal."

"I didn't imply it. I straight out said it," Theo snaps back. "This whole trial of yours is just some vainglorious, bullshit ego-stroke for you. If—"

"I've completed three entirely successful procedures in the past six weeks. Three patients, all completely recovered and healed, returned to their families. Their symptoms have been improving daily, as their swelling goes down. I have every hope that Sorrell's procedure will go just as well."

"Three patients? Out of how many?"

Dr. Brighton looks like she'd love to slap Theo again, but she thinks better of it. "*Three*," she says coolly. "Three out of three. A one hundred percent success rate."

Theo's mouth snaps shut.

* * *

"The headaches you've been suffering from, as well as some of the extreme lethargy, are all side effects of the contusion on your brain. This area here," Dr. Brighton says, drawing a circle with a stylus around a darkened area on the image of the brain—*my* brain—that is displayed on her computer screen. "This is your frontal lobe. This is the area of your brain that's responsible for your personality. For things like emotions, mood and judgment. These areas here are the hippocampus and the medial temporal lobe. These are the areas responsible for making and storing memories. As you can see, this small shadowy area sandwiched between the frontal and the medial temporal lobe is darker than the rest of your brain. This is what is causing your issues. We were worried that it was the beginnings of a glioma—a tumor caused by the trauma you suffered during your accident. Our scans have subsequently discounted that, though, which is excellent news. We now know that this is more than likely a fibrotic lesion scar, putting pressure on very delicate areas of the brain, which is obviously causing some very serious complications. I would like to perform a lesionectomy using an exoscope and a new tubular retractor system—"

"Snake oil," Theo hisses through his teeth.

Dr. Brighton rolls her eyes. "This is a common procedure, Theo. I'm not reinventing the wheel here."

"Right. But you haven't explained to her yet that the area you're trying to resect in her brain is incredibly deep. The complications associated with screwing around in that area of the brain are—"

"Are noteworthy, yes, and not to be made light of. If you'd stop interrupting me, then I'd love to go through the procedure with Sorrell, step by step, from start to finish. I'll explain the associated risks that come with each of those steps, as well as the overall recorded outcomes, and perhaps *then* you can air your grievances."

Theo is clearly unhappy about it, but he allows Dr. Brighton to describe the procedure. I'm covered in a cold sweat by the time she's finished, and more than a little confused. Neurosurgeons get paid the big bucks because that shit is hard. But my takeaway once she's done is this: the surgery is dangerous. It will take about four hours. I could wake up with some of my memories, or all of my memories returned to me, but there *is* also a chance I might not wake up at all.

"With the recent improvement in our practical techniques and the subsequent successes we've had at the center, outcomes are much higher than we might have expected even a couple of months ago," Dr. Brighton says.

"If that's the case, then would you care to explain what happened to Henry," Theo demands.

Again, Ru—urgh! *Dr. Brighton* casts a disgusted glance at Theo. He's a pest to her. An inconvenience she could well and truly do without. "Henry's death was very unfortunate. The trauma to his brain was less considerable than Sorrell's, but the placement of his scar tissue was far more complicated. We didn't realize the extent of it until he was lying on the table—"

"And once you had drilled a hole in his fucking head and had him on that table, and you *did* see the scope of his scar tissue, do you think it was ethical to roll the dice and continue with the procedure, without consulting his parents or performing more comprehensive scans? I mean, why wasn't every scan in the book carried out already? It's a miracle you still have a license to practice medicine. I hope you have a good lawyer, 'cause I hear Mr. DeKosky is just itching to sue the living fuck out of you—"

"Then you'd better hope, for both of your sakes, that Sorrell opts to undergo the surgery as quickly as possible," Dr. Brighton says, without even the smallest flicker of emotion. "Falcon House is the only facility equipped to deal with cases like Sorrell's, and I'm the only doctor willing and experienced enough to help."

"If you do open me up and things look worse than anticipated, would you halt the procedure? Close me back up so we can game plan?" I ask.

Dr. Brighton looks displeased, but she nods. "If that's your wish."

Theo practically leaps out of his chair. "You can't *seriously* be considering this, Kid."

I ignore him. "And there is a chance that I'll get my memories back? All of them?"

"We will primarily focus on alleviating the pressure to your frontal lobe first, to ensure that the issues you've been experiencing with your judgment and personality are stabilized first. Once complete, we'll move on to resect the deeper area of the lesion that's affecting your memory centers. I'm very confident that we'll be able to address both matters to a satisfactory standard."

Closing my eyes, I shake my head. "I'm not looking for confident or satisfactory. I'm looking for a definitive."

"Even if the odds of success were much, much higher, I wouldn't be able to offer you a definitive. There are always associated risks, even to the safest surgeries. I couldn't in good conscience—"

"Oh, *please!*" Theo erupts. "Like you have a conscience!"

Dr. Brighton blows out a frustrated breath; she slumps back into her chair, slowly setting her stylus carefully back down on her desk. "I'm afraid that I've had enough of you for one day, Mr. Merchant. I'm going to have to ask you to leave."

"I'm not leaving her here with you," he spits. "God knows what you'll get her to agree to."

Frustration vibrating from her, Dr. Brighton turns her sharp eyes on me. "Sorrell, you're an intelligent young woman. I trust that you can make your own informed decisions. Is there anything else you'd like to ask me before we end our appointment today?"

There's only one question that's been bothering me since I found out what role this woman plays in my story. I feel ridiculous putting it into words, but my own curiosity compels me to ask. "Why? Why did you play along with—with my delusions? I turned you into some kind of savior. I thought you were training me to come and hurt Theo. You came all the way out to Toussaint. I—I don't understand why you'd go along with *any* of that."

Dr. Brighton tucks a rogue strand of hair behind her ear. "I wouldn't categorize the fantastical memories your mind created in order to protect you as delusions. They were a very authentic reality to you. You believed that reality was true. It would have been dangerous to repeatedly jar you from that reality. Certainly counterproductive. It was no problem for me to play along with your reality as you saw it, or to oversee your physiotherapy. I wanted to make sure you were physically fit and capable of going back to school yet again. It's quite normal for patients to perceive their doctors through the lens of some kind of...god or savior—"

"Jesus *Christ*," Theo mutters.

"The very nature of our work means that we hold life and death in our hands on a daily basis. It isn't surprising that your mind assigned me an authoritative role in your life. I came to Toussaint because your principal was concerned that if you left Toussaint for a fourth time, you'd lose any progress you'd made and that you were running out of opportunities to heal in a safe environment. I was happy to come and perform an assessment. Additionally, your health insurance is *very* comprehensive, and I was compensated handsomely for the long-distance appointment."

Well. This woman might not be the hardened, distant foster carer I made her into in my mind, but she is certainly just as cold and unfeeling as I seem to remember. I can't help it—I know who she is now, and that she has only been doing her job, but some innate, ingrained part of me who always sought her approval is stung by the callousness of her reply.

"Was there anything else?" she asks.

"No. Thank you. I think I've heard everything I needed to hear."

Dr. Brighton opens the top drawer of her desk and takes out a business card. She snaps it down onto the desk and slides it over to me. "I'm fully booked for the next few months but let me know if you'd like to proceed. I'm eager to further my research, so I'm sure my schedule could be rearranged if you decide to go ahead."

SORRELL

"There we go. Booked." Theo closes his laptop with a flourish. "Flight doesn't leave until two tomorrow, so we won't have to rush. We can grab some breakfast and take our time getting to the airport."

"*Mmm.*" I stare out of the hotel room window, feeling a strange sense of detachment when I realize that I can see the Hollywood sign on the hillside in the distance. So freaking bizarre. I thought I knew this city, but I don't. The past I created for myself here feels like a weird dream now, half constructed and full of holes. Most of the time I've spent in Los Angeles was all at the hospital, recovering from my injuries.

The bed dips when Theo comes to sit next to me. "You okay?" he asks, brushing my hair back from my face. "You've been pretty quiet since we left Brighton's place."

"Yeah, I don't know. I don't know what I expected. I just…I didn't expect her to be so cut-throat."

"I warned you."

He did. And I believed him. "It just feels so strange," I tell him. "Everything. All of the time. It never seems to stop." There's only one way to lift this miasma of confusion I live in, but I keep that to myself. Theo doesn't want to hear it. He wants us to go back to Toussaint and roll with the punches. Let nature run its course and see if my brain heals itself on its own. No other option seems to satisfy him. As far as he's concerned, too many risks have already been taken, and this final risk is just too much. I understood how he felt before, and now, having properly met Dr. Brighton, I can see why he has no interest in letting her root around inside my head with a scalpel.

"Let's go out and get some food," Theo says, grinning. "And when we get back... I vote we do something to get you out of your head." He teases a light touch down the side of my neck, and my body responds to him, as it always does.

My bones feel heavy, my heart too light to be contained within my chest.

This boy.

This *man*.

He's the answer to a question I wouldn't even begin to know how to ask.

He's a balm to my tattered soul, the medicine that makes me complete. And I *am* complete with him, even without the surgery. Dr. Brighton's knives won't change that. He is the stars in the night sky. The oxygen in my lungs. He is every beautiful and vital thing in the world for me. Without him, my soul is a cracked, shriveled thing that cannot exist.

The light flooding in through the floor-to-ceiling windows is lovely as honey, so different from the lonely, mournful light of the Pacific North-West. It gilds his face, plucking every spun filament of gold from the liquid amber of his eyes and making them burn. Theo is a breaking storm at Toussaint. Here, he's the first light of dawn. No matter where he is in the world, it's as if Mother Nature seeks him out and vows to make him glorious.

I cup his cheek in my hand, smiling at him, my worries already fading away to smoke. "You're all I need to get me out of my head," I tell him.

He turns his head, leaning into my hand, so that he can kiss my palm. His eyes bore into mine, his gaze so potent that it makes me shiver. "Yeah?" he asks, his voice soft. It's amazing how he can lace just one word with so much suggestion. "'Cause I'm starving in every way imaginable, Voss. But there's one hunger I always want to cater to first, before anything else." My heart trips over itself, squeezing frantically, when he proceeds to lick my palm. The sight of him trailing the tip of his tongue upward, over the heel of my hand, up the inside of my wrist, his eyes still locked with mine... Holy fuck, what is happening right now? How he can turn me on so dramatically, so immediately is a mystery to me.

I was sinking low into a bog of self-pity a moment ago. Now, all I can do is burn.

"Theo," I breathe. "God, you're going to break me."

Slowly, he shakes his head, and the sunlight catches on the curls and flicks of his hair, warming the black a little. "Nothing can break you, Sorrell Voss."

Out of nowhere, a flash of a memory comes to me, painfully in focus and so unexpected that it takes my breath away.

Theo, walking down in a hallway somewhere, laughing. Judging from the crazy, colorful carpet and all of the numbered doors, we're in a hotel. He's wearing nothing but board shorts and flip flops. He has only a couple of tattoos—the outline of the sun currently marks his chest, and his right arm is covered with his sleeve. His whole face is commandeered by pure joy. The sound of his laughter echoes from the walls, loud and boisterous, and my body floods with the warmest, most beautiful heat.

"Careful, Voss. You're treading on thin ice," he tells me.

"Oh, am I?" I laugh, too. The giddiness of the feeling makes my eyes prick. "How are you going to punish me if I don't give you what you want?"

He charges me, and I turn and run, squealing at the top of my lungs. I don't get very far; he catches me, swooping me up into his arms, pretending to bite my neck like a savage, so that I scream even louder. "I'm going to finger you under the table at dinner, while you're trying to make small talk with Lani. She'll be whittering on about One Direction or some shit, and you'll be trying not to moan while I make you come."

"You wouldn't dare!"

He grazes my neck with his teeth again, this time nipping at me so a flash of pain fires down between my legs. "Try me."

"Theo! Put me down!"

"Say it."

"No!"

He bites me harder. "*Say it.*"

"I won't!"

I go limp when he sets me down and spins me around, shoving me up against the wall, kissing my neck instead of biting it this time. *Fuck. Oh fuck, oh fuck, oh fuck.* He runs the tip of his nose along the line of my jaw, breathing heavily. "Say it, Kid," he growls, roughly cupping my breast through my bikini top.

"You drive me crazy," I pant.

He pinches my nipple. "Try again."

"You make me come *so* fucking hard."

He smirks devilishly, wetting his bottom lip with his tongue. "That's good. But it's not it. Try again."

"You're the hottest fucking guy alive!"

Theo raises his eyebrows, biting his bottom lip now—a warning. He nods, and then drives his fingers down the front of my bikini bottoms. In less than a second, he's discovered just how wet I am, and has begun rubbing small circles around my clit. It feels fucking amazing.

"Theo! Anyone could see us!" I pant, trying to wriggle free. He's not letting me go anywhere, though.

"You think I give a shit if someone sees me making you squirm, Kid?" he laughs. "I don't."

"Ahh! Ahh, Theo, please!" I don't want him to stop. I never want him to stop. I would like to take this somewhere a little more private, where his parents might not walk around the corner and find us, though.

Rather than heeding my pleas, Theo makes things infinitely worse by sliding his fingers back and slipping one of them inside me. I go still, jaw hanging open, my fingernails digging into his back. Theo purrs, very pleased with himself indeed.

"You want me to fuck you, baby?" he asks.

I can only nod.

"You wanna come on my dick?"

"Y-yes."

"Say it, then."

"All right. All right. Oh my god. Ahhh shit! *I love you, Theodore William Merchant! I fucking love you!"*

He withdraws himself from me, eyeing me fiercely as he removes his hand from my bikini bottoms and sucks his index and middle fingers into his mouth. "Good, baby girl. That's what I like to hear."

I snap out of the memory, breathless and overwhelmed. I'm back in this hotel now, and a heavy kind of frustration sits on my chest. I want the rest of that memory, damnit. I want to remember what happened next.

Theo isn't licking the inside of my wrist anymore. He's sitting back on his heels, watching me, a small frown tugging his brows together. "You just remembered something, didn't you," he says.

I nod. "We were in our swimsuits, in a hotel somewhere. You were pinning me up against a wall. You, uh…you wanted me to tell you something," I admit shyly.

A brief, brilliant smile flares across Theo's face, wiping his frown away. "Right. Yeah. I remember that hallway," he says, nodding. His eyes spark with humor. "I *liked* that hallway. I liked it a lot."

"I think I liked it, too."

"You liked the shower afterwards better," he says, his right eye scrunching up a fraction. He blinks hard with both eyes, and I can't help but laugh. "What?" he demands, poking me in the thigh.

"You're ticklish *and* you can't wink?"

"Hey! Even perfection has its flaws sometimes!" He sobers. "Come on. Let's eat. I'll give you a reenactment of the Tijuana hotel shower once we get back. And hey?"

"Mmm?"

"That's a really good sign, Sorrell. You remembered a lot there. Seriously. That's real progress."

SORRELL

You can't get better than Urban Ramen.

Once we're back at the hotel, stuffed to the gills, I run a bath for Sorrell, only when I head back into the room to tell her it's ready, she's passed out, tucked tight into a ball in the middle of the huge king-sized bed. I don't have the heart to wake her, even though my raging boner is adamant that I do otherwise. There'll be plenty of other times for bathtub sex once we're home, though.

Instead, I order room service and drink a coffee, determined to stay awake for as long as possible. I want to watch her sleep. Fucking sue me. I don't care how much of a stalker that makes me. I've spent a long time watching over Sorrell, lying in a bed with her eyes closed. She wasn't sleeping then. She was in a fucking coma, barely alive, and staring at her beautiful face then, her eyes ringed with bruises, was pure fucking torture. She looks peaceful now. Healthy. There are no dark shadows beneath her eyes anymore, and I can tell by the way her fingers twitch in her sleep that she's dreaming. Until the day I die, it will always make my heart soar to see this girl dream instead of lie there, inanimate, hovering on the brink of death.

I stroke her hair softly, unwilling to wake her. I must fall asleep eventually, because when I start awake, Sorrell's standing by the night stand on my side of the bed with her hand on the lamp's switch. She turns it off, the room falling into darkness.

"What are you doing? Come back to bed," I mumble.

"I have to pee," she whispers back. She kisses me lightly on the forehead. "Won't be a second."

I drift back into the void of my own sleep, hand hanging off the side of the mattress, reaching for her, waiting for her to take it when she comes back.

* * *

It's daylight. Broad fucking daylight.

My eyes snap open, and ah, shhhhhit! My arm's dead. I've slept with it hanging over the side of the bed. God*damn*, that hurts. I flex my fingers, trying to get some blood flow back to them, and pins and needles explode up my arm.

The digital clock on the nightstand reads eight forty-eight am. How the fuck did we sleep in so late? Rolling onto my back, I rub my eyes, stretching out my back. "Guess what time it is," I say, my voice scratchy from disuse.

Sorrell doesn't answer.

Lazy bones.

I smile as I open one eye, and then the other. Sunlight dapples the ceiling, bouncing off the windows, sending ripples of white undulating up the walls. It's beautiful. It's also warm. Not hot by any stretch of the imagination, but *warm*. Sumner was tiptoeing just above freezing when we left two days ago. It may be winter in the rest of the Northern Hemisphere, but Southern California doesn't seem to have gotten the memo.

"God. I'm almost sad we're leaving today," I say out loud. "Maybe we can swing by the beach for an hour before we leave or somethi—" The second I roll over and see that the other side of the bed is empty, I know.

I fucking *know*.

I expect there to be a note, but there isn't. She probably didn't get a chance to write one when she was sneaking around the room in the middle of the night like a fucking cat burglar. It isn't as if I need a note to tell me where she's gone or why though, is it. I know perfectly well where she's gone.

I get dressed, pulling on a pair of jeans and the t-shirt I planned on wearing to the airport, and I am out of the hotel room in seconds. Seconds.

Do not check out.

Do not pay your bill.

Do not pass go.

I figure trying to flag down a taxi will be quicker than ordering an uber, but I am so fucking wrong on that front it isn't even funny. There are no regular cabs left in Los Angeles. Rider share apps are the only option available now, and it's peak commute time in the heart of the city. I pace up and down on the sidewalk, alternating between chewing my nails and aggressively kicking the trunk of a palm tree as I wait for Josh to arrive in his silver Toyota Prius. I'm halfway to Falcon House when I think to see if Sorrell sent me a text. And she has. God, I'm such an idiot.

From: The Kid
Received: 4.08 am

I can't see the screen on this thing so I ho9pe I don;t fuck this up. I know you're probably angry and Im sorty. I can't get back on the plane without trying this. I can't stand the thought of missing half a life with you, even if we do get to share the rest of this one. If I could gau=uarantee that we *would* spend the rest of our lives together and I wouldn't be waiting to just turn into someone else, then maybe. But that isn't how things are. I love you, Theodore William Merchant. I have faith that this is all going to work out. I'm so, so sorry if it doesn't.

"Whoa, man. You okay back there? You look like you're about to punch the damn window out or something." Josh the uber driver is very astute. I see him watching me in the rearview and do my best to marshal the combination of anger and absolute terror that's currently splitting me in two.

"If you could just step on it, that'd be awesome," I say through gritted teeth.

Josh laughs. "You're kidding, right? Rush hour traffic in L.A. doesn't move for anyone, buddy. We'll be there in eighteen minutes."

Eighteen minutes is too fucking long. "How far to the destination? How many miles?"

"Uh, one point four miles."

Yeah. Fuck this. I'm not sitting in a car for sixteen minutes to travel one point four fucking miles. "Let me out."

"We're moving, man. I can't just—"

"LET ME OUT OF THIS FUCKING CAR RIGHT FUCKING *NOW!*"

Josh immediately pulls over to the side of the road. No one even bothers to honk; we were crawling along, anyway. "You're gonna get charged for the full ride, dude!"

"I don't care." The second the car stops, I rip the door open and I run. Following the directions on my phone, it takes me a little over nine minutes to reach my destination. I'm sweating and dizzy as fuck when I tear across the parking lot of Falcon House.

Gaynor is sitting outside the entrance on a park bench, waiting for me.

The expression on her face is fraught with worry when she spots me tearing toward the sliding doors . "Stop!" she shouts, leaping up from her seat. I attempt to bypass her, but she blocks the path that leads inside.

"It's too late! You're already too late," she hisses, planting her hand in the middle of my chest.

Horror grabs hold of me and takes me out at the knees. I can't breathe. "What do you mean, *I'm too late?*"

"Brighton rushed her in as soon as she got here. I didn't even know she was coming. She made me promise not to call you. I'm sorry, I just couldn't."

"She's already inside? Or...or she's already in pre-op, or—"

"She's already in the O.R."

"What? *WHAT?*" I'm gonna pass the fuck out. "Brighton doesn't have new scans. She has no idea what Sorrell's lesions look like right now!" She's going in blind, just like she did with Henry. This is precisely what I was worried about. "I'm gonna fucking kill her," I snarl. "I'm gonna grab her out of that operating room and rip her fucking head off."

Gaynor grabs me, yanking me back. "And what good's that gonna do, huh? Your girlfriend is already on the table, Theo. She's gone all in. Cause trouble with Dr. Brighton now and where does that leave Sorrell?"

I quit fighting to get to the door, a broken gasp leaping out of my mouth. She's right. She's fucking right. My hands are tied. I can't interrupt the surgery now. Sorrell is the only one who'll suffer for it. I sink to my knees, right in the middle of the path that leads up to the building, and I cover my face with my hands.

Gaynor rubs my back, doing her best to comfort me. "It's gonna be all right. It is. It's gonna be all right. The only thing we can do for Sorrell now is hope and pray and have faith that everything will be all right."

* * *

"I didn't think I'd be seeing *you* again."

I look up and there is Father Simmons, lighting the biggest candle I've ever seen, up by the lectern. He's exactly how I remember him—face weathered, hands gnarled, eyes bright. In his early sixties, he looks a lot older than his years. I suppose a lifetime spent trying to alleviate other people's pain and suffering will age a man beyond his years.

"Have you come to pray?" he asks, approaching the pew where I sit.

I laugh derisively. "Nope. Just a big fan of really hard, really uncomfortable wooden seats."

Father Simmons' laughter is far more genuine. "Y'know. Back in the early nineties, we replaced all of the wooden benches at my last church with these really nice new ones. Upholstered benches. Seat pads. Cushioned backs. They were so comfortable. Too comfortable, really. Within two months we had to go back to the original seats. The parishioners kept falling asleep during mass."

I snort, picking at my fingers. "She's in surgery again," I say quietly.

"I think I heard something about that. Is there anything I can do for you, Theodore?"

I think about his question. Really think about it. There's nothing he or his God or anyone else can do for me at this point. I let my head fall back, working hard not to fall to pieces. "You can do something for *her*," I say quietly. "You can pray."

SORRELL

It settles over you like a weight sometimes—the knowledge that something is wrong. It's happened to me before, but never with the same certainty as it does today. I'm sitting in the waiting room, listening to the sound of the inane reality TV show the nurses have on in the background, my mind skipping from thought to thought, when a ten-thousand-pound stillness falls over me. I'm glued to my seat, too afraid to breathe, or blink, or move a muscle. If I stay here, like this, locked in place, then maybe the bad news never comes. Maybe I can just exist here, in this state of limbo, and I'll never have to face the fact that my life is about to go up in flames for the fifteen millionth time.

But of course, it's damn near impossible to hold back a forest fire once it's caught momentum, and this blaze has been raging for years now.

"Theo?"

Do not look up.

Do *not* look up.

I'd do anything not to, but there is no hiding from this. Eventually, I lift my gaze and steel myself as I meet Gaynor's eyes—eyes that are brimming over with tears. "I'm sorry, Theo. I'm so, so sorry."

"Tell me she's fine. Tell me she's already sitting up in a bed back there, asking to fucking see me. Tell me anything other than you're fucking sorry."

"I—I don't know what—" A broken sob flies out of Gaynor's mouth.

Breathing in a ragged breath, I fix her with a hard stare. "Is she dead? Just tell me, did she fucking die back there without properly saying goodbye to me?" If she did, then I swear to God, I will hold a grudge for the rest of my day. Since the universe hates me, I'm probably going to die an old man in my bed, having lived a long and torturous life without Sorrell Voss, just waiting to be reunited with her. The moment I *do* kick the bucket, and I find myself entering into whatever afterlife may exist for us once we shuffle loose this mortal coil, I will find that girl who died and took my heart with her, and I will give her the ass-kicking of the century.

Gaynor can't talk around her crying.

"Gaynor, please! For fuck sake! Tell me she isn't dead!"

"She—she *isn't* dead."

Relief. Breathtaking relief. I've never known anything like it. But I can tell from looking on Gaynor's face that there's something else. I get out of my seat, and my legs buckle. This will crush me. After everything, if she's not going to make it…

"Explain what's going on. *Now*. Use as few words as possible."

Gaynor wipes her mouth with the back of one hand. She steps forward, placing her arm on the top of my shoulder. "Dr. Brighton managed to resect the lesion. The surgery was going well, but at some point, a vessel was nicked and there was a bleed. We don't know how bad it was, but Sorrell hasn't woken up yet."

* * *

They won't let me see her. They won't let me go anywhere near the ICU ward. I threaten to break a security guard's neck, at which point I'm told that if I don't calm down, I will be forcibly ejected from the hospital.

Dr. Brighton is nowhere to be found. Surprise sur-fucking-prise. I promise myself, the universe, and every false deity and god ever created by the fragile minds of men, that Dr. Ruth Brighton will not live to see another day if Sorrell hasn't regained consciousness in the next six hours.

I pace the hallways. I drink so much coffee that I give myself a panic attack, and then I have a complete fucking meltdown in the restrooms, hyperventilating into my hands, desperately trying to keep my shit together. This is not my first rodeo. I've been here before. How messed up is that? But just because I've been here before, doesn't make this any easier. There is no situation or reality where something like this is ever *easy*.

At five o'clock, ten hours after Sorrell first entered the operating room, I finally see Dr. Brighton marching her way down the corridor toward me. I leap out of my seat, the fires of hell blazing in my eyes. "Well? What's going on? You're *finally* coming to give me an update?"

"Excuse me, Mr. Merchant. You seem to be blocking the exit."

"I'm sorry?"

"I'm leaving for the day, Theo. Please step aside."

Words fail me. I open my mouth, grappling with my tongue, trying to figure out which insult I want to hurl at her first. "What do you mean, you're *leaving?*"

"I have a birthday party to get to."

"A birth—a *birthday party*? Are you out of your fucking *mind?*"

"Sorrell called me in the middle of the night, and I dropped everything for her. Do you have any idea how long other patients have to wait to undergo a surgery like this? I have some patients on the East Coast who've been waiting months just for an assessment—"

"You fucked up," I snap. "Just like I said you would. You went in there blind and hacked at her brain like a fucking psychopath. You don't give a shit about any of these people, do you?"

"I assure you, I do give a shit about my patients. I care about them very much. There were complications with Sorrell's surgery. It's not uncommon for issues to arise once we open up people's brains. You know this already. I'm not a butcher. I'm a neurosurgeon, at the top of my game. I get paid extraordinarily well for what I do. There's a reason for that. I'm one of the only people in the country who can perform this type of surgery, and I won't be spoken to like some sort of monster."

"You opened up a fucking vessel, for fuck's sake. That's a rookie error. And now you're just sauntering out of here to go to a fucking *party* like you work a goddamn nine-to-five. You're not going anywhere. You need to tell me exactly what's happening, and then you need to get back in there and figure out how to fix whatever it is that you broke."

"In case you've forgotten, *I* am the one with a medical degree and twenty years of experience behind me. No mistakes were made. The procedure was executed to the letter. Sorrell needs some time—"

"You've said that before!"

"And she was fine! I don't have to justify my decisions to you, and I certainly don't have to justify my actions in the operating room. You're not Sorrell's next of kin. You're not her husband. You're not even a blood relative, and even if you were, there *is* nothing to report beyond what you have already been told. Now, you can wait here all damn night if you like and perhaps Gaynor will give you an update out of the goodness of her heart, but I have a birthday party to get to and I'm not going to be late. There's nothing else for me to do here until Sorrell's situation changes. Now get the hell out of my way."

* * *

I don't sleep. How can I? Gaynor brings me some crappy hospital food when dawn breaks, but I don't eat it. I sit in the waiting room, picking at my nails until they bleed, trying to make sense of this situation. Other kids go to high school. They fall in love. They have normal relationships. They fight, and they fuck, and they fall in love, and they either stay together or they don't. They go off to college, and they finish their degrees, and they either get married or they don't. Either way, they don't find themselves in and out of hospitals, trying to make it from one day to the next, their hearts shredded in a meat grinder over and over again, just when it looks like things might be getting better.

I fucking hate this.

God help me, but a part of me just wants to leave. It wants me to get up and walk out of here, to catch a ride back to the airport, to go home and to never look back. This isn't the first time I've felt this way. I'm a human being. Sure, I've thought about bailing on this mess a million times over the past couple of years. There is a limit to how much pain and suffering any one person can take, and I've hit that wall too many times to count. I have climbed the wall, or smashed my way through it, or dug beneath it with my bare fucking hands, though, and I have never given up.

When I fell in love with Sorrell, I knew there were consequences. I am neither fickle nor inconsistent. Once I told her that I wanted to spend the rest of my life with her, that was it for me. She is the be all and end all of my existence, and, just like I told her back in that bathroom at Toussaint, I will navigate all seven circles of hell to be there for her, by her side, when she needs me.

That doesn't mean I've got to like any of this.

At ten in the morning, Lani calls and leaves a voicemail, asking why we didn't make it back to the academy yesterday. At three in the afternoon, my mother leaves me a voicemail, telling me that an administrator at the hospital called on Dr. Brighton's behalf, requesting that she speak with me regarding my aggressive behavior. At the end of the voicemail, my mother tells me that she thinks it might be time for me to come home. She's been trying to get me to move on and go to college ever since Sorrell was first injured. The woman doesn't understand love. If she did, she'd never ask this of me.

Dr. Brighton.

Weak ass, stupid Dr. fucking Brighton.

She knows I won't back down—that I'll keep giving her shit until I find out if Sorrell is okay—so she has someone call my *mom*?? Fucking pathetic.

Finally, at nine pm, Gaynor bustles through the double doors that lead into the ICU, and I can tell something's happened. The dark shadows underneath the nurse's eyes are far worse than they were yesterday. Unlike Dr Brighton, Gaynor hasn't slept. She hasn't even gone home to freshen up. I thank every star in the sky for this woman, who has waited by Sorrell's side, even though her shift ended hours ago. She may like look crap, but at least…wait. She's smiling?

"What is it? Has something happened?" My voice cracks, but I'm too anxious to be embarrassed.

Gaynor sheds exhausted tears as she pulls me into a hug. "Nothing short of a miracle, sweetheart. Nothing short of a miracle."

SORRELL

THREE YEARS AGO

Snowflakes dance in the air, hovering as if suspended there by magic. New York City has been a winter tempest for the past four days, and Theo and I have been stuck indoors, staying warm beneath our blanket, watching back-to-back Marvel movies. Now that the blizzard that seemed so set on ruining our trip has broken, we've bundled ourselves up in the thickest jackets we can find and ventured out into the world, on a mission for coffee.

Massive winter boots; thick, bright pink mittens; a multicolored scarf; I can barely see Theo underneath the weird, mismatched array of warm clothes he's wearing. He spins on me, narrowing his eyes at me over the top of his scarf. "You'd better not be laughing at my outfit, Voss," he growls.

"Wouldn't dream of it," I tell him, stifling back a snicker. "I think you look very cute. Very prepared for your surroundings. There's nothing sexier than a man who knows how to dress for the weather."

"Knew I should have worn that mankini," he grouses. "How are you supposed to think I'm hot when you can't even see my ass properly?"

"Oh, I can see your ass just fine, and it's still soaking wet!" Theo slipped and landed on his ass not two steps out the front door of the Brownstone we've been staying in. He tried to laugh it off, but I think it actually hurt. I promised to kiss it better when we get back, which I'm pretty sure he's looking forward to, though. Pulling a face at me, he grabs my arm and threads it through his, yanking me playfully to his side.

"If I go down again, you're coming with me," he says.

"Happily," I agree. "Always. Wouldn't have it any other way." I check the time on my cellphone; it's only midday.

Clouds of fog bloom like flowers made of smoke as we head across Brooklyn, giggling like idiots and clinging onto each other for dear life when we nearly slip on patches of ice.

"We've passed eight cafes, Kid. Why the hell do we have to walk halfway across the city to get a coffee?" Theo complains.

"Because I said so." I grin at him cheekily. "Also, the coffee at this place was Uncle Ray's favorite." Uncle Ray, with his wiry grey moustache, and his fifteen pairs of brown corduroy pants, and his obsession for going out to grab a copy of The New York Times every morning, without fail, even though he never, *ever* read it. A pang of sadness washes over me at the thought of him. When Mom and Dad died, moving across the country to stay with a man I barely knew seemed like the end of the world. It didn't take long to warm to him, though. He was funny and eccentric; his quirkiness endeared me to him almost immediately. I still laugh over the fact that the man had tenure at one of the most prestigious colleges in the country and still couldn't figure out how to the use the TV remote.

Theo squeezes my arm, nudging me with his shoulder. He's always been so good at reading my mood. "You miss him," he says. "Fine. If we have to cross the Arctic Circle to order a coffee at Uncle Ray's favorite coffee shop, then so be it!"

We reach the coffee shop thirty minutes later. Miraculously, neither of us have fallen again, but our toes are numb and there's a chance we both have frostbitten noses. When the waitress brings us our coffee, Theo takes one sip of his and nearly spits it across the table. "Fuck me, Voss, that's *terrible*."

"I know," I say, grimacing as I take a sip from my own mug; the ink-black liquid inside tastes and smells like burnt hair. "I said it was Uncle Ray's favorite. I didn't say it was *good*."

Theo's eyebrows rise. "We passed *so* many Starbucks." He winces again as he manfully swallows down another mouthful of the coffee.

I check my watch again. Twelve forty-three.

"That's, like, the fourth time you've checked your watch since we woke up this morning, Voss. You got somewhere to be?"

I bite the tip of my tongue, grinning. "No. I just don't want to get caught outside after dark is all. It's gonna start snowing again."

He looks at me like I'm crazy. "We have plenty of daylight left, Kid."

The coffee we punish our way through tastes awful but it's as strong as fuck. We're cracked out and loopy when we leave. Theo lobs a snowball at me as we're crossing a road, and very quickly we're embroiled in a full-blown snowball fight that four other passersby randomly join in on, too. We're almost back to the Brownstone, laughing breathlessly, cheeks raw from the cold, when Theo grabs me by the arm and drags me toward a bodega. Rather than selling pretzels and hot dogs, this particular bodega sells tourist trinkets: mini 'Statue of Liberty's; 'I HEART NYC' t-shirts; Empire State Building key chains; a million different snow globes.

"Don't look. I'm getting you a gift."

"I lived here, Theo! I don't need a souvenir!" I laugh.

Theo grabs my mittened hands and slaps them over my eyes. "Do as your told."

"Ohh, so *bossy*."

His breath is warm and smells like mint, which isn't a surprise after all the gum he chewed to rid himself of the foul coffee taste. "You have no idea *how* bossy I'm gonna be with you later," he whispers.

A nervous shiver races up my spine at this; we've been skirting around sex for so long now that I think I'll go insane if I have to wait much longer. We've both been teasing each other senseless, but we're getting to the point now where stopping before things go too far is proving difficult.

Theo bumps the end of my nose with his. "Don't move."

I stay very, very still, mittens still clapped over my eyes, while Theo jokes and barters with the bodega salesman. "Get the snow globe!" I shout.

"I'm getting you the damn snow globe," Theo growls playfully.

A minute later, he returns—I can *feel* his presence, my body so aware of him—and he tugs on my coat sleeve, pulling my hands away from my eyes. "Here," he says. The glass orb in his hands is a little larger than your average snow globe. Inside is a miniature version of the Manhattan skyline, dusted with tiny little flecks of white. More of the fake snow swirls around inside, mimicking the air that surrounds us now. Silver and gold glitter flashes inside the globe, too. It's beautiful—a city filled with magic and wonder.

"I love it. It reminds me of Christmas. I used to sit in the window and watch it snow, and daydream about you showing up out of the blue to surprise me."

"Stalker."

I thump him in the arm. "What's that there?" I try to tap the glass but I can't with these cursed mitts on.

"Where?"

"The little pirate's chest." There *is* a little pirate's chest in there, at the foot of the mini Empire State Building.

"It's a little safe. Look at the bottom. You can slot a tiny gift or a letter in there."

I gape at him, eyes wide, mouth open. "Did you put something in there?"

"I did."

"What's inside, what's inside!"

"A secret," he says. "You can't open it yet. You have to promise me you won't—"

"Oh my god, dude, seriously? I'm gonna die of curiosity. You're not gonna tell me?"

Theo's eyes are made of molten chocolate and honey. They spark with amusement as he flattens his lips into an apologetic smile and slowly shakes his head. "Patience, Kid. Promise me."

"Urgh. Fine. I promise."

When we get back to the Brownstone, I check the time again. It's one fifty-three.

Theo grabs me from behind, making me scream as he lifts me up the bottom step, setting me down on the second. "Okay, enough already. Bad girl. Tell me what's going on with the clockwatching or I'm gonna bite you."

"Where are you gonna bite me?"

"On the ass," he says. "*Hard*."

"All right, all right, fine! Jeez! I got you a present! It was supposed to get here yesterday but with the snow—" My heart is in my throat. I've been nervous about this all week. Ever since I came into the money my parents left for me, I've been wanting to buy this gift for Theo, but it required that we come to New York to collect it. I've been waiting and waiting...

Theo squints at me suspiciously. "There's something in there? For me?"

"Yes."

"How did it get in there?"

"I gave someone a key."

He's trying not to smile. "That was incredibly risky. What is it?"

"Well, I don't think I should tell you now, given the fact that you're keeping your little secrets from *me*," I say, waving the snow globe in his face.

Theo pulls a face, then turns and hurtles up the stairs. He has the door unlocked by the time I catch up with him and he's shoving his way inside. "Where is it?"

"In the living ro—Theo, *wait!*" God, he is such a child. I kick off my snow boots in the hallway before chasing after him. In the living room, Theo stands stock still, staring at the black instrument case resting on the thick plush rug. Across the front of the case, the name *'Charles Rufino'* is delicately painted in beautiful gold script.

"You're fucking with me," Theo whispers.

I'm suddenly very, very shy. "If you don't like it..."

Snowflakes melt on the ends of Theo's hair, turning his waves to curls. He sinks to his knees, fingers shaking ever so slightly as he unfastens the catches on the case and carefully lifts the lid.

The cello inside is astonishing.

It's Theo's *dream* cello.

"This is custom," he breathes, holding his hand out; his fingers hover an inch above the neck of the instrument, as if he's afraid to even touch it. The wood is so dark that it verges on black; tiger-striped and polished to a high shine, it's a singular thing. It even makes *me* want to reach out and make it sing.

"This is—" Theo whispers, shaking his head in disbelief. "This is thirty thousand dollars' worth of cello, Sorrell."

It isn't. Okay, it was thirty-*four* thousand dollars, but I don't want him knowing that. "Is it all right?" I ask anxiously.

There are tears in Theo's eyes when he stands. He just stares down at the cello. Stares and stares.

"If you don't like it, I can always—"

"I'm so in love with you," he whispers.

"What?"

"I said I'd wait until you were ready for me to love you, Kid. I tried to stop myself, but I'm *embarrassed* by how hard I failed." He faces me, and it's there on his face—sheer, absolute, overpowering love. It's a look I've seen on his face many times before, but he's not trying to hide it anymore. Stepping forward, he cups my face in his hands. "Tell me that you're in love with me, too, and I swear I'll make you fucking happy," he says.

It isn't even a question. I've imagined telling him that I'm in love with him a thousand times, but I've always been petrified of the admission. Afraid that I'll sound stupid, or I'll fuck up the moment when I try and get the words out, stumbling all over myself. In the end, the words come out easy, though, simply because they are true. "I'm in love with you," I whisper.

His eyes fall closed. "Tell me that you're in love with me, and I'll worship you every day for the rest of your life."

"I'm in love with you."

"Tell me that you're in love with me, and we'll be each other's forever."

"I'm in love with you."

"Tell me that you're in love with me..." He rests his forehead against mine, fingers twining into my hair, "...and we'll never leave each other's side."

"I'm in love with you, Theodore William Merchant. I'm in love with you. I'm in love with you. I'm in love with you."

* * *

I remember.

I haven't even opened my eyes yet, but I remember.

So many things are right there—images, events, feelings all fanned out at my fingertips like the cards of a rolodex. I flip through them, skipping from one to the next, tiny fragments of my past falling into place as I do so. My mother—she was *so* beautiful!—greeting me from school, crouching down to hug me. My father, singing to me from the front seat of the car. A much smaller, much ganglier version of Theo, sharing his candy, laughing at me when I fell off my skateboard, getting mad at me when I beat him for the first time at Mario Kart.

My parents' funerals.

Theo, sitting at the back of the class, my first day at Toussaint. How the sight of him had stolen my breath away. How my heart had lifted right out of my chest.

Theo, kissing me in the hallway at Kieran Davis' house.

Theo sneaking me into his bedroom late at night. Us, devouring each other, sharing hot breath, making each other come for the first time.

So much joy and so much pain, all demanding to be felt at once. It's almost too much to bear.

Over and over again, my trip to New York with Theo repeats itself, forcing its way in between these snapshots of other times and places, demanding to be *seen*. That moment he and I shared in that Brownstone was a cornerstone; so much has pivoted around that moment, where Theo officially told me he was in love with me for the first time, and I reciprocated. That was our point of no return. We made promises that have kept us irrevocably anchored to one another, but have cost us so much in the process.

I know *where* I am. I know *who* I am. I roll onto my side and tuck my knees into my chest, silently sobbing as *everything* comes back to me. Even the things I don't want to remember.

My time as Amelia.

My time as Rachel.

These memories are strange, distorted things. I see them as if I'm observing them from outside my body. Like they don't really belong to me. I suppose they don't. I cry even harder when I tiptoe through my time as Catherine. The drugs. The screaming. The fights. My god, the amount of shit I put Theo through is unimaginable. I can't even begin to process any of that, so I quickly shut it all down. I'm going to have to face it at some point, but for now, the onslaught of it all is just too much.

"Hey, Kid."

The soft sound of Theo's voice makes me tremble.

Oh god. I can't face him. Not like this, after I snuck out on him in the middle of the night, to do something he so desperately didn't want me to do.

"*Sorrell.*"

I am the worst human being alive. I bury my face into the bleached sheets of the hospital bed.

"Shhh, it's okay." The gurney groans as he climbs up onto the mattress behind me. Deftly, he slides his arm around me, navigating the IV and all of the wires that are attached to me, and then gently holds me to him. His whispers into my hair, his breath skimming the back of my neck. "You nearly gave me a heart attack. *Again,*" he murmurs.

"I'm sorry," I moan. "I'm so fucking sorry."

"Don't be. You're okay. You're gonna be okay."

"You're not mad at me?"

After a long second, I feel him shake his head. "No. Not you. I'm mad at myself. You were brave. You came and did this by yourself, 'cause I was too scared to even consider it. I should have been here for you. I should have held your fucking hand—"

'Don't you *dare*." I spin around in his arms, needing to see him. My heart shatters into a million pieces when I lay eyes on him, though; with his bloodshot eyes, and the massive hollows under his eyes, and the deathly pallor of his skin, he looks like he's been through hell and back. "Don't you *dare* feel bad for not being here." I grit the words out, each one desperately painful. "You'd suffered through enough. I didn't want you to have to hold my hand and kiss me goodbye before they wheeled me into that O.R. I couldn't do it to you. It was selfish of me, too. So, so fucking selfish, but I don't regret it. Not now that I remember how many times you've already had to—"

Theo goes stiff, his eyes widening. "Wait. Wait, wait, wait. You *remember*?"

The hope in his eyes nearly breaks me. My anchor. My home. He's never faltered. Never once let me down. Even when I got it into my head that I needed to murder him, for fuck's sake. He's never walked away. I have no idea how I'll ever be worthy of him...but I'm damn well going to try to be.

"Tell me you're in love with me, and I'll risk death to find my way back to you," I whisper.

He sits bolt upright in the bed, staring down at me. "Sorrell?"

"Tell me you're in love with me, and we'll survive anything. Together."

His eyes shine, full of tears. "I'm in love with you," he says.

"Tell me you're in love with me, and I'll—" I don't get a chance to finish. Theo cuts me off with his mouth, kissing my words away. He's gentle, handling me as if I might break. And there's a good chance I might. I feel like hammered shit. My head has never hurt this badly before, and my body feels so unbelievably weak, but with Theo kissing me, holding me in his arms again, I've never felt more invincible.

EPILOGUE

Toussaint is a puzzle box, revealing its secrets to me slowly. A flower, blooming, unfolding its petals one at a time. I belong here. I have history here. So many moments that I never thought I'd get back steal out of the woodwork, sneaking up on me, taking me by surprise.

I loved being here with Theo. It wasn't just about him, though. I had a love affair with Toussaint itself. The vaulted ceilings, and the creeping ivy across the old leaded windowpanes. The smell of wood smoke at dawn, and the pristine blanket of snow across the lawns on winter mornings. I loved the library and sitting on the hearth of the fireplace in the Great Room, reading a book while the crackling fire toasted my back.

Toussaint is unbearably romantic, now that I see it through these new slash old memories. The special moments Theo and I have shared here are innumerable.

I have great memories with other people here, too.

"Lani said you were looking for me?"

I look up from the book I'm reading, and Beth is standing on the other side of the table, hip popped, chin raised defiantly. Her eyes are hardened steel. She's beautiful, of course, her blonde hair braided and pinned into a crown, lips painted blood red. The library is empty tonight, but the very stacks themselves seem to hold their breath when the two of us face each other.

"Well? Did you want to see me or not?" she demands.

"Will you sit down a second?"

She rolls her eyes, and I figure she's going to refuse...but then she pulls out a chair, the legs screeching on the stone flooring, and sits heavily opposite me.

"Rocking the side shave, I see. How edgy of you," she mutters.

I laugh stiffly. "Yeah, well. They tend to get a little trigger happy with the clippers when you go in for brain surgery." The scalp was patchy as hell when I first got out of the hospital. Since then, Lani's tidied it up for me. She did her best to tame it into some kind of style, but in the end, she resorted to buzzing the left side of my head. It's far from a professional job, but I reckon I'm rocking it.

Beth pouts, choosing not to respond to that.

"I know you've been waiting on this," I say, tapping the envelope sitting next to my textbook. I've already given one just like it to Sebastian, and another to Ash. I've been waiting to give this one to Beth, because...well, I've been conflicted as hell about talking to her if I'm being honest.

Beth's gaze darts quickly to the envelope, then away again.

I slide it toward her, knowing she isn't going to reach out and take it if I don't; she waits a second before casually collecting it. I watch her open it up and slide the check out, her eyes scanning the details of it, and then she swallows, sliding it away again.

Most people would react if they saw that many zeros on a check, but not Beth. No, she's a master of concealing her emotions. "Is that all?" she asks.

"No, actually, it's not." I sit back in my chair, dropping my pen onto my notebook, letting out a long breath. "I wanted to thank you first."

"What *for?*"

"You agreed to stay on at Toussaint until I was better. You've had a million opportunities and plenty of reasons to leave over the past couple of years, but you didn't. And I—well, I appreciate it."

Beth gives me a shrewd sidelong look. "Being loaded has it's perks, I guess. I couldn't go until you were well enough to sign that check. Your executor was pretty clear about that when she set this whole thing up."

My executor, Marylin Bishop, was my mother's best friend from high school. My parents left detailed instructions regarding the money that would be bequeathed to me in the event that they should die. The house was to be left to me, and Marilyn was to safeguard my inheritance until I turned twenty-one. In her wisdom, Marilyn apportioned out a percentage of my money and used it as an incentive to persuade Beth, Ash and Sebastian to stay on here at the school to help me while I recovered. She hadn't stipulated how long they'd have to stay. Just that *I* had to sign the money over, and to be able to do that, I had to be of sound mind and body. It was a tricky play on her part, but the girls and Seb were the ones who took the deal. They chose to stay for as long as they did.

I do not feel good about *any* of it.

"Regardless. I'm grateful to you. Thank you." I imbue my voice with as much sincerity as I can muster. "I know how badly this whole thing must have sucked for you guys."

She snorts, as if that is the understatement of the century.

"Secondly…I wanted to apologize."

Beth's attention snaps back to me.

"The things I said in the hallway, when I came back here this time around—"

"Stop." Beth shoves her chair back, rising. "I have no interest in rehashing—"

"I should never have said those things, Beth. I remember you telling me about that stuff a very long time ago. You told me in confidence. And I know how—how conflicted—"

"Can we just *not*?" she hisses. "I don't wanna talk about it."

I'm not surprised. Beth's liaisons with her father's business partner started an age ago. It was an abusive situation that I regret not saying something about back then, but I'd been young. Beth had bragged about the whole situation. Said it was kinky and made her feel good. I wasn't old enough to realize how badly she was being manipulated, or how very wrong it was that her father would watch her. I have no idea if it's still going on or not, but I definitely don't want to pressure her into talking about it if she doesn't want to. I hold my hands up in a placating gesture.

"Okay. All right. I'm sorry. But please know…I was *really* confused, Beth. My head was *so*…" I can't even explain where my head was at. I could try, but it still wouldn't make any sense to her. "I would never have normally said that stuff, though. I hope you know that. Things were weird between us before the accident, but I'd never have said—"

"It's okay. I know you wouldn't have. We're good. I'm not holding it against you." Beth inhales, looking around the library. "I can't tell you how glad I am to be getting the hell out of here," she says. "But… it's weird. It feels like home now, doesn't it?"

I survey the library, seeing all of the things she's seeing, too. We've spent so much time here. Learned. Struggled. Suffered. Grown. "It does," I agree.

"I hear you're moving back to Sumner. Back into your parents' old place tomorrow," she says abruptly. "You and Theo."

"Yeah. We are."

"You're gonna graduate early, and then go to Columbia next year?"

"Yeah, well I've taken three runs at my senior year. Turns out I knew enough of the syllabus to pass all of my exams with flying colors."

Beth mulls on this, looking terribly awkward.

"And you? You're going to be modeling?"

She purses her lips, wrinkling her nose. "Yeah. For Givenchy. Perfume and make up mostly."

"That's really cool. I hope…I hope it makes you happy, Beth."

"Yeah, thanks. And likewise. With Columbia. And…Theo."

"Thank you."

"Anyway. I guess I'll see you around." Beth leaves, her heels clicking against the stone tile as she goes. It isn't until she's vanished through the mahogany doors that I hear him clear his throat.

Theo.

He's been waiting for me.

He sits on the other side of the stacks in a leather armchair, slouching so badly that he's almost horizontal. His feet are kicked up, resting on the edge of a table. On his chest, a thick book is splayed open, the pages ruffled like a fan. His eyes flick to me, a small smile quirking up the corners of his mouth when he sees me.

My body hums like a struck tuning fork when I see *him*. He's fucking incredible. Gone are his long-sleeved shirts. He wears short-sleeved shirts now, his ink on full display, even though it's the dead of winter and Toussaint is *not* the warmest of places. The grey shirt he's wearing tonight is much tighter than anything he used to wear. I just stand there and take a moment to appreciate just how damn hot he is. The man is made of sin. He shouldn't be fucking legal.

"Enjoying yourself?" He arches an eyebrow at me cockily.

"Immensely."

Closing his book, he drops it to the floor beside him. "Come here," he commands.

"Oh, I don't know about that. We're in a *very* public place."

"You'll get your ass over here and sit on my cock if you know what's good for you, Sorrell Voss."

We've been making up for lost time ever since we came back to Toussaint, and I've loved every last second of it. I've had Theo's fingers (not to mention his dick) inside me in some seriously scandalous places. The library's one place we haven't fucked yet, though.

He holds his hand out to me, gesturing for me to go to him. "I'm getting impatient." Holy mother of Mary, his voice is rough as raw silk. "I'm not leaving this place until I've made you come all over me in this chair, Kid. My dick's been hard as fuck since I snuck in here."

I take one teasingly small step toward him. "Oh, yeah?"

"Yeah. And you're gonna milk it with that pretty little pussy of yours."

Another tiny step. "I don't know about that."

"Lift up your skirt," he demands.

"Someone could come in."

"We're leaving tomorrow. Who fucking cares? Lift. Up. Your. Skirt."

I raise it just an inch, toying with the hem line. "Like this?"

He smiles at me, slow and suggestive, his eyes shuttering until they're half closed. "Am I gonna have to get up and deal with you? Are you gonna make me?"

"Maybe?"

"I won't be gentle if you won't behave."

A bigger step this time, closing more of the gap between us. He's full of threats, this one. And he carries them out when he isn't obeyed, too. I catch my lip between my teeth, lifting my skirt, flashing the ludicrously see-thru panties I put on this morning in the hopes that he'd do exactly this; after all, Theo can't resist me in a skirt.

He looks up at me, a fire blazing in his hooded eyes. "Touch yourself," he orders. "Through your panties."

"And what are you going to be doing while I touch myself for you?"

He puts his hands behind his head, making himself comfortable. "Oh, I'm gonna watch."

There was a time when I'd be nervous to do something so graphic in front of him, but that was another lifetime. I tease my fingertips lightly over the front of my panties, heat building in my veins—a siren song, urging me on, galvanizing me, begging me to comply with his demands.

Gradually, I apply pressure between the apex of my thighs, working my fingers over the tightening bud of nerves there, setting free a small, breathless pant. Theo growls out his approval, his eyes avidly fixed on what I'm doing with my hand.

"Good girl. Faster."

I do as I'm told, moving my fingers in a small circle, rubbing harder.

Theo wets his bottom lip. "How does that feel?"

"Good. It feels...really...good."

"Are you wet yet?"

I let out a shaky laugh, nodding. "Yeah. I am."

Theo moves languidly, like a cat, drowsy from laying out in the sun. He reaches for his waistband, unfastening his jeans. I can't avoid staring at his cock when he takes it out—erect, straining, the head swollen. He's amazing to watch as he leisurely runs his hand up and down his shaft, all the while watching me. "Pull your panties to the side. Wet your fingers for me. Show me."

I maneuver my underwear to one side, my breath hitching a little as I slide my fingers between the folds of my pussy, stroking myself. When I withdraw my fingers and hold them up for him to see, they're slick and wet with my arousal. Theo catches hold of me by the wrist, eyes alive with desire. Holding onto me tight, he pulls me to him until I'm standing right next to the chair, and then he slowly guides my fingers into his mouth.

He sucks on them, eyes boring into me, licking me clean. "You taste fucking amazing," he groans. "I could bury my face in your pussy and never come up for air." Now that I'm so much closer to him, he grabs hold of my panties and rips them down my legs. I yelp when he sits up, taking hold of me by the hips, manhandling me so that I have no choice but to straddle him. With my skirt bunched up around my hips, it's only a matter of seconds before he has me right where he wants me. The tip of his cock butts up against the entrance of my pussy for a moment, and then he's pulling me down onto him, spearing me with his erection.

He's so big, so fucking hard, I—*fuck!* "Oh my god! Holy shit, Theo!" I dig my fingers into his chest, through his t-shirt, holding onto him for dear life. He's so deep. *So* fucking deep! I can't breathe around the sensation of him, as he *somehow* grows even harder inside me.

"Jesus wept," Theo pants. "I thought you didn't want to kill me anymore!"

"I—" I laugh breathlessly. "I *don't!*"

"Tell that to your pussy. You're gonna make me come too fast, and then I'm gonna die from embarrassment."

I try to laugh again, but Theo grits his teeth, rocking himself up inside me, pulling me down onto him by my hips at the same time, and my smile dies on my face. This is no laughing matter. "Oh god! Oh my…oh my fucking God! Theo!"

He's full of shit. This man can hold off an orgasm for over an hour when he wants to, and then be ready to fuck again three minutes later. It's me who spontaneously climaxes whenever he fucking touches me. Pure ecstasy rockets through me as Theo repeats his actions, slamming himself up into me, and the world fades away.

He reaches up, tearing my top down, exposing my breasts, and it's all I can do not to scream when he leans up and sucks one of my nipples into his mouth.

This guy. This fucking guy.

He will be the death of *me*.

I rock against him, enjoying the delicious friction our bodies create, the flat, muscled plane of his stomach rubbing against my clit as I ride him.

A wave of pleasure begins to rise inside me, burning between my legs, begging to be unleashed. I can't, though. Not yet. I need to relish every second of this. I need to savor it, commit to memory so well that no matter what happens, I will *never* forget this moment.

Theo bites my breast, teeth grazing over bare skin, and I cry out—the sound of my bliss ringing out through every hollow corner of the library.

"You're holding back," Theo growls. His fingers gouge into my hips, forcing me to rock harder against him. Faster. "Soak me, Sorrell. Let go. Come."

"*No!* I—"

He bites again, sinking his teeth into my flesh, and the sting of the pain and the heat of his mouth has me whimpering into his hair. He snarls, bodily lifting me so that I slide up his cock, and then the world ignites when he drives himself home. The orgasm tears me to shreds. My nerve endings riot. My vision strobes with explosions of light. Mouth hanging open, I cradle Theo's head, crushing him to my chest as I rock against him, too blinded by what's happening inside my body to even think straight.

By the time I come down from my high, Theo's pulled back a little and is looking up at me, eyes on my face, studying my features. "You are so fucking beautiful when you come," he tells me, his tone rough with need.

"I want to feel *you* come," I pant.

"And you will. But I'm not done with you yet."

"Wait, wha—what are you *doing!*" I barely have time to wrap my arms around his neck; he stands, holding onto me, smirking ruinously as he hitches his jeans up *just* enough so that they won't fall down… and he heads for the exit.

"You're still *inside* me!" I yelp.

"And you'd better keep it that way." He nips and nibbles at me, kissing my neck as he carries me through Toussaint's dark hallways, and proceeds to carry me up the ever-loving stairs. I nearly come all over again by the time he reaches the second floor; the friction between us feels far too good, but the way he's teasing my neck his tongue could make me fall apart all by itself.

I'm a trembling wreck by the time he kicks open my bedroom door and carries me inside. "Fuck, Theo. Please. Please, please, *please*."

He chuckles darkly as he lays me down on my bed, sliding out of me. "Please what?" He tears his shirt off over his head. In a flash his pants are off, and his boxers are gone.

"Please fuck me!"

His body is fucking glorious. The muscled wall of his stomach. His arms. His sculpted thighs. I can't stop touching him. I *have* to stop for a second when he strips me out of *my* clothes. I help as best I can, but I'm so turned on and desperate for him that I can't seem to make my hands work properly. Once I'm naked, Theo pins them above my head. "You want me?"

"Yes! Fuck! Please!"

"You want me to make you come?" He hovers above me, nestled between my legs, his cock rubbing agonizingly lightly against my clit.

"Yes! Holy *shit*"

He loves bringing me to breaking point like this. But just when I'm about ready to lose my mind…he slams himself into me, showing no mercy, and I see fucking stars.

"*Fuck*," he hisses through his teeth. Setting a punishing pace, he drives himself into me again and again, until we both can feel it—the point where neither of us could stop, even if we wanted to. It comes on swift and powerful. We climax together, me robbed of all breath, him roaring, and for ten brilliant heartbeats we are the only two people who exist in the world.

After, once we're capable of movement again, Theo carries me into the shower and washes every inch of me, meticulously cleaning up the mess that he made of me. Again, he teases yet another orgasm out of me, and the feel of my climax ripping through me with hot water pummeling my skin, is sheer, unadulterated heaven.

When I come out of the shower, wrapped only in a towel, I find Theo laying on my bed, unashamedly naked, holding the snow globe he bought for me in New York in his hands. Beside him sits the notebook he was always scribbling in under the tree, back when the winter hadn't fully captured Toussaint in its grasps yet. He grins at me like a little kid, shaking the snow globe, sending the little flakes of plastic snow inside swirling around the little buildings.

"Remember when I bought this for you?" he asks, offering it to me.

I take it from him, smiling suspiciously. It feels like a miracle that I get to say yes to his question. "Mmhmm. The day I gave you your cello."

"You asked what the little pirate's chest in there was for. And I told you I'd put something in there for you?"

"Yes, and you made me promise not to open it," I say, feigning annoyance.

"Right. Well." Theo props his chin on his hand, looking at the snow globe. "I want you to open it."

"Now?" I flip the snow globe over, looking down at its base, but Theo stops me.

"No, not yet. There's something I want you to read first." He pats the notebook, looking a little rueful as he does so.

"What is it?"

"Ahh, y'know. Just every lame, heartbroken thing I ever wanted to say to you when I couldn't. It makes for terrible reading, but..." He shrugs. "I understand if you don't want—"

"Give me that notebook right *now*, Theodore! I demand to read every last word!"

He laughs unapologetically, shunting himself to the end of the bed. He leaves the book on my pillow. "I'm going to raid the kitchens and find us some food while you dip your toes into that, then. Do you want sweet or savory?" he asks.

My heart thumps a little at the question. I have a theory about

Theo. How the guy that I'm in love with is the perfect mix of sweet and savory. Light and dark. Good and bad. I wouldn't have him any other way. "Both," I tell him. "Always both."

"*So* greedy. "He huffs, amused, pulling on his jeans. I nearly weep when he puts his t-shirt back on, covering up his beautiful body. Stopping by the door, he frowns as he stoops down and collects something from the floor.

Looks like mail.

He turns it over in his hands. "Huh."

"What is it?"

Theo plucks up an orange Post-It Note, reading it quickly.

"Well?"

Wearing a slash of a grin, he hands me the stack of letters and the Post-it Note. "See for yourself."

I suppose you're not so bad, Voss.

We never did it for the money.

Three envelopes.

Three envelopes, with three checks inside.

Sebastian, Ash and Beth *all* returned them?

"My faith in humanity is *almost* restored," Theo says, heading for the door. "I'm still not forgiving Seb for the coke can incident, though."

"You have to," I tell him. "I have. And if I'm not mad at him for being a dick anymore then you can't be, either."

Theo grins, his smile taking over his whole face. "Just read the book, Kid. I'll be back soon."

Nervous as hell, I crack open the notebook once Theo leaves, my heart climbing up my throat. I know this is going to be hard. *So* hard, but I want to know what Theo was thinking, all of those times I saw him scribbling in this notebook beneath the tree. I owe it to him to understand everything he went through, and—

I stop dead on the first page.

The handwriting is familiar, but it isn't Theo's.

Darling Sorrell,

Messages from the dead are macabre, but I felt like I had to write at least this one to you. I have so many hopes and dreams for your future. You are the brightest star in my sky, and I adore you so very much. I couldn't leave this life without stealing one last opportunity to tell you just how honored I am that I got to be your mother.

I've given this notebook to Lorelei, because, despite our differences, she will one day honor my request and give it to her son, and he will write all of the wonderful things I can't say in it for me. He'll tell you how proud he is of you when you graduate. He'll tell you what a beautiful young woman you've turned into. He'll tell you how much he adores you, and he'll fill these pages with love.

From the moment you two could walk, it was obvious that you were made for each other. Lorelei will never admit it, but you and Theo have always gravitated toward each other in a way that could never be explained. From the moment you could walk, you were these two gorgeous little magnets, always doing your damnedest to snap back together and find your way home.

There are people in this life who are sent to us as gifts, to complete our experience on this earth and bring us joy. The universe sent me you, *Sorrell. But I wasn't meant to keep you. It also sent you to Theo, and him to you. I might not be here to witness it first-hand, but I already see the wonderful life you two will have together, and it makes my heart soar to know that you'll be happy.*

I have left the ring your father gave to me the night he proposed in Lorelei's keeping as well as this notebook. One day, she will give it to Theo, and I just know that he'll find some special, silly way to ask you if you'll wear if for him.

I hope you say yes.

Don't waste the precious moments you have with one another.
Be good and kind to one another.
Love, and be loved.
Always.

Mom x

WANT MORE?

WREN JACOBI BONUS CONTENT!

I have an extra-special little surprise for you over the coming pages, but FIRST! **If you loved Requiem, please make sure leave to a review for the book!** It makes an author's day to read your thoughts about their stories, and it would make me so unbelievably happy to hear what YOU thought of Sorrell and Theo's journey.

Now...

In celebration of Requiem's release, I've included a very special extended bonus chapter for Wren Jacobi from Riot House!

Be warned. MAJOR spoilers lie ahead if you haven't read Riot House, so please do not proceed if you are yet to check out the Crooked Sinners' Series.

Be advised, the following chapter contains male/male content.

WREN'S BONUS CHAPTER

"I wanna fuck you."

The class falls silent, smiles falling off a dozen previously grinning faces. Fitz's tone was playful and teasing a second ago, but the intensity in his voice now has stunned everyone to silence. It even has me peering at the English Professor over the top of my sunglasses.

Way to go, Fitz. Finally. *Something to spice up an otherwise terminally boring syllabus this semester.*

Outside, rain sweeps across the lawn, obscuring the rose garden and the entrance to the maze. A mournful wind buffets Wolf hall, moaning through the cracks in the old academy's mortar, forcing the thermostat down so perilously low that there were spiderwebs of ice on the inside of the windows half an hour ago, when I entered Fitz's den and slumped down onto the battered old leather sofa. The temperature has risen considerably since then—so many bodies crammed into one small space will generally have that affect—but by the sounds of things, Fitz has decided to hike the heat up a couple of notches all by himself.

"I want to devour you. I want your body on my body, and your blood on my lips. And your come..." He pauses a beat, surveying the room; his eyes land on me. "On my tongue," he finishes.

Well, well, well.

The boring bastard nearly made me sit up.

Nearly.

"I want to suck on your toes. I want your hair wound tight 'round my fingers, so it cuts the skin. I want to drink your breath, and eat your light, and feed you to the stars," Fitz continues, sidling around his desk.

There's a battered book in his hands. I doubt anyone else has noticed it, too stunned by the carnal words issuing from Fitz's mouth. He glances down, shoving his glasses back up the bridge of his nose, looking at the book now, though; on the floor beneath the window, Dash sits, crossing his legs at the ankle, shifting as Doctor Fitzpatrick begins to slowly walk around the room, coming amongst us like Jesus preaching to his precious disciples.

"I want to bathe in your sweat and drown in the flood of you. Drown, and drown, and drown."

I drop my head back into the cushion I'm lying on, closing my eyes behind my Wayfarers, the boredom that Fitz almost dispelled creeping back in again.

"I want your rigid cock in my mouth. To feel you swell and to burst. I want the salt of your body to christen my throat, and your ecstasy to deafen my ears—"

"Is this the shit you read to get off, Fitz?" a disgruntled voice asks. "Gross. English teacher porn. Talk about over-sharing. We can give you some privacy if you like."

It's Pax.

Of course it's Pax.

I huff out a laugh, lacing my fingers together and resting my hands on top of my chest, waiting for Fitz's dour comeback; it arrives right on cue. "Mr. Davis. Hilarious as always. If you'd bothered to listen to anything I've said this morning, you'd know that this is a piece from Rostom Booth's most recent book of poetry on—"

"Sounds like a bestseller. What's it called?" Pax snipes.

Fitz clears his throat. I deign to crack an eyelid to see what's going on; the man standing next to Mara Bancroft unfolds the book's cover, holding it up for him—for all of us—to see. The thin book's cover is plain black. The title is two words, printed in bold white lettering: *'Hate Fuck.'*

"Catchy. I'll add it to my TBR." Sitting next to Dash, back leaning up against the wall, Pax runs his tongue over his teeth, narrowing his eyes down to a vicious glare. There's no love lost between Davis and our English Teacher. Dash has never cared for him, either. I've been casually indifferent towards the guy since he showed up at the beginning of the year to take over the English department. I've barely paid him any mind at all, but I've got to say, his choice of poetry is pretty fucking entertaining.

Doctor Fitzpatrick dons a professionally bland smile; his eyebrows rise an inch. "That's great news, Mr. Davis. Although, I am surprised to hear it. I wasn't aware that you could read."

Ahhh, Jesus.

I swing my legs over the side of the couch, slowly dragging myself into an upright position. I don't want to miss what comes next. The sunglasses even come off.

Pax looks like a deranged inmate, newly released and spoiling for a fight. He bares his teeth, cracking his knuckles one by one, staring down the teacher. Next to him, Dash has adopted a careful, cool expression, but his eyes are alight, interested and alert. Must be amusing to have Pax turn this particular fury-filled expression on someone else and not him for a change.

My two best friends couldn't be more different. One, the direct relative of the Queen of England, austere, buttoned up so tight he might burst. The other, a rabid dog that's slipped its chain, always growling and ready to bite. They bait each other. Fight. Chalk and cheese. Even they don't see how much they rely on one another.

Pax has worn his shit-kicking boots today; I think I'm about to witness him insert the right one up Fitz's ass. "God. I bet you cry after sex, don't you? You probably need to be held like a baby or something. Limp-dicked, asshole, motherfu—"

"While I'm okay with a little profanity in my classroom, Pax, I do have to draw the line on occasion. You're about three millimeters away from crossing that line and seriously pissing me off. *Tread carefully.*"

Lord, the man doesn't have the sense he was born with. If he did, he'd roll his eyes and ignore Pax. This won't end well for him if he tries to exercise power over my roommate. It'll result in Pax crouching over him while he sleeps in his bed, gripping a knife between his teeth, contemplating where he should cut first.

"I'm pretty clumsy," Pax admits. "I've never been very mindful of where I put my feet." He appears disinterested, but I know him better than anyone else—better than Dash, even—and right now he's brimming over with manic delight. Things are about to go sideways, real fucking fast.

I lazily get to my feet.

Pax won't be expelled from Wolf Hall. Not with the disgusting amount of money his mother pours into this place every year. Her 'donations' to the academy are dressed up to look appropriate and charitable, but let's face it: they're bribes. Meredith Davis does not want to have to find another school willing to take in her wayward son. The amount of money she pays in addition to the academy's fees every year reflects that and then some. That's not to say that Harcourt won't temporarily suspend Pax for being a dick. And if he's suspended, he'll be moping around the house *I* paid for, getting his grumpy ass into all kinds of trouble, for god knows how long. I don't feel like walking through the door of Riot House to find the place trashed, with a naked, half-dead hooker in the basement.

Time to diffuse this situation.

I should have gone to military school like my father wanted; I could have joined the fucking bomb disposal team and had done with it. Roadside IEDs are far less unpredictable than Pax. I look down at my friend, avoiding Fitz's incredulous stare. "Come on. Time we were leaving."

"I'm not going anywhere." Pax shrugs. "I'm enjoying this healthy little debate. You're enjoying it, too, aren't you, Fitz?"

The English professor slaps the book of poetry against his palm, laughing. "Christ Almighty, you're a glutton for punishment—"

I kick Pax's feet. "*Now.*"

"I don't know what the thought process is here, Mr. Jacobi, but contrary to popular belief, this class is not voluntary. It's a mandatory part of the syllabus. Attendance is also mandatory. You can't just come and go as you pl—"

"I doubt *Hate Fuck* is a mandatory part of the syllabus," I counter. "Does Principal Harcourt know that you're reading us such provocative filth? She thinks we're in here studying Little Women, and you're strolling around the room, waxing lyrical about tasting my come."

Fitz blanches; it takes a lot to make him react to anything, but this comment has him turning the color of a fresh bleached flour. "I'm trying to make an English class more interesting for a bunch of horny teenaged idiots. If you'd rather be working on a three-thousand-word essay on Jo March and feminism, then be my guest."

Dash hasn't said a word throughout all of this. His gaze is desultory as he looks around the room, eyes skipping over the stacks, and the over-stuffed armchairs, and the rapt faces of our classmates. I gesture to Fitz, quirking an eyebrow at him. "Care to weigh in on any of this?" I shouldn't be annoyed, but the bastard's been distracted of late. There's a girl involved. I *know* there is. I just haven't figured out which one yet. I haven't allocated much of my attention toward the problem.

Dash blinks, eyes snapping to me. It takes him a second to get his bearings. And then: "Oh. I'd say it's all rather moot at this stage." He drawls this, his English accent peppered with distaste. He throws Fitz a displeased sidelong glance.

Fitz crosses his arms over his chest, his dark brown eyes gunning down all three of us. "And how do you figure?"

Dash doesn't respond. He holds up his index finger…and two seconds later, the sound of the bell's shrill ringing can be heard out in the hallway. "We're *all* free to go now," Dash says. The slow, taunting smile that creeps across his face is satisfying as hell. I consider donning one of my own but decide against it. Sometimes, a neutral, flat expression is far more effective than showing your hand.

Doctor Fitzpatrick surprises me by cracking a smile; the guy's only in his early thirties, and he's a good-looking dude. Works out. When he grins like that, I find myself questioning why he chose to become an English professor and not an actor, or a model like Pax. No one who looks like Fitz *chooses* to become a teacher, unless all other doors are closed to them.

The other students perched on their fainting couches and sprawled out in their armchairs come to life. Books are packed into bags. Conversations explode around us—most of which are about the scandalous poetry Fitz just chose to read out loud. On the other side of the room, Mara Bancroft calls something out to Pax. She winks at him, and he reacts the way that Pax always reacts: he flips her the bird.

"All right, all right. Quiet as you leave!" Fitz claps his hands together. "Listen. *Listen!* I want an original piece of poetry from each of you by Monday afternoon. You can load it up onto the portal or you can drop it in my cubby. Shock me. Surprise me. Give me lust, give me greed, give me power, give me sex. Elicit a reaction from me. Show me the power of the English language! Bonus points if you can do it without using a single curse word!"

A chorus of grumbling replaces the laughter and amused chatter.

"Oh. And Wren? Stay back a second. You and I need to have a discussion about the mechanics of hierarchy and authority."

"I know perfectly well how both function."

His expression cold, eyes flinty and sharp, brook no argument. I've faced down my father, though. General Jacobi is more intimidating in his sleep. If Fitz wants to cow me, he'll have to try a hell of lot harder than this. But…fuck it. What the hell. I have history next, and I can't imagine a fate worse than having to sit through another interminable (and factually incorrect) lecture about the second world war. Amusement sparking in my veins, I slap Dash and Pax on the shoulders, jerking my head toward the exit. "It's fine. I'll meet you outside later."

Last year, Pax decked our previous English teacher so hard, he fractured his orbital socket. The guy had suggested that Pax might benefit from tutoring; Pax chose violence. He missed his midday coffee at lunch today, though. His energy levels must be running low. Rather than throwing a fist at Doc Fitzpatrick, he mutters under his breath. "I learned how to blow up a car on YouTube this morning. Want me to practice?"

He *would* blow up Fitz's car. Take a highly intelligent, extraordinarily belligerent, deeply bored individual and trap him in a boarding school on top of a mountain in the middle of bumfuck nowhere, and there are bound to be explosions.

I smirk, shaking my head. "All good, Davis. I've got this."

I perch my ass on the edge of a desk while I wait for the rest of the class to leave. Fitz packs up his leather record bag, cleans off the white board, tidies his desk. Once the door closes after the final trailing student, he turns to face me, sliding his hands into his pockets. His head tips back, his jaw lifting.

"Why is it that the three of you have to fight me on everything?" he demands.

I look to my left. Look to my right. "Three of me? Hate to break it to you, but I'm just one guy."

"Don't get smart with me. You know what I'm talking about."

Assessing him, I take in the way he's clenching his jaw, and the way his shoulders are straining against his white cotton button-down, and I come to the conclusion that he's pissed. Poor, poor Fitz. He was all smiles and cool comebacks, but it seems like we got to him after all.

"If you're asking me why Dash and Pax give you a hard time, then I'm afraid you're going to have to ask them. They're their own guys. I'm not their mouthpiece."

"Bullshit you're not. They both watch you like hawks. The tiniest tic or movement from you and they react. It's toxic as fuck. Fascinating to watch, but like I said. *Toxic*."

The smile I give him teeters somewhere between derision and pity. "You're mistaken. They don't look to me for anything. We're all equals. We all play our part. The dynamic between us more...*symbiotic*."

Fitz rolls his eyes. "I'm not arguing semantics with you. Just tell me what the damage is so we can all move past it."

I laugh, shaking my head as I look down at my feet. "I can't speak for them," I repeat. "But since we're being blunt, I can give you my response. *I* don't like you because you understand the order of things. You know your position here is weak at best. You know that we're untouchable. We come to class to fill the day, Doc. We literally have nothing better to do. We do our assignments and complete the work you give us...because it *suits* us to. We'll graduate at the end of our tenure here because that's what our parents expect to happen, and there's no way in hell Harcourt would dare disappoint them. And yet you *still* think you have it in you to browbeat us into submission. I don't resent it. I mean, I'm sure this whole situation would make me feel fucking impotent if I were in your shoes. Not that I would ever allow myself to be in your shoes, but whatever, you get the point. It's entertaining, watching you try to wrestle with us. To win us over. To get us to *like* you." I can't keep the sneer from my voice. "But it is desperate, Wesley. It's impossible for us to like you. There might have been room for us to respect you. But now?"

I say no more. My words have hit their mark; a burning anger simmers behind Fitz's normally calm eyes. The muscles in his jaw work and flex as he chews the inside of his cheek. "I worked at a school in Texas before I came here, y'know."

"I *do* know," I shoot back.

He doesn't ask how I came by this information. It's inferred: *I did my homework on you before you even stepped foot inside this little den you've made for yourself here, asshole. I know everything there is to know about you. I make it my business to* know *things about people.*

Fitz smiles sourly. "There was a kid there. She was just like you. Stubborn. Arrogant. Spoiled. Treated me like shit because she thought she could get away with it."

"Let me guess. You showed her otherwise?"

His gives his response with his eyes rather than with words. Fury roils beneath his composed exterior, and I'll admit, the sight of it there does pique my curiosity a little. Does Doctor Fitzpatrick, with his too-cool blazers, and his hipster record bag, and his expensive tailored shirts, and his sensational poetry books have something a little more interesting lurking beneath the carefully curated front he puts on? I highly doubt it…

"I don't lose, Wren," he says. "You say that you're untouchable, but you can't be that stupid. There are plenty of ways for me to make your time here really unpleasant."

I tip my head to one side, pouting mockingly. "You really think so?"

"You know the gazebo? The one at the center of the maze?"

"Sure."

He spins around, turning his back on me, returning to his desk to collect his bag. "Meet me there tonight," he says. "I have something I want to show you."

"Sorry, dude. I have plans."

Fitz sighs heavily when he faces me again; he looks weary, like this back-and-forth sniping match between us is growing tiresome. "Then you'll cancel them," he informs me.

"I won't."

"Yeah." He heads for the door. He opens it, then stands there with his hand resting on the handle. "You will."

"Right." I chuckle darkly under my breath. "And what makes you so sure?"

"Because you love a good fight, don't you, Jacobi? You love when someone refuses to acknowledge that you're their better. Because you're bored out of your mind, stuck on this mountaintop, and anything that interrupts the monotony of your existence sounds like a good time. Am I wrong?" He waits. One second. Two. three.

I grin, rocking on the balls of my feet.

"Yeah. That's what I thought."

* * *

The gazebo is off-limits to students, but since when did telling a bunch of teenagers not to go somewhere ever work out well? The last time I bothered to venture out here, the small one-roomed structure at the center of the maze had been boarded up. Where the boards had come loose or been pried free, the windows had been smashed in their frames. The inside of the gazebo was little more than a breeding ground for mice, rats and a slew of other small rodents. The wallpaper had been peeling from the walls like a tree shedding its bark. The floor, concrete, sunken in the middle, collected a pool of standing water every time it rained, which stank to high heaven.

The place is entirely different now. The boards are gone. The graffiti that used to cover the pale stonework has been scrubbed away. The windowpanes are once more whole within their frames, which have been painted white, as has the brand-new wooden door that has a yale lock on it instead of the old metal latch the previous door relied upon to keep inquisitive academy students out.

Freshly planted rose bushes dot the perimeter of the gazebo, but who knows what color their blooms will bring; their buds are tiny and green, furled tightly shut against the cold and the rain. They won't be open for a long while yet.

Still thoroughly bemused from the conversation I had with Fitz earlier, I approach the entrance, shivering against the icy breeze, wondering how this is all going to play the hell out. Fitz said he wanted to show me something. If I know him at all, then it'll be a book. Some fancy first edition, signed by the author. An American classic poet? Something written by one of the literary greats, that's for sure. Twain. Whitman. Hemingway. He thinks he's got me pegged—that he can win me over with some rare tome that I'll be desperate to get my hands on. I'm not so easily bought. It'll take more than one special fucking book to sway my opinion of him.

There are lights on inside the gazebo already. Fitz didn't specify a time to meet him, so I left it late. It was eleven when I set off. Closer to eleven forty-five now. I left the house without a jacket, which wasn't so smart, but even despite the cold, I was in no hurry to get up here. I was curious to see how long he'd wait for me to show. I refrain from knocking and try the door handle, confident that it will be unlocked for me.

It is.

I stand for a second, taking in the newly decked out interior, silently impressed by what I find. The space is transformed. The bare concrete floor is now polished floorboards, covered with a plush, thick rug. Low bookshelves skirt the interior walls, loaded with different fiction titles and academic texts. A large sofa and two armchairs take up the lion's share of the floor space. Artwork hangs from the walls—contemporary and complex pieces that catch my eye. I'll stop and study them up close later, but for now I feign indifference as I cross the room toward the renovated fireplace, where a fire burns, cracking happily in the grate.

This is not what I was expecting.

Fitz sits on the massive three-seater sofa, leaning forward, elbows resting on his knees as he types on the laptop sitting on the coffee table before him. The lenses of his glasses reflect the brilliant white flare of the laptop's screen. His dark hair is swept back, styled, the sides cropped closer than they were this morning, almost buzzed to the skin.

I slump down into the armchair closest to the fire, kicking my feet up onto the coffee table. "See you went and made yourself pretty for me after work," I say.

He stops typing. Looks at me briefly before going back to his whatever the fuck it is that he's doing. "I assume you're referring to the haircut?"

"I am."

"Well. Y'know. I do like to maintain my appearance. When was the last time *you* had a haircut?"

I make a show of yawning. Like I haven't heard this shit before. My father insists I get a crew cut every time I see him, and I never do. If I won't cut my hair for him, then a sly dig from this asshole isn't going to send me running to the barber's. "Show me what you wanted to show me, Fitz. I lost interest in this whole thing about a mile down the road."

"Patience," Fitz says.

"I have none."

He sighs again, much like the tired sigh he let out back in his den. Closing his laptop, he scoots himself forward to the edge of the couch, then slowly gets to his feet. He's not wearing one of his flashy three-hundred-dollar button-downs tonight. His plain white t-shirt is conservative in comparison. And his black jeans…hah! Never thought I'd see the guy wearing jeans, period. He steps towards me, then roughly knocks my feet off of the coffee table, sitting on the edge of it, right in front of me.

He's weirdly close. Weirdly intense. He looks a hell of a lot younger than normal in his civilian, off-duty teacher clothes. I'm surprised by the sight of a black swirl of ink on his forearm. Definitely wouldn't have thought Fitz would have tattoos.

Narrowing his eyes at me, he leans forward, resting his elbows on his knees again, but this time his focus is all on me. "How old were you when you lost your virginity?" he asks.

"Excuse me?"

"How old?"

"Is that a suitable question for a teacher to be asking a student?"

Fitz rolls his eyes. "I'm gonna say thirteen. I bet you acquitted yourself admirably, didn't you? No coming in the pants for Wren Jacobi. You're not a two-pump chump, either. No, I'm betting she was older. Quite a bit older. More experienced. But I bet you held her down and fucked the living shit out of her, didn't you?"

I can see why he didn't want to have this conversation inside the academy. I laugh quietly, making myself comfortable in the chair. "Thirteen, huh? That's what you think?" I cluck my tongue, wagging a finger at him. "That kinda talk will get you arrested, Wesley."

His eyes flash. "Don't call me Wesley. I haven't given you permission to call me that."

"I don't need your permission. I'll call you a goat-faced donkey-fucker if I want to. We're not *technically* on academy grounds right now. It's also well passed school hours."

The annoyance I saw simmering in Fitz's eyes earlier resurfaces, boiling over. "You keep baiting me with that tongue of yours and you're gonna find yourself without it," he snaps. "Get up."

"I'm comfortable here, thanks."

"What's the point in being here if you're not going to do what I tell you?"

"I didn't realize that by coming here, I was agreeing to obey your every whim."

He glowers, interlacing his fingers. "All right. Be willful. Be stubborn. *I'll* get up." He does, and he's so close to me, wedged between the coffee table and the armchair I'm occupying, that his knees wind up touching mine. I'll be damned if I give him the satisfaction of moving. I'm confident enough within my own skin not to jump back in retreat when someone else's body makes contact with mine. Fitz looms over me, tall and broad, his glasses reflecting the dancing flames in the grate now instead of his laptop. I can barely see his eyes through them.

His hands move to his waist band.

I flash a warning smile up at him, wolfish, all teeth. "What the fuck are you *doing*, Doc?" I do not move. Do not blink. The professor doesn't flinch away from the sharp edge of my tone. He pops open the button on his jeans and lowers the fly.

"If you want to engage in a dick measuring competition with me, this might be the quickest and easiest way to settle the score between us," he says flatly. Before I can even laugh at the ridiculousness of his statement, he shoves his pants down over his hips, all the way to his knees.

Apparently, the guy doesn't wear underwear.

He's soft, but not for long. He palms his dick, working his hand up and down the length of it, and in seconds he's huge and erect, the head of his cock jutting out of the top of the fist he's made around himself.

"Seven inches," he says. "I wouldn't have made much of a career for myself in the porn industry, but I'm still in the upper percentile when it comes to dick size. Decent girth, too. What d'you think?"

Now I can't stop myself: a bark of laughter bursts out of my mouth, bouncing off the stone hearth to my right. If he thinks shock tactics will work with me, he's sadly mistaken. "This is your problem, Fitz. Yeah, you have a big dick. Very nice. Congratulations. On paper, it's a real people pleaser. But what good is a massive cock if you have no idea what the fuck you're doing with it?" I watch him, smiling an open-mouthed smile, entertained by the sight of him still shuttling his hand up and down his erection. Wonders will never cease—never in a million years did I expect this man to drop his pants and start jerking off in front of me. At least this evening's trip has been eventful.

"You think your position at Wolf Hall automatically entitles you to my respect," I continue. "You expect compliance because you're older, and you schlepped your way through a doctorate like a good little boy. But the toolkit you brought with you to this academy does not equip you to deal with the likes of me, Wesley. It never will. Just like that." I nod my head towards his admittedly impressive hard-on. "How does *that* benefit you if you keep trying to fuck the wrong holes with it?"

I expect embarrassment. At least a little shame. But Fitz quickens his pace, shaking his head. "I've never met a hole I can't fuck with this thing."

Ahh.

Wow.

I'm a very astute human being. I can usually see this kind of shit a mile away, but somehow I overlooked this possibility. This just keeps on getting weirder and weirder. I look up at him, leaning against the chair's arm, propping my head up in my hand as I consider him. "Did you bring me here to try and fuck me, Fitz? Is that what's happening right now?"

Tension fills the little cabin, building and building. Fitz doesn't break eye contact with me. The silence that stretches out between us carries many unspoken words. Words that, once said, could end his fucking career and potentially get his ass thrown in jail. I luxuriate in that silence, relishing the conflict that I feel building in him. If he acts now, if he speaks, he's risking *everything*. And he has no idea how I'm going to respond. What I'm going to do. What my reaction will be, if he comes out with it and directly propositions me.

He's a fucking coward. There's no way he's going to do it. I sit up, about to move, but—he shifts to his right, blocking my exit. "I didn't bring you here to *try* and do anything. Yeah, I brought you here to fuck you," he states. "You really didn't think that might have been on the table when you came here?"

I take it back. Fitz is dead set on surprising me tonight. "Honestly, it never occurred to me. Not even for a second. I would never have thought you had it in you, old man."

"I'm not that old. And you're not that surprised. Come on. Stand up."

"I won't let you boss me around a classroom. What in the fuck makes you think I'll let you boss me around a bedroom? Or..." I look around. "A gazebo?"

"The bravado's an act, Jacobi. You lash out at people because you think that being subservient and deferring to another human being makes you weak. But you're tired of it. Don't you wanna know what it would feel like to relinquish control to someone else for a change?"

"God. You really..." I can't even get the words out. "You *really* think you know what makes me tick, don't you? As far as I know, your qualifications don't extend to psychology. But might I suggest you go see one? This is...this is..." I puff out my cheeks, throwing my hands up in the air.

"Excuses. You're giving me excuses. Have you never been with a guy before, Jacobi? I would have thought that worldly wise Wren Jacobi, with his *'fuck you'* attitude and his unparalleled arrogance, would have tried everything by now."

"That's your tack? Try to *goad* me into fucking you? Jesus Christ. Weak, Fitz. I would have expected better, honestly. If you were doing this to a girl right now—"

"What difference would it make? Why does it matter if you're a girl or a guy?"

"It makes a difference because I'm bigger than you, motherfucker, and I could knock your teeth down your throat if I felt like it. If you put a girl in this position and stood over her, groping at your own cock like some depraved, grotesque ape, that would make you the worst fucking human on the face of the fucking planet. Doing it to *me* just makes you the stupidest."

He doesn't even flinch. "Does it?"

"Yes."

"I'm not holding you down. I'm not restraining you in any way. I'm not physically preventing you from leaving. You're right. You are bigger than me...by *one* inch," he adds. "There's nothing I could do to keep you here. If you weren't intrigued by this situation, you'd already be out of that door and half the school would know about this. But you're still sitting there. Watching me. Look at yourself, Wren. Look."

He points down at my crotch, and low and behold, the outline of my own dick is visible there, straining against my jeans. Well, isn't that just fucking perfect? I roll my shoulders back, shifting in the seat, unfazed. If anything, the angle I'm now sitting at emphasizes the fact that I'm hard rather than concealing the fact.

"I'm seventeen, asshole. You can literally say the word fuck and my dick will get hard."

He ignores me. "Have you never even made out with a guy before?"

"Sure. We're very inclusive in our games of *'Seven Minutes In Heaven'* these days."

"I mean properly. Like you fucking mean it."

"Back the fuck up, Fitz." I've reached my limit with this now. I fill my eyes with fire, gunning him down with a murderous stare.

Fitz mustn't be that stupid after all, because he takes a step back. I don't lower my gaze as he slowly hitches his jeans back up. He doesn't fasten the button on them, though. I get up, irritation burning hot in my veins. He brought me up here and wasted my time for this? Goddamn it, a first edition signed book would have been far less trite. I stalk for the door, ready to bail and leave this nonsense in my rearview, but then Fitz speaks.

"I have to say, I'm disappointed. I didn't think you'd freak out quite so badly."

I spin around, incredulity shocking the air right out of me. "*Excuse me?* What the fuck did you just say?"

"What? You look pretty freaked out to me. And all because you were hit on by a—"

"Idiot. I've been hit on by a thousand guys. I don't give a shit that we're the same fucking gender. Have you considered the fact that I might just be embarrassed for you, and I'm just not fucking attracted to you?"

"No," he says flatly, adopting a defiant stance. "I'm really hot."

Hah. And there was me thinking Pax had the market cornered on this level of arrogance. It's been a long fucking time since I was this turned around by anything. Not confused, but rather…on the back foot. I wait for him to panic and rush for the door, to make me promise I'm not going to tell anyone about this, but he remains stoically standing in place, arms folded across his chest, watching me as I…as I…what the fuck am I doing? Just standing here, in the middle of the room, waiting for something to fucking happen? Not leaving? Not staying?

Fitz shoots me half a smile, and I read the amusement in it. He's not scared. He's not panicking over how badly I could upend his life right now. He's *enjoying* this.

"You know what? Fuck it." I cross the room and slam myself into him, carrying him forward with my momentum. To his credit, he doesn't stumble. Isn't surprised. His back hits the wall, and one of the paintings I admired when I came in here falls from its hook, crashing to the floor. Fitz waits, lips parted, eyes bright—

His eyes grow rounder as I wrap my hand around his throat and squeeze. A second later, my mouth is on his, and his breath is fanning out across my face, and my tongue is in his mouth, and...

Fuck. Me.

He was clean-shaven this morning. Always so clean-cut and well put together for class. His barber didn't give him a shave when he went to get his hair cut, though; his stubble scrapes against my own, grazing against my lips and my cheeks as I drive my tongue further into his mouth, forcing him to open wider, for him to hand over more of himself to me.

He kisses me back, his tongue tangling with mine, tasting and exploring *my* mouth, and my dick hardens further, rock solid and painful. It's with a strange and burning curiosity that I realize I can feel his erection butting up against mine, his length pressing down hard on mine. We're so close in height that our bodies line up almost perfectly. Our mouths, our chests, our hips...

Fitz lets out a breathless groan, the muscles of his throat straining beneath my hand; he's trying to protect his airway, fighting to sip down some oxygen, but I'm done being played with. He brought me here to mess with me. Time I messed with him back. I close my hand tighter around his throat, applying a brutal amount of pressure to his windpipe. I kiss him deeper, harder, fighting with him, waging a war that he cannot fucking win—

I go very still when I feel his hand on me. Not over my pants. *Inside* them. I've been so possessed by this madness to acknowledge that he was unfastening my jeans. It's a difficult fact to ignore with his hand is wrapped around my dick; he squeezes me as hard as I'm squeezing his neck. It doesn't hurt, of course. It feels fucking good, and I despise the fact that it feels good, and—

"You want me to pass out, Jacobi?" Fitz hisses, grinning at me.

"Maybe. If it'll make you shut the fuck up," I retort. But I relax my grip on him, letting him go. He reacts at the same time, grabbing the back of my neck, pulling me back in to kiss him.

Nothing about this is gentle. When I fuck a girl, I don't tiptoe around the task. I don't caress or tease. I *fuck* them. I'm a storm that they weather, and I'm not fucking tender about it. They give as good as they get a lot of the time. But this is different. There's a strength and a power here that I'm not used to. A roughness and an unexpectedness that's...fuck. It isn't better. It's just *different*.

Every muscle in my body tenses when Fitz begins to stroke his hand up and down my cock. He doesn't jerk me off the way a girl might. There's an intimate knowledge in the way that he's touching me. Knowledge that doesn't come from experience in jerking guys off, but from *having* a dick and knowing personally how it feels to be touched.

"Fuck." The word escapes me unbidden. I'd love to get through the entire interaction without utter another word, but the way he's stroking me, cupping my balls... "Holy *fuck!*"

Fitz chuckles mercilessly into my neck as he spins me around, reversing our positions so that I'm the one who's pinned. He takes hold of my jeans at the waistband with both hands. I know what he's going to do. If I want to stop him and put an end to this insanity, now's the time to do it.

I hold my hands up, out of the way, letting him have at it.

Next thing I know, my pants are around my ankles and Doctor Wesley Fitzpatrick is yanking my Converse off my feet, chucking them over his shoulder, one and then the other. My jeans are gone not long after. He attempts to stand, to get back up, but only gets so far. On his knees, he places his hands on my hips and stares at me—at my *dick*—like it's the holy fucking grail.

In turn, I look down at him and a weird spark of anger sparks in my gut. "Well?" I stroke my hand down the side of his face, running the pad of my thumb along his jaw, roughly shoving it past his lips and into his mouth. "You know how the saying goes, Fitz. It isn't going to suck—"

The world ignites.

His mouth is hot and so wet. Tight. He's done this before. My god has he done this be-fucking-for. I let my head fall back against the wall, stifling a groan as he licks and sucks at me, kneading my balls as he swallows my cock. I go rigid for a second when he slides a finger back, using it to tease my asshole, but I relax quickly. I'm no prude. I've had a finger in my ass before. Just not my English professor's.

He knows exactly what he's doing when he curls his finger forward inside me, stroking it against my g-spot, and plunges down onto my dick so deep that I feel myself butt up against the back of his throat. How easy it would be to come right here and now. It would only require a momentary lapse of concentration, and he would have me. I'd explode in his mouth and give him what he wanted. But I'm not about to do that.

His hair is much shorter than it was this morning, but it's still long enough; I fist it, wrenching his head back, off my dick. I yank him back further, so that he has to look up at me, and when our eyes meet, what little authority he *did* have over me fades away.

I have *him*. The delight, and excitement, and desire on his face all confirm this. I'll admit, that look of desperation is intoxicating, and makes my dick pulse hungrily, wanting to be sunk back into the heat of his mouth. The heavy ache in my balls intensifies when Fitz strokes his finger inside my ass again, reminding me that it's there, and I release a shuddering breath. *"Up."* I issue the command, using the handful of his hair that I'm still holding to urge him to his feet. Fitz obeys me like a good boy.

His finger slides out of me as he stands, and the sensation of that alone nearly has me coming undone. My need to come is powerful as all hell, but I refuse to give in to him. I'll die first. "You're going to do it," Fitz murmurs. He turns his face into me, kissing the inside of my wrist. "You're going to let me fuck you."

I don't know if he's trying to convince himself or me of this. It won't work. I let go of his hair, using both hands to grab his t-shirt and tear it off over his head. He rips mine from me. Stripped naked, the orange glow cast off from the fire dancing on our skin, we circle each other like two predatory cats both waiting to strike. Fitz's eyes skip from my face, down my chest, over my stomach, lingering on my dick; he struggles to tear his gaze away for a moment.

"I knew you'd be big. I *knew* you'd be perfect," he rumbles. "Your body's incredible, Wren. Every inch of you is perfection. You're like something out of a dream. Beautiful and terrible."

His own body is impressive to say the least. His arms are corded with muscle. His chest and stomach are packed with it, too. He's sculpted and toned in a way that speaks of hard hours spent in the gym. His thighs are solid and huge, every part of him flawlessly executed. I can see why the girls at the academy are obsessed with him. The sight of him, naked, his cock jutting out from his body, massive and straining, the muscle in his broad shoulders tensing, his eyes alight with fire—yeah, I get it. He's an incredibly attractive guy. I'm excited by the nearness and the nakedness of him in a way I haven't experienced before. It feels both right and wrong—a set of scales teetering so precariously in the balance, tugging me in two equally opposing directions. I want him. I want to hurt him. I want to make him pant, and beg, and bleed. I want to soil him, and coax him into his climax, and I want to watch him weep.

"I don't need romancing," I growl. "You wanted to make me hard. You succeeded. You wanted to make me come. I'll give you that, too. But there's only one way you're having me, Wesley, and that's on all fours with your ass in the air. Is that how you want this thing to go?"

He sets his jaw. "I can accept that for now. But I *will* have you, Wren."

"Maybe one day. If you keep me interested long enough. But tonight..." I spin my finger, power coursing through my veins, as I gesture for him to turn around. If his goal was to bring me here and dominate me tonight, then this can't feel too good right now. He's resigning more of his power to me in doing this, but I can read it all over him: his need for me is stronger than his pride. His body is aching for mine. He inhales sharply, turns, and sinks to his knees.

"I said all fours."

He laughs tightly. "You really know how to fucking torture someone, don't you?"

"I've had practice. Now do it."

Slowly, Fitz lowers himself, resting on his hands, following my command.

"Good." I stand behind him. My hand hovers over the smooth skin of his back, an inch away from making contact; aside from choking him and kissing him, I haven't touched him yet. I'm not afraid to. It a moment worthy of taking note, though. Fitz shivers as I finally trail my fingertips along the dip of his spine. It's dizzying, seeing him like this, in such a vulnerable position, exposed to me. I've taken plenty of drugs over the past few years and none of them have felt as heady as this.

"God, Jacobi. Just fucking *do* it," Fitz groans.

He's right. This has gone on long enough. Moving quickly, I shove his legs apart, making room for myself between them, pressing myself up against him; my dick slides between his ass cheeks, thrusting up between them, and both the visual and Fitz's response sets my blood on fire.

"Fuck, Wren. For fuck's sake! Please!"

"All right. All right."

I'm not gentle about it. Pulling my hips back, I position myself and thrust forward. Not just the tip. Not just a couple of inches. I drive myself forward all the way to the hilt, until all of my shaft is buried inside him and my swollen balls are pressed flush with his flesh. I enter him so roughly that he shouts out, his fingernails clawing at the rug underneath him. "Shit! Holy shit. Oh my god," he pants.

I need a second to compose myself. Just one. And then I fuck him. Again, and again, and again, I slam myself home, griping hold of his hips, using his body as leverage to drive myself deeper. Fitz groans, his breath coming in fast, animal, primal sounds working free from his throat. I feel him tighten around me, know that he's close, but I ease back, keeping him from his release. He deserves to suffer for this a little.

"Wren. Wren. Fuck, Wren..." He chants my name like it's a goddamn prayer. "Please..."

I curve over him, grabbing another handful of his hair again, using it to guide him up so that he's kneeling. Quickly, I let go and wrap the hand around his throat, choking him from behind. With my other hand, I reach around his body and take hold of his cock, grabbing him so hard that he yelps.

From this angle, with his back flush to my chest, it feels like I'm jerking myself off in a way. His flesh slides with my palm as I work my hand up and down his dick, and Fitz begins to tremble. His shaking grows worse when I rock my hips back, drawing myself out of him, and then push myself back into him, wickedly slow.

The sensation of being inside him like this is earth-shattering. He clenches around me, spasming, his body trembling so hard, and a cruel kind of delight crawls its way up my spine. To control him, to tease him, to fuck him like this… I see why he wanted to do it to me now.

Hastening my speed, I fuck him harder, faster, my grip on both his throat and his cock tightening as I set to work.

He's not the only one close to coming now. I can feel it, building inside me. My balls tighten, drawing up close to my body, ready to empty.

Again, again, again, I slam myself home.

Fitz is a knot of muscle, rigid, back arched, every part of him tense. He isn't breathing. His hands scramble against my legs, trying to grab hold of me, to pull me into himself harder.

"Okay. You're gonna come now. Are you ready?" I growl into his ear.

He nods frantically.

I'm brutal with him. Vicious. I fuck him so hard that I see stars, working my hand up and down his dick, and within seconds he's jerking, his ass clenching, and he's spurting wet hot jets of come all over my hand.

I pull out of him, determined not to give him the satisfaction of coming inside him, either. Instead, I erupt all over his back, my own come painting his skin as he moans and pants, falling forward, back onto all fours.

Sinking back onto my heels, I swallow, trying to catch my breath, processing everything that just happened. Fitz doesn't say anything. Doesn't move.

Well, shit. That just happened, I guess.

I scrub my hands through my hair, over my face, shaking my head, trying to get my brain to function. Goddamn. That escalated *quickly.*

Time for me to get the fuck out of here, I think. I get to my feet, legs feeling decidedly wobbly, and I get dressed. While I'm doing so, Fitz rolls onto his back, resting his hands on his chest, and blinks up at the gazebo's wooden beams overhead, like he's in shock and trying to recover himself.

"You'll be back," he announces, as I head for the door.

"Maybe. Probably," I admit.

He laughs hoarsely, turning his head toward me, still lying there on the floor. "What's it going to take to get you to submit to me, Wren Jacobi?"

My mouth twists up into a wretched smirk as I open the door and walk out of it. "A *very* cold day in hell."

SPOTIFY PLAYLIST

DO YOU LOVE HEARING THE SONGS THAT INSPIRED
A BOOK?
CHECK OUT THE REQUIEM PLAYLIST ON SPOTIFY
RIGHT HERE!

ALSO BY CALLIE HART

A EMOTIONAL, DARK, TWISTED STANDALONE.

DARK, SEXY, AND TWISTED! A BAD BOY WHO WILL CLAIM BOTH YOUR HEART AND YOUR SOUL.
Read the entire Blood & Roses Series
FREE on Kindle Unlimited!

LOVE A DARK AND DANGEROUS MC STORY?Check out the Dead Man's Ink Series here!

Read the Dead Man's Ink Boxset
FREE on Kindle Unlimited!

WANT TO DISAPPEAR INTO THE DARK, SEDUCTIVE WORLD OF AN EX-PRIEST TURNED HITMAN?
Read the Dirty Nasty Freaks Series
FREE on Kindle Unlimited!

WANT A PLOT THAT WILL TAKE YOUR BREATH AWAY?
Read Between Here and the Horizon
FREE on Kindle Unlimited!

WANT A NYC TALE OF HEARTBREAK, NEW LOVE, AND A HEALTHY DASH OF VIOLENCE?
Read Rooke
FREE on Kindle Unlimited!

FOLLOW ME ON INSTAGRAM!

The best way to keep up to date with all of my upcoming releases and some other VERY exciting secret projects I'm currently working on is to follow me on Instagram! Instagram is fast becoming my favorite way to communicate with the outside world, and I'd love to hear from you over there. I do answer my direct messages (though it might take me some time) plus I frequently post pics of my mini Dachshund, Cooper, so it's basically a win/win.

You can find me right here!

Alternatively, you can find me via me handle @calliehartauthor within the app.

I look forward to hanging out with you!

JOIN MY READER GROUP!

If you'd like to discuss my books (or any books, for that matter!), share pictures and quotes of your favorite characters, play games, and enter giveaways, then I would love to have you over in my private group on Facebook!

We're called the Deviant Divas, and we would love to have you come join in the fun!

TAKE ME TO THE DEVIANT DIVAS

Printed in Great Britain
by Amazon

84624325R00197